Shoot-Out in Hell

THE COMPLETE LOU PROPHET, BOUNTY HUNTER SERIES

The Devil & Lou Prophet
Dealt the Devil's Hand
Riding with the Devil's Mistress
The Devil Gets His Due
Staring Down the Devil
The Devil's Lair
The Graves at Seven Devils
Helldorado
The Devil's Winchester
The Devil's Laughter
Hell's Angel
The Devil's Ambush
Bring Me the Head of Chaz Savidge!
To Hell on a Fast Horse

LOU PROPHET, BOUNTY HUNTER

SHOOT-OUT IN HELL

A WESTERN DUO

PETER BRANDVOLD

FIVE STAR
A part of Gale, a Cengage Company

Farmington Hills, Mich • San Francisco • New York • Waterville, Maine
Meriden, Conn • Mason, Ohio • Chicago

LIBRARY OF CONGRESS CATALOGING-IN-PUBLICATION DATA

Names: Brandvold, Peter, author. | Brandvold, Peter. Devil's bride. | Brandvold, Peter. Devil's fury.
Title: Shoot-out in hell : a western duo / Peter Brandvold.
Other titles: Devil's bride. | Devil's fury.
Description: First edition. | Waterville, Maine : Five Star Publishing, a part of Cengage Learning, Inc., [2017] | Series: Lou Prophet, bounty hunter | Description based on print version record and CIP data provided by publisher; resource not viewed.
Identifiers: LCCN 2017007829 (print) | LCCN 2017012659 (ebook) | ISBN 9781432835422 (ebook) | ISBN 1432835424 (ebook) | ISBN 9781432835439 (ebook) | ISBN 1432835432 (ebook) | ISBN 9781432835521 (hardcover) | ISBN 1432835521 (hardcover)
Subjects: LCSH: Bounty hunters—Fiction. | GSAFD: Adventure fiction. | Western stories.
Classification: LCC PS3552.R3236 (ebook) | LCC PS3552.R3236 A6 2017b (print) | DDC 813/.54—dc23
LC record available at https://lccn.loc.gov/2017007829

First Edition. First Printing: August 2017
Find us on Facebook– https://www.facebook.com/FiveStarCengage
Visit our website– http://www.gale.cengage.com/fivestar/
Contact Five Star™ Publishing at FiveStar@cengage.com

Printed in the United States of America
1 2 3 4 5 6 7 21 20 19 18 17

For Larry Gebert,
fellow Minnesotan and western lover,
with warm regards and many thanks.

CONTENTS

THE DEVIL'S BRIDE 9

THE DEVIL'S FURY 185

★ ★ ★ ★ ★

The Devil's Bride

★ ★ ★ ★ ★

Chapter One

As the stagecoach abruptly slowed, the driver bellowing profanely at his poor horses, Mathilda Anderson, formerly of St. Paul, Minnesota, flew forward off her stagecoach seat and nearly ended up in the lap of the burly gent sitting across from her.

The only thing that prevented the young woman's body from pressing up against that of the burly gent was the leather strap dangling from the ceiling and which young Mathilda grabbed just in time to prevent catastrophe. She did, however, find her face pressed up within five or six inches of that of her fellow traveler.

She was so close to the man that she could see every pore in his sun-bronzed cheeks, every broken blood vessel giving his skin a blotchy-purplish tint above his ragged beard, every line around his dark-blue eyes deeply recessed beneath heavy brows and a jutting forehead, pale where his hat shielded it from the harsh western sun.

The burly gent's tobacco-encrusted mustache lifted as he spread his lips back from his brown, cracked, and crooked teeth. The man's breath pushed, rank and hot, against Mathilda's face. Though she had no experience in such matters, she imagined the odor akin to that emanating from the cave of some wild forest animal.

The stench was so strong, it nearly took Mathilda's own breath away and caused her eyes to water.

"Oh, dear god, I beg your pardon!" Mathilda cried, finding the hasty retreat she so desperately wanted to make nearly impossible given that the stage was still slowing so rapidly that she felt as though a large hand were thrusting her forward into the fellow's lap.

The burly gent's knees, clad in patched denim, were pressed against her own knees, and, twisted sideways as she was, sort of dangling from the straps, her own bottom was a mere three or four inches from the man's thighs. A fleeting, horrified glance told her there was a slight swelling behind the man's buttoned fly.

The burly gent reached toward her with an insinuating grin. "If you wanted to get cozy, dearie, you might have just said so instead of raisin' such a ruckus!"

He winked as he began to close his hands around Mathilda's waist.

Thank god the stage rocked to an abrupt but steadfast stop at just that moment, throwing Mathilda back into her own seat.

"Gosh darnit!" lamented the burly gent, who wore a large revolver on his right hip and an equally large and savage-looking knife on his left hip, jutting above his coat flap. "I thought we was gonna have us a fine old time!"

The other three men sharing the coach with the young woman laughed as they began gaining their feet and grabbing their hats and baggage, most of which consisted of small accordion bags or carpetbags. None obviously was a gentleman. Not a single one waited for the coach's sole female occupant to de-stage before they fairly swarmed to the door like cattle desperate to leave an abattoir.

Dust was already billowing in and around the coach, and the men's reckless scurrying only kicked up more of it, so that Mathilda choked and waved a hand in front of her face, futilely trying to clear the air.

In seconds, the young woman sat alone in the stage.

She felt a little dizzy and sick to her stomach from the long and trying ride from the railroad station at Gunnison. The coach had bounded up and over steep mountain passes, the air growing colder and colder, jostling young Mathilda and the men around her like dice in a gaming cup.

She knew the men to each side of her hadn't minded the hectic ride nearly as much as she had. In fact, they'd taken the utmost advantage of the times—and many there were!—in which they'd been thrust up against her. The rotund fellow on her right had kept giving her a seedy, slant-eyed grin, tipping his head back so as to get as good a look as possible into the white shirtwaist of her burgundy velvet traveling frock.

Now, when the dust had settled somewhat, Mathilda rose, grabbed her carpetbag containing a few female necessities and the leavings of a light lunch, and made her way out of the stage. She directed the driver—a small, foul-mouthed, leathery-skinned man whom she'd heard addressed only as Big Time—to set her luggage consisting of a portmanteau, a black leather accordion bag, a triple-decker steamer trunk, and two carpetbags on the stage relay station's front porch.

A sign jutting from the porch on pine posts announced in large, blocky red letters: DEAD SKUNK GULCH, COL. TERR.

When the driver and shotgun rider had gone into the relay station cabin while two other men had walked out from a large log barn to lead the coach and team away, Mathilda found herself standing alone in front of the porch, looking around. There appeared no one else out here except a small dog chasing horses around in the corral connected to the barn, and yapping.

The smell of wood smoke, cigarette smoke, and liquor emanated from the relay station cabin, pushing out the front door that was propped open with a rock. Mathilda studied the black rectangle of the open door reluctantly. Finally, glancing at her luggage and wondering if it would be safe out here unattended, she climbed the porch steps and moved cautiously into the cabin.

She blinked as her eyes adjusted to the heavy shadows of the place's interior.

Men, including those mongrels she'd shared the coach with, were sitting at tables scattered here and there about the shabby hovel. A group of five was playing cards to Mathilda's left. Three men stood at a bar that ran along part of the room's rear wall. As she looked dubiously around the room, she saw that all eyes were on her, cast with customary goatish male lust.

Mathilda felt her insides recoil.

Trying to ignore the brash gazes of the men, she studied each face in turn. Finally, clearing her throat, she announced, "Shep Hatfield?"

There was no response. The men continued to stare at her. One leaned toward another and whispered, but Mathilda could not hear what he'd said.

She looked toward the bar. A big, fat man standing behind it wearing an orange apron lifted his arms and shoulders in a shrug, and said, "Ain't seen hide nor hair of ole Shep in weeks." Behind him was an open door through which she could see a gray privy standing in the backyard at the end of a well-worn path.

Mathilda turned her mouth corners down in defeat and walked back onto the porch to sit on her steamer trunk, staring off toward a trail that entered the yard from the northwest, through a gap in the thick pine forest. Surely Shep Hatfield would come for her soon.

Why wasn't he here? He should have been here, waiting for her. *She* certainly shouldn't be waiting for *him*. No gentleman would leave a young lady waiting in the midst of so many hardened and soiled characters—some half-drunk!—loitering around a remote stage relay station.

"Pssst!"

At first, Mathilda thought the sound had merely been the wind caroming around the cabin's eaves. But then she heard it again, louder. She turned to see a man in a shabby, ill-matching three-piece suit standing off the cabin's front corner, to her right.

He beckoned frantically, looking bereaved. He was a little man with a considerable paunch bowing out his shabby, orange and brown checked vest. Greasy gray hair hung down from his ragged bowler.

Mathilda felt her insides recoil again. She turned away from the man, pretending she hadn't seen him.

"*Pssst*—please, Miss. I need your help, if you will."

Mathilda turned to the little man again, frowning curiously, apprehensively. "I'm sorry, but—"

"Please. You look like a smart young lady. It's my dog. He seems sick and I'm worried about him. I thought maybe you'd come and have a look."

"I know nothing about dogs, sir."

"Please." The seedy-looking little man beckoned again. "My partner wants to shoot him, but I'd like you to take a look at him and see if you can't figure out the problem."

"I told you, sir . . ."

Mathilda let her voice trail off. There was something so guileless and sad in the little man's eyes that she found her resolve losing its mortar.

"Please, Miss—hurry. I think there might be somethin' caught in his throat. My hand's too big—it won't fit down there!"

Mathilda looked around.

Finally, she stood reluctantly and moved down off the porch steps. As she strode toward the little man, she said, "I'm certainly not going to stick my hand down a dog's throat. He might bite me." She paused by the little man, staring down the side of the cabin toward the rear, seeing only stacks of split firewood. "Where is he?"

The little man walked down the side of the cabin and gestured toward a gap in a large stack of stove wood. "He's right here. Lyin' down against the wall here. Poor li'l thing. Please take a look at him—oh, won't you, Miss?"

Apprehension drew Mathilda's shoulders together. Just the same, she found herself walking toward the little man. She moved slowly, cautiously, ready to scream if she saw that she was being led into a trap. Surely one of the men from inside the cabin, gentleman or not, would rush to an imperiled woman's aid . . .

She moved forward, tilting her head to stare into the gap, toward the cabin. "There really isn't much I can do—"

Mathilda stopped abruptly. The burly man from the stagecoach stood in the gap, his back to the cabin wall. He was grinning lewdly, eyes slitting, his shoulders jerking as he laughed.

The seedy little man was snickering, as well.

Mathilda glowered curiously. She didn't know what the men were laughing at until she followed the burly gent's own gaze down past his belly to see his mottled red manhood angling up out of his open trouser fly.

"Pet the doggy, miss," sang the man with the exposed organ. "Pet the doggy now. Give him a kissy-kiss!"

Mathilda recoiled, slapping a hand to her chest.

"Disgusting!" she cried and swung around to start running back toward the front of the cabin.

The seedy little man grabbed her from behind.

"Oh, no you don't, you little bitch!"

"Leave me . . . let me *go*!" Mathilda cried, trying to wrestle out of the seedy man's grasp. But then the man with the exposed organ was on her, too, pulling her toward the gap. She could smell the rancid sweat and sour whiskey stench of both men as they grappled with her.

She had turned toward the front of the cabin, but now they'd turned her around to face the gap.

"Come on, you little bitch!" cajoled the burly gent. "You're gonna suck us both off, and don't you think—!"

"All right, fellas—that's enough."

Mathilda had looked up to see a tall, broad figure move toward her from behind both her attackers a second before she'd heard the man's mildly admonishing voice. He stood a whole head taller than the seedy little man and the burly gent. He wore a badly weathered, funnel-brimmed tan hat, and a buckskin tunic stretched so taut across his brawny chest as to appear barely able to contain his considerable bulk.

"Stay out of this, you son of a bitch!" snarled the seedy gent. "You can have her after *we're* done!"

As both he and the burly gent continued to pull Mathilda into the gap, the big man grabbed them by their shirt collars, gritting his teeth. "You might find a girl who looks a little more willin' than this one, you dunderheads!"

He jerked them apart and then back toward each other. Their heads crashed together with dull wooden thuds. Instantly they released Mathilda, who jerked free so suddenly, she lost her footing and went flying backward, hitting the ground on her butt with a grunt.

"Oh-*ow*!" cried the burly gent, his exposed organ flopping around the open fly of his pants. He crouched, grabbing his head.

"You son of a bitch!" cried the seedy little man, clutching his own head in both hands and leaning forward, squeezing his eyes shut.

The burly gent shook his head as though to clear it, and

glared at the big man facing them, fists on his hips, feet spread a little more than shoulder-width apart.

"Prophet, this ain't none of your affair, you son of a bitch!"

The burly gent swung his right fist at the man he'd called Prophet. The big man swatted the burly gent's fist out of the air as though it were no more than a fly. Then he buried his own right fist in the burly gent's belly. As the burly gent leaned forward with a groan, Prophet slammed his fist into the side of the burly gent's head.

As the burly gent flew sideways into the gap, the seedy little man picked up a chunk of split stove wood and bounded toward Prophet, swinging the wood toward Prophet's head. Prophet blocked the seedy man's arm with his own, then punched him three times, hard.

They were straight, short jabs. Each one made an awful smacking sound. With each blow, the little man's head jerked back. He stumbled backward, moaning, clutching his hands to his bloody mouth. He stumbled over some trash, twisted around, and fell in a heap.

Rubbing his bloody right fist against the palm of his left hand, the man called Prophet turned toward the burly gent, who was down on all fours, breathing hard and shaking his head. He appeared neither willing nor able to continue the fight, if you could call what had just transpired a fight.

Prophet turned to Mathilda. That's when she saw another man steeling up quickly but quietly behind him, stretching his lips back from his teeth and raising a shotgun in both his gloved hands.

"Oh, look out!" Mathilda screamed.

Too late.

The man behind Prophet smacked the back of Prophet's head with the shotgun's butt. The big man staggered forward, wincing, squeezing his eyes shut. His hat tumbled off his shoulder. He dropped to his knees, fought to keep his head up, but then lost the battle and pitched forward onto his face.

He tried to push up but dropped flat with a groan and lay still.

Chapter Two

Sitting on her butt in the dirt near the inert, prone figure of the man called Prophet, Mathilda looked up in horror at the man who'd laid him out.

This man was as tall as Prophet, but older and not as broad through the shoulders. His long face was carpeted in a thin gray beard through which several large, ugly moles were visible. Dressed almost entirely in grimy black wool, he held the shotgun on his shoulder as he glowered down at Mathilda.

"Please," Mathilda heard herself beg in a thin, wheedling voice, recoiling at the tall man's raptor-like gaze. "Oh . . . please . . . don't . . ."

She thought for sure the assault was about to begin anew, with three men now instead of two. But then the tall man with the raptor's eyes walked over and delivered a hard kick to the seedy little man's left thigh.

The little man rolled over, cursing and groaning.

"Get your ass up, Bell. You, too, Hotchkiss," he added, walking into the gap where the burly gent was rising to a squat.

Hotchkiss held up his hands in supplication as he leaned back against the cabin wall, and the tall man reached down and jerked him to his feet. "We got more important business here than trifling with"—he glanced at Mathilda, making a sour expression—"backcountry harlots. Now, both you corkheads get your asses back inside. I didn't call you up here for nothin'. We got business to discuss!"

"What's the damn hurry, Cade?" asked Bell, dabbing at his smashed lips with a handkerchief. "We was just wantin' a little pleasure. Shit, I ain't had a woman since—"

"I said shut up and get your asses inside!"

"Well, hold on," said Bell, drawing the pistol he wore in a holster on his right leg. He clicked the hammer back and aimed the weapon at the back of the unconscious Prophet's head. "I wanna shoot this big bastard. Been wantin' to clean his clock ever since I first saw him in Abilene, and that was awhile back."

Mathilda shrank back, poked her fingers in her ears, and squeezed her eyes closed, steeling herself for the imminent carnage.

"No," Cade said, grabbing Bell by the arm and shoving him toward the front of the cabin. "We don't want the trouble it might attract. Hurry up, Hotch. Goddamnit, if I gotta tell you again . . . !"

"All right, all right—I'm comin'." Hotchkiss set his tall, black hat on his head and started following Bell and Cade toward the front of the cabin. He paused beside Prophet, glaring down at the unconscious man.

He cursed bitterly as he swung his right leg back and forward, burying the toe in Prophet's right side.

"Ohh!" Prophet said, suddenly conscious and wincing as he rolled onto his back, clutching his battered ribs.

As Hotchkiss walked past Mathilda, he spat down at her, the gob of filth barely missing her left cheek to plop onto the ground beneath her.

"Nasty man!" she reviled him when he'd slipped past the cabin's front corner. She brushed a hand across her cheek. "And I am certainly no *backcountry harlot,*" she added indignantly, pushing onto her knees and brushing dirt from the sleeves of her dress. "Backcountry harlot, indeed! I'd have nothing to do with the likes of such barbarians . . ."

She let her voice trail off when Prophet sat up, grunting and groaning. Her hat had come off during the dustup with Bell and Hotchkiss. She saw it lying at the base of the woodpile, near the boots of Prophet, who was muttering under his breath as he rubbed the back of his head.

Tentatively, Mathilda rose to her feet and, watching Prophet as though he were a wounded wild animal, she stepped wide around him and crouched beside her hat. She was in front of Prophet now. This close, she could see that he was not an unattractive man, though certainly not in the more refined, eastern sense of that word.

He was big and rawboned, his face included, which was almost handsome when viewed from certain angles. He fairly emanated raw, savage power. His nose appeared to have been broken several times and not set right. Below his forehead, which had been shaded by his hat, his skin was brick red from the sun. His leathery cheeks owned a two- or three-day crop of sandy beard stubble.

He lifted his head and opened one light-blue eye, directing his gaze at Mathilda, who was gathering up her poor, abused hat. She supposed she should say something to the man—he'd helped her, after all—but his brash masculinity and size, as well as the big pistol strapped to his thigh, made her feel nearly as vulnerable as she'd felt in the clutches of Hotchkiss and Bell. The hide-wrapped handle sticking up from under his shirt collar must belong to another weapon. Possibly, a knife . . . ?

Mathilda clutched her hat against her breasts and rose. She stood staring down at the big man, wanting to take her leave and return to her luggage, but her natural propriety compelled her to linger.

"Can I . . . can I get you a drink of water, perhaps?" she asked.

Prophet spat to one side. "I don't suppose you got any

whiskey on you, do you?"

"No."

"That's all right. I got business to tend to, anyways."

Mathilda frowned. "Business?"

"Yep." The big man heaved himself to his feet and brushed himself off. "Business."

He swung around and strode toward the front of the cabin. Mathilda watched him sort of stagger with a proud resolve—chin up, shoulders back—around the corner until he was out of sight. She could hear his boots stomping up the cabin's front steps, spurs ringing, then thumping across the porch.

Deciding her hat was in such bad repair that she could no longer wear it until she could take a needle to it, Mathilda held it down by her side as she strode, a little weak-kneed and spongy-footed from the shock of what had happened, back around to the front of the cabin. Again, she looked around for the man who was supposed to meet her here, wishing now more than ever that he would hurry.

There was no sign of him, however—whoever he was. She really didn't know anything about him except his name.

Shep Hatfield.

She stopped at the bottom of the porch steps when what sounded like several arguments erupted simultaneously inside the cabin. There was the unmistakable sound of a man's fist slamming into a face. Mathilda jerked back with a start, slapping a hand to her chest.

There was a savage, bellowing roar followed by a string of curses that lifted a flush in the young woman's cheeks. Several sets of boots stomped loudly. There was the thunderous scrape of chairs being slid across wooden puncheons. Raucous shouting.

Smack!

Smack!

Smack-Smack!

A man came flying through the window left of the cabin's open door in a gale of breaking glass and splintering sashes. Hotchkiss lay moaning amidst the rubble of the broken window.

More shouting, the thunder of stomping boots, the revolting *smacking* sounds of fists on flesh.

Another man came hurtling through the window to the right of the open cabin door. When the glass had settled, Mathilda stared in horror at the seedy little man, Bell, writhing on the porch floor amidst the rubble of the broken window, cursing and spitting glass from his lips.

A bellowing yell erupted from inside the cabin.

Mathilda stared through the open door to see a dark figure fairly flying toward her. The man called Cade was hurled through the door as though he'd been propelled by a catapult. He crashed onto the porch with a loud bang and a wafting of dust and a splintering of porch boards. He rolled wildly down the steps, arms and legs flailing, and into the yard. He didn't stop rolling until he was a good ten feet beyond the steps.

Mathilda stood frozen to the left of the porch steps, a hand on her breast, mouth agape, as she stared at the rumpled, dusty figure of Cade writhing before her. "Oh, my goodness! Oh, my goodness!"

Boots stomped loudly. Mathilda looked from Cade to the cabin. Prophet strode out the door. He leaped down the steps and into the yard just as Cade gained his feet. Keeping his head down, arms spread wide, Cade stormed into Prophet, bulling the big man off his feet. Dust billowed as Cade and Prophet hit the ground a few feet beyond the porch steps.

Blinking against the wafting dust, Mathilda retreated several steps from the spot of the melee. "Oh, my gosh! Oh, my gosh!"

As Cade and Prophet rolled around, kicking and punching each other, Hotchkiss and Bell ran down the porch steps, cursing, blood dribbling down their cheeks and oozing from rips in their ragged clothes. Several more men followed from inside the cabin, and Mathilda moved even farther away from the swarm of cursing, punching men.

The thudding of a horse's hooves and the rattling of wagon wheels lured her gaze away from the small horde of fighters. She looked toward where the trail entered the yard from a break in the evergreen forest. A horse and battered farm wagon was just then emerging from the forest and entering the yard, the driver turning the horse toward the cabin.

Mathilda gazed at the driver hopefully.

He was a dark-haired, dark-eyed man wearing a black felt hat that had seen better days. The hat owned a braided leather band from which a brown hawk feather protruded. His dark-brown beard showed traces of gray, especially on his knoblike chin.

The man looked over the head of the red-brown horse before him, toward Mathilda, frowning, then glanced at the fighters, who were continuing the foofaraw about fifteen feet to Mathilda's left. They were all on their feet now and exchanging blows, blood glistening on smashed lips. They all seemed to be ganging up on Prophet, but so far he was holding them off and making each one pay for getting close enough to throw a punch at him.

The wagon driver swung the rig in a broad semicircle, skirting the edge of the fighters, none of whom so much as glanced at him, so involved were they each in his savage, grisly pursuit. The driver pulled the horse and wagon up sideways in front of Mathilda, the horse's head aimed generally back toward the trail from which it had entered the yard.

The driver shoved the iron brake handle forward and turned to stare down at Mathilda. He wore a dark, plaid shirt, suspenders, and dark-green canvas trousers. The cuffs of his trousers were stuffed down into high-topped, moccasin-like boots. He wore two pistols on his hips, and a rifle rode beside him on the wagon seat.

His dark, narrow-set eyes were too crowlike and his face too sternly and haphazardly chiseled for him to be called handsome, but given the circumstances, Mathilda still hoped he was her ride.

The crow's eyes studied Mathilda closely, flicking up and down. They remained too flat for her to tell if the man behind them approved of what he saw.

"You Mathilda?" he said, the words coming out like a grunt, deep lines spoking around his eyes.

"Y-yes," Mathilda said. "Are you Mister Hatfield?"

He nodded once and glanced over his shoulder at the fighters. Smacks and shrill curses were still emanating from the heart of the ruckus, dust rising when a man hit the ground and rolled before scrambling back to his feet.

"What the hell's that all about?" Hatfield asked.

"It's a long story," Mathilda said, wincing when she glanced over to see a man get around Prophet and leap up onto the big man's back. "Could we discuss it on the trail to your ranch?"

Hatfield jerked his chin with an annoyed air. "Come on up."

Mathilda turned to look at her gear heaped on the porch. "But my luggage."

He looked at her baggage and then glanced quickly—anxiously?—toward the fighting men. "Fetch it. Hurry it up."

"I'm . . . I'm going to need some help, Mister Hatfield."

"What?"

"It's quite a lot of baggage. I did pull up roots, after all."

Again, Hatfield looked at the baggage before shuttling his crow's eyes to the fighters. He muttered something under his breath and then climbed quickly down the opposite side of the wagon. While the fight continued, the smacks resounding and men flying and dust billowing, Hatfield made two quick trips up the porch steps to retrieve the young woman's luggage and stow it in the back of his wagon. In his haste, he tossed them into the box without care.

Mathilda opened her mouth to voice a mild rebuke, for she'd packed a few breakable pictures and trinkets in the steamer trunk, but given the man's testy demeanor, she thought better of it. He walked over to her side of the wagon, grabbed her around the waist, and tossed her up into the box—also without care. She might have been a child he'd lost patience with. Mathilda gasped against the pinch of his big hands but again reconsidered a possible objection.

The last thing she wanted was to be left here at this wild and savage stagecoach station to fend for herself.

As Hatfield climbed up the wagon's opposite side, she glanced behind to see that two men were holding Prophet while two others punched him in turn.

"Oh, my goodness," Mathilda muttered into her hand.

"What is it?" Hatfield asked, releasing the brake.

"That man . . . the one they're beating . . . he helped me earlier."

"Don't mind him." Hatfield glanced over his shoulder at the savage festivities, then turned forward and shook the reins over the horse's broad back. "He can fend for himself or go to hell!"

As the horse and wagon lurched forward, Mathilda was thrown back in the spring seat. She studied Hatfield, who kept his gaze directed at the trail opening ahead of them.

"Do you know that man?"

Hatfield turned to her with that frowning, impatient look. "Huh?"

"I asked you if you knew that man—the one they're . . . treating so poorly."

"Hell, no," Hatfield said as the wagon entered the trail, the shade of the fragrant pines striping them. He whipped the reins harder over the horse's back, and the mount broke into a gallop.

Mathilda grabbed the iron sides of her seat to keep from being thrown overboard.

Chapter Three

While Shep Hatfield's clay-colored horse negotiated the steep mountain trail and Mathilda held onto the unpadded wagon seat for dear life at the sharp corners, she cast quick, furtive glances at her dark-eyed, irascible driver.

She was trying to reconcile the last letter she'd received from the man, responding to *her* response to his newspaper ad for a bride. The letter had not been long, but it had been written in a flowing, attractively masculine hand with few misspellings. The words and phrasing hadn't been poetry, for sure, but they'd been evocative and even tender and amusing at times, just as his two previous letters had been.

Hatfield had described himself as "middle-aged and fit as fit goes for my years," and "while I am admittedly getting a little soft around the middle," he was "certain that splitting wood for the long mountain winter ahead would trim the tallow off my rack."

"However, Miss Anderson," he'd added, whimsically, "if you're a good cook, you can only hold yourself to blame if I'm as big as Santa Claus come spring. Hah!"

Could the man riding beside Mathilda on the wagon seat, scowling out over the horse's bobbing head with his little, dark, crow's eyes have been the man who'd penned those jovial, literate missives? If so, he'd certainly been in a far different mood than the one by which he was currently struck. Why he was so dark, Mathilda had no idea. She'd expected to find her new husband happy at the prospect of starting a life with his new bride. Couldn't he at least have worn a nice jacket and brought her a simple spray of mountain wildflowers, if not a smile?

Maybe Mr. Hatfield had enjoyed the anticipation of starting a new life with a new woman, but the practical reality of sharing his cabin after several years alone was giving him second thoughts. In one of his letters, he'd said that his wife had died "some years ago." Mathilda thought it possible that those years, while often lonely, had also cultivated in him a pleasing independence and appreciation for solitude.

Yes, that must be it. The poor man was merely having a bout of cold feet. Mathilda would have to do her best to set him at ease. Then the man who'd written those whimsical letters would make an appearance, and all would be right with the world. She'd always thought it both curious and wonderful how much a smile could change a person's overall demeanor.

A mere quirking of the lips . . .

Mathilda would simply have to give Mr. Shep Hatfield a reason to move his lips and loosen those stony muscles in his cheeks.

She did so herself as she looked up at him sitting so rigidly beside her, scowling out over the trail. "You don't have to be frightened, you know."

He glanced at her, eyes hard beneath his heavy brows. "What?"

"Not to worry. This is going to work out just fine for both of us. You'll see."

Suddenly, as though the clouds were parting and the sun shone after hours of heavy rain, the man's mouth corners rose. His eyes almost sparkled as they flicked up and down the length of the young woman's body. "You're right as rain there, sweetheart."

He winked and then cast his gaze out over the galloping horse once more. He laughed once and shook his head.

There, you see? Mathilda told herself, ignoring a slight apprehension that was like a sip of sour milk in her belly. *That's all it took. Just a few reassuring words!*

The wagon hammered out of the forest and into a broad valley carpeted in small, teal-colored, wiry shrubs. Beyond the forested ridges that hemmed in the valley, steeper, rockier ridges vaulted toward a cobalt sky, some streaked with the ermine teardrop shapes of what must be old snow.

The vastness and raw beauty of this remote, up-and-down country made Mathilda a little light-headed. She'd been born and raised in St. Paul, Minnesota, and she'd been no farther west than the headwaters of the Mississippi River. Being this far from her home and finding herself in such a savage land was at once frightening and intoxicating.

The trail curved off to the right and rose through hills stippled with more scattered evergreens. After about another mile of pitching, swaying travel, a welcome sign of man's presence showed itself in the form of a house and a barn and several corrals constructed of wooden rails. This must be the ranch.

Mathilda had seen several on her way by rail to Denver from Minnesota, and the little farm-like settlements of similar fashion had been pointed out to her by friendly fellow passengers. Most such ranch steads had been fronted by two poles straddling the entrance trail, and a wooden cross beam attached to the tops of the poles with either a family name or a brand burned or carved into the beam. The "portals," as they were called, were a ranching tradition in the West.

The tradition continued even here to this little dwelling in the "high and rocky," as such remote places were called.

The red-brown horse pulled the wagon under the portal straddling the two-track trail. Into the crossbeam HATFIELD RANCH had been burned and the antlers of some large elk or deer mounted. As she rode beside her future husband, Mathilda glanced at the log barn to her left but paid most attention to the log house set straight ahead on the far side of the yard and flanked by another steep, dark-green rise that rose to a peak from which a steady *whoosh* of wind sounded.

The house looked humble but sturdy. It appeared to have two stories and was tight enough, its logs chinked and the shingles intact. The flowers and shrubs planted out front of the veranda were a sorry sight, but some cultivation and water and a woman's touch would go a long way in bringing back vibrancy to their drooping petals and leaves.

Mr. Hatfield pulled the wagon up in front of the house, and set the brake.

"Moon!" he called, looking around.

He called the name again.

A small, log outbuilding sat back in the brush to the right of the corral. Gray smoke rose from a tin chimney. The building's side door opened slightly, and a long, horsey face appeared, staring out.

"Get over here!" Hatfield called, beckoning impatiently. "Tend the horse and wagon!"

Muttering curses under his breath, Hatfield climbed down from the wagon and immediately started unloading Mathilda's luggage from the box. She looked at her prospective husband expectantly over her right shoulder. As he lifted her steamer trunk off the wagon bed, he glanced at her, and scowled.

"Oh, fer chrissakes!" Hatfield set down the steamer trunk and walked over to the side of the wagon. As he pulled Mathilda brusquely down from the driver's boot, he said, "You're on a workin' ranch now, girl. You're gonna have to learn to fend for yourself. I ain't gonna be here to horse you around whenever you need—"

"Mister Hatfield, I am no shrinking violet!" Mathilda cried, indignant. "This gown makes it not only difficult but downright dangerous to climb in and out of high buckboard wagons. As soon as I am more properly attired, I assure you that you will not need to *horse me around,* as you say, and that I am completely capable of fending for myself!"

"All right, all right," Hatfield said, smiling down at her. He'd kept his hands on her waist as his little crow's eyes flicked across her again in an unseemly manner, making her innards recoil. "Don't get your drawers in a twist . . . though I gotta admit I wouldn't mind seein' what that looks like."

Mathilda twisted her body to the right and left as she removed his hands from her hips. "Seeing what *what* looks like?" she asked, beetling her brows skeptically.

"Your drawers," Hatfield said, chuckling. "In a twist!"

Mathilda stepped back, aghast. She opened her mouth to castigate the man but closed it when she saw the man from the outbuilding walk up to the wagon. He had a pronounced limp, seemingly favoring his left leg. He was maybe in his mid-forties with thin, gray-blond hair dropping down from beneath his soiled Stetson, and several days of beard stubble carpeting his horselike face. He wore gloves, a denim work shirt, suspenders, and leather leggings. His legs were as bowed as a rain barrel. A working cowboy, Mathilda opined. His eyes were cautious, a little befuddled, as he glanced from Mathilda to Hatfield.

"Haul her bags up onto the porch," Hatfield ordered the man he'd called Moon. "I'll take 'em from there."

Hatfield grabbed two of the lighter bags, turned, and headed for the cabin's front door. Mathilda stared after him, incredulous, embarrassed. She'd expected Hatfield to introduce her to his hired man, not simply walk away and leave her standing there with the onus of the introduction on Mathilda herself.

Mr. Hatfield not only needed a woman's touch around the place, he needed to be taught a few manners, as well. Such social blunders would not do. As Moon limped around to the back of the wagon, Mathilda stepped forthrightly up to him, extending her right hand.

"Hello, there, Mister Moon," she said, smiling. "I'm—"

She stopped when Moon, stooping to grab her steamer trunk, merely glanced at her perfunctorily; then, lifting the trunk off the ground with a grunt, swung away and followed Hatfield to the cabin.

"Well, for all the saints in holy heaven," Mathilda said in hushed exasperation, "I don't know that I've ever seen such discourtesy!" She stared in awe toward the cabin into which Hatfield was pushing while Moon continued lugging the heavy steamer trunk toward the veranda. "Good grief!" Miranda cried, grabbing one of her carpetbags from the wagon box and striding into the yard.

When Moon met her on his way back to the wagon, he didn't so much as glance at her. Mathilda shook her head in amazement. She stepped past the steamer trunk and walked into the cabin, which she was surprised to find not so shabbily appointed.

Hatfield's wife might have been dead for several years, but evidence of her presence remained in the form of decorative wall hangings, tasteful bric-a-brac owning a feminine flavor, and even a small piano sitting in a corner of the parlor, which took up the left side of the first story.

Gold sconces with white candles on an embroidered length of muslin adorned the piano. The kitchen, with its whitewashed cupboards, sink wet with water pump, large range, and oilcloth-covered eating table, was to the right. A narrow, unenclosed stairway divided the kitchen from the parlor.

Unfortunately, despite the tasteful furnishings, the place was a mess. It looked as though a man without comportment and no head for organization had had the run of the place for too long. The table was littered with dirty pots and pans and plates heaped with food leavings. A Winchester rifle leaned against the table near the door, and ammunition was spread across the oilcloth. A dead potted plant sat on the windowsill.

In the parlor, a pair of saddlebags hung over a side of the piano, and two pairs of shabby pants, a ragged shirt, and wash-worn longhandles had been hung to dry from a rope strung between ceiling beams.

"Oh, dear lord," Mathilda said, wrinkling her nose at the man-stench. "This place badly needs airing out . . . and cleaning up!"

She released the door handle, leaving the door wide. Boots thumped in the second story, and she looked up to see Mr. Hatfield standing atop the stairway. He no longer had her carpetbag and accordion bag in his hands.

"Our room's up here," he said. He turned slightly sideways and canted his head to indicate the hall behind him. "Come on up." There it was again—a lusty twinkle in his left eye.

"*Our* room," Mathilda muttered under her breath as she climbed the stairs. "We'll see about that . . ."

As she gained the second-floor hall, she caught Hatfield gazing at her with a seedy quirk to his mouth. She slipped past him, making sure their bodies did not make contact, and strode down the hall, surveying the wall hangings and two bracket lamps.

One of the lamps had a cracked mantle, as though someone had bumped it out of the sconce or perhaps fell against it in passing. There were two doors—one to each side and one at the end. The door at the end of the hall stood open.

"What are these other two rooms?" Mathilda asked, glancing back over her shoulder at Hatfield staring after her, arms crossed on his chest.

"Storage."

"I see."

Frowning, tentative, Mathilda stepped into the large main bedroom. The man-stench was even stronger in here. She made a sour expression, wrinkled her nose, and looked around. The large double bed with mahogany posters was unmade. On a delicate, cherry-wood dressing table stood an unlabeled bottle, half-filled with what was obviously liquor, and several shot glasses and two trays filled to overflowing with ashes. Two scatter rugs lay twisted on the floor amidst discarded socks, underwear, and several airtight tins and a beer bottle.

"Never been much for keepin' up a place," Hatfield said, stepping into the doorway behind Mathilda.

"Mister Hatfield, you've obviously been, uh . . . dwelling in here. But there is only one bed. You do mean to turn this room over to me, don't you?"

He leaned against the doorframe and canted his head. There it was again—that insinuating leer as the crow's eyes flicked her up and down. "What're you talkin' about? We're man and wife now."

He stepped toward her.

Chapter Four

"No," Mathilda said, raising her hands palm out and taking one step back. "Stop right there, Mr. Hatfield."

He stopped, placed his hands on hips, and scowled down at her. "Look, now—"

"No, you see here, Mister Hatfield. I am no doxie. That, despite its current state of disarray, is a marriage bed. I will not share a marriage bed with any man until I am married to him. Now, I will take this room—alone—until the minister arrives to marry us. Then you may move back in."

"Ah, hell, we don't hold with such form in these parts!"

"I do, Mister Hatfield. I will not lie with a man until I am married to him. Now, according to your letters, you were looking for a respectable woman to marry. I am that woman. I am not a . . . a . . . *parlor girl*!"

Hatfield opened his mouth to speak but she shut him up with: "I suppose you could take me by force. You are much bigger and stronger than I am, and, indeed, you come off as rather rough. Frankly, you're not at all what I expected after reading your letters. But if you were to take me against my will, I will guarantee you that I will not stay here afterwards but will ride or walk down off this mountain, if walk I must, and report such savage incivility to the nearest authority. I know there must be laws against rape even out here!"

"Oh, don't get your neck in such a godawful hump!" Hatfield intoned. "Christ almighty, woman, I don't see what difference it's gonna make if a man in a black shirt and a white collar reads words out of a book, but if that's what it's gonna take for you to act like a proper wife—all right, I'll ride down to Cormorant first thing in the mornin' and fetch us a sky pilot."

"Why don't we both ride down to this Cormorant place and have a decent church wedding?"

"There ain't no church down in Cormorant. It's a shaggy little minin' camp. There's more dogs than people and more whores than men. But there is a sky pilot. He preaches in a saloon every Sunday mornin', when he's sober enough to. That's his church. A saloon. Now, you wouldn't wanna be married in a saloon, would you?"

"Why, no!"

"Then I'll ride down to Cormorant and fetch the preacher, and we'll make everything decent and proper, and wrap a damn bow around it. In the meantime, I hope you can cook, 'cause I'm right hungry after that long damn ride to Dead Skunk Gulch and back!"

"I told you in my letters I can cook, didn't I? I am not a liar, Mister Hatfield. First, I'd like to straighten up a bit around here"—she glanced in horror around the messy bedroom—"and have a bath. I haven't had a proper bath since eastern Nebraska. Then I'll see what food you have to eat, and I will cook it."

"Christalmighty!" Hatfield grunted as he stomped out of the room.

"Mister Hatfield?" Mathilda called.

He stopped halfway down the hall, and turned back to her. "What is it? You want me to skin out of the county while you take a bath?"

"That won't be necessary. I'm wondering where I'll find a washtub."

"A what?"

"A washtub?"

"Well, hell . . . I don't know where a washtub is. I been taking my weekly baths in the creek out yonder."

"Surely, you have a washtub, Mister Hatfield."

"Surely, I do," Hatfield said, scrunching up his devilish little eyes at her and leaning slightly forward at the waist. "But I ain't used it in so long, I don't remember where it is. Why don't you look around the place and see if you can kick it up? Me—I got some chores to do."

He swung around and descended the stairs angrily, shaking his head.

As her mind turned to a badly needed bath, she remembered that the bulk of her clothes were in her steamer trunk.

"Oh, Mister Hatfield?" she called.

Silence.

Then, testily: "Yes?"

"My steamer trunk, if you please."

Though weary from her long trip and the unsettling attack at the stage relay station in Dead Skunk Gulch, Mathilda went back downstairs to stoke the stove so she could heat water for a bath.

Then she got busy straightening her room. She scoured it clean of useless debris, dumping it all into an empty flour sack she'd found by the range and tossing the sack out a window. She then piled Mr. Hatfield's gear in a corner.

She replaced the bed sheets, pillowcases, and quilts with fresh ones she'd packed in her trunk, and then set water to boil on the stove. She found a washtub hanging from a nail in the house's rear outer wall, and carried it upstairs.

Mr. Hatfield wasn't around—she wasn't sure where he'd gone, exactly—but even if he'd been near, she wouldn't have asked him for help, given the surliness of his demeanor. Besides, she was glad to have some time alone.

The bedroom was nowhere near clean, but a thorough sweeping and scrubbing would have to wait until tomorrow. She felt a desperate urge to scour her body from head to toe, cleansing it of days of trail filth. When enough water had heated, she filled the tub and adjusted the temperature with cold water from the pump. She closed the bedroom door and, grateful to find a locking bolt on it, slid the bolt into its slot in the doorframe, locking herself in. She didn't trust Mr. Hatfield farther than she could have thrown him uphill against a howling blizzard.

She hoped that his goatishness was merely due to his having been alone so long and not the symptom of some deeper character flaw. The more she thought about it, though she didn't want to think about it much at all, Mr. Hatfield didn't seem like the man who would have written those letters she'd received. Or *could* have written them. He didn't strike Mathilda as even *literate.*

Maybe, desperate for a wife, he'd coaxed someone else into writing the missives. If he himself hadn't written them, what other explanation could there be?

Yes, that must be it, she thought. The poor illiterate fool had coerced a literate neighbor to write the letters for him. Anyway, it was best to not think too deeply into the situation. When she'd decided to set her hat for marriage to a man in the Colorado Rockies, Mathilda had broken all of her ties to St. Paul. She'd quit her job as a bank clerk, said goodbye to her elderly aunt and uncle, and caught the west-heading trail.

This ranch was her home now. She had nowhere else to go. Shep Hatfield did not seem like the man she'd corresponded with, just as he did not seem like the kind of man she'd care to have much to do with at all—much less marry!—but she was here, now, and Mr. Hatfield was going to be her husband.

And that was that.

She had no choice but to make the best of it.

She shucked out of her clothes, pinned up her hair, sank into the steaming tub, and leisurely scrubbed herself. When she felt refreshingly cleansed of the travel filth, she sank back against the side of the tub, rested her head on the edge, and gazed absently around the room. The walls were covered in tan paper printed with yellow, pink, and purple flowers clinging to green vines against a backdrop of green leaves.

As she looked around the room, a frown stitched Mathilda's brows together. There were no pictures of people on the bedroom walls. And she couldn't remember seeing any pictures on any of the other walls in the house. There were homespun oil paintings and the sorts of decorative tintypes that could be purchased in mercantile stores, but there were no pictures of people.

No pictures of Hatfield or his wife or anyone else in their family.

However, a nail sprouted from the middle of the wall on the far side of the bed. Something had once hung from that nail. The fact was even more obvious given the slightly brighter color of the wallpaper where the hanging had hung. The paper around a lighter, fairly large, oval-shaped area had faded from the light striking it.

Since this was the marriage room, perhaps a wedding photo had hung from that wall. Had Hatfield removed it so as not to make Mathilda feel uncomfortable? That seemed odd, given that he'd been uncouth enough to leave the rest of the cabin in utter disarray.

But maybe it was the one thing he'd felt sensitive about . . .

When Mathilda climbed out of the tub and dressed and brushed out her long hair and pinned it into a roll atop her head, she primped a little and then went back downstairs. She looked around at all the walls. No pictures of people down here, either. But there were three empty nails poking out of the whitewashed logs.

Again, apprehension tickled the back of Mathilda's neck.

As she walked slowly around the parlor, frowning, arms crossed on her chest, she glanced out the front window to see her betrothed sitting on the veranda, leaning back in a wicker chair, his boots crossed atop the rail before him. She poked her head out the open door, leveling a quizzical look at the man.

"Mister Hatfield, why aren't there any pictures of your family on the walls? Surely, you must have family . . . beyond your wife, I mean. I can understand if you wanted to remove her pictures . . . for my comfort . . ."

"Huh? What? Pictures?"

He looked befuddled. Mathilda saw that there was a bottle on the floor by his chair, and a glass on the small table at his side. He was also smoking a hand-rolled cigarette.

"Yeah . . . that's it." He took a drag off the half-smoked cigarette, and blew smoke out his mouth and nose, answering, "Just didn't want to make you uncomfortable is all. I had ole Mam and Pap up, and some other kin, but they're all dead, so I thought I'd make room for you to hang whatever pitchers of whatever kin you still got."

He smiled as he took another drag from his quirley, as though mildly surprised as well as pleased by his answer.

"I see."

"Say, you look purty in that dress."

Mathilda looked down at the simple frock she'd donned, and flushed. "Oh . . . well, thank you."

"Right purty."

His eyes were on her breasts pushing out from behind the muslin of the frock's simple bodice. Crossing an arm over the rich mounds, Mathilda turned back into the kitchen.

"Say, I'm right hungry, and it's dang near my suppertime,"

Hatfield called behind her testily.

"I'm going to get started on supper right now," Mathilda said, glancing around the house once more. She saw that a cartridge belt and two holstered revolvers hung from a peg near the door, beside another peg from which a long, tan, canvas coat hung nearly to the floor.

The guns bothered Mathilda. So did the man's answer to her question about the missing photographs. A quiet voice inside her head was asking a troubling question, the gist of which was: *Had the man on the veranda taken down the photographs to conceal the fact that he was not, alas, Shep Hatfield?*

If he was not Shep Hatfield, who was he?

And where on earth was the actual Shep Hatfield?

The possibility that Mathilda was sharing the house with an imposter was too troubling to think about. So instead of thinking about it further, she set to work straightening up the kitchen, figuring out where all the utensils and spices were stored, and then taking an inventory of the food stores.

There wasn't much, but there was enough canned meat and tomatoes—and she found an onion and enough shriveled potatoes in an outdoor cellar behind the house—to cook a hearty stew. While the stew bubbled on the range, Mathilda mixed together the ingredients for biscuits.

While she worked, sweating in the warm kitchen with the ticking range, her fear-constricted heart beat quickly, painfully, despite her trying not to think about her possibly perilous situation.

Many times as she toiled, she cast glances onto the veranda where Hatfield sat, smoking and drinking. She could hear him moving around out there, shifting in his chair, drinking from his glass, sucking on his cigarette, occasionally coughing. Once he rose from his chair, and Mathilda felt herself shrink until she saw that he was stepping down off the veranda and into the yard.

As she removed the biscuits from the range, she watched Hatfield stride leisurely, heavy-footed from drink, over to the corral near the barn. She frowned as he faced the corral, moving oddly, bending his knees slightly, holding his hands down low in front of himself. Then he turned to one side, and she saw the stream of his water glisten as it made an arc in the bright but fading sunlight.

Hatfield . . . or whoever he was . . . turned his head toward her, grinning devilishly. Mathilda sucked a breath and turned away, cheeks warming.

"Say, where you goin' with that?" Hatfield asked her later, after they'd supped together in silence at the freshly cleared table.

Mathilda had filled an extra plate and held it steaming now by the door. She'd donned a cap against the evening's penetrating chill.

"I'm going to take a plate of stew to Mister Moon," Mathilda said, feeling her insides recoil again as Hatfield regarded her critically. When he'd taken his last bite of supper, he'd refilled his whiskey glass and rolled a fresh cigarette. His eyes were red.

"You didn't need to bother with that," Hatfield said. "Ole Moon can fend for himself. Come on back. Sit down. Let's play a game of poker. You know poker, don't you? If not, I'll teach you."

"I made enough stew to feed Mister Moon," Mathilda insisted. "And feed him I shall!"

She wasn't sure where she'd found the steel to put into her retort, but she was relieved to hear Hatfield laugh as she opened the door and carried the cloth-covered plate out into the cool, dark night. She drew the door closed behind her, still hearing Hatfield laugh as though both amused and impressed by the backbone she'd shown him.

She hurried across the yard toward the small, log outbuilding set back in the brush near the corral. She wanted to talk to Mr. Moon. She wanted to talk to him very badly . . .

Chapter Five

Mathilda could see a wan, guttering light in what appeared the cabin's only window, to the right of the door. She walked slowly toward the cabin, along a well-worn path, wincing when she kicked a couple of discarded airtight tins.

She knocked on the cabin door.

On the other side, a man grunted as though he were rising from a comfortable position. There was a scraping tread, and the door latch clicked. The door opened slightly. Mathilda could see the silhouette of Mr. Moon's face in the crack. His hair was rumpled.

"What do you want?" he asked gruffly, his breath frosting in the cold, dark air. A watery light shone behind him.

Mathilda held up the plate. "I brought you some supper."

Moon shook his head. "Nuh-uh. You just go on out of here. Leave me alone. I want no part of you."

He closed the door.

"Mister Moon," Mathilda said, flabbergasted. "I only wanted to bring you some food, and . . . and to ask you a few questions."

"Nuh-uh," Moon said on the other side of the door. "You go on out of here. Hurry, now—before he catches you over here!"

"He knows I came, Mister Moon. I told him I was bringing you some supper. He had no objection," she added, under the circumstances forgiving herself for the half-truth.

When Moon didn't respond, Mathilda tilted her head to the

door, listening. There was only silence.

"Mister Moon," she said, glancing cautiously back toward the house. "Who is he?"

Again, only silence.

She waited, but Moon offered no response. It was doubtful she would receive one. The man seemed petrified.

"All right, then, Mister Moon," Mathilda said with a sigh. "I'm going to set the plate outside your door here. I'm going back to the house."

She set the plate on the worn patch of ground fronting the door, turned, and strode back toward the lighted windows of the cabin. When she came to within a few yards of the house, she could see Hatfield inside, his back to the front windows, raising and lowering his shot glass and then pouring more whiskey.

Terrified now in light of her non-visit with Mr. Moon, Mathilda moved back inside. As she closed the door and stepped into the kitchen, Hatfield turned to her but didn't say anything. He merely looked up at her and winked over the rim of his shot glass.

He was laying out a game of solitaire. As he continued to play the solitary game, having apparently forgotten about the poker he'd offered to teach Mathilda—thank god!—she quietly, deliberately cleared the table and scrubbed the dishes. After drying them, she put them back where she'd found them. Hatfield did not speak, so neither did she.

As she worked, he laid out his cards and flicked each one down with little *snicking* sounds, considering each move carefully, sometimes muttering softly to himself. He sipped from his glass and smoked one cigarette after another.

The silence hung as thick as a cold fog.

When Mathilda finished her chores, she reached behind her back to untie her apron. "Well, it's late, and I'm weary from travel, so I think I'll . . ."

She let her voice trail off as she turned to see Hatfield slumped over his cards, right cheek on the table. One arm hung down below the table while the other one rested atop the table, beside the sleeping man's head.

His cards were still in his hand. She could hear him breathing. His breaths were growing gradually louder, making raking sounds in his throat. Soon, he would likely be snoring.

Mathilda's heart quickened.

She glanced up and behind the man to where his pistols resided in the holsters of the pegged shell belt. Her mind was a whirlpool of anxiety. She stared at the guns. What was she considering? Shooting him while he slept?

Certainly not. She'd never fired a gun in her life, much less *at* someone! She might, however, take one of the firearms upstairs with her, in case he woke up and tried to assault her. She nixed that idea, too. Since she didn't know how to wield such a weapon, she'd probably only shoot herself. Besides, his waking up and spying one of the pistols missing might spur him into doing the very thing she was so afraid of—attacking her.

He'd said he was going to leave first thing in the morning to fetch the minister from Cormorant. While he was gone, she'd figure out what she was going to do. Maybe once he was gone, if only for a few hours, Mr. Moon would feel safe enough to answer her questions about the man she was beginning to doubt more and more was really the man who'd fetched her out here to marry him.

What if he was, in fact, not that man?

What options did that leave Mathilda? What would she do? Where would she go? It was getting so late in the year, with winter on the way, that travel would soon be hazardous. She'd heard that the western mountains often received as much as or even more snow than her native Minnesota did, and it could get just as cold—which was *cold,* indeed. Certainly cold enough for a person without shelter to die very quickly from exposure.

Besides, Mathilda had little money—only the seventeen or so dollars left of the original nest egg she'd saved to help her travel west to be married. That certainly wasn't enough to get her back to Minnesota, even if she still had a home there, which she did not. Her aunt and uncle had rented out her room to a young woman attending the teaching academy.

When she'd made her way back to her room, and bolted the door, Mathilda crawled beneath the bedcovers without undressing. She felt vulnerable enough with that man nearby, whoever he was, without being half-naked, as well. He could probably break down her door with just one vicious kick.

She wasn't going to make it any easier for him to rape her than she needed to.

"Oh, god," she muttered aloud, her voice quavering in the semidarkness. She'd turned the lamp merely low, not out. "What in the world am I going to do?"

Even if the man downstairs was Shep Hatfield, Hatfield was not the man he'd purported himself to be in his letters. The man downstairs was a no-good ruffian. If he'd written those letters or coerced someone else to write them for him, he'd lured Mathilda here with lies.

He hadn't wanted a wife. He'd wanted a *whore.*

Nothing more, nothing less.

She had a feeling, however, that his story was even darker than that . . .

She lay awake for a long time, staring at the ceiling, feeling as frightened and alone as she had when she'd first been orphaned many years ago. The cold, dark universe seemed to want to suck her up into its vastness and obliterate her.

When the oil in the lamp bottomed out, the flame sputtered with a hissing sound, issuing black smoke up the chimney from the wick. The flame died. Darkness, like the ragged wing of a giant black bird, settled over the bed.

Mathilda had no idea how it had happened, but she must have slept. As though time had skipped ahead during a single heartbeat, she was aware of golden morning sunlight pushing through the curtained windows. She pushed up onto her elbows and looked around fearfully, as though expecting to find the man who called himself Shep Hatfield lying beside her, having had his way with her while she'd slept.

But she was alone in the room. The door was closed, the locking bolt residing in its catch.

Mathilda held her breath, listening. The house was silent. The only sounds from outside were the chirping of birds.

Mathilda rose from the bed and slid the curtain away from the near window, looking out into the ranch yard. Nothing moved except birds wheeling over the yard, and a thin column of gray smoke rising from the chimney pipe of Mr. Moon's cabin. The sun was up, which meant Mathilda had slept far later than she'd expected to. It must be eight-thirty or nine o'clock.

Where was Mr. Hatfield?

Mathilda tucked her hair back up into the roll she'd pinned after yesterday's bath. She adjusted her wrinkled frock, smoothing it across her thighs, donned her side-button shoes, then threw the locking bolt. She twisted the knob and opened the door, wincing at the squawk of the rusty hinges.

She gazed straight out along the hall toward the stairs. She neither saw nor heard anyone moving about the house. Opening the door farther, she stepped into the hall, unconsciously crossing her arms on her breasts. She stole along the hall and stopped at the top of the stairs, surveying the first story below.

Empty.

On the kitchen table was a bottle and a shot glass as well as a tray overflowing with ashes and cigarette butts.

"Mister Hatfield?" Mathilda called.

No response.

She called the man's name again, louder.

Still, no response.

She smelled him, though. The stench of unwashed man and whiskey and cigarettes was cloying. She felt her insides contract against it.

Mathilda moved on down the stairs. She swept her gaze around the parlor and then turned toward the kitchen washed by the golden rays of the morning sun pushing through the house's front window.

Hatfield was not here. She knew a moment's relief, but that relief was vanquished by her acknowledgment that just because he wasn't here now didn't mean he wouldn't be back. And she still had the problem of her possibly—no, *probably*—being held here by an imposter, a man who'd lured her here merely to satisfy his darkest desires.

In the corner of her right eye, Mathilda spied movement in the yard. She jerked with a start and turned to gaze out the sun-bright window left of the door.

Mr. Moon was leading a mottled gray horse toward the house. The horse was saddled and a blanket roll was strapped behind the saddle. Moon wore a hat, gloves, leather leggings, and a denim coat that hung down past his waist. He also wore a cartridge belt and holster from which a six-gun jutted.

As Moon led the horse up to the house, he stared off to the west with a dark, cautious cast to his gaze.

Brows furrowed, Mathilda stepped out onto the veranda, and cast her puzzled gaze at Moon, who was looping his horse's reins over the tie rail fronting the house. "Mister Moon," she said. "Are . . . you going somewhere?"

When she'd stepped out, he'd jerked a quick, startled look at her, as though his nerves were drawn as taut as hers were.

"Hell, yeah, I'm goin' somewhere," Moon said, chuckling darkly as he limped up the veranda steps. He looked down at her and shoved his hat back off his forehead. "I'm gettin' the hell away from that devil."

He gave her a scampish grin, his eyes twinkling beneath his hat brim. "But, first . . ."

"But first what?" Mathilda said, turning as he brushed past her into the house. When Moon did not reply but stood just inside the kitchen, looking around, Mathilda said, "I don't understand. Where is Mister Hatfield?"

"Huh?" Moon said, glancing over his shoulder at her as though nudged from a reverie. "Hatfield? Shit, he's dead!"

"Dead?" The word knocked Mathilda backward. Her heart thudded.

"Dead and buried in a shallow grave behind the house," Moon said, walking around the parlor and casting his gaze about anxiously, as though looking for something. "That man in here last night . . . that wasn't Shep Hatfield. Told me his name was Beauregard. Frank Beauregard."

Mathilda fought to remain calm, licking her lips. "Where . . . where is Mr. Beauregard now?"

Moon paused in his desperate scouring of the parlor to cast Mathilda his baleful grin again. "Frank's done ridden down to Cormorant to fetch a preacher. And lay in a supply of whiskey, most likely." He laughed as he raked Mathilda's heaving chest with his goatish gaze. "He's done gonna have a fine ole time with you this winter. He intends to hole up here, let his trail cool. He expects me to run the ranch, keep things in trim, the herds gathered and whatnot, so no one will suspect poor ole Shep Hatfield is dead until spring . . . at which time Frank'll likely cut your throat and head for Mexico!"

Again, Mathilda gasped and stumbled backward.

"Me?" Moon said, loudly. "Shit, I'm splittin' ass outta here right now—this mornin'! If I stayed around here all winter, I'd be as dead as you're gonna be come spring."

"I knew . . . I knew he was an imposter!"

"Really?" Moon said, chuckling as he resumed his frantic search of the house's first story, crouching to look under furniture and tossing books from shelves, opening cabinet doors and rummaging around inside. "What was your first fuckin' clue?"

"Oh, my god, Shep Hatfield is *dead*?" Mathilda cried as the realization struck her with the full force of its implications. *"Really?"*

"Sure enough," Moon said. "Frank rode in here a week ago, let ole Shep fix him supper, serve him whiskey. Shep was generous that way. He never saw no man as a stranger. But as soon as Frank had his fill of Shep's hospitality, Frank shot him in the heart and buried him out back. He'd have shot me, too, except he decided to hole up here . . . and decided he needed someone to run the ranch . . . tend the stock for him. I suppose he figured a man with a bad leg wouldn't give him any problems."

Moon, having given the first story a thorough search, started up the stairs, dragging his bad leg. He paused to look back down at Mathilda. "Ole Shep would have enjoyed you." He shook his head as though with genuine sadness. "He was awful lonely since Bonnie died three summers ago. He read me the letters he wrote you, really wanted to get the words right. He was lookin' forward to you comin' and gettin' all hitched again. Too bad. He'd have made a good husband. And you . . ." Moon's eyes brightened as they strayed back down to Mathilda's swollen corset. "You woulda made one hell of a wife!"

"Mister Moon, you can't leave me here alone!" Mathilda yelled as Moon climbed the stairs. "Please," she cried. "You have to take me with you!"

Moon said nothing as he clomped down the hall.

Mathilda hurried up the stairs, lifting her skirts above her ankles. Moon was in the main bedroom, stomping around like a bear in a cage. Mathilda strode into the room and yelled in frustration, "What are you *looking* for, Mister Moon?"

He rummaged around in the armoire, muttering, "Gotta be somewhere. He'd have wanted to keep 'em close."

Mathilda ran to Moon, grabbed his arm with both her hands, and fairly shouted, "Please, Mister Moon—you must take me with you. You can't leave me alone here. If what you say is true, that . . . that Mister Beauregard is a cold-blooded killer!"

"That he is, sure enough," Moon said. "And I'd love to have you along for the ride, believe me." He chuckled lustily. "But you'd only slow me down. Soon as I find them saddlebags, I'm . . ."

He let his voice trail off. He'd wrenched his arm free of her grip and stooped to open a steamer trunk sitting on the floor at the end of the bed.

"*What* saddlebags?" Mathilda asked in frustration.

"These saddlebags right here," Moon said, lifting a pair of leather saddlebags from the trunk. He turned to her, dreamy-eyed, clutching the bulging bags against his chest like a mother with a newborn babe. "These bags right here, sure enough."

He opened one of the flaps and looked inside. His eyes brightened and a smile of pure rapture blazed on his unshaven face. He held his wide-eyed gaze on Mathilda as he dipped his hand into the pouch. He pulled out a packet of greenbacks bound with a brown paper band, and looked at it.

"Mercy, look at that! Oh, mercy, look at that!"

Moon brought the packet to his mouth and kissed it. He hopped a jig and slapped his knee.

"Now, ain't that a sight for sore eyes?" He jostled the bags against his chest. "This here is the twenty-five-thousand dollars ole Frank and his bunch stole off the midnight Atchison flier between Denver and Cheyenne last month—yessir! I heard about it when I drove down to Cormorant for supplies. Not a week later, ole Frank rode into Hatfield's yard, and if you don't think you coulda knocked me over with the petal of a dead daffodil! Ha!"

Moon dropped the money back into the pouch, buckled the flap, slung the bags over his left shoulder, and headed for the door. "I'd love to stay and chat with you, honey, but I'll be headin' for Juarez. The fillies down there maybe can't cook good as you, but they don't just lay there and chew their knuckles." He laughed. "You fill out a frock right nice an' all, but I had you pegged for a knuckle-chewer the second I laid eyes on you!"

The thunder of his raucous laughter echoed around the hall.

"No, please, Mister Moon!" Mathilda ran after him. "You must take me with you. You can't leave me here alone with that—!"

She cut herself off when Moon stopped at the top of the stairs and stared down toward the first floor. Mathilda froze halfway between the main bedroom and Moon. She stared in trepidation at the man's back. He stood so still that he might have been a statue standing there, chin dipped, saddlebags on his shoulder.

A statue of a man frozen in shock.

There was a faint dripping sound. Mathilda looked down to see water dribbling down from Moon's right pant leg onto the toe of his boot.

Chapter Six

Mathilda stole slowly up behind Moon, who remained at the top of the stairs, staring in hang-jawed horror. While Moon continued to evacuate his bladder down his leg, the urine pooling on the floor around his boot, Mathilda peered over his shoulder.

Her heart dropped into her stomach.

She knew who she was going to see standing there at the bottom of the stairs, but she still wasn't prepared for the sight of Mr. Hatfield . . . er, Frank Beauregard . . . glaring up at her and Moon. Beauregard stood with his head canted to one side, one boot cocked forward, hands on his hips. His pistols bristled on his thighs. His long canvas coat was pushed back behind the holstered weapons.

Mathilda's face slackened in shock. She felt the blood drain out of it, and her knees turn to warm mud.

Beauregard didn't say anything. He just stared up at Moon, within whom Mathilda heard a low moaning sound begin to rise as though from deep in the man's chest. The sound started out very low but slowly built into a keening wail on the heels of which Moon raised his gloved hands in supplication toward Beauregard, and said, "N-now . . . now . . . now . . ."

"Walter," Beauregard said, lowering his flinty gaze, "you done pissed yourself."

"Now, Frank, I—"

"I what, Walter? Let's hear it. I what?" Beauregard paused. "I don't really have the saddlebags filled with that stolen train loot draped over my shoulder, Frank. Is that what you're trying to say, Walter?"

"Now, Frank."

"Come on down here, Walter. Let me take a look at them bags. They sure look like the same ones I was storin' in that steamer trunk at the end of"—he glanced at Mathilda and grinned—"the marriage bed."

"Oh," Mathilda said, the hall and the stairs slowly turning around her. "Oh . . . Mister Beauregard—oh . . . please . . ."

"Come on down," Beauregard said, returning his gaze to Moon and raising and lowering his chin. "Come on down. Let me have a look at them bags."

Moon stepped forward and, like a frightened dog being hailed by a cruel master, began moving down the stairs. He was fairly sobbing as he stopped at the bottom step and stared at Beauregard standing before him, in the same position as a minute ago.

"Now Frank," Moon said, whining and holding his hands up in front of him, palms out, "I wasn't gonna . . . really . . . I wasn't . . ."

"Wasn't gonna do what, Walter?" Beauregard opened the flap of the pouch hanging down Moon's chest. "You wasn't gonna skin out fer Mexico with my loot?"

"Frank," Moon moaned. "Oh, Frank . . ."

Beauregard ripped the saddlebags off Moon's shoulder and tossed them onto the floor. He glanced up at Mathilda and said, "Was you gonna take my darlin' bride, too? My money and my woman?"

"No, Frank," Moon said, slowly shaking his head, "no . . ."

Mathilda swallowed the hard knot in her throat, and said, "Mister Beauregard . . . please . . . don't . . ."

Beauregard swept up his left hand toward Moon's face. Moon gasped and lowered his head, like a cowering dog, and Beauregard swept his hat off his head.

"No, Frank!" wailed Moon.

Beauregard grabbed Moon by the front of his jacket and jerked him around and thrust him toward the door standing open behind him.

"Mister Beauregard!" Mathilda screamed as Beauregard followed Moon out onto the porch.

She ran down the stairs on quivering legs, her heart racing. Just beyond the door, Beauregard shoved Moon down the porch steps and into the yard.

"Don't shoot me, Frank," Moon begged, sobbing, throwing his arms up and backing away. "Oh, please don't shoot me. Show some mercy!"

"I just had me a feelin' as soon as I left the yard you'd be up to somethin'," Beauregard said, dropping down the steps and strolling slowly toward where Moon was still backing away from him. "You and"—he glanced over his shoulder at Mathilda—"her."

"No, Frank!" Moon urged. *No!*"

"Please don't do anything irrational," Mathilda cried, moving toward Beauregard. She was more afraid for her own life than she'd ever been, but she felt compelled to try to save Mr. Moon. "There's no point in doing anything you might regret."

"Regret what?" Beauregard laughed. "Regret shootin' this dung beetle that was trying to rob me blind? Hell, I'm not gonna regret that at all."

"There is no point in bloodshed," Mathilda said, grabbing Beauregard's left arm, trying to stop his progress toward Moon.

"Sure, there is," Beauregard said, turning and giving Mathilda a hard, violent shove.

She screamed as she hit the ground and rolled up against the bottom of the porch steps.

"Sure, there's a point in bloodshed," Beauregard said, turning back to Moon, who continued backing away from the aggressor, his hands raised shoulder high. "The point is dyin'. The point is, see—he tried to rob me, steal my woman."

"No, he didn't!" Mathilda said, sitting up, dazed. "That part was my idea, Mister Beauregard. Not his."

"He just wanted the money—that it?" asked Beauregard, keeping his eyes on Moon.

"Please don't shoot me, Frank!" Moon pleaded. "Oh, please don't shoot me! I'm just a thirty-a-month-and-found cowpuncher! I send five dollars a month out to my old ma in Nevada!"

Beauregard stopped walking. Between his spread legs, Mathilda could see Moon beyond him, backing away.

Beauregard thrust his right arm toward Moon. "Stop!"

Moon stopped so quickly that he almost fell.

His back to Mathilda, Beauregard placed his fists on his hips. "You might as well make a play, Moon. Don't make this so easy for me. What have you got to lose?"

"I ain't gonna get in no draw down with you, Frank. Why, just lookin' at you and them pistols, I can tell you're faster'n greased lightning!"

Beauregard laughed, pleased. "Still might as well make a game of it. You don't wanna die with your pistol in its holster, do you? That's no way for a man to die."

Mathilda sat back against the steps, breathing hard, one leg curled under the other one. She watched the two men in speechless horror. She was about to see a cold-blooded murder. The fact was as cold as a Minnesota snowstorm. It froze her brain and sucked the wind out of her lungs.

She stared in horror at Moon from between Beauregard's spread legs.

Moon looked at Mathilda. It was a quick, dark, frantic look. Then he lifted his gaze to Beauregard and, crouching, whipped his right hand down to the pistol holstered on his hip. He screamed as he raised the pistol. It belched smoke and flames.

Beauregard jerked his head to one side, as though he'd been slapped. At nearly the same time, Mathilda heard the roar of Moon's gun as well as a hard thumping sound in a support post behind her.

Beauregard had also jerked his own pistol from his holster, and a sixteenth of a second after Moon's revolver had barked, Moon's did, as well. Moon stumbled backward, drawing his stiff arms across his belly.

He gave a ghastly howl, stretching his lips back from his teeth. He stumbled back once more, then began raising his pistol again.

Beauregard walked toward him, firing his own gun two more times, each shot punching Moon two more steps backward, wailing. Moon lifted his chin skyward and gave one more tooth-gnashing howl before he fell to his butt, dust billowing around him. He slumped backward and to one side, and lay on his hip and shoulder, quivering.

Beauregard stood over Moon. He aimed his pistol down in front of him, and fired once more. Moon's head bounced violently. The man's body tensed. He sort of arched his back, digging his heels into the ground as though he were trying to rise. He raked his arms up and down across the ground, as though he were making dust angels.

Then he slumped back down, made a gurgling sound, and lay deathly still.

Smoke from Moon's gun wafted in the midmorning sunlight.

Beauregard turned back toward Mathilda, rubbing the heel of his left hand across that cheek. A long line of blood shone. As he walked toward her, he chuckled dryly.

"That's what I get for foolin' around. Bastard was faster'n he thought he was!"

Mathilda stared up in horror as the killer strolled toward her, grinning. He holstered his smoking revolver. Mathilda gave a warbling cry of terror, knowing by the glint in the man's eyes what would happen next. She scrambled to her feet. Twisting around, she lunged up the veranda steps.

She'd just gotten to the top when he grabbed her right ankle, tripping her. She slammed face down onto the veranda floor, an anguished grunt punched out of her throat.

She tried to rise but then the full weight of the man's body was on her, pressing her down. "Weddin', my ass!" Beauregard laughed. "I wasn't goin' for no preacher. I was goin' for whiskey over to the old tradin' post . . . to celebrate our union . . . but then I got to thinkin' that it might not have been such a good idea, leavin' you and Walter here alone"—he raised his eyebrows—"with my nest egg."

Beauregard grabbed the hem of her skirt and tore the frock vertically up to her hips with a savage exclamation. Instantly, Mathilda felt the cool morning breeze on her pantaloon-covered legs. With another savage grunt, Beauregard pulled the undergarment as well as her bloomers down to her ankles, and she could feel the air's assault on her bare skin.

"Oh, god," Mathilda said, her cheek pressed against the rough wooden floor. "Oh, no. Oh, please, don't!"

Beauregard laughed. Keeping one hand on her back, holding her down, he laid his unshaven cheek against her bare bottom. His beard bristles raked her. He sniffed her, like a dog. She gave another moan as he slid his hand between her legs. His fingers probed her most private regions.

Mathilda squeezed her eyes closed and sobbed, tears dribbling down her cheeks and onto the floor.

"Beauregard!" came a man's distant voice.

Beauregard's fingers stopped probing. Mathilda could feel her attacker's body tense on top of her.

"Beauregard, you devil—leave that poor girl alone, hear?" came a voice that sounded oddly familiar.

Beauregard rose and whipped around. Mathilda saw him reach for his holstered revolver.

A distant gun thundered.

Beauregard screamed and flew back on top of Mathilda once more. She craned her head around to see him staring down at her, his eyes and mouth wide in horror. He was a dead weight on her back. Through her dress, she could feel the oily wetness of blood leaking out of his chest.

Beauregard raised his left hand slowly and raked his dirty fingers across Mathilda's cheek. He winced, convulsed in pain, and then said throatily, weakly, "We . . . coulda . . . had us . . . a good time . . . you an' me . . ."

His hand fell away from her face. His chin dropped to her shoulder. His eyes remained riveted on Mathilda's, but they quickly turned as opaque as dusty windows.

Mathilda stared in shock at the suddenly dead man on top of her. Crunching footsteps approached. Spurs rang. A shadow, as though death's own, passed over the back of Frank Beauregard. A tall, broad-shouldered man in a funnel-brimmed hat stood over the dead man and Mathilda, staring down.

His face was silhouetted against the sun behind him.

He shook his head in disgust and then grabbed Beauregard's shirt collar, and rolled the man off of Mathilda. The repulsive sensation of oily blood remained on her back. She looked up at the big man. In silhouette against the sky, he appeared as large as a mountain and as dangerous as a summer storm.

He held out his hand to her. It was huge and brown. There was blood on it. In his other hand he held a rifle. Smoke curled from the barrel.

Mathilda looked at Frank Beauregard lying on the ground beside the steps. His eyes reflected the bright sunlight. A large bloodstain glistened on his chest.

Another wave of terror and revulsion rolled through Mathilda. Blood and deadly violence were everywhere.

"No, no, no!" she cried as she scrambled to her feet, tripping. She paused to pull up her underwear and thrust her torn dress down over her legs. *"Nooooo!"* She ran into the house and up the stairs. *"Leave me alone!"*

Blood and deadly violence . . .

She wanted only the safety of the bedroom. She wanted to stay behind that locked door forever, and never come out.

She dashed into the room and threw the bolt.

Chapter Seven

Lou Prophet watched the young woman scamper into the house and up the stairway.

About halfway to the top of the stairs, she tripped on the hem of her dress and dropped to a knee with a yowl. Desperately, as though the devil's seven hounds were on her heels, she bounded back to her feet, jerked up her dress, and continued climbing. Her stamping footsteps dwindled into the second story, and there was the crack of a door being slammed and the rake of a bolt being thrown.

Prophet scratched the back of his head, nudging his badly weathered hat low on his broad forehead. "I declare," he said in his petal-soft, rich, deep-southern accent, turning to where Frank Beauregard lay staring sightlessly up at him, "you made a wreck of that girl, Frank. Her nerves are stretched tight as a buxom nun's corset. Too bad you're not still alive so I could kill you again."

The big bounty hunter prodded Beauregard's side with his boot toe. "That's the problem with killin' a bastard like you—once you're dead, a feller can't kill you again. And if ever a man deserved a second killin', that son of a bitch is you. I reckon the world's just cockeyed that way. That and some other ways . . ."

Prophet let his voice trail off. He was just babbling, anyway. Procrastinating. Now that he'd killed Beauregard, the real work began—the unpleasant task of getting the sorry bastard out of the mountains to Denver so Prophet could claim the reward money. Wells Fargo was offering a good-sized bounty, a full thousand dollars, for the capture or killing of Frank Beauregard and the safe return of the money he and his gang stole from their express car between Denver and Cheyenne.

There was a thousand-dollar bounty on each of the other gang members, but a posse out of Camp Collins had taken care of most of them, who were snuggling now with angleworms and diamondbacks.

Only two of the gang had escaped into the Front Range mountains—Frank and the Missouri gunslick, Norwood Cranston. Frank and Norwood had split up somewhere around Idaho Springs. At least, that's where their trails had diverged. Knowing there was little honor among thieves, the bounty hunter recognized the possibility that either Frank or Cranston might have absconded with the bulk of the loot.

Prophet hoped his partner, the pretty but surly Louisa Bonaventure, was either closing on Cranston by now or had overtaken him. Whether Cranston had the loot or not, they could use that extra thousand dollars on Cranston's head to get them through another long western winter.

Prophet stepped out away from Beauregard's bloody carcass, looking around the humble ranch yard. He wondered if anyone else was here. Anyone living, that was. He'd seen the other man lying dead in the yard, halfway between the house and the barn.

"Hello?" Prophet called. "Anyone else here?" Besides the girl upstairs in the house, he meant. Whoever she was, whatever her place here was . . .

He called again, louder, but the chirping of birds and the sowing of the wind in the brush around the buildings was his only response.

He looked at the second dead man in the yard. Prophet had seen Norwood Cranston's likeness inked on a wanted dodger, so he knew this man wasn't Cranston.

The young woman's husband?

Prophet would likely find out sooner or later. If she ever came out of her room, that was . . .

In the meantime, Prophet dragged both dead men into the barn. He'd prepare Frank for transport later. He had to find out who the other man was. It was only right. He hadn't killed him, but if the woman was alone here, Prophet should take it upon himself to give the gent a proper burial. A lot of bounty hunters wouldn't do that, but such men gave bounty hunting a bad name. Prophet was above their ilk.

He would remain here until he'd buried the second gent. He and his horse needed a rest. They'd traveled far over the past several weeks, kicking up squirrels in every "hoot an' holler," as the southern saying went, looking for signs of the train robbers.

Beauregard's gang had robbed the train nearly a month ago. Most of the others in the bunch of seven had gotten themselves run down and beefed, but Frank and Norwood Cranston were wily. Their horses had seemingly sprouted wings.

Prophet was nothing if not persistent, however. Persistence often paid off in a profession overcrowded with shilly-shallying types. If a bounty hunter took down only the easy quarry, he'd soon find himself having to supplement his income swamping saloons or digging privy pits. Prophet had worked enough in both trades to know he didn't want to work in them again. Beauregard's cold trail warmed every now and then when Prophet, asking around, ran into someone who'd seen a rider fitting Frank's description.

So now with Beauregard dead and ready to be wrapped in a saddle blanket, Prophet would cool his heels and rest his horse, Mean and Ugly. Thinking of the horse now, he whistled. A minute later, the lineback dun galloped into the yard, his reins wrapped around his saddle horn. Prophet's double-barreled coach gun, a Richards ten-gauge shotgun, sawed off just above the stock, was also bound to the saddle horn by its leather lanyard.

He reserved use of the savage but efficient weapon for tight-quarters work. The Richards was no good at more than fifteen feet. That's when his Colt Peacemaker or Winchester '73 came into play.

Prophet stripped the gear off the horse and hazed him into an otherwise empty corral, one closed off by a gate from the one in which four ranch horses and one mule milled. Prophet was glad for the empty corral. As per the dun's name, Mean and Ugly didn't get along well with others, especially when a mare was present. Mean had been gelded, but he tended to forget, and he'd fight a stallion for a filly's attentions . . .

When the bounty hunter had tended the horse, rubbing him down and feeding him fresh oats and hay from the barn and water from the windmill, Prophet clomped up the porch steps and peered through the house's open door. He tapped his knuckles on the door, clearing his throat.

"Ma'am?"

No response.

Louder, he said, "Ma'am, I might look big and owly, but I'm no *real* threat."

He supposed the fresh bruises on his face from the previous night's dustup at Dead Skunk Gulch didn't make him look any less dodgy. One eye was swollen half-shut, but it didn't hurt any worse than what he was accustomed to. He'd fought for the Confederacy, and there hadn't been much for soldiers to do in winter bivouac after they'd wearied of pitching horseshoes and playing euchre except to box or wrestle or play an especially violent form of leapfrog.

Prophet moved inside and stopped at the bottom of the stairs. "Ma'am?" he called again, directing his voice up the steps, holding his hat in both hands in front of his broad chest.

"Ma'am, the name's Prophet. We met back at the . . ."

He spied a pair of saddlebags lying on the parlor floor, six feet to his left. He squatted over the bags, unbuckled the flap over one of the pouches, and looked inside.

"Well, I'll be hanged if the old coon ain't treed."

When he looked in the opposite pouch, he smiled again, then rose and draped the bags over the back of a chair at the kitchen table. He was going to leave the bags there, but then he cast a cautious glance through a front window, into the yard, and reconsidered.

There didn't appear to be anyone around, but he hadn't come all this way to get the bags stolen out from under him.

He draped the bags over his shoulder and climbed the stairs. He strode down the hall, wincing at the stamping of his boots on the wooden floor. He tried to lighten his tread but it didn't do much to squelch his thunder and the chiming of his spurs.

He'd seen the young woman go into the room at the hall's end, so he paused outside that door, canted his head to listen, then, not hearing any sounds, rapped three times lightly.

"Ma'am . . . uh . . . miss?"

"Go away!" she cried on the other side of the door. He could tell from the pinched, quavering sound of her voice that she'd been sobbing.

"I just wanted to assure you I mean you no—"

"Oh, go away, won't you? Please go away! I want to be left alone!"

"Just one thing, ma'am . . . er, miss. I'm wonderin' who that gent—"

"Oh, please, go away! Please go away and leave me alone!"

Prophet sighed. He set his hat on his head. "All right."

He turned and strode back down the stairs and into the yard. He looked around, pondering where to stow the saddlebags.

Finally, he went into the barn and dropped them into the oat bin. That's likely the first place anyone would look—if anyone came calling, that was—but he didn't want to hide them so well he wouldn't be able to find them again himself. Besides, they wouldn't be there long, and he'd keep a sharp eye out for interlopers.

He climbed up onto the corral near where Mean and Ugly was contentedly munching hay from a crib, and rolled a smoke. Mean whickered and switched his tail in greeting, and kept on munching.

It was only noon, so Prophet had the day and night to kill. Tomorrow, with the train loot and Frank Beauregard in tow, he'd head down out of the mountains toward Denver. He'd likely meet his comely partner, the Vengeance Queen herself, somewhere along the way. If their trails didn't naturally converge, they'd agreed to meet at the Larimer Hotel in Denver.

Pondering his situation, Prophet licked the quirley closed, fired a match to life on his holster, and touched the flame to the cigarette. He'd like to know who the second dead gent was so he could decide what to do with him. He'd like to have that poor gent taken care of so he could concentrate on Frank and the loot, but that would have to wait until he could lure the woman out of hiding.

She'd probably dry up soon—even women had only so many tears to shed—and drift downstairs. In the meantime, he'd smoke his cigarette and maybe find a creek—he'd thought he'd heard one rushing when he'd ridden around the perimeter of the yard, getting the lay of the land—and have a good soak.

He smoked the cigarette, then mashed it out in the dirt with his boot. He grabbed his war bag and walked off to the southeast and found a broad, shallow stream curving through pines. He walked along the stream a ways to the east, through the soughing pines, and found a dark pool.

He looked around carefully, making sure he was alone out

here, and then dropped the war bag and kicked out of his boots.

He tossed his hat down in the brush, removed his shell belt and revolver as well as the bowie knife sheathed behind his right shoulder, and emptied his pockets of what little he had stowed in there—a few coins, an old rabbit's foot he'd carried during the war (and which he supposed had brought him luck in that he hadn't died, though he'd watched hundreds of others, including several of his own cousins, turned to red jelly by Union Minie balls and grapeshot), and a tarnished silver pocket watch that had been creased by an Apache arrow a few years back in western Texas.

He grabbed a soap cake from his war bag, walked over to the edge of the bank, drew a deep breath, squeezed his eyes closed, and stepped off the bank, plunging into the pool. The water was a good five feet deep here. He crouched to let it wash over his head, soaking his grimy trail clothes. He stayed under for a time, hearing his heart beating in his ears, the stream gurgling hollowly around him, and then lifted his head above the water, drawing air into his lungs.

He thrashed around for a time, twisting and turning and kicking, giving his dirty, sweaty duds a good scouring, and then waded into the shallower water upstream a ways. He sat down on the bank and skinned out of his sodden clothes. He laid the clothes out to dry on a log near the stream's edge, then, naked, he lathered every inch of his brawny body. He reached as far behind as he could to lather his back.

The cool water and cleansing soap felt so good as it ground away at his sweat- and dirt-chafed skin that he threw his head back and sent a howl careening toward the pine tops. A crow cawed in answer. Prophet howled again and shook his head, his wet, sandy hair flopping across his forehead.

"Hot damn!" he intoned. "This feels so good it's a wonder a feller don't take the plunge more often!"

When he was white and froggy with gossamer soap bubbles, he tossed the soap onto the bank, near his war bag, and plunged back into the deeper pool, rinsing himself off. He lay in the shallows for a time, having a good soak, and then climbed up onto the bank and lay down in the tall grass, in a patch of radiant sunlight, to dry off.

His eyelids grew heavy, and soon he was snoozing, vaguely hearing his own snores competing with the calm forest hubbub of the breeze, birds, tumbling pinecones, murmuring water, and chattering squirrels.

The snores died with a gurgling grunt, and he snapped his eyes open.

He drew a deep, calming breath despite the unnatural sound he'd heard among the din, and gained his bare feet. Calmly, keeping his head down but rolling his eyes around, surveying his surroundings, he made as though to pluck his longhandles off the log they'd been drying on.

Instead, he grabbed his Winchester '73, slammed a cartridge into the chamber, dropped to a knee, and fired.

Chapter Eight

The man bearing down on Prophet with a Sharps carbine fired his own rifle as Prophet's bullet punched into his chest, causing him to jerk his rifle up and his bullet to blast a pinecone out of a bough arching over him.

The shooter screamed and stumbled backward, falling.

Standing naked with his smoking Winchester, Prophet racked another round into the action but held fire. His assailant had tossed the Sharps wide and he wasn't reaching for the pistol jutting on his right hip. He lay in the short grass and pine needles, writhing and bellowing as he flopped his arms and legs.

Prophet looked around for more shooters. There were only the slanting columns of sunlight and inky forest shadows. Behind him, seventy yards away, he glimpsed the barn and cabin turning dull gray in the waning light of the late afternoon. Aiming the Winchester one-handed from his hip, the bounty hunter strode forward, wincing at the pine needles and broken twigs nipping at his bare feet.

He stopped and glowered down at a middle-aged man with a thin, gray beard that could not mask the large, brown warts on his lean, badly bruised face. One of his eyes was swollen shut, and his nose was fat and purple. Both lips were badly torn and crusted with dried blood. His left hand was wrapped in white, bloodstained flannel knotted at the palm.

The hole in his upper left chest was oozing frothy blood.

"Well, well, 'Hound Dog' Chuck Hagen—fancy meetin' you here."

Hagen's pain-bright eyes focused on Prophet, and the man hardened his jaws.

"You didn't get enough of me back in Dead Skunk Gulch—eh, pard?" Prophet asked.

"Fuck you, Prophet—you son of a bitch. You killed me!"

"You killed yourself when you followed me up here." Prophet dropped to a knee and leaned on his rifle as he glared down at the man who'd been about to trim his wick. "You did follow me up here, didn't you, pard? I take it you didn't come for the fishin'."

Hound Dog Hagen cursed him again. Hagen cursed Prophet's mother and his father separately and then both of them together, until blood licked over his ruined bottom lip.

Prophet chuckled and poked his finger in the hole his bullet had punched in the man's chest.

Hagen bellowed and flopped violently.

"How many others came with you?"

"Just me! Just me! Oh, please, stop doin' that, you rotten Rebel bastard!"

Prophet glanced around and pulled his finger out of the bloody hole.

"Why did you follow me?"

Between ragged breaths, Hound Dog said, "Seen . . . seen you pull out of the Gulch early this mornin'. None of the others was up yet. They was sleepin' off all the whiskey they drank after you beat holy hell out of us."

Hound Dog licked his bloody lips. "You looked like a dog on a scent . . . so . . . so I followed ya. Ever'body knows that jasper, Beauregard, is up here somewhere. Figured you must've . . . must've sniffed out where." He writhed violently. "Oh, shit—I'm in a bad way, Prophet!"

Prophet chuckled. "If you and the others wasn't so damn intent to clean my clock yesterday, you might've seen him, too. He drove into the yard of the relay station, and picked up the girl. I recognized him from the wanted circulars."

Hound Dog stared up at Prophet, incredulous. He cursed again.

"I'm too old for this kinda work," Hagen said. "A few years ago . . . I woulda given you a run for your money, you big bastard."

"Instead, you turned to bounty poachin'," Prophet said, shaking his head. "That makes you lower than a snake's belly in a wagon rut. A few years ago, that would've been above even you, Hound Dog."

"Prophet, do me a favor?"

"What's that?"

Hound Dog chuckled despite the pain in his eyes. "Put some clothes on, will ya? I don't want the last thing I see on this earth to be your big hairy naked hide!" He laughed again, stretching his lips back from his large, tobacco-stained teeth.

Then the light leeched out of his eyes and he lay still, eyes and mouth wide as though in eternal horror of his grisly end.

Prophet sighed and wiped blood from his finger on Hound Dog's canvas trousers. He rose and sighed again. "Damnit all, Hound Dog. You was never worth much, but you was once worth somethin'."

Over the years, Prophet had crossed a few of Hound Dog's trails, also a bounty hunter. They'd played a few hands of poker together and even shared a cook fire up in the wilds of Montana Territory when they'd both been shadowing owlhoots.

Prophet had found the former Union artillery gunner a braggart and blowhard—especially when talk turned to the war. And he could be meaner than a wet panther when he imbibed.

Still, while Prophet wouldn't have taken the time to bury

most men who'd tried to kill him and poach his bounty, Hound Dog had been a fellow soldier despite their being on opposing sides. A few years ago, Hound Dog wouldn't have tried the fool stunt he'd tried here today. But Prophet knew that age often did strange things to men, and Hound Dog wasn't as young as he used to be.

Neither was Prophet.

For those reasons, Prophet felt an obligation to bury him instead of just leaving him here for the coyotes and wolves to pull apart and scatter.

"Damn you, Hound Dog. I'm as hungry as a starvin' goat, but now I gotta take the time to bury your fool ass. I *shouldn't.* Most men *wouldn't.* But I wouldn't sleep if I *didn't,* damn your warty old hide!"

Prophet turned away and began to gather his freshly laundered and nearly dry clothes and to dress. By the time he'd finished digging a hole north of the house, on a peaceful rise he'd found near a tributary of the creek—a spot which he himself might have deemed worthy of his own final, eternal rest—the sun had vaulted behind the western ridges.

Darkness was quickly closing down, and a chill rose. Prophet stuck the shovel, which he'd found in the barn, into the mound of dirt he'd heaped behind Hound Dog's grave, and turned to where the dead, fellow bounty hunter lay, glaring skyward in death.

Prophet stopped.

He'd spied something just beyond the dead man.

Frowning, he stepped between some spindly evergreen shrubs, and stopped. "Bless my pea-pickin' heart," he said, raking a thumbnail down his unshaven jaw. "What in the hell do we have here now?"

A man's pale, stiff hand stuck up out of the ground, fingers and thumb slightly spread. A wrist with a blue shirt cuff was attached to the hand. There was probably also a body under there, somewhere, for the mound appeared to be a grave. Obviously a shallow one. The sour stench of putrefaction touched Prophet's nose, making his eyes water.

He looked around. The grave bore no marker. There was just the low mound of dirt and rocks roughly forming the shape of a man's body.

Light footsteps sounded behind Prophet.

He swung around, instinctively raking his Peacemaker from its holster and clicking the hammer back.

"Oh, god!" exclaimed a woman's voice. There was a dull *clink* as she dropped the cup she'd been holding. "Please don't shoot me!"

Prophet saw the young woman's silhouette in the near-darkness. He drew a deep, relieved breath, depressed the Colt's hammer, and dropped it into its holster. "Shouldn't walk up on a man like that," he said, chuckling to soften his words. "Not in this country."

She stood about ten feet away, one arm crossed on her chest, the other splayed across her neck, as though to choke herself.

"I saw you walk this way with the shovel, carrying the dead man. I figured by now you could use a cup of coffee. My god, I didn't think a person could smell so awful so soon after death!"

Obviously, she thought the stench was from the man Prophet had just buried. It was also obvious that she thought the man he'd just buried was the unknown dead man he'd found in the yard earlier—the one Frank Beauregard had shot.

Her second false assumption was fine with the bounty hunter. She didn't need to know about Hound Dog Hagen.

"The stink is from a man who was already out here," Prophet said, crouching to retrieve the cup she'd dropped. "He was buried shallow. Some critter dug part of him up. You know who he is . . . or, *was* . . . ?"

"Oh, my gosh—that must . . . that must be"—her voice pinched and trembled with emotion—"the man I came all this way to marry." She covered her mouth with her hand. "That must be Shep Hatfield." She gave a single sob, clamping her hand more tightly over her mouth.

"The man you came all this way to *marry*?"

She nodded, lowered her hand, but kept her gaze on the shallow grave behind Prophet. "Mister Hatfield and I exchanged letters. He'd placed an ad . . . an ad for a bride . . . in the St. Paul newspaper."

"Oh." Prophet had wanted to say "Oh, shit," but he'd managed to censor himself for the lady. "I'm sorry to hear that," he added.

"Dear god, what a nightmare!"

"I reckon so. Did Frank kill him?"

She nodded. "Mister Moon said that Mister Beauregard rode in and rewarded Mister Hatfield's hospitality by shooting him after they'd spent a night dining and conversing."

"Was Mister Moon the other man in the yard earlier?"

The woman sobbed briefly, then sniffed and crossed her arms on her chest again, composing herself. "Yes. Frank left Mister Moon alive to tend the ranch for him. He was going to hold up here for the winter . . . let his 'heels cool,' as Mister Moon had put it, and then head for Mexico in the spring. Mister Moon was crippled. I guess that's why Frank didn't count him as a threat."

"Ole Frank was going to hold up here with Hatfield's mail-order bride." Prophet gave a sardonic snort. "That devil. He had it all worked out, didn't he?"

"Except I guess he didn't think a crippled man capable of greed."

"Ah."

"Are you a lawman, Mister Prophet?" the girl asked in a

hopeful tone. "I don't see a badge."

Prophet shook his head. "Bounty hunter. I'm up here after Beauregard."

The corners of her mouth dimpled with disappointment. "Would you please give Mister Hatfield a proper grave, Mister Prophet? From his letters, I could tell he was a good man. He didn't deserve the death he received by that . . . that devil, Frank Beauregard, as you so appropriately deemed him."

"I will do that, Miss . . ."

"I'm Mathilda Anderson."

"I reckon we weren't properly introduced, Miss Anderson. I'm Lou Prophet." He extended the empty cup to her.

"I wish I could say it was a pleasure, Mister Prophet," she said, accepting the cup.

"I know what you mean. You're lookin' better, though. I mean, for all of that earlier . . ."

"I wish I could say I felt better."

"Did he hurt you?"

She shook her head quickly, averting her gaze. "Just rattled me." Turning away, she said, "I'll bring you another cup of coffee."

"No need to fuss."

"It's no fuss. I need something to do. I'll try to scrounge up something for us to eat, but I warn you, there's not much in the house. Frank Beauregard wasn't much of a hand at keeping the larder stocked, I'm afraid."

"Just so happens, I shot a couple of jackrabbits, ridin' up here. I'll skin 'em and cook 'em. You lie down and rest for a while."

That he'd shot the rabbits was a lie. He'd found the jacks, gutted and still warm, hanging from Hound Dog's saddle horn, on the mouse-brown dun he'd found in the woods near where he'd first spotted Hound Dog. The dead bounty hunter had probably shot the jacks on his way up here, but since Prophet didn't want Miss Anderson to know about Hound Dog, she couldn't know the truth about where the rabbits had come from, either.

"You skin them and I'll cook them. I'm a hand at cooking rabbits, Mister Prophet."

"All right, then. I'll be in soon."

She drifted away in the darkness.

Prophet started digging a new grave for Shep Hatfield.

After Miss Anderson had brought him the fresh coffee and returned to the house, he went over and laid Hound Dog in his own hole and covered him. Then he finished the grave for Hatfield.

Digging up the rest of the dead rancher's body and laying him in the new, four-foot-deep grave was a grisly, smelly task, one that made Prophet appreciate the cool breeze that rose while he was working, tempering the eye-watering stench lifting from the bloated corpse. Ninety minutes after the girl had brought out the fresh coffee, which he'd drunk during a five-minute break, he finished his chores for the night and returned the shovel to the barn.

He kept it handy, for he still had another man to dig a grave for in the morning. He'd try to finish that chore before Miss Anderson rose.

Grabbing the dead rabbits off the nail he'd hung them from, he headed to the house. Smoke rose from the tin chimney pipe, which meant Miss Anderson had stoked the stove to cook supper. He knocked on the door before he entered, and found the young woman scrubbing the kitchen table with a soapy brush and a bucket resting on one of the chairs.

He hadn't gotten a good look at her until now. Earlier, her face had been masked by either misery or the night's darkness. Now he found himself studying her fondly as he stood just inside the door, holding the dead rabbits by a hemp cord. Mathilda Anderson wouldn't be what one would call traditionally beautiful, but there was something beguiling in her features.

She was a well put-together young woman, with a heart-shaped face, rich lips, a full bosom, and gently rounded hips. Her brown eyes were prettily expressive, intelligent. There was a flush in her cheeks now as she scrubbed, and Prophet liked the way her breasts jostled inside the corset of the pale yellow dress she wore, buttoned to her throat.

She'd pinned her brown hair into a schoolmarm's roll atop her head. The hairstyle contrasted with the smooth youthfulness of her face, enhancing it. The bun shook and quivered as she moved, and the skirt of her frock bustled around her slender legs.

She appeared freshly scrubbed and even robust, despite the horror she'd endured earlier at the hands of Frank Beauregard. She'd have made Shep Hatfield a fine wife, Prophet opined. Too bad about Hatfield. He'd no doubt been lonely, living way out here without a woman for who knew how long. This bright young flower would have put some spring back in his step.

The girl—she seemed somewhere between girlhood and the full flower of womanhood—glanced at Prophet, then gasped and fell back against the table. She regarded him, terror-stricken, as though he were a specter who'd materialized out of the chill autumn night.

"I didn't realize you were just standing there," she cried, bosom rising and falling sharply. "My god—what are you *doing*?"

Her start had given Prophet himself a start. "Hell, I was just . . . I was just . . . watchin' you, Miss Anderson. I didn't mean—"

"You were *ogling* me!"

"I wouldn't call it that!"

"Well, you should . . . because that's what you were doing!" Miss Anderson glanced toward the windows and doorway, which were nearly totally dark, with only a smudge of gray-green light left in the ranch yard. "My god, we're all alone out here, aren't we?" she said, her voice low but brittle with fear.

She swung her gaze to Prophet once more, and her eyes flung little, sharp javelins of castigation at him. "I hope you don't intend on savaging me, Mister Prophet, now that night has fallen and no doubt your goatish male desires are rising! You're a big man, much bigger than I, and you could no doubt have your way, but a gentleman would—"

"Oh, for chrissakes," Prophet said, kicking the door closed behind him. "My desires ain't one bit goatish. Besides that, I've never taken a woman by force in my entire, pea-pickin' life. Never had to, thank you very much."

He chuckled proudly as he tossed the rabbits onto the cutting table near the wet sink. "Now, I'm sorry for your lousy luck, Miss Anderson, but as long as I'm here, you will be in no more danger—from me or anyone else. I'll double-dee guaran-damn-tee you that, and it's known far and wide across Dixie that the word of any Prophet is as good as bond!"

He cast her a resolute look over his shoulder. She stood, regarding him thoughtfully, one brow arched skeptically, from the other side of the table. Prophet gave her his back as he reached up behind his right shoulder and slowly slid his bowie knife from its hard leather sheath. He made no quick moves, so as not to excite the girl further, and held the knife up to show her.

"I'm just gonna skin the rabbits with this, that's all. I ain't gonna use it to help satisfy my goatish desires."

She stared at him. Gradually, a look of chagrin passed like a cloud shadow across her brown eyes. "I'm sorry. I acted foolishly, I know. It's just that as soon as I de-staged in Dead Skunk

Gulch, so much trouble started to appear from every quarter that I keep expecting more to appear at any moment."

"The trouble is over, Miss Anderson."

"Oh, Mister Prophet—do you promise?"

Prophet smiled. "I promise. You can let your guard down. You're safe here now."

She smiled.

Prophet's heart warmed at the glitter in the girl's relieved gaze.

A shadow flicked across the window to his left. There rose the screech of breaking glass, and then, as Prophet glimpsed a rifle barrel sprout like some ominous steel flower through the dark furrow of the broken window, he shouted, "Ah, shit—get down!" and vaulted himself over the table.

Chapter Nine

Mathilda screamed as the big man in the skintight buckskin shirt hurled himself at her, the giant, savage-looking knife clenched in his right fist.

He was still in the air over the table, slanting toward her like some giant, man-shaped bird, his eyes wide, lips stretched back from his teeth, when the thunder of a rifle assaulted the room.

Mathilda saw the red-blue flashes to her right, and heard a man's jubilant, bellowing cries with each deafening screech of the gun.

Prophet hammered into Mathilda, wrapping a big arm around her shoulders and driving her to the floor. Somehow, he managed to get one of his own shoulders and a hip under her, cushioning her otherwise hard fall to the floor.

He tossed her aside and lurched to a crouch, his right arm whipping up so fast that it was a mere blur to Mathilda's shocked gaze. She spied what could only have been Prophet's large knife hurling end over end through the lantern-lit corner of the kitchen, flashing dully in the flickering light.

As the man firing into the room through the broken window turned his rifle as well as his pinched gaze and grinning mouth toward Mathilda's and Prophet's side of the kitchen, the knife thumped into his forehead with a crunching thud.

The hide-wrapped handle jutted from about three inches above the bridge of his nose, which had a thick, white bandage over it. Around the bandage, the man's nose was red and puffy.

The man's rifle dropped from his hands to the floor, and he gritted his teeth and squeezed his eyes closed with sudden agony as he tried to draw his head back out the broken window.

He didn't make it. He collapsed against the bottom frame from which glass shards jutted. His head and arms drooped to the floor. A thick wash of dark-red blood oozed down the papered wall from his neck, which the glass shards must have torn.

Mathilda stared in horror at the man's jerking head, flapping arms, and gushing blood. As she did, the door to her left blasted open, and a man in a black wool coat and a ragged, broad-brimmed black hat burst into the house, shouting, "You're a dead bastard, Prophet!"

He fired once seemingly without aiming, then swung toward Mathilda, pumping his rifle's lever and grinning devilishly when he saw Prophet to Mathilda's right.

"Stay down!" Prophet yelled, shoving Mathilda against the floor as he reached for his short, double-barreled shotgun hanging from a chair back.

The newcomer, whom Mathilda had recognized as the burly man from the stagecoach, fired his rifle toward Prophet, who cursed and jerked to one side before raising his savage-looking shotgun in both hands. Mathilda poked her fingers in her ears and squeezed her eyes closed, pressing her cheek hard against the floor.

Still, the shotgun's blast sounded like a canon, causing the floor to literally bounce. When Mathilda opened her eyes and removed her fingers from her ears, she saw the burly man writhing on his back on the floor clear on the other side of the house's parlor area. He was howling and clutching his bloody belly from which what appeared red snakes were trying to escape.

Prophet's cannon-like gun belched again, wickedly, to Mathilda's right. This time she hadn't muffled her ears. The gun's cannonade was like God's own thunderclap inside Mathilda's head, instantly causing loud bells to toll behind her eyes.

She'd seen the shotgun's flames lance toward the far side of the parlor, where the shotgun's bullets blew out the glass and shredded the curtains of the window in that wall. It also caused another rifle and a man's head to disappear. Agonized screams rose from that side of the house.

"Stay here and stay down!" Prophet yelled, though he'd sounded far away beneath the bells clanging inside Mathilda's head.

Prophet tossed his smoking shotgun onto the still-wet and soapy table, and unholstered his sidearm as he strode quickly out the open door and into the night.

Outside, the cracks of a pistol sounded—again, again, and again.

Mathilda jerked each time she heard them, though they were little more than dull thumps compared to the blast of the shotgun. Men shouted. The shouts diminished, as though the shouters were moving away from the cabin.

Mathilda had instinctively pressed her hands to her ears on the heels of the shotgun's second blast. Little good it had done her. Now she lowered her hands as she lifted her head from the floor, looking around the cabin dully. She felt as though she'd suffered a severe blow to her head. She felt dizzy, disoriented, and numb.

The ringing in her ears only added to the confusion.

But when she turned to the man whose head and arms hung down over the windowsill to her right, and she saw the thick mass of liver-colored blood painting the wall below him, the sharp, wickedly cold lance of fear impaled her once again.

"Oh, my god!" she cried, pressing the heels of her hands to her temples. "Oh, my god!"

The words exploded out of her as though from small explosions inside her own soul.

She rose to her feet and looked at the burly man who now lay still but with his insides appearing like blood-basted snakes dribbling down his sides as though trying to make their way to the floor.

"Oh, my god!" Mathilda heard herself shriek, though beneath the clattering and ringing in her head it sounded like little more than a whisper. "Oh, my god! Oh, my god! Oh, my god!"

She scampered up the stairs, seeking the safety of her room. She fell three times, her feet slipping off the risers in her haste to remove herself from the carnage that seemed to be clutching at her, trying to drown her in its horror.

She ran into the room, slammed the door, and threw the bolt.

Prophet triggered a third round as the third attacker ran, stumbling, into the woods behind the house. The runner grunted. There was a flash as the man returned fire, but having received an unhealthy dose of Prophet's buckshot through the window, he was in no condition for accurate shooting.

Aiming toward the flash and leading slightly as he heard his quarry continue running, Prophet stopped and emptied his Colt into the darkness.

On the heels of his sixth fired round, a shrill scream sounded. It was followed closely by the cracking of a branch and a dull thud as the runner hit the ground.

Prophet continued striding forward, dumping out his spent shell casings and quickly reloading. When he had all six chambers filled with fresh brass, he flicked the loading gate closed, spun the cylinder, and moved through the scattered pines until he saw the dark lump of a body on the ground before him.

He stopped and kicked the man onto his back.

The man's face was a mess. In fact, half of it looked like finely ground beef. Starlight glistened on a mask of blood and viscera. One eye had been blown out by the buckshot. Still, Prophet recognized his third attacker.

"Renfield Bell. You stupid son of a bitch."

Bell did not respond. The little man only glared up at Prophet through his one remaining eye, lips stretched back from his little brown teeth. His chest was not moving. Bell had gone to his reward, which was probably a piping hot coal shovel somewhere in the bowels of the devil's own hell.

That's where wayward bounty hunters went.

Prophet would be heading that way himself, but not because he was anything like Renfield Bell. He considered himself one of the few honorable bounty hunters. Prophet would be shoveling coal for ole Scratch throughout eternity because, after the prolonged misery of the War of Northern Aggression, he'd sold the fork-tailed devil his soul in return for plenty of whiskey and women on this side of the sod before he was turned under.

"You, too—eh, Bell?" Prophet shifted his gaze from Bell to the lit windows of the house and the darkness of the ranch yard behind him. "How many others from Dead Skunk Gulch got the same silly notion as you, Bell, you copper-riveted dunderhead?"

He'd recognized the second man he'd killed inside the cabin as George Hotchkiss. He hadn't gotten a good look at the man in whom he'd drilled a third eye with his bowie knife, but he'd bet gold nuggets against fish bladders that it was Raymond "Scurvy" Jenkins, another no-account outlaw from Bell's and Hotchkiss's native Texas Panhandle.

They must have gathered in Dead Skunk Gulch because they'd heard the same rumors that the misbegotten and dearly departed Hound Dog Hagen had heard—that Frank Beauregard was haunting this neck of the mountains with twenty-five-thousand dollars in stolen greenbacks.

Figuring that Prophet had been at Dead Skunk for the same reason, they'd followed him—or at least they'd followed Hound Dog following Prophet—up here to the Hatfield ranch. Some so-called bounty hunters found it easier to follow other, more experienced bounty hunters to quarry than to actually track the quarry themselves.

How many others had followed?

Would follow?

Prophet hadn't taken a close count of the other men at the Dead Skunk Gulch station, but he'd estimate now that there'd been a good dozen. Only a handful had been "career" manhunters. Prophet hadn't known the others personally, but he'd judged them to be general no-accounts who hunted men when the opportunity presented itself—an opportunity like a single outlaw riding into their near vicinity carrying twenty-five-thousand dollars and a sizable bounty on his head.

Most were likely still stinging from the dustup out in the yard. But Prophet had to assume the others—or most of the others—would be along soon. Word must have spread that Prophet was on Beauregard's trail, and he himself had left a warm trail from Dead Skunk Gulch.

He left Bell in the brush. He wouldn't bury him or his ilk. They didn't deserve it. Returning to the cabin, he was not surprised to find Miss Anderson nowhere in sight. He knew a moment's chagrin. He'd promised that she was no longer in danger. Ha!

Sometimes he had to admit he was way too much in love with himself. Served him right now to look the fool in front of the girl.

He cursed under his breath, then walked over to the man hanging down over the windowsill on the right side of the kitchen. Blood had turned the paper beneath the sill and all the way to the floor a deep, dark red. It was still running down the wall and pooling on the floor.

Prophet reached down and grabbed the handle of his bowie knife. He used the knife to lift the head until two little, coal-black eyes gazed stupidly up at him.

"Sure enough—it is you, Scurvy. I'd thought you had more sense than Hotchkiss and Bell, since you're originally from Dixie an' all, but this just goes to prove that all my fellow Confederates ain't as smart as I give 'em credit for. I'm gonna have to adjust my outlook accordingly."

He lifted Scurvy's head a couple of inches higher, until he heard the bones in the man's neck crack. He pressed his right boot toe over Scurvy's mouth and tugged on the knife. It was soundly embedded in Scurvy's head. Prophet had to grit his teeth and pull hard and listen to the grisly cracking of broken skull bone until the blade pulled free.

"Christ, there's gotta be a better way to make a livin'," Prophet opined, letting Scurvy's head drop and cleaning the blade on the dead man's scalp.

When he'd slid the knife back into its sheath, Prophet kicked the man's head and arms back out the window and heard the body drop with a thud in the yard. Then he went out and dragged Scurvy out to lie beside Bell. He dragged Hotchkiss out there, as well.

When he had all three sons of bitches lying in a neat row, their open eyes glistening in the starlight and the milky luminescence of the rising powder-horn moon, he retrieved his rifle from the barn and gave the yard a thorough scouring, checking to see that no more bastards like Hound Dog and the most recent three were near.

He returned to the cabin, silently vowing to keep a better guard for the rest of the night. Neither he nor Miss Anderson needed any more surprises. The ambush by Hotchkiss and the other two was downright embarrassing for a man of Prophet's experience and expertise. He should have expected something like that.

He hadn't had a woman in a while, so maybe the girl had dulled his instincts. She was right easy on the eyes, he had to admit.

He hoped that was all it was, and he wasn't just getting careless.

He blew out the lamp, then waited for his eyes to adjust to the darkness tempered by starlight and moonlight slanting through the windows; then he stoked the stove and finished skinning his rabbits, chopping them up, seasoning with salt and pepper, and frying them in a cast-iron skillet popping with lard.

When the meat was done, Prophet carried a plate upstairs to the girl's closed door, but his offer of a meal was met with a pouty, "Oh, go away!"

So he took the plate outside and ate the meal himself, kicked back in a wicker chair, boots crossed on the porch rail.

He'd spied a bottle in the house, and dumped a goodly portion of whiskey into a speckled tin cup. The tangle-leg was of the rotgut variety, which Frank Beauregard had no doubt supplied, and to which Prophet was not unaccustomed. It did an acceptable job of washing the rabbit down while sanding the sharp, splintered edges off his nerves but not overly compromising his night vision nor his hearing.

He followed the meal up with one more shot of whiskey and a quirley, which he enjoyed in the chair on the porch, his rifle resting across his thighs, his shotgun laid across the porch rail.

He set the empty plate on the rail and smoked and sipped the whiskey, keeping his ears skinned. He heard nothing more disturbing than the breeze, an occasional owl, and an intermittent coyote chorus rising from a distant ridge.

When he'd finished the cigarette and the whiskey, he went

back inside and stoked the stove once more. It was a chilly night and would likely get chillier. The frosty mountain air would slide through the two broken windows unimpeded. Prophet could weather a cold night, but he was thinking of the girl.

The bounty hunter sat at the table, near the door, which he kept cracked so he could keep an ear to the yard, and allowed himself a couple of hours of shut-eye. It was an intentionally shallow but refreshing slumber. When the eastern sky began paling, Prophet stole outside with his rifle and investigated the yard once more.

Deeming it free of interlopers, he dragged the body of Hatfield's hired man, Walter Moon, out to the rise near Hatfield's final resting place, and buried the poor cuss. By the time he'd finished mounding the grave with rocks against predators, the sun was a swollen, orange, liquid ball rising between two eastern ridges that stood furry black to either side of it.

The sun had crested those ridges by the time Prophet had fed, watered, and saddled Mean and Ugly as well as one of the horses in Hatfield's corral—a stocky roan with a white ring around its left eye and a white-tipped tail. He wrapped Frank Beauregard in two saddle blankets, wound rope around the blankets and Frank's slack, stiffening carcass, and tied the bundle over the saddle of the spare horse.

The top of Frank's balding head poked out of a slight opening in the blankets, and a few light-brown strands of his thin hair waved in the chill morning breeze.

Prophet slung the saddlebags containing the train loot over his own bags, behind the cantle of his saddle, and shoved his rifle into its scabbard. He slung the Richards behind his back, and turned out a stirrup. As he swung into his saddle, Mathilda Anderson stepped out of the house.

Prophet scowled curiously. The young woman was dressed as

though for travel in a blue dress and ruffled white shirtwaist. She even wore a picture hat adorned with phony flowers. On her hands and arms, all the way to her elbows, were gloves as white as fresh mountain snow. She set two carpetbags onto the porch and lifted a hand to shield the sun from her eyes as she cast her gaze toward Prophet.

"Where's my horse?"

Prophet's scowl cut deeper lines across his forehead, beneath the funneled brim of his badly weathered Stetson. "Where's . . . ? What're you talkin' about?"

Chapter Ten

The young woman studied Prophet skeptically from beneath the gloved hand shading her face. "Surely, you're not intending on leaving me here?"

"Where do you expect me to take you?"

"Where are you going?"

"Denver."

"Well, then, I guess I'll go to Denver. I can't very well stay here."

"Why not? Hatfield brought you out here to be his wife. Too bad he's dead, but, hell, I reckon the place is yours."

"I have no rightful place here, Mister Prophet. Mister Hatfield and I were not married. I never even met the man. Besides . . ." She looked dubiously around the ranch yard flooded now with buttery morning light. "What would I do here . . . alone?"

Prophet shrugged. "I don't know. I reckon you could get you some chickens. Find yourself another man." He looked her up and down, feeling the warmth of his own lust. "Shouldn't be too hard for a gal who wears a dress like you do."

Mathilda's eyes sharpened. "Now, you see there! That's just the reason I can't stay out here by myself! That and the fact that I have no claim to this place . . . even if I did know what to do out here in the middle of nowhere!"

Prophet beetled his brows. "I don't understand. Why can't you stay out here by yourself?"

"Because of men like you! My god, the frontier must be chock full of goatish reprobates who think that all a woman's good for is . . ." She bunched her lips and jerked her head as though trying to find a proper way to articulate the graphic and reprehensible concept.

"I'm sorry to tell you, Miss Anderson, but that is about all most women are good for out here. Unless they're married or have a ranch. Now, I don't see no reason under the sun why you can't just make like you have the ranch and a man, and stay here and sink a taproot."

"A tap . . . *what*?"

"Because you sure as hell aren't goin' nowhere with me dressed like that. My god, woman, how in the hell do you think you could sit a saddle in a getup like that? You'd either break somethin' on your lovely person tryin' to get mounted, or you'd tear that skirt to shreds!"

"Maybe you could hitch up a wagon? Besides, wouldn't that be an easier way to get Mister Beauregard to Denver?"

"Frank's just fine where he is. And so am I. And so are you. I'm not drivin' no wagon out of these mountains."

"Why couldn't you do that for me? You know the spot I'm in."

Prophet growled a sigh through a grimace. "Miss Anderson, in case you hadn't noticed, I ain't the only bounty hunter who's been after Frank Beauregard. Now there are some who'll give credit where credit is due, and yield to my having gotten to Frank first and not contest the bounty. But there are some, not unlike those rabid human coyotes who kicked up such a fuss last night, who don't care if an owlhoot's already done been captured. They'll try to capture him again, and shoot the rightful owner of the bounty."

"I understand that, Mister Prophet. I am not stupid. I was here, remember? That said, I'd rather take my chances on the trail with you than stay out here where I'll no doubt be prey to any and all *rabid human coyotes* who happen by. While you're obviously a lusty southern man with brutish ways, you don't seem to be a rapist and cold-blooded killer. At least, you haven't raped and murdered me yet. It is testament to the sorry state of my current circumstances that with a man such as you I feel the most secure!"

Her face crumpled and she sobbed, shoulders jerking.

"Ah, shit—stop that."

"No, I will not stop it," she sobbed. "I have every right to cry."

"What I was gettin' at about the wagon . . . or lack thereof . . . is that since I am liable to be hound-dogged by cutthroats all the way back to Denver, probably right *up to* and maybe even *inside* the Wells Fargo district office!—I can't travel by wagon. I'm going to need to take back trails . . . horse trails . . . when I follow any trails at all. And I'm gonna need the option of speed. No wagon can outrun a man on the back of a good horse." Prophet shook his head. "A wagon's out, Miss Anderson. I am sorry, but you're better off right here."

He pinched his hat brim to her. "Good day."

He turned his head away from her and touched spurs to Mean and Ugly's flanks. As the gelding lurched into an eager trot, ready to be moving again, Prophet held the reins of the stocky roan carrying Frank Beauregard. Prophet did not glance behind as he and the horses left the yard. He could feel the young woman's eyes on his back. They felt like two warm buttons pressing against his skin.

Still, he did not look back.

"Christ, she must have gone inside by now," he said aloud when he was a hundred yards away from the house.

He let Mean take four or five more strides before he glanced over his left shoulder. She was still out there, staring toward him. She looked so lost and defeated, standing out there on the porch, staring toward him, that the fist of guilt reached inside and twisted his guts.

"Goddamnit."

Prophet reined Mean to a halt. He sat his saddle, one fist on his thigh, the other hand on the reins, staring straight out ahead of him.

Finally, he cursed under his breath, reined Mean and the packhorse around, and galloped back into the yard. He drew up before the porch. The girl stared at him much as she'd stared before, only now her eyes were growing slightly wider as though with hope.

"I'll tell you what I'll do," Prophet said. "I'll take you as far as the stage relay station in Dead Skunk Gulch. All right? You can wait there for the next stage."

"But Mister Prophet, I don't have enough money to get back to St. Paul. I doubt I have enough for the fair back to Denver."

Prophet was exasperated. "Well, where in the hell did you have it in your head you were going, then?"

Mathilda threw up her hands. "Anywhere but here! I don't know. Denver! Cheyenne! Maybe I could get a job waiting tables in some café. I just very much need to be away from here, Mister Prophet. I can't live out here all alone."

Prophet nudged his hat down low on his forehead and scratched the back of his head, thinking it over. He glanced at the bulging saddlebags riding behind him.

"I'll get you to Denver and on the train back to St. Paul," he said. "Just in time for the first winter snowstorm." He chuckled, for he himself hated the northern cold and couldn't understand how so many people managed to live up there, winter after winter. He supposed it was those long, cold, oyster-shriveling winters that gave the Yankees such sour dispositions. That's likely why they talked so fast. They couldn't keep their mouths open long enough to pronounce words correctly because if they did, they'd likely freeze their tonsils.

"How would you do that, Mister Prophet—get me back to St. Paul?"

"I'll take the fair out of the loot I'm carryin'. I'll tell the Wells Fargo agent in Denver to take what I took out of my reward." Anything to get rid of her.

Mathilda gasped and clasped her hands over her rich-lipped mouth. "Oh, for goodness sakes, Mister Prophet. I can't thank you enough!" Her eyes glistened.

"All right, all right—let's get movin' before you cloud up and rain again. I tell you, that cryin' of yours is startin' to get on my nerves." Prophet swung Mean toward the corral. "You go inside and get changed into somethin' more fittin' for a long ride, and I'll saddle you a horse."

"Wonderful!"

"Yeah, wonderful," Prophet growled as he booted Mean across the yard toward where the Hatfield horses were eyeing him skeptically.

"Oh, Mister Prophet?"

Prophet swung down from Mean's back and turned to the girl again. "What is it?"

"How are we going to carry my steamer trunk and portmanteau?"

Prophet scowled. "How are we going to . . . ?" He snorted, incredulous. "We're not!"

A half hour later, as Prophet and Mathilda and their three horses followed a switchback trail down a fir-stippled mountain slope, the young woman glanced behind her as though at the ranch yard, and said forlornly, "You have no idea how many valuables I left back there, Mister Prophet."

"You'll live without them, Miss Anderson," Prophet said, holding Mean's reins high against his chest, as the horse picked its way down the trail. He had the reins of both the packhorse and Mathilda's horse tied to Mean's tail, as Mathilda had confessed to knowing little about horsemanship and Prophet hadn't had time to teach her.

"In the steamer trunk alone were quilts and woven coverlets—family heirlooms from Norway! My mother's wax doll. Her wedding dress. In the portmanteau are Father's collection of pipes, and I'm not even going to mention how many dollars' worth of my own clothes!"

"Like I said," Prophet said, "you'll live without 'em." He glanced at her over his shoulder. "And your next stagecoach driver won't curse you, neither." He winked at her.

But her mind was still on the loss.

She looked down at the gown she was wearing—dark-green wool with a ragged tear up her right leg, revealing the dark stocking and pantaloons beneath it. "This skirt cost me nearly six dollars at Miss Dagover's shop, and you simply tore it up like it was nothing more than an old newspaper!"

It wasn't as though she were castigating the bounty hunter but merely recounting his bewildering actions in hushed disbelief.

Prophet had torn the skirt because, while it had been her idea of something more sensible to wear than the silk and velvet frock she'd originally donned, it would still have been too cumbersome for riding astraddle. Even if Prophet had found a sidesaddle in Hatfield's barn, he wouldn't have fiddled with the ridiculous contraption.

So he'd merely slitted the wool skirt to make it easier for the girl to ride astride.

He'd chosen a mild-eyed steeldust mare in Hatfield's corral for her. After tying her two carpetbags to the horn of her saddle, he'd tossed her up onto the steeldust's back, and they'd ridden out of the yard.

Mathilda hadn't had a decent hat for outdoor weather, so Prophet had found her a battered gray Stetson in Hatfield's bunkhouse. Probably having belonged to a former hired hand, the hat was too large for the girl, but it had a handy horsehair thong, which dangled down the front of her cream cambric blouse and the man's wool mackinaw she wore open, and it did a more than adequate job of keeping the sun off her head. It would protect her from any rain or even snow they might run into on their transmountain journey.

She'd found the mackinaw herself in the house. It had no doubt belonged to her dead betrothed, Shep Hatfield. She'd made a face when she'd put it on, and Prophet hadn't blamed her for that. He had to admit that he himself did not cotton to wearing dead men's clothes. He and his people were superstitious mountain folk. It must have been even more bizarre for the girl, however—donning the clothes of the dead man she'd been slated to marry but hadn't even met . . .

The mackinaw was too big for her, too, but it did the job.

They rode in silence for over half an hour before Prophet drew his horse to a halt and stopped both Mathilda's mare and the packhorse, as well.

"What is it?" Mathilda said, sharply, edging her voice with fear.

Prophet stared straight ahead, listening. Mean and Ugly did, too, twitching his ears apprehensively.

"Mister Prophet?" Mathilda said, grinding the words out with trepidation.

"I don't know," Prophet said. "Maybe nothin'. Maybe somethin'." He reined Mean and the other two horses off the trail and into the woods. As he did, he freed the keeper thong from over the hammer of his Peacemaker. "But we'd best figure it's somethin' . . ."

Chapter Eleven

"Oh, no," Mathilda said, closing her hands over her mouth as Prophet led her horse into the woods. Tears glazed her eyes and began to dribble down her cheeks.

Prophet pressed two fingers to his lips, shushing her.

He pulled Mean and the other two horses up behind a large deadfall lying over another fallen tree. He swung down from his saddle, then pulled Mathilda off the mare.

"Stay here and stay low," he said quietly.

As Mathilda sagged onto a low branch of one of the dead trees, Prophet swung his shotgun around in front of him and stole back to the trail. When he saw the trace slanting down the side of the mountain, he dropped behind a mossy boulder about ten feet away from it.

He could hear men's voices now as well as the thudding of horses' hooves and the squawking of tack. Bridle chains jangled. Shortly, a group of riders appeared, moving toward him on his left, trotting their horses along the trail up the mountain. As they came within forty yards and continued closing on him quickly, Prophet doffed his hat and crouched lower behind the boulder, sliding his left eye around the rock's left side.

There were six—no, seven—riders. The lead rider wore a black bear coat over a black suit. He had long, dark-brown hair and a matching, dragoon-style mustache. To his bear coat was pinned a nickel-plated badge in the shape of a shield.

That would be a Pinkerton's badge.

Prophet recognized the rider as the gun-for-hire, Leonard Kilroy.

Prophet scanned the other riders as they drew even closer, and saw that the others also wore the Pinkerton shield. Several of the men were conversing in low, casual tones, and one of them chuckled and spat to one side as they passed as a group. Prophet pulled his head back behind the boulder as the wad of chaw the rider had spat smacked against the rock's other side.

The dark-brown goo splashed off the edge of the boulder and into the dead leaves and pine needles to Prophet's left.

He could smell the leathery-sweet stench of the spent plug tobacco.

As the hoof thuds dwindled on up the mountain, Prophet slid his gaze around the boulder's right side. The Pinkertons drifted away through the pines, turned to follow a turn in the switchback trail, and were gone.

Prophet glanced at the tobacco staining the leaves and pine needles, then cast his gaze back up the mountain toward where the Pinkertons had disappeared.

"Crude cuss," he muttered, picking up his hat and setting it on his head.

He walked back over to where Mathilda hunkered behind the deadfalls, staring wide-eyed at him.

"I heard the horses," she said.

"Seven Pinkertons."

"Seven who?"

"Pinkerton detectives. Wells Fargo must've hired the Pinkertons to go after the train loot. These men aren't detectives, though, I got a deep suspicion. Like Kilroy, they're likely all hired guns."

"Who's Kilroy?"

"Just a fella I'm distantly acquainted with."

Mathilda's light-brown eyes flashed hopefully. "But the

Pinkertons . . . they're like lawmen, aren't they?"

"Some. Sorta."

"Thank god." Mathilda frowned. "Why didn't you summon them, tell them you had the money as well as the man who not only stole it but murdered Shep Hatfield and Walter Moon?"

Prophet chuckled as he placed his hands around Mathilda's waist and hoisted her back up onto the mare's back. "I said they're lawmen of a *sort.* That don't mean I trust 'em. Especially not seven of 'em led by Leonard Kilroy . . . when a woman as well as twenty-five-thousand dollars in stolen loot is involved."

"If you can't trust lawmen, Mister Prophet," Mathilda asked, scowling down at him, "who can you trust?"

Prophet gave a sardonic chuckle as he toed a stirrup and swung up onto Mean and Ugly's back. He gave Mathilda a pointed look as he slid the Richards behind his shoulder and adjusted the set of his hat. "There ain't no one I trust but myself."

"That's a rather cynical viewpoint."

"It's the only one I got, Miss Anderson."

Prophet led her horse and Frank Beauregard's back onto the trail.

Prophet didn't like the idea of riding back into Dead Skunk Gulch so soon after the dustup with the other bounty hunters. Some of the same men might still be there. And Teague O'Malley, the Irishman who ran the place, held grudges. Roughing up the place, as Prophet and the other man-hunters had done the other day, was definitely grudge-worthy.

Besides, there might still be men who called themselves bounty hunters lurking around there who had the same itch as the now-dead man-hunters up at the Hatfield ranch. The itch to relieve Prophet of Frank Beauregard and the saddlebags of stolen loot.

Any way you sliced it, Dead Skunk Gulch was a place to be avoided, and Prophet would have steered around it if it weren't for Miss Anderson.

Roughly an hour after they'd left the Hatfield ranch, Prophet led the girl and the dead man into the yard. He stopped fifty yards away from the cabin to get the lay of the place and to slide his Richards around to his belly, in case he needed it.

Fortunately, the relay station was quiet. Only three horses were tied to the hitchrack out front. The only person Prophet saw anywhere around the yard was the portly O'Malley himself, sweeping off the front porch, a soiled orange apron buffeting around his thick legs, a meerschaum tightly clamped in one corner of his gray-mustached mouth.

Prophet clucked, and Mean trotted across the yard. As Prophet and the girl and Frank Beauregard drew to a stop out front of the cabin, O'Malley turned his gaze toward the newcomers, and frowned. O'Malley's pale, freckled face blossomed red as apples, and the Irishman's blue eyes fairly burst into flame. He removed the meerschaum from his mouth and thrust it toward Prophet, his knuckles turning white around it.

"Goddamn your worthless, bloody hide, Prophet—what the hell are you doin' here? I reckon your wooden head was still reeling when I banned all you bruisers from the premises for the rest of your bloody worthless lives the other day—is that it? Well, let me tell you here and now, boyo—*you are banned for the rest of your natural-born life from this establishment! Now, ride on and keep ridin'. When you see the red fires of hell, then you can stop!*"

"Ah, don't get your drawers in a twist, Teague," Prophet said. "Christalmighty, look at you. Why, you're swollen up like a big Irish deer tick! I ain't here for me. I'm here for the girl. She needs fare back to Denver. I'm just gonna leave her here and mosey on down the trail." He turned to Mathilda and said,

"Miss Mathilda Anderson, this charming Mick is Mister Teague O'Malley, and he's going to set you up . . ."

Prophet let the sentence die on his lips when O'Malley shook his head. "The stage ain't due again till next week. In the summer, it comes through twice a week. Startin' on September first, it comes through only once a week. Since September first was the day it came through here last, it won't be coming through again till next Tuesday. Now, since I don't run no hotel, Miss Anderson can't stay here for five days. Out of the question. Me, personally—I wouldn't mind."

O'Malley's eyes glinted amorously across the girl. "But I don't think Mrs. O'Malley would approve one bit."

"Ah, hell," Prophet grumbled.

O'Malley tipped his head to one side, scrutinizing the load draped over the back of the roan. "Say, now, what . . . or *who* . . . you packin' there? Is that—?"

O'Malley glanced back toward the open front door as a man strode through it. He was a black man in a long, gray coat hanging open over a gray plaid shirt and suspenders, a deputy U.S. marshal's badge pinned to his breast pocket. He was middle-aged and medium tall with a slight paunch bowing out the front of his shirt.

The black lawman stopped at the top of the porch steps and set his brown Stetson on the bald crown of his coffee-colored head. "Why is it that every time I hear the name 'Prophet,' it's never whispered but always shouted? Shouted in anger, more times than not."

The deputy U.S. marshal placed his fists on his hips and leaned slightly back at the waist, chuckling, flashing nearly a full set of large, white teeth, his molasses-black eyes glinting in the sunshine.

"I thought I smelled a rat," Prophet grumbled. "Should know by now that whenever I smell that fetor, an especially rank one, it's usually you, Roy."

"Prophet's one o' them that broke up my place," O'Malley said, pointing the bowl of his pipe toward the mounted bounty hunter. "Arrest him, Marshal Dodd! He's the one that instigated the whole damn thing, an' I got a busted table, three busted chairs, two busted lamps, a mess of broke glasses and spilled whiskey, and two busted tables out of the whole bloody mess. Took me half the night to set things straight!"

Ignoring O'Malley, Roy Dodd glanced around Prophet at the horse carrying the dead man. "What brings you here, Proph? With such a pretty woman. Say, that wouldn't be who I think it is ridin' so uncomfortable-like behind you, there, would it?"

"I don't know," Prophet said, as two more men walked out of the cabin to stand on the porch behind Dodd. "Who do you think it is?"

"I think it might be the man me an' Gunderson and Halcon are here for," Dodd said, naming the two men—a tall, stoop-shouldered white man and a short Mexican Apache—standing behind him, both holding Winchester carbines.

Sam Gunderson was also a deputy U.S. marshal, about ten years younger than Dodd, who was in his late forties. Halcon, who'd been an Apache scout for Crook in Arizona, was Dodd's tracker. Dodd had been a buffalo soldier. Halcon wore a patch over his left eye. The story went that Halcon, a Chiricahua tracker, had had that eye carved out by a Navajo scout in the sutler's store at Fort Bowie late one night when the *tizwin* had been freely flowing.

"Whose shadow's been draggin' you boys up and down these mountains?" Prophet asked Dodd, good-naturedly.

"Frank Beauregard's."

"Ain't that a coincidence?" Prophet said, chuckling and jerking his head toward the roan. "Got him right here."

"Pshaw!"

"Sure, I do. He's covered up by the blanket. Go have a look for yourself, if you don't believe me."

Dodd glanced at the two men flanking him. "Boys, let's take us a look. I can't believe Prophet took down Frank Beauregard all by his lonesome."

"That purty li'l blonde who everyone calls the Vengeance Queen probably helped him," said Sam Gunderson as he followed Dodd down off the porch steps. "Where is she, anyway? She's purty to look at—not that the one you got with you is hard on the eyes." He snickered as he lingered a look at Mathilda.

"That blond viper an' me forked trails a ways back," Prophet said. "I'm sure we'll cross 'em again before too long. Sorry to disappoint you, though, Sam. I know you an' Louisa have a special relationship."

A year ago, in a Denver hotel, Louisa had kicked Gunderson in the balls when, pie-eyed, he'd hidden behind a potted palm while Louisa had crossed the lobby toward Prophet, waiting for her near the front door. Gunderson had stolen up behind Louisa and covered her eyes with his hands, inviting her to guess who he was.

Obviously remembering the incident now, Gunderson gritted his teeth as his cheeks above his thin, light-brown beard turned rosy. Halcon chuckled while his round, flat face remained expressionless. Dodd walked over to the roan gelding, crouched, and peeled the horse blanket away from Frank Beauregard's head. Dodd jerked his head up and stumbled back, eyes wide, running his hand across his mouth in disgust.

"Jumpin' Jehosaphat, his eyes are still open!"

Gunderson, still annoyed by Prophet's reminder, laughed at the black man's squeamishness. "Christalmighty, Dodd—it ain't like you never seen a dead man before!"

"No, it ain't, but that always catches me off guard—their eyes stayin' open like that," said Dodd, planting his fists on his hips and staring down in disdain at the dead man's head. "Ole Frank looks like he's just layin' there, takin' a nap. Exceptin' that his face is as white as a redheaded whore's ass!"

Dodd chuckled, then turned to Prophet, who was smiling at Halcon, who had not bothered to inspect Beauregard but stood about six feet in front of Mean and Ugly, cradling his Winchester in his arms while he scowled moodily up at Prophet. Prophet wasn't sure what he'd done to crawl the Chiricahua's hump. As far as he could recollect, he and Halcon had never exchanged so much as a single word, in anger or otherwise, during the several times they'd encountered one another.

Nevertheless, Prophet knew in the way men did that Halcon had it out for him, and that sooner or later they were going to have to settle the unspoken enmity between them.

Dodd looked up at Prophet. "I reckon if anyone could take ole Frank Beauregard down solo, that'd be you, Proph."

"Where's the Vengeance Queen?" Gunderson asked Prophet mockingly, biting the top off a tobacco braid he'd produced from his shirt pocket. "I want to talk to her about Denver."

Dodd said, "O'Malley says there was a whole passel of others after Frank. You didn't run into any of them up there in them mountains, did you, Proph?"

"As a matter of fact, if you ride an hour thataway, followin' the main trail, then branchin' off onto the second secondary track you come to, you'll find the buzzards fat and happy."

"Marshal Dodd?" All eyes, including Prophet's, turned to Mathilda, who'd spoken for the first time. Her voice was halting, timid. "It . . . it is Marshal Dodd, isn't it?"

Dodd turned to the woman and smiled proudly as he slid the lapel of his long, gray coat away from his badge. His voice was low and syrupy. "Why, sure enough it is. And may I be so bold as to inquire the name bestowed upon such an eye-pleasing waif as yourself, Miss?"

Ah, Jesus, Prophet inwardly groaned.

Chapter Twelve

"I am Mathilda Anderson from St. Paul, Minnesota," Mathilda told Deputy U.S. Marshal Roy Dodd, sliding a lock of dark-brown hair back from her cheek and tucking it up beneath the crown of her oversized man's Stetson. "I came here after an exchange of letters with Mister Shep Hatfield. I came here to be married to Mister Hatfield, in fact."

"You don't say?" Dodd said, a curious frown bulging the skin between his black brows. "One o' them mail-order affairs, I fathom . . . ?"

"Yes, indeed," Mathilda said. "Unfortunately, the man who met me right here at this very place, after the stage pulled in only yesterday, was Mister *Beauregard.* He was posing as Mister *Hatfield.*"

"Oh, my gosh!" intoned Dodd, slapping his thigh, looking as horrified as he had when he'd seen Beauregard's death-glazed open eyes.

"Can you imagine?" Mathilda's voice climbed in volume as she continued her tale. "He drove me back to Mister Hatfield's ranch and continued posing as Mister Hatfield until it became very clear to me that he could simply *not* be the man with whom I exchanged such tender and amusing correspondences."

Prophet saw Dodd share a quick, conspiratorial glance with Gunderson while maintaining a sober expression, albeit with effort.

"And what was it exactly that brought you to that conclusion, Miss Anderson?" Dodd asked.

Gunderson brushed a fist across his nose and mouth, stifling a snort, as he kept his eyes riveted on the girl.

Mathilda leaned toward Dodd to impart the grave information in a tone of hushed horror. "He shot Mister Hatfield's hired man, Mister Walter Moon. Now, to be clear, Moon was no angel. Beauregard had feigned leaving the ranch to fetch a minister who would marry us—as he'd still been passing himself off as the man I'd traveled all this way to marry!—and while he'd been away, Mister Moon had stolen into the house to steal the money that Mister Beauregard stole from the train."

"I'll be jiggered," said Dodd.

"Yes!" said Mathilda, relieved that someone else shared her incredulity, as Prophet had apparently been way too mildly accepting of the events she'd found so catastrophic. "Mister Beauregard, having anticipated Mister Moon's ploy, returned and shot Mister Moon outright!"

The young woman's eyes glazed with wavering tears, and her voice faltered. "I saw the whole thing. He shot Mister Moon outright! Oh, it was terrible! I'd never seen anything like it!"

"Shot him *outright*?" exclaimed Gunderson, sliding a quick glance toward Dodd.

"Yes, it was terrible," Mathilda said, fingering a tear from her right cheek. "Then . . . he attacked me like some rabid, amorous dog . . . and that was when Mister Prophet stepped in."

"Stepped in, did he?" said Dodd, glancing at the bounty hunter. "Fed him a load of buckshot, eh, Lou?"

"Forty-four slug," Prophet said. "From what I've heard regarding Frank's reputation, he had one o' them comin' for years. But I only shot him when he drew on me. Miss Anderson will vouch for that. Just like the others. They attacked me . . . er, *us,* I should say—didn't they, Miss Anderson?"

"Oh, yes, of course," Mathilda said in a pinched voice. "I've never been so terrified." She turned to Dodd. "Marshal, you will see to Shep Hatfield, won't you?"

"See to him?"

"Yes, I mean, see that he gets a proper funeral, that a minister is summoned to say a few words over him. He was a good man. I know from his letters. He did not deserve to die in such horrific fashion. He should have a good Christian funeral."

"Oh, of course, of course," Dodd said, running a hand along his cheek. "A Christian funeral."

"And whatever family he has . . . they should be notified," Mathilda said.

"The family," Dodd said. "Right, right. Say, Miss Anderson, if you'll excuse me for enquirin', what're you doin' with the big man here?" He canted his head at Prophet. "You throwin' in with ole Prophet now, are you?"

Dodd gave a coyote grin.

Mathilda beetled her brows uncertainly and glanced at Prophet. "Throw in with him? You mean, as in . . . oh, certainly not! Mister Prophet is a bounty hunter. He hunts men for money. I certainly wouldn't throw in with such a . . . such a man as that. He's simply chaperoning me down out of the mountains. It isn't safe here, as I've become very soundly convinced after the savagery of the last couple of days.

"I intend to head home to St. Paul and try to pick up where I left off, if at all possible." She cast another indignant glance at Prophet. "Throw in with such a man as this? Certainly not." Her features softened when, as though in afterthought, she quickly added, "Though I do so much appreciate his shepherding me out of these mountains, however."

Prophet gave a snort and pulled Mean's head up by the reins. "Well, I'd love to stay and chin with ya'll, fellas, but we're burnin' daylight and I wouldn't want Miss Anderson to have to endure my man-huntin' presence any longer than she has to."

"Say, now, Miss Anderson," Dodd said, walking up to the head of Mathilda's horse and grabbing the bridle strap running along the beast's jaw. "There's no point in turnin' back after you've come so far. Why, there's plenty of men in these mountains who could use a good wife."

"Sure," said Gunderson, grinning up at Mathilda. "There's plenty of men in these mountains who'd appreciate a young, sweet gal who's as easy on the peepers as you are. Take me, for instance."

Dodd glowered at the taller deputy marshal. "You?"

"Hell, yes, me," Gunderson said. "I ain't been married in two years. My last wife ran off with a sky pilot, if you can believe that. Since then I been chasin' outlaws so hard, I ain't had time to slow down and marry up again!"

"Ah, hell," Dodd said. "You'd do best to choose Halcon there. That dog-eatin' Chiricowy's got him five wives, and there ain't a one of 'em I ain't never seen without a smile on her face this wide." The marshal held up his hands three feet apart. "I got a notion he must be hung like a damn bung starter!"

Halcon finally cracked a grin—an ugly one, given the grisly state of his teeth and gums—but a grin just the same. His mud-brown eyes were on Mathilda.

"All right, fellas," Prophet said, reining Mean and Ugly toward the southern trail, "been nice jawin' with ya. Lookin' forward to doin' it again sometime!"

As he and Mathilda and the dead Frank Beauregard loped across the yard and onto the trail around which tall pines jutted high, the two deputy U.S. marshals laughed raucously, slapping their thighs. Prophet glanced back to see Halcon still grinning and thrusting his hips lewdly toward Mathilda.

The girl, leaning forward to grasp her saddle horn, regarded Prophet as though stricken, tree shadows dancing over her bleached features. "Those men were actually *lawmen*?"

"Yes, ma'am."

Mathilda opened her mouth and shook her head, deeply befuddled. "How can *lawmen* act so . . . so *vile*?"

Prophet gave a dry snort and turned his head forward. He kicked Mean into a faster stride. Mathilda gave a clipped scream. He glanced back to see her sliding down her left stirrup fender. She managed to haul herself back upright and to hunker low over the horn, which she was clenching with both hands. She wore her hair down, and it blew in a wild mass about her shoulders beneath the oversized hat.

She looked up beseechingly. "Please, Mister Prophet, must we go so fast?"

"Might as well get used to it," Prophet told her, raising his voice to be heard above the thundering hooves. "We'll likely be traveling this fast and faster most of the way to Denver!"

Fifteen minutes later, after dropping down the backside of a steep hill, Prophet checked the horses, curveting Mean and swinging down from the saddle. Nearly lying prone across her saddle pommel, Mathilda looked up at him, cheeks flushed and hair badly disheveled.

"What . . . where are you going?" she asked as he strode past her.

Prophet didn't respond as he climbed to the top of the hill and stared in the direction from which they'd come. After a time, he strode back down to the horses, pensively chewing his bottom lip.

"What were you looking at?" the girl asked.

Prophet reached under her horse's belly to tighten the latigo. "I wasn't lookin' *at* nothin'. I was lookin' *for* those scurvy devils—Dodd and the others."

"Why? Do you think they'll follow us?"

"I'd put money on it."

"Why would they follow us? You mean, to make sure the

money arrives safely in Denver?"

Prophet chuckled without mirth as he rammed his fist against the mare's belly, to force the beast to exhale as he tightened the cinch. "Yeah, that's it."

"I don't understand, Mister Prophet. Why are you acting so cross with me? I can't help it that the stage won't pull through Dead Skunk Gulch until next week!"

Prophet secured the strap and scowled up at her. "You wouldn't throw in with a man such as *me*, huh? A bounty hunter? Ain't that what you told Dodd?"

Mathilda flushed. "Well, I . . . I wouldn't want anyone to think that . . . that . . . I . . ."

"Would have thrown in with me if you'd had a choice?" Prophet's face burned. A vein throbbed in his forehead. "Well, throw in with me you did. *Forced* yourself on me, is more how it was. Believe me, I wouldn't be riding with you, either, the . . . the"—he glanced at where Frank Beauregard lay sprawled belly down across the roan—"the mail-order bride of that outlaw devil!"

"Bride of that outlaw devil?" Mathilda intoned, mouth and eyes drawn wide in shock.

"The bride of that outlaw devil!" Prophet repeated. "The reason you're here, enduring my soiled presence, is because I felt sorry for you. But I now see that you and Frank were two peas in a pod. Too bad I had to come along and spoil Frank's fun. Too bad ole Frank couldn't have lived to marry you. The son of a bitch deserved a spoiled, uppity little brat like you. That would have been the best punishment in the world for ole Frank. Even better than shovelin' coal in hell. Shit, he got off lucky!"

"I will thank you to not swear in my presence, you brigand! And how dare you call me a spoiled brat. I am anything *but.* I have worked hard all of my life. And uppity? I never!"

"And here I am, having saved your snooty ass, payin' the piper for it." Prophet swung onto Mean's back and cast his fiery gaze at Mathilda once more. "I should've left you at Dead Skunk Gulch with Dodd!" He swung Mean around and booted him down the trail, the other two horses loping along behind. He laughed bitterly. "Got shed of one snooty female only to fall into the trap of another. Where in the hell did my luck turn south?"

"You are uncouth, foul-mouthed, and ill-tempered," Mathilda castigated his back, her voice quavering as the mare lunged beneath her. "Just like every other man I've so far met on my ill-fated western sojourn. I told Marshal Dodd that I appreciated your assistance, but instead you prefer to focus on something I said only in *passing.*"

"*Only in passing* to make sure Dodd, that privy-feedin' no-account rat from Alabama, knows your rightful social station." Prophet chuckled ironically and shook his head. "As though Dodd would know a snake from a boll weevil!"

"I can't hear what you're saying," Mathilda called behind him, clinging for dear life to her saddle horn. "So if you're saying something for my benefit, you'd best speak louder!"

Prophet glanced over his shoulder at her. "I said hold on, we're headin' cross-country!"

He neck-reined Mean and Ugly off the left side of the trail and into the forest. The other horses followed. Behind Prophet, Mathilda screamed. He glanced back to see the girl tumbling in the brush beside the galloping mare, hat whipping in the air around her head.

All Prophet could see as she rolled ass over teakettle were glimpses of her flying brown hair and whipping hat and then her side-button shoes and then her hair and hat again, inside a thickly roiling dust cloud. She disappeared with a crunching thud in a chokecherry thicket.

Then all the bounty hunter could see of the girl was the sunlit dust she'd kicked up, sifting around the shrubs.

Chapter Thirteen

"Oh, shit," Prophet muttered, reining Mean and Ugly to a halt.

The other two mounts stopped behind him and turned to peer warily back toward where Mathilda had disappeared in the shrubs. Dust still sifted in the sunlit air. The roan carrying Frank Beauregard snorted and flicked his ears.

Mean and Ugly looked at Prophet dubiously and shook his head, rattling his bit in his teeth.

The horses appeared to be reprimanding him for his dunderheaded move. Inwardly, he castigated himself as he walked slowly, tentatively toward the shrubs. The shrubs were not moving. Prophet couldn't see the girl inside them. Since the shrubs weren't moving, she probably wasn't moving either.

"Oh, shit," Prophet said. "Oh, shit."

He stopped at the edge of the shrubs. "M-Miss Anderson?"

No response.

Prophet stepped into the bushes, elbowing branches out of his way. He called to her again. Anxiety was a tight fist wrapped around the base of his spine. He'd let his temper get the better of him. He shouldn't have turned the horses so fast into the trees.

What did he think would happen?

"Damn fool," he scolded himself, stealing himself for what he was afraid he might find—the girl lying in the chokecherries with a broken neck.

He took another three steps, following Mathilda's own course into the thicket marked by bent and broken branches and ripped leaves. He stood looking down at her, stretching his lips back from his teeth in dread.

She lay belly down, head turned to one side. Her man's hat partly covered her head, still attached to her neck by the rawhide thong. Her hair was sprayed across her shoulders and exposed right cheek and the flattened brush to both sides.

"Miss . . . ?"

He let his words trail into silence when he saw that her shoulders were moving. They were jerking slightly. Then he could hear her broken, watery sobs. He hunkered beside her and slid the hat aside so he could see her face. Her lips were stretched back from her teeth as, squeezing her eyes closed, she sobbed.

Prophet placed a hand on her shoulder. "You, uh . . . you all right, there, Miss Anderson?"

She drew a raking, phlegmy breath, then pushed up onto her hands and knees.

"You barbarian!" she cried, and flung herself at him, punching him with her clenched fists, sobbing. "You're a barbarian! A barbarian!"

Despite the bruises he was still wearing from his dustup with the other bounty hunters at Dead Skunk Gulch, he let her get several good licks in, hoping they might make her feel better. Him, too.

"Bastard!" she yelled, laying a hard right across his jaw. "You're a bastard!"

She was strong for a woman, but he had a hard head, and he deserved the punishment. Finally, he grabbed her wrists and held her out before him so he could get a look at her. She hung her head, sobbing.

Her bottom lip was cut and her clothes were soiled and mussed. There were a couple of other scrapes on her cheeks and forehead. Though none of the abrasions looked deep, each was like a dagger to his heart.

"You don't look too bad," he said as she continued to sob, her face hidden by the dusty, leaf-speckled screen of her hair. "How do you feel? Do think anything's broken?"

"I don't know," she cried, shaking her head. She lifted her chin and fired volleys of pure hatred with her eyes. "You're a bastard! Every bit as bad as the others! You're right—I would have been as well off with Beauregard!"

"Come on," Prophet said, rising and gently pulling her up with him. "Stand up and let's check you out, see if anything's broken."

"Get away from me!" She pushed him away, swung around, and stomped out of the shrubs. "I hate you!"

"I don't blame you a bit," Prophet said. "Come on over here, and let me . . ."

He'd heard something. He turned his gaze in the direction of the trail. He couldn't see any movement out there, but he could hear men's voices and the thuds of galloping hooves.

Prophet pushed through the shrubs and strode quickly over to where the girl was standing, sniffing, rearranging her clothes and brushing her hair back from her face.

"Come on," he said, grabbing her hand and jerking her toward him. "We gotta go!"

"Leave me alone," she cried. "Get away from me. I want nothing more to—" She gasped. "What are you . . . *what do you think you're doing?*"

Prophet had picked her up in his arms and was striding around the shrubs toward the horses.

"Shut up—someone's comin'."

Mathilda craned her head to look around Prophet toward the trail. "I didn't hear anything."

"I did."

"Well, I—wait! What're you doing?" Prophet had lifted her onto his saddle.

"Since you have such a damned hard time sitting a horse without help, you're gonna sit mine until we've lost whoever's shadowin' us."

Prophet grabbed the reins and climbed up onto the saddle behind her.

"Wait—this won't do!" Mathilda cried.

Ignoring her, Prophet touched Mean with his spurs. The dun lunged off his rear hooves, jerking the other two mounts along behind.

Prophet held his arms around the girl, holding Mean's reins in front of her, feeling her hair blow back to whip against his cheeks, an oddly arousing sensation given the direness of their situation. She leaned forward slightly, gripping the saddle horn, but as Mean climbed a low hill, tall pines whipping by on both sides, she fell back against Prophet's chest.

Mean gained the top of the hill and suddenly they were plunging down the steep opposite side. Prophet wrapped his left arm more tightly around the girl's belly, pulling her back against him as the sure-footed dun picked his way down the steep declivity. The two trailing mounts raced to keep pace.

When they gained the bottom of the ridge and Mean was galloping across a meadow peppered with aspens and young firs, Prophet glanced back up toward the ridge crest.

He could see no riders.

Had they lost them already? Maybe whomever he'd heard on the trail wasn't after him and Mathilda, after all.

Maybe. But he couldn't take that chance. He was only one man trying to get a dead man with a lucrative price on his head and twenty-five-thousand dollars in train loot back to Denver. And he had a girl to protect. In other words, he had a job of work ahead of him, and he couldn't afford to take any chances.

He and the girl crossed the meadow and started up the next forested ridge. This was a steep one as well as a long one, and when he thought they were halfway to the top—though it was hard to tell because of all the trees—he stopped to rest the horses. As he did, he stared back down through the forest toward the bottom of the ridge.

He could neither see nor hear anything except birds and the chittering of angry squirrels. The forest duff smelled sweet around him. Rays of warm sunlight dappled the soft, thick, pine-needled turf.

Prophet glanced at Mathilda before him. She wasn't moving but only staring straight ahead.

He nudged her. "You all right?"

She did not turn to look at him but only nodded. She felt warm against him. He could feel the curve of her breasts against the top of his left arm. He tried not to notice the sensations but it wasn't easy, their bodies pressed against one another as they were. He felt the stirrings of arousal, and an embarrassed flush rose in his cheeks.

"Come on, Mean," Prophet said with annoyance, pulling the grazing horse's head up and turning him toward the upslope. "Time to go!"

They topped the rise and Prophet found himself on a broad, windy ridge crest almost barren of trees. Another, rocky ridge rose in the east, roughly a hundred yards away. Prophet headed for it. When they'd topped the rise strewn with talus and boulders and over which the wind howled like an enraged witch, Prophet reined the horses to a halt in a hollow a ways down the ridge's lee side.

He swung down from the saddle and then reached up and gently pulled Mathilda down, as well.

"What are we doing?" she asked, raising her voice to be heard above the wind.

"I'm gonna see if we're bein' shadowed. Stay here with the horses."

Prophet shucked his Winchester from its scabbard and his spyglass from his saddlebags, and then walked back up the side of the rise. A few feet from the top, he dropped to all fours and crawled until he could see over the crest. He doffed his hat, secured it to the ground with a rock, and then, lying belly down, raised his spyglass to his eye and adjusted the focus.

He stared back along the broad plateau they'd just crossed, toward the dark-green forest on the other side. It was hard to keep the glass in focus with the wind hammering against him, but he continued to scour the plateau with his gaze for nearly twenty minutes, until he decided no one was back there. If someone were shadowing him and the girl, they were lying far enough back as not to be an imminent threat.

Prophet collapsed the brass-framed glass, returned it to its sheepskin sheath, donned his hat, and strode back down into the hollow, where Mathilda sat on a rock near the grazing horses. Her hat hung down her back, and her long hair blew in the wind.

As he returned his spyglass to the saddlebags, Mathilda looked at him worriedly. "Anything?"

Prophet shook his head. "I think we're all right. We'd best keep movin', though. Get down out of this wind."

Mathilda rose and looked around, frowning bewilderedly. "Where are we going? Which direction are we riding?"

"Denver's east."

"Yes, but . . ." She continued to look around at the vast, lumpy, forested landscape stretching around them, under a clear blue sky from which the sun fairly hammered its harsh, high-altitude light against them. "How do you know the . . . way . . . ?"

"We're gonna head over Bull Elk Pass." Prophet wrapped his

hand around hers, and pulled her to her feet. He pointed. "See that purple ridge over yonder, to the northeast?"

"To the left of the one with snow on it?"

"That's the one. That's Bull Elk Pass. We're gonna take the pass over to the valley of the Arkansas, then follow the Arkansas down out of the mountains to the eastern plains. Then we'll ride north to Denver . . . and get you on a train to home."

"My god," Mathilda said, so softly that Prophet could barely hear her above the wind. "It looks so far."

"Only another day's ride." Prophet led her over to her horse. "You can ride your own mount now."

She looked at him, holding her windblown hair away from her face with her hand. "You promise not to throw me again?"

Prophet nodded, turning his mouth corners down sheepishly. "I promise."

"Okay, then."

As she started to turn toward the horse, reaching for the apple, he drew her back toward him. "Let me see that."

"See what?"

"Your lip." Prophet inspected the cut on her lower lip. "Hold on," he said, and walked over to retrieve his canteen from his saddle. He pulled a red handkerchief from his back pocket, moistened the cloth from the canteen, and dabbed at the girl's lower lip.

She jerked and turned away. "Ouch!"

"Sorry."

"You had no call," she chastised him, gently.

He sighed as he dabbed at her lip again. "I said I was sorry. What more can I do?"

"You can *not* do it again."

"I won't."

When he had most of the blood cleaned up, he lifted his gaze to her eyes. She was staring into his. She wore a strange expression. It was almost as though she were trying to look deep into him, to see who he really was.

"Don't worry," Prophet said. "I'm not going to hurt you again. I promise." He raised the canteen. "Drink?"

She kept her mildly skeptical eyes on him for another five seconds before she accepted the canteen, lifting it to her mouth. She took a long drink. He watched her pale, slender neck move as she swallowed. She had a small, barely perceptible mole to the left of her voice box. He suddenly found himself yearning to press his lips to it. Warm blood pooled in his belly.

"Here," she said, shoving the canteen against his chest, nudging him from his wanton reverie. She scowled at him as though reading his mind. "I'm done."

He took the canteen and then helped her turn out a stirrup and mount her horse. He didn't keep his hands on her for long. He didn't like what the sensation of her body was doing to his insides, and he sensed she could sense it in him.

Come on, Proph, you goatish bastard, he inwardly scolded himself as he shoved his Winchester into its scabbard.

Get a damn hold of yourself!

Chapter Fourteen

"Are you really going to haul Mister Beauregard's body all the way back to Denver?" Mathilda asked Prophet just after midday. Earlier they'd stopped for a half hour's rest and a pot of coffee brewed over a low fire.

Prophet had removed Beauregard's body from the back of the horse packing it, so the roan could rest, and then he'd hoisted it back over the saddle. Mathilda had watched him work with a disgusted scowl.

"You bet I am," Prophet said. "All the way back to the Wells Fargo district office in Denver. Some bounty men will just bring the heads back, but that's too damn bloody for me. I seen enough blood in the war. If I can bring back the whole carcass, that's what I'll do."

"Oh, my god!" He could hear her gag behind him. "I can't imagine doing what you do," she added thickly. "Yours is a disgusting profession!"

As they rode along a broad, deep valley hemmed in with tall, forested crags, following an old Indian trail along the Moose River, which cleaved the canyon down the middle, Prophet glanced over his shoulder at her. She was getting on his nerves again. He was glad. He felt better being annoyed with her than randy for her.

The former emotion seemed more dignified—not to mention understandable.

"You have anything against lawmen, Miss High and Mighty?"

"Marshal Dodd and his ilk excepted, of course not."

"Well, how is what I do any different from what a lawmen does? I hunt bad men down and bring 'em to justice."

"Yes, but you do it for money, Mister Prophet."

"You mean lawmen don't get paid?"

"Well, certainly they do, but . . ." Mathilda scowled at him, flushing slightly. She gave a frustrated chuff. "There's a difference, Mister Prophet. I can't put my finger on it just now, but I know there's a difference!"

Prophet snorted ironically and turned around to stare up the trail. "You let me know when you do, Miss High and Mighty."

"And please stop calling me that!"

"All right," Prophet said, lowering his voice and grinning as he added, "Miss High and Mighty."

"I heard that!"

They continued riding along the river for the rest of the day. The valley seemed endless and relatively unchanging from mile to mile.

When the sun began falling behind the western ridges and deep-purple shadows stretched out from the high ridge walls, Prophet found a prime camping spot along the stream. The river made a continuous, low rushing sound. Pines and aspens shielded the camping spot from the trail. Chickadees and nuthatches cheeped in the branches. Pinecones dropped with dull thuds.

When Prophet had unsaddled the horses and tied them to a long picket line close enough to the river that they could drink from the shallows, he grained them and rubbed them down carefully. He inspected and cleaned out their hooves and shoes and cut burs out of their tails with his bowie knife. He was glad to have stopped early enough in the evening that the horses would have a long rest. They'd have a long, hard pull climbing Bull Elk Pass over the next two days, and he wanted them in the best possible condition.

With the horses situated, he hid the saddlebags containing the loot beneath a blowdown cottonwood a ways from the camp, away from prying eyes. He dragged the blanket-wrapped bundle of Frank Beauregard near the slight clearing in which he intended to bivouac. Mathilda was gathering sticks and brush for a fire. As she dropped another load onto the small pile she'd already gleaned, she cast Prophet a repelled look, and crossed her arms. "Does Mister Beauregard need to be so close to where we'll be dining? Surely you two have been close enough all day that it might be beneficial to spend some time apart . . ."

"Truth to tell, I'm tired of Frank," Prophet said, pulling the stiffening carcass up against the base of a large fir whose branches didn't start until six feet up from the ground. "And I'm likely to get a whole lot more tired of him . . . when he starts to get a little whiffy on the lee side, especially."

"Oh, please!" Mathilda groaned.

Prophet chuckled. It was not to his credit that he found humor in scandalizing the girl. "But I want him close enough to keep an eye on. He's worth two thousand dollars, Frank is. Not only to me, but to anyone who can get him to Denver." He straightened and brushed his hands together. "Wouldn't want to have trailed him all this way just to get him stolen out from under me."

"No," Mathilda said, wincing as she sagged a trifle stiffly onto a deadfall log. "No, I suppose you wouldn't."

"What's the matter?"

"I'm . . . I'm a little stiff." Her cheeks flushed.

"Ah." Prophet chuckled. "I don't reckon you've spent much time in the saddle until now."

"You would reckon right," she said with a groan, arching her back and massaging her hips with her hand.

"You'll get used to it."

"Yes, but probably not until just before we arrive in Denver."

Prophet chuckled again as he dropped to a knee beside his saddlebags. He rummaged around for a time, muttering, then pulled out his slingshot, inspecting it to make sure the rabbit-gut thong was still attached to the Y-shaped knob of mountain ash.

"What are you going to do with that?" Mathilda asked, leaning from side to side, stretching.

"I'm gonna bring us down a couple of squirrels for supper."

"Squirrels, wonderful." Mathilda sighed, obviously not overjoyed at the notion. "Why don't you use one of your several firearms? Lord knows you have enough of them."

"Because I don't want anyone to know we're here. That's the beauty of a slingshot. Soundless. Besides, I'm as good with one of these as I am with any of my so-called firearms. I learned to nail a squirrel with a rock before I was out of swaddling clothes."

"Swaddling clothes, really?" Mathilda laughed, skeptically.

"Swaddling clothes—sure enough!"

Prophet winked at her, then turned to stride off through the trees, swinging his head to inspect the branches for prospective supper.

A half hour later, he returned to the spot of their bivouac, three squirrels dangling by their tails from his left fist. He cooked the squirrels on a hastily woven willow spit he erected over the fire Mathilda had built while he'd been hunting. She'd also put coffee on to boil. The woman made a good pot of belly wash, the bounty hunter decided, after she'd poured him a cup and he slouched back against his saddle to sip the brew and tend the meat.

His estimation of the young woman instantly climbed.

Night came quickly to this high county hemmed in by jutting crags. A cool breeze shepherded bright yellow aspen leaves around the camp and tossed them gently onto the ever-sliding—and darkening—stream.

Prophet ate the succulent squirrel hungrily with his hands, washing the greasy meat down with frequent sips from his cup. Mathilda was hesitant at first, eating the first bites of the meat tentatively with a fork from a plate. After she'd consumed a sizable portion, however, she glanced across the fire at Prophet, cocked a brow, and grinned, slipping another chunk of the still smoking meat between her pretty lips with her fingers.

"Good, huh?" Prophet asked, chewing.

"Not bad, Mister Prophet," she said, her cheeks dimpling beautifully. "I must say."

"There—see, now?"

"See what?"

"I ain't so bad, after all."

Mathilda smiled across the fire at him again, saucily, slipping another chunk of meat into her mouth. "No, you're not so bad, Mister Prophet. I do apologize."

"Ah, hell."

"No, I really do," she said, frowning seriously over the flames at him. "You saved my life. Twice. Possibly more. And I rewarded you with condescension if not outright disdain."

"I know a way you can make it up to me, Miss Anderson."

She turned her head slightly to one side, studying him dubiously. "And . . . how is that, Mister Prophet?"

He slid his coffee cup around to her side of the fire. "Refill?" He snorted.

Mathilda chuckled. "Of course." She used a couple of leather swatches to pour the still-smoking, coal-black brew into his speckled, dented, and scorched tin cup. Finished with his meal, he sat back against his saddle, sipped his coffee, and watched the girl admiringly as the night closed in around them.

Later, they each washed their dishes in the stream and prepared for bed. Prophet had packed Mathilda the bedroll he'd found in the hired hand's cabin, and helped her roll it out on the far side of the fire from his. She turned her saddle over so that she could use the woolen underside for a pillow.

When he'd rolled out his own blankets and arranged his saddle at the head of them, he poured himself and Mathilda each another cup of coffee from the fresh pot she'd brewed. The young woman sat stiffly onto the deadfall log, her freshly brushed hair copper-tinged by the low, snapping flames. Prophet set his cup down on the log and then began rummaging through his saddlebags.

"What are you looking for?" she asked him over the steaming lip of her cup, which she held in both hands clad in knit gloves.

Prophet strode back toward her, prying the lid off the small tin in his hands. He sat beside her on the log, about two feet away, and offered her the tin. "Arnica. Best put some on that lip and those cuts on your forehead there. It'll take the sting out and help you heal faster."

"Thank you." Mathilda took the tin and smeared a little of the arnica on her lower lip. She dipped her finger back into the tin and raised it uncertainly. To Prophet, she said, "You wouldn't happen to have a looking glass, would you?"

Prophet chuffed a laugh. "With my ugly mug?"

Mathilda smiled. She held the tin out toward him. "Would you mind, then?"

Prophet took the tin uncertainly. "And . . . ?"

"Smear some on my cuts. You managed to clean the blood from my lip earlier."

"Oh . . . right." Prophet's ears warmed with embarrassment. Why? Like she'd said, he'd had no problem cleaning her lip for her. For some reason, he felt more awkward around her now.

"Here—use this." Mathilda held out the finger on which she'd dabbed the salve.

Prophet looked at her finger. He lifted his hand and stuck

out his own finger, his ears turning warmer. He swallowed, glanced away, and then tried to rub his right index finger against hers, but missed.

Mathilda chuckled.

Prophet chuckled, too, and tried it again, managing to connect the tip of his finger with hers this time. They both chuckled at the same time, and now her cheeks flushed as she glanced away.

Prophet dabbed the arnica on a light scrape-blemish above her left brow and more on the small gash on her left temple, just below her hairline. As he did, he glanced down to see that she was staring at his chest. Her own chest was rising and falling slowly, heavily beneath her man's plaid wool coat. She'd tucked her hair back so that he could see that her ears were mottled red.

He pulled his hand away from her face, smearing the excess salve around between his thumb and index finger.

"Mister Prophet," she said. It was almost a whisper.

"Might as well call me Lou, I reckon."

"All right, then—Lou?"

"Yes?"

"I find your mug very handsome indeed." The corners of Mathilda's mouth quirked a wry smile. "Just so you know."

"Why, thank you, Miss Anderson. I find your countenance a right pleasing one to gaze on, myself."

"It's Mathilda. Mattie for short."

"All right, then. Mattie."

"Lou?"

"Yes, Mattie?"

"If it weren't for you, I would be dead. Many times over."

"Oh, I don't know if I'd go that far, Mattie."

"If you left me right now, I would likely be dead by this time tomorrow night. I have no idea where I am or how to get home.

Even with a horse, I would merely ride in circles and likely fall prey to the kind of men you rescued me from or to wolves or to Indians."

"Not too many Indians out here these days," Prophet said. "Most are on the reservations. I'll admit that some still—"

Mattie reached up and placed two fingers on his lips, silencing him. "My point is this—I know that you are a man with a man's . . . urges. I saw how you were . . . well, looking at me earlier."

"Oh, now, that . . . that was just—"

Again, she placed two fingers on his lips. "I will lie with you tonight, Lou . . . if you promise that whatever happens, you will not strand me out here."

Hot blood surged in Prophet's loins. He swallowed the knot in his throat, trying to ignore the male urges, as she'd called them, which were fairly battering him. He shook his head.

Mattie's eyes widened with alarm. *"What?"*

"No," Prophet said. "I ain't gonna lie with you. Not for that."

"For what, then?"

Prophet gently cupped her face in his hands. "You gotta admit you want me as much as I want you." His lips spread with a faintly challenging grin.

Mattie's cheeks grew bright red, and her eyes blazed as though his words had deeply offended her. She opened her lips to give a swift, sharp retort, but the words didn't make their way across her vocal chords. She lurched toward him, wrapping her arms around his neck and closing her mouth over his.

They kissed there on the log for several minutes. Then Prophet moved her down onto her bedroll and began unbuttoning her coat. He lifted his head up suddenly, looking around. "Hold on."

"What is it?"

Prophet kissed her, gazing into her eyes. "I'm gonna have a

look around, make sure we're alone. You think it over, and if you still wanna continue by the time I get back, we'll continue." He winked at her, then rose and grabbed his rifle.

He checked on the horses, none of which seemed alarmed about anything, which was a good sign. Prophet could usually count on Mean and Ugly to keep a good night scout.

Still, he circled the bivouac area slowly, investigating the woods around the river with his own keen vision and hearing. Relieved when he found nothing amiss, no one about, and could see no distant campfires from the low knoll he'd climbed, he returned to the camp. The fire had burned low. He leaned his rifle against a tree and walked over to where Mathilda lay curled in her blankets.

"All clear," he said, doffing his hat. "Now, if you're still of a mind, let's get down to . . ." He stared down in horror at what he'd thought was Mathilda. She was not here. Her blankets were twisted around so that they'd only assumed the shape of a human figure.

Prophet's heart clanged like a hammer on a blacksmith's anvil.

Mattie was gone.

Chapter Fifteen

Prophet looked around, drawing a deep breath to calm himself. She'd only gone into the woods to tend to nature, he told himself. "Calm down, fer cryin' in Grant's whiskey, old son."

Raising his voice, he called her name. When he did not receive a response after five seconds, the short hairs bristled across the back of his neck. He cleared his throat and raised his voice a little higher, so that she could hear him above the river's steady, dull *whoosh.*

"Mattie?" Prophet waited. His heart beat slowly but heavily, painfully. Even louder: "Mattie?"

Prophet turned his head, raking his gaze in a complete circle around the camp, seeing only the fire's dull glow pulsating out against the formidable darkness. He could see only the wan light and the silhouettes of breeze-jostled branches. A thud sounded behind him. He whipped around, his Colt in his hand. The hammer clicked back as he aimed into the darkness.

But the thud had only been a pinecone dropping from a branch.

Prophet tightened his grip around his revolver's walnut grips. "Mattie, goddamnit, if you're out there, answer me."

Suddenly, he felt foolish. She was a dignified young woman. She might have only strolled out beyond where she could hear him above the river's wash, to perform her night's ablutions. Prophet again told himself to settle down. She'd likely be back in a minute or two.

He depressed the Colt's hammer, slid the revolver back into its holster, snapped the keeper thong into place over the hammer, and picked up his rifle. He moved a ways back from the fire and gave his eyes to the darkness until shapes formerly obscure became clearer.

He stood cradling his rifle in his arms, looking around and listening to the night, which was dominated by the river's endless whisper above the intermittent rake of the breeze. In the far distance there rose the mournful wail of a wolf. After a minute, the first call was answered by another call from a little farther away than the first.

The air against Prophet's face grew chill. It smelled like cold steel tinged with the tang of pine resin.

An owl hooted.

A night bird gave a cry. There was the following screech of a rabbit dying violently. Prophet felt the backs of his legs tighten as the screeches continued before dwindling to grisly silence.

He swung his head from right to left and back again, his vision so keen now that it was almost as though a moon were on the rise, though there wasn't one. If anyone moved within fifty yards of him . . . or her . . . he'd see that person. But there was nothing. Nothing moved except the branches being nudged by the breeze.

When Prophet finally turned back toward the camp, there was only darkness in that direction, as well. He walked back toward his and Mattie's bedrolls. The fire had gone out. The night had closed down like a black glove over the bivouac. Prophet looked around. Mattie's blankets were as he'd last seen them—twisted and vacant.

Hot blood pooled again in Prophet's belly. It was not the heat of lust now, however. It was the heat of dread. He'd been standing away from the camp for over half an hour, maybe closer to an hour, and Mattie hadn't returned. She'd either wandered so far away that she'd gotten lost, or someone had taken her.

Again, Prophet heard the ominous screech of the hunting night bird.

Again, the rabbit gave its high-pitched wail.

Wait.

Prophet held his breath, listening, pondering. He could hear the thud of his heart in his ears.

That had been no hunting bird. No dying rabbit.

"Halcon," Prophet said, releasing his held breath, flaring his nostrils.

The Mexican Apache trapper had Mathilda. And he was toying with Prophet. Mocking him.

It had to be Halcon. He was the only man in these mountains who could have stolen into Prophet's camp and taken the girl without Mean and Ugly winding him and sounding the alarm. Prophet had heard the stories about Halcon. It was said he was as stealthy as any full-blood Apache. In fact, he was known to be a better scout and tracker than most. That's why Dodd had ridden with him for so long.

Halcon made easy prey of almost any veteran outlaw.

Now, Halcon, Dodd, and Gunderson had taken Mathilda out from under Prophet's nose. They'd probably glassed the camp from a distance. Not seeing the loot, they'd decided to take the girl instead, and hold her for ransom—Beauregard's body and the Wells Fargo money.

Humiliation mixed with fear and frustration flowed like black pools of burning oil in the bounty hunter's blood. They'd likely hold her for a while and let Prophet think good and hard about what he'd do to save her.

They knew, of course, that eventually he'd turn over the money as well as Beauregard's carcass. They knew that Prophet, his soul having been broken by the war, would have no choice in the matter. He couldn't let her die. He may have sold his soul to the devil, but not his honor.

Dodd would give him time to think about his situation. A good time to think about what they might be doing to her . . .

"Bastards," Prophet muttered, hardening his jaws and squeezing the rifle in his gloved hands. He drew a deep breath, threw his head back, and shouted, *"Bast-arrrds!"*

The echoes vaulted away, dwindling, toward the cold glittering stars.

Then there was only the lonely silence of the night.

Prophet jerked his head up from his chest, lifting the Winchester that had been resting across his thighs, and jacked a round into the chamber.

He aimed out into the dull light of early morning.

He blinked, easing the tension in his trigger finger.

Nothing there but the gray light of dawn sifting through the inky pines. A chill breeze rose, shuttling leaves across the ground. Prophet's breath frosted in the air around his head. A light hoarfrost dusted the grass. It outlined the soles of his boots and glazed the slack of his denim trousers. His butt was cold. He felt as though he'd been sitting on ice.

Depressing the rifle's hammer, he lowered the Winchester and looked around. He was sitting against a tree about forty yards from the camp. He hadn't intended on sleeping but only waiting out the night for morning, as he hadn't expected movement from Dodd, Halcon, and Gunderson until the sun had risen. He had no idea what strategy Dodd's group was figuring on.

Would they bring Mathilda to Prophet, or were they going to let Prophet ride to them and Mathilda?

Looking around cautiously, Prophet built a low fire over which to brew coffee. While the fire sparked and crackled to life, he saddled the horses and strapped Beauregard over the roan's back. He had a quick cup of coffee and a few bites of jerky and hardtack, then kicked out the fire.

He looked around, waiting.

Would they come?

Finally, when the sun was high enough to offer sufficient light, he scoured the outlying terrain for sign. He doubted the half-breed had left any spoor, but he had to look. On his third time around the camp, he found Mathilda's hat lying about sixty yards to the east. The grass around the hat was slightly dented, forming a faint, spotty trail leading farther east.

Few blades of grass had been disturbed. Halcon had learned how to move with the slightest disruption to the terrain around him. He'd likely been carrying Mathilda, who probably had something tied over her mouth to keep her from calling out.

Prophet stared east. Anxiety was a cold knife twisting in his belly. Around the knife, fury burned.

East was the direction Halcon had taken Mathilda, so east was the direction Prophet would ride. Since they hadn't shown up here, they were likely waiting up the trail for him. Maybe near the pass.

He retrieved the loot from the cavity beneath the blowdown, and slung the saddlebags over Mean's back. He took one more cautious glance around him, making sure he was alone, making sure no one was drawing a bead on him, then mounted up and rode back out to the old trail.

He hadn't ridden far when something caught his eye. One of Mattie's knit gloves lay along the trail's left edge. Prophet dismounted and scooped the glove off the ground. His heart quickened.

He'd wondered if the hat had fallen by accident, but now he doubted it. The glove told him that Halcon was leaving a trail for him. A little farther on, he saw where the man had mounted a horse. The horse's shod tracks continued east along the winding trail tracing a route along the river, heading toward Bull Elk Pass looming ahead.

A half hour later, Prophet reined Mean and Ugly to a halt near a pile of gray ashes mounded inside a ring of fire-blackened stones. Two eyes and a mouth curved in a smile had been drawn across the pile. The stick that had been used to draw the mocking leer lay across the stones.

Prophet clenched his jaw in anger. He swung down from the saddle, removed a glove, and poked a finger into the ashes. Warm. Dodd's men had pulled out a couple of hours ago, likely heading up the pass. Prophet knew that Dodd took his lawdogging assignments out of the federal building in Denver. That's where he was heading, stringing Prophet along with the loot, using Mathilda for bait.

"You better not have hurt her, you bastard," Prophet growled, pulling his glove back on. "Because that badge of yours won't deflect double-aught buck, you son of a bitch!"

He swung back into the saddle, turned Mean out to the main trail, and, with Mattie's mare and Beauregard's roan trailing by their reins tied to the dun's tail, began the slow climb up Bull Elk Pass.

The trail had originally been excavated by prisoners from the Colorado Territorial Pen to provide stagecoach passage from the Arkansas River Valley to the Western Slope. The eight-foot-wide, rutted, pine-needle-carpeted trace zigzagged up the side of the pass, hemmed in on both sides by tall firs, pines, spruces, and tamaracks. Occasionally, the trees disappeared to either side, and a deep, rocky chasm yawned below, providing a breathtaking view of the river valley Prophet had traversed to get here.

Turning aspens provided color. Through the early part of the morning, the air was cooler than it had been below, but as the sun climbed, it warmed considerably so that about two-thirds up the mountain Prophet removed his mackinaw and tied it around his bedroll.

He rested the horses for a time, letting them draw water from a spring chuckling up from a nest of rocks, and looked around.

He had the feeling he was being watched. Following the trail made him vulnerable to a bullet fired from ambush. But something told him that Dodd wouldn't risk an errant shot, incurring Prophet's wrath and a possible bellyful of ten-gauge buckshot. Far less risky to exchange the girl for the loot. Then both parties could be on their way—one considerably richer than the other.

Dodd would not only get the bounty for the loot and the bounty on Frank Beauregard, he'd also draw the admiration of his superiors and newspaper writers. Roy Dodd had always been an ambitious, attention-seeking cuss. It was well known that he rode both sides of the law. There would be little Prophet could do about the poaching of his bounty. It would be his word against Dodd's, Halcon's, and Gunderson's.

He rode for another hour and was just making his way around another switchback, when a rifle belched shrilly. Prophet jerked his head down with a start, and reached for his Winchester.

"Leave the long gun in its sheath, Prophet!" a man's voice bellowed.

Prophet released the Winchester's butt, and straightened, holding his reins taut in his left hand, looking around. He saw three horses standing on a bald, rocky rise upslope and on his right, mounding above the pines and aspens. He reached behind him and fished his spyglass out of his saddlebags, quickly unsheathing it. He raised the glass to his right eye, adjusted the focus, and brought the rise into focus.

Dodd sat his horse beneath a sprawling dead aspen that capped the knoll. Gunderson sat his horse to Dodd's right, near the stagecoach trail that skirted the knoll. Halcon sat his own mount a little down the knob and in front of Dodd. Halcon tipped his head slightly back, moving his mouth. The sound of the attacking bird and dying rabbit rose on the wind. As it faded, Halcon lowered his head to grin down the slope toward Prophet, whose heart thudded hotly.

He slid the glass toward Mathilda.

Again, his heart thudded.

The girl was riding double with Dodd, sitting behind the black marshal. She had a noose around her neck. The noose was attached to a rope snaking up over a thick branch of a lightning-topped aspen under which she and Dodd sat. Mathilda's arms were pulled back, her wrists likely tied or cuffed behind her. The rope was tied off low on the dead aspen's bole.

In the sphere of magnified vision, Prophet could see Dodd spreading his lips in a toothy grin of fiendish delight. Mathilda's shoulders jerked as she sobbed.

"You bastard," Prophet muttered through his own clenched teeth. "You fork-tailed, snake-eyed bastard!" He pointed and yelled: "You hurt her, I'll cut you up in little tiny pieces, Dodd!"

Dodd tipped his head back and opened his mouth wider, laughing.

"Leave the rifle in its scabbard, Proph!" he yelled. "Dismount and slap the horses on up the trail. When we've got what we want, I'll send yours and the girl's horses back down to you. I'll send the girl, too—her pretty li'l ownself!" He laughed again.

Prophet cupped his hands around his mouth. "You'd better!"

He wrapped his reins around his saddle, dismounted, and dropped his spyglass into his saddlebag pouch. He stared up the slope. He had to rise onto his tiptoes to see the men and young woman on the knob, as the trees obscured his view.

"No tricks, Dodd!" Prophet shouted. "Or I'll hunt you down and shoot you like a rabid dog!"

He slapped his hand sharply against Mean's butt. The horse gave an indignant whinny and galloped on up the trail, pulling the other two mounts along behind.

Chapter Sixteen

Mathilda sat so tensely on the back of Dodd's horse, behind Dodd, that she thought her spine would splinter. Tears of horror rolled down her cheeks. The noose knotted around her neck was coarse and scratchy.

She lifted her chin to look at the branch around which the rope hung. The view of the charred branch against the deep blue sky made her dizzy. The world turned around her. More tears rolled down her cheeks as she lowered her gaze to the horse she and Dodd straddled. The mount shifted its weight, drawing the rope tighter around Mathilda's neck, momentarily pinching off her wind. Her heart shuddered.

She gasped.

"P-please, Marshal Dodd," she begged the man before her. "You can't . . . you can't do this. Why, you're . . . you're a man of the *law*! You're *all* men of the *law*!"

She heard Dodd chuckle. He placed his black-gloved hand on her right thigh, squeezed, and glanced over his shoulder at her, narrowing one eye. "Honey, you're gonna see how much man I am around tonight's fire!"

Mathilda's eyes widened in shock. "You said . . . you said you'd release me . . . just as soon as you had Beauregard and the loot!"

Dodd gave his head a slow shake and smiled, narrowing his coal-black eyes to slits. "Darlin'-honey, I only said as much to Prophet. I told *you* I'd let you go when me an' the boys have done had our fun."

"What kind of a lawman are you, anyway?" Mathilda shrilled.

Dodd turned to brandish another evil leer. "A lonely one!"

He and Gunderson laughed. The short, stocky, Indian-featured man who'd stolen her out of camp last night, as silent as a ghost, stared to the right, where the trail curved toward the knoll from the west.

Prophet's horse was trotting out of the pines, the other two horses in tow. Frank Beauregard's blanket-wrapped body jostled across the roan's back, edges of the red-and-blue-striped blanket rippling in the wind.

"Here they come," said the Indian throatily.

Mathilda knew a half-second's relief when she saw the horses. She thought she knew Lou Prophet well enough by now to know that he would do everything he could to keep her alive, even if that meant turning over the Wells Fargo loot and Frank Beauregard's valuable body to the brigands masquerading as lawmen.

Still, she hadn't known him all *that* long. She'd been visited by an unwelcome lingering, agonizing thread of doubt.

What if she'd misjudged him? What if he had simply taken the loot and Beauregard's body and, steering wide of her and the so-called lawmen, continued up and over the pass to Denver, leaving her to the virtual wolves?

Now, seeing the horses, that doubt was gone. But the horror was not. The crooked lawman, Dodd, was not going to uphold his end of the deal . . .

Another sob raked her.

Gunderson had walked to the horses now lined up at the base of the knob, beneath Mattie and Dodd, and checked both bulging saddlebag pouches. He turned to Dodd, grinning. "We got it." He patted one of the pouches. "Looks like it's all here."

He turned to the Indian, Halcon, who'd dismounted and was

standing a ways away from him, holding his rifle in his thick arms. Halcon grinned, too.

Another sob bubbled up out of Mattie's chest. Hope had risen quickly, and just as quickly fallen.

"Not to cry, li'l honey." Dodd reached back to lift the noose up over Mattie's head. "Looks like you ain't gonna be the guest of honor at a necktie party, after all." He let the noose swing free, chuckling. "Nah—you're gonna be the guest of honor at another kind of party." He chuckled louder.

"What do you say we dump ole Beauregard?" Gunderson suggested, looking down at the slack, blanket-wrapped body hanging down over the side of the roan. "He's gonna be stinkin' to high heaven by the time we reach Denver."

With the saddlebags draped over his left shoulder, Gunderson leaned down and parted the folds in the blanket, until a tuft of light-brown hair shone in the sun's crisp shine. He grabbed a fistful of the hair and jerked up the head, until the slack face was tilted toward him. "Ain't ya, Frank?"

The eyes snapped open. The nostrils flared. "Ouch! That's no way to treat a dead man, you disrespectful bastard!"

Mattie gasped. In front of her, Dodd gave such a violent start that the horse beneath them started, too.

Gunderson leaped nearly a foot back away from the talking dead man, shouting, *"Ohhh!"*

The saddlebags tumbled off his shoulder as he reached for one of his holstered pistols. "It's Prophet!"

The blanket moved violently as Prophet threw it back off his right shoulder and raised his shotgun, gritting his teeth and twisting his body slightly as he hung down the side of the roan.

The shotgun roared, lapping gray smoke and red flames.

Gunderson was lifted three feet up and punched six feet back, triggering his revolver wildly. As he hit the ground and rolled, the roan jerked, lifting a shrill whinny.

Shouting something unintelligible, Halcon ran toward Prophet, who hurled himself, still half-wrapped in the saddle blanket, off the lunging roan's back. As the bounty hunter hit the ground, Halcon stopped and fired his rifle at him, missing Prophet by a hair's breadth. All three horses galloped off as Halcon shrieked crazily and fired again, his second bullet pluming gravel a foot to the left of the bounty hunter, who threw the blanket aside and rose to a knee.

Gritting his teeth, Prophet raised his shotgun again.

BOOM!

Halcon screamed as he was blown backward as though lassoed from behind. His head struck a boulder as he fell. He bounced off the rock, landed on his side, and lay shivering as though deeply chilled.

"Hy-ahhh!" Dodd shouted, grinding his spurs into his horse's flanks.

The horse bounded toward Prophet, who tossed his smoking shotgun behind him and turned, wide-eyed, toward the black lawman galloping toward him. Dodd was reaching for the gun holstered on his right hip.

Mathilda lunged forward and sunk her teeth into the lawman's right shoulder.

"Bitch!" Dodd shouted, leaning forward, then twisting around and ramming Mathilda with his left elbow.

Mathilda screamed as she went flying off Dodd's mount.

Prophet was reaching for his Peacemaker when the girl flew toward him, her mouth and eyes wide. She was screaming. Prophet raised his arms, and the girl flew into them, knocking the bounty hunter, unprepared for a hundred-and-ten-pound woman hurled at him like a human cannon ball, off his heels.

He stumbled backward, his face buried in her bosom, and fell, hitting the ground on his back, Mathilda groaning and squirming on top of him. He threw the girl to one side, flinging aside the folds of her gown as he'd tossed away Beauregard's saddle blanket seconds ago. Dodd, trying to control his skitter-hopping mount, drilled a round into the ground a foot to Prophet's right.

As Dodd's horse crow-hopped, spinning, Prophet bolted to his feet and shucked his Peacemaker. Dodd and the horse spun back toward Prophet, Dodd raising his own revolver, cursing.

Prophet narrowed one eye, aiming.

His Colt roared.

The bullet punched into Dodd's chest, knocking him back in his saddle. His right arm flew high, and his pistol careened out of it. Dodd began to slump forward. His horse pinwheeled once more, throwing the lawman out of his saddle. As the dappled bay galloped down the knob, trailing its bridle reins, whinnying shrilly, Dodd landed in a cloud of dust fifteen feet from Prophet and the girl.

As the dust cleared, Prophet saw that Dodd was unholstering a pearl-gripped Bisley. The lawman started to aim the gun toward Prophet. Prophet aimed and fired his own Peacemaker, and Dodd yelled shrilly as he triggered the Bisley straight up at the sky before flopping over backward where he lay writhing like a landed fish.

Prophet turned to Mathilda. She lay on her side, facing away from him. Her hands were handcuffed behind her back. He placed a hand on her arm and looked worriedly down at her. "You okay, Mattie?"

She nodded dully, staring in shock toward Dodd. "I . . . I think so, Lou."

He touched the cuffs. "I'll fetch the key."

Prophet walked over to where Dodd lay scowling up at the sky, the dust still falling softly around him. The black man was breathing hard, grunting, blood oozing out of his mouth to form two thick streams down his chin. More blood welled from the two ragged holes in his pinstriped shirt, just beneath his red bandanna.

His enraged, horrified eyes found Prophet. "Y-you just . . . killed two lawmen . . . and a federal tracker," he told the bounty hunter, sneering.

"Bullshit," Prophet said, dropping to a knee to rummage around in the man's pockets. "You're no more lawman than I am, Roy." He grinned as he pulled from the man's vest pocket a rabbit's foot with two small gold keys attached to it by a slender chain. He held up the rabbit's foot. "And your luck just ran out."

"You go to hell, you Rebel bastard!"

Prophet rose and stood glaring down at Dodd. "I'll see you there."

Dodd opened his mouth to speak but only a grunt issued. A terrified light filled his gaze. His bloody lips shaped a snarl, and he threw his head back, stiffening. A last breath sighed out of him.

He gave one last jerk and lay still, staring up past Prophet at the sky.

Prophet hurried back to where Mattie lay on her side, and removed the cuffs. "I'm sorry, Mattie," he said. "I shouldn't have—"

"Oh, Lou!" Her wrists free, she sat up and threw herself against Prophet's chest, wrapping her arms around him. "Oh, Lou, as big and uncouth as you are, I think I love you!"

Chapter Seventeen

Prophet built a small fire in the shade of a spruce tree.

The shade offered sanctuary from the blasting, high-altitude sun and the chill wind. The fire offered warmth. It also offered coffee, which Mattie boiled and sipped while Prophet dug a shallow communal grave for Dodd, Gunderson, and Halcon.

Finished digging, Prophet rolled the bodies into the three-foot-deep hole at the base of the knob from which Mattie's would-be hanging tree jutted. Three feet was all the deeper he cared to dig the grave in the hard, rocky soil for three men who'd been about to hang Mattie. He'd found himself feeling as protective of the queenly Miss Anderson as he often felt about another young woman she in some ways reminded him of.

The Vengeance Queen herself, Louisa Bonaventure, who Prophet often rode the long coulees with, hunting killers. Of course, Mattie didn't have the Queen's kill-savvy and rugged independence, nor Louisa's hunger to kill every bad man who crossed her trail—especially those who harmed women and children, like the gang who'd murdered her own midwestern farming family several years ago.

But there was a salt-of-the-earth innocence and proud dignity in Mattie that Prophet had once recognized in Louisa before Louisa had taken down so many deserving men . . . and even some women . . . and left them howling.

As in Louisa, there was strength in this girl, as well. Despite all the danger and harm that had come to her on her journey west to be married, she hadn't buckled. Oh, she'd sobbed plenty, but after the danger had passed, she'd always quickly recovered her composure and set about doing what needed to be done.

It was the same now. When Prophet finished covering the grave with the folding shovel he always carried on his saddle, and had started gathering rocks to keep predators from scavenging the bodies, Mattie came up from the spruce to hand him a steaming, overfilled cup of coffee.

She placed her hand on his shoulder and said, "You take a break and drink some coffee, Lou. I'll finish up here." She pressed her fingers into his shoulder with a warm, soothing intimacy, lightly kissed his cheek, and began gathering rocks that had tumbled down from the knob.

He liked the wet spot she'd left on his cheek. Her lips were warm and soft.

"All right, then," Prophet said, watching her admiringly. "Don't mind if I do."

When Mattie had finished mounding the grave with rocks, she dusted her hands on her skirt, swept her long, messy hair back from her cheeks, and turned to Prophet, who sat back against the spruce, boots crossed, empty cup resting on the ground beside him.

Mattie frowned, troubled.

"What is it?" Prophet asked her.

"They were lawmen," the girl said, glancing at the grave and then back to Prophet. "Bad lawmen, but lawmen just the same. Won't there be trouble for you, Lou?"

"There would be if anyone learns about all this." Prophet rose with a weary grunt, and shoved the cup back into his saddlebag pouch. "Even if you and me wrote a . . . a, uh, hickymadoo . . . an affidavit . . . the federals likely wouldn't believe either one of us. At least, I wouldn't trust 'em. Most are Yankees, and I don't trust a Yankee any farther than I can throw 'im uphill in a Texas twister. I've known too many just like Roy Dodd and that human hookworm, Gunderson."

He tossed his saddlebags over Mean's back. He'd retrieved Frank Beauregard's body from the clearing where he'd left him when he'd switched places with the dead outlaw to get the jump on Dodd, and now all three horses were gathered in the spruce's shade. He'd turned the lawmen's horses loose to forage on their own.

Prophet tightened Mean's saddle cinch. "Nah, we'd best keep it between ourselves. None of 'em had any family. At least, none that I ever heard of. If they did, said families are better off without those badge-totin' scalawags. They'd likely be glad they're gone."

Standing by the rock-mounded grave, Mattie nodded pensively. Wisps of her brown hair blew around her face in the breeze. She laughed and looked at Prophet, her eyes sparkling.

"What is it?" Prophet said, looking over his shoulder at her as he tied the reins of Beauregard's mount to Mean's tail. She was normally a tad plain, but, God, she was beautiful when she smiled!

"When you opened your eyes as Frank Beauregard, I almost had a heart stroke!" Mathilda laughed harder. "Gunderson nearly jumped out of his boots. I swear, Dodd leaped a whole foot out of his saddle!" She paused, bending forward, holding herself, shoulders quivering. She looked up at Prophet, lines of humor creasing her forehead. "The horses even jumped!"

Prophet threw his head back, bellowing, "I thought ole Gunderson's eyes were going to leap plum out of his head!" He leaned forward, slapping his knee.

When his laughter dwindled to head-waggling chuckles, he glanced at the grave behind Mathilda, who'd dropped to her knees and was sitting back against her heels, no longer laughing but smiling with amusement.

"That'll teach 'em," Prophet said.

"Teach 'em what?" Mattie said, chuckling.

"Well . . . yeah, I reckon you're right. There's not much more they can learn now except how to shovel coal. But if those fellas had kept a closer eye on me in the clearing, they would have seen me bolt after the horses. Once me and Mean and Ugly were in the trees, I exchanged places with ole Frank."

Prophet pulled his shirt out from his chest, and sniffed. "Phew! I'm glad he wasn't any riper than he was."

"We're gonna have to find you a bath," Mattie said.

"Yeah, I reckon this is a two-bath month," Prophet said. "Come on, girl. Let's get a move on. We'd best get over the pass before nightfall. Gets cold up here after sunset. Hell, this time of the year it could even snow."

Mattie began to rise, and winced.

"What's the matter?" Prophet walked over to her.

She pushed off her haunches again, giving a pained expression. "I reckon it takes a girl's backside, if you'll forgive my salty language, some time to conform to the western stock saddle."

Prophet took her hands, pulled her to her feet, then crouched, and threw her over his back.

"Oh, Lou!"

Prophet chuckled. "I got a feelin' by the time we reach Denver, you'll be an old hand at forkin' leather. You'll probably decide not to head back to Minnesota, after all. Hell, you'll probably decide instead to look for ranch work in eastern Colorady!"

Prophet set her on her saddle.

Mattie laughed. "I doubt that. I'll probably be so stiff and sore, I'll need a whole month's bed rest before I'll even be able to consider another long train ride."

"If that's so," Prophet said, resting a hand on her thigh and gazing up at her, "I'll tend your every need."

She held his gaze. Her cheeks colored slightly. "Will you?"

Prophet winked at her, then turned to his own saddle.

"Lou?"

Prophet stopped and looked back at her.

"I think I'd like to try steering my own horse. After watching you, I think I got the hang of it."

"By all means." Prophet untied the mare's reins from Mean's tail, and handed them to Mattie. "That's a well-trained horse," he told her. "The lightest touch across her neck will do. She's gotten used to followin' me and that ewe-necked cuss of mine. Think she's even taken a shine to Mean an' Ugly." He chuckled. "After we've ridden a ways, you'll see how she does."

Mattie nodded as she adjusted her grip on the ribbons.

After they'd ridden fifteen minutes, heading on up the pass, Mattie said behind Prophet, as she rode easily in the saddle, "Lou?"

"Yes, my dear?"

"Who is this Vengeance Queen Dodd was talking about the other day? He also called her . . . what was it—Louisa?"

"The Vengeance Queen, indeed," Prophet said. "Louisa Bonaventure. My sometime-partner, on the rare occasion I find myself bathing in the glow of her good graces, that is. That's gettin' rarer an' rarer as the years go on."

"You two aren't married, I take it."

Prophet chuckled. "Hell, no." Though they'd discussed it a time or two in the past.

"How did she come to be called the 'Vengeance Queen'?"

Prophet told her about Louisa's family being murdered by the savage gang led by Handsome Dave Duvall and how she and he had thrown in together to hunt the killers, eventually blowing the wicks of the entire depraved, grave-deserving bunch.

"You've been through a lot together, in other words," Mattie said.

"I reckon you could say that."

"Where is she now?"

"She's probably waiting in Denver for me and Beauregard and the loot. She went after another member of the gang. Knowing Louisa, she's probably got ole Norwood Cranston hog-tied by now. Or snugglin' with the diamondbacks. She might've even decided to follow my trail into the mountains. Louisa's the fidgety sort. Doesn't like sitting around over much."

"How old is Louisa?"

"Oh, a little older than you, I reckon. You remind me a little of her." Prophet smiled over his shoulder at her. "Only of her better traits, I hasten to add."

"Is she pretty?"

Prophet ears warmed a little. "Pretty? Oh, well . . . yeah, I guess you could say she's pretty. In fact, I reckon that's what made her such a successful man-hunter. Her china-doll looks rock men back on their heels. While they're oglin' her and tryin' to come up with ways to get her on her—well, you know—she turns 'em toe-down."

He chuckled dryly, shaking his head. "Louisa don't like takin' prisoners overmuch, unless they got a price on their heads that's just too good to pass up."

Mattie frowned at him curiously. "Do you love this girl—this Vengeance Queen—Lou?"

Prophet pondered the question for a few paces, chewing his lip. "I reckon I do."

"I see," Mattie said quietly behind him.

Prophet looked at her over his shoulder again. "No, you don't see. I love her, but not in the way you're talkin' about. I did at one time, but Louisa an' me—we're cut from the same cloth.

The cloth that chafes. We're both pig-headed and contrary and think we know everything there is to know about everything. We get along all right for a few hours. But after those few hours, we're each like coal oil on the other's fire."

Prophet paused. "Nah. I don't love her—not anymore. Not in the way you mean. We're like brother an' sis, Louisa an' me."

"I see," Mattie said again behind him, with a little more volume this time.

They rode up above the tree line, where the jade grass was short and pikas peeped amongst mossy rock nests. At the top of the pass, dirty snow still streaked the leeward sides of knobs and ridges. They paused to take in the awesome view of jutting mountains and rolling valleys layered like the pleats in an elaborately stitched dress. The earth vaulted away in a complete circle, the yawning distance enough to make even Prophet, accustomed to such views, dizzy.

Chilled by the cold wind despite the intensity of the sunshine, they rode on down the eastern side of the mountain.

Several times, Prophet glanced behind to see how the girl was handling the mare. She rode a little too stiffly, and she sometimes looked tentative, but mostly her eyes were confident and determined beneath the broad brim of her man's hat. She was getting the swing of it.

They left the sun on the west side of the pass. Dropping down the east side, they rode through the mountain's heavy shadow.

"We'll stop soon," Prophet said. "I know a good place along a stream."

"I'm hungry," Mattie said.

"I'll see about supper, too." Prophet had seen no one climbing the pass behind them, so he thought he could safely bring down a deer. Both he and Mattie could do with a rich, plentiful meal.

"You're pretty much the perfect man—aren't you, Lou?" Mattie said.

Prophet glanced over his shoulder at her. She smiled shyly, chin down, a corner of her bottom lip sucked in. "Now, those are words I can't say as I ever heard before!" Prophet said with a chuckle.

Mattie laughed.

A few minutes later they arrived at the spot, well off the trail, that Prophet remembered from previous trips as a good one for a night's camp. He untied Beauregard's horse from Mean's tail, then, leaving Mattie to gather wood and start a fire, rode Mean upstream in search of game.

He came upon a small, young buck half an hour later, brought it down with one shot, field-dressed it, and dragged it back downstream. Mattie had a big fire going. Prophet dressed out the deer, quartering it, and fried up the tenderloin with wild onions. He wrapped the rest, including the liver, which he'd save for breakfast, in burlap.

He shoveled two big, smoking portions of chopped tenderloin onto tin plates, and he and Mattie ate with the zeal of overworked gandy dancers, sitting Indian style on the same side of the fire. They washed down the succulent meal with frequent sips of coffee. Prophet had spiked his own mud with Beauregard's whiskey.

"I was right," Mattie said, dropping her fork onto her cleaned plate and leaning back against her saddle. "You are the perfect man, Lou Prophet."

"You're just sayin' that 'cause your belly's full."

"I'm going to be lost without you—back in Minnesota."

Prophet looked at her. She sat back against her saddle, regarding him sadly.

"Now, that there is another thing I never heard before," Prophet said, trying to keep the mood light, though he himself was no longer in a hurry to get shed of Miss Mathilda Anderson, either. She'd grown on him.

He knew a moment's pang of guilt. *Louisa.*

Remembering how testy their partnership had grown despite the enjoyment they still occasionally took in each other's bodies, the guilt quickly fled. It had become clear that Prophet and the Vengeance Queen were no longer anything but occasional bounty hunting partners, occasional casual lovers . . .

Prophet rose and rummaged around in his saddlebags. When he found his sliver of lye soap wrapped in waxed paper, and a sorry-looking towel scrap, he turned to Mattie.

"Follow me."

She frowned in the firelight, knees drawn up to her chest, arms and gloved hands wrapped around them. "What are you talking about?" She glanced at the night pressing close about the fire's pulsating glow.

"It's this ole Rebel's time for a bath. I'm tired of smelling ole Beauregard's death stench on myself." Prophet grinned. "I need you to wash my back."

"A *bath*?" Mattie was incredulous. She gave a shiver, and chuckled. "It's cold. Why . . . there'll soon be frost on the pumpkins, my dear crazy man!"

"Maybe so." Prophet pulled her to her feet. "But we'll be as warm as two toads in a Georgia bog . . . under a log!"

"Oh, my goodness . . . you are crazy," Mattie said, breathless, chuckling nervously as he pulled her along by her hand, tramping out away from the fire. Prophet glanced at Mean, eyeing him skeptically from where the beast stood hobbled with the other two mounts. "Keep an eye on things, old son. If you see any skulkers, give a whicker!"

Mean snorted, rippled his withers, and shook his head, breath frosting gray in the dark air around his head.

Chapter Eighteen

"Lou, we shouldn't be out here," Mattie complained as she followed him, occasionally tripping over fallen trees and branches, dead leaves and pine needles crunching beneath their feet. "It's dark . . . and cold . . . !"

"Just about there."

"Just about *where*?" Mattie sniffed. "What's that smell? Smells . . . salty . . . or rotten. Like a ripe pond."

"Sulfur."

"Sulfur? The smell's getting heavier. What's that sound?"

"Running water."

"Oh, your creek. You're crazy, Lou, if you think you're going to . . ."

Mattie let her voice trail off as Prophet stopped at the edge of the water, along the surface of which steam writhed like torn scraps of an old wedding dress billowing in a silent breeze. Starlight glistened on the steam and rippled on the pond's nearly smooth surface. The water made soft sucking sounds against the shoreline.

"Why . . . it's warm," the girl said when she'd dropped to her knees and slid her hand into the water. She looked up at Prophet, curious. "How can that be?"

Prophet kicked out of his boots. "A hot springs. An old Injun introduced me to it not long after I came west, after the war. Him and me worked on the railroad for a time, before we headed this way to hunt the bounty of a man who killed several workers in an end-of-track saloon. The Injun was a Ute—Three White Bones, was his name. This is Ute country."

Prophet had removed his shirt and cartridge belt, and was hanging the coiled belt from a knobby branch. As he began to shuck out of his denims, grunting with the effort, he said, "The springs is good medicine, according to ole Bones. Come on—skin out of them duds, darlin'. You're gonna wash my back!"

"Oh, gosh—I don't know," Mattie said, taking a step back and lifting her hands to her neck, regarding the water apprehensively.

"No one but us out here." Prophet unbuttoned his wash-worn balbriggans, sliding them down his chest and arms and then on down his legs.

He tossed them away.

Naked, he walked over to Mattie, who looked up into his eyes, color rising in her cheeks. Prophet pressed his lips to her forehead, winked at her, and then swung away and stepped off the shore and into the warm, steaming pool.

The salty liquid pressed against him, warm as a womb. It rose to his chest. The bottom was sandy, lightly pebbled. He bent his knees, pulling his head under, and came up blowing and wiping water from his eyes.

He lay back, gave a kick, and gently backstroked to the pool's opposite side, about twenty feet from Mattie, who remained standing tentatively at the edge of the pool, near Prophet's discarded clothes.

"If you ain't gonna come in," Prophet called, "throw me that soap, will you? I set it on my shirt, on the log to your left."

"No," Mattie said, gazing at the water. "No . . ." She looked at Prophet, and smiled. "I'll bring it to you."

Prophet lolled against the opposite bank, arms stretched across the mantle-like shelf of stone behind him, and smiled. He watched her undress. She kept her back to him until her clothes were piled around his, and then she tied her hair up on top of her head and turned to the pool. Her full breasts jostled in the starlight as she walked up to the edge of the water.

"I'm terrified to contemplate what my aunt and uncle would think if they saw me now . . ." she said, and stepped off the bank.

She plunged into the pool, the fog dancing around her. She swam over to Prophet and he put his arms around her, groaning inwardly when he felt the soft pressure of her breasts against his chest.

He kissed her. She returned the kiss, her lips pliant.

"Bones told me that this pool was where the young Indian maidens used to come to swim and frolic with their beaus."

Mattie's eyes widened, her lips spread. "Oh . . . I see. I guess I should have asked more questions before I allowed myself to be led off into the forest . . ."

"Hey," Prophet said, frowning at her, "you forgot my soap."

Mattie smiled and opened her hand, showing him the soap. "Later."

Prophet ran the tips of his fingers down her slender back, which tapered beautifully to her rounded hips. "The Utes say that the spirits of those maidens return here from time to time . . . to the spot of their bliss . . . to frolic with the spirits of the braves they once cavorted with."

"Oh . . ."

"They say the sounds you hear, when you're here at the pool, are actually the calls of the spirits who once frolicked here. They're calling because they want to come back here and relive the joy . . . so quickly gone."

Just then a bird's screech ripped across the night.

Wings made a sinewy sound as the bird flew out of a near tree.

"Oh!" Mattie cried with a start, and threw herself against

Prophet's chest. She looked up at him. "Do you think . . . that was . . . ?"

"Most like." Prophet wrapped his arms around her shoulders and kissed her. She tipped her head back, accepting the kiss and returning it, letting his tongue caress her own. Her breasts swelled against him. Her nipples pebbled.

Mattie pulled her head back from his. "Do you think that our spirits will return here, Lou?" She glanced around. "To this place of our . . ." She turned to regard him, narrow eyes dancing serenely, glinting in the starlight. ". . . first frolic?"

"I reckon we'll just have to see," he said, and groaned as she reached down between them to wrap her warm, soft hand around him and slide him inside her.

Prophet lifted his head from his saddle, heart pounding.

He hadn't heard anything but the clanging in his own head. The din had kept him from sleeping a wink in the hour since he and Mattie had returned to the camp and built up the fire to dry out in the flames' warm caress.

They'd made love again by the fire and then Mattie had curled up and gone to sleep. She slept now, breathing softly, deeply to Prophet's right, her forehead pressed against his shoulder. Prophet looked around. All—except the buzzing whine inside his own head—was still and quiet.

He cursed.

He wanted to sleep for at least a couple of hours, but it wasn't looking good.

He rose quietly, pulled his clothes on, and stepped into his boots. Mathilda groaned and rolled onto her other side. She gave a sigh, smacked her lips, and was soon breathing deeply again, sound asleep.

Prophet shrugged into his coat and gloves. It was damned cold. His breath was a heavy cloud billowing around him. He laid a single branch on the fire that had burned down to glowing umber coals, and set the half-full coffee pot on a rock near the fire's base to rewarm it. When the coffee had chugged and gurgled for a minute, steam issuing from its spout, he poured himself a cup of the hot brew and sat on a log on the opposite side of the fire from Mathilda.

He removed his gloves to roll a quirley from his makings sack. When he had the cigarette sealed, he scratched a match to life on a rock forming the fire ring, and lit the quirley, blowing smoke out into the night. He picked up his coffee cup, leaned forward, sipped the coffee, and smoked the quirley, gazing across the low, softly snapping fire at the girl who was a crooked shadow against the ground on the other side of the orange flames.

Her hair glistened like burnt copper in the firelight.

She was the reason he couldn't sleep.

He couldn't get her out of his head.

Why?

She'd be gone soon, on her way back to Minnesota by rail, and he'd go about his business of hunting bounties for a living. Why did the thought of her leaving fill him with such dread?

He smoked the cigarette and sipped the coffee and stared at her lying on the other side of the fire, thinking it through.

He was at war with himself, he realized. Mathilda was tugging at him hard, and he was resisting her pull. She was tugging without even realizing she was tugging, but he'd be damned if he hadn't fallen for her. Fallen for her like he'd never fallen for another woman except for maybe the Vengeance Queen herself.

Maybe he'd fallen for Mathilda even harder than he'd fallen for Louisa. It felt like a primal pull. As intoxicating as it was undeniable.

They'd made love as though it hadn't been their first time together. They'd frolicked in the water and then on the shore, bathed by the pool's warm steam, and then here again by the fire . . . as though they'd been enjoying each other's bodies for years. As though they were more than the relative strangers they really were.

Odd.

Damned odd. It was time to quit thinking about it. He had to let her go. He'd had to let Louisa go, because his settling down just hadn't been in the cards.

Or . . . maybe it just hadn't been in the cards for him and Louisa.

Maybe, having had his fill of man-hunting, he'd been waiting for the right opportunity—the *right woman*—to come along. To give him a reason to hang up his shooting irons and sink a taproot.

Well, maybe she had come along.

Maybe the real reason he'd sold his soul to ole Scratch was because he wanted to live long enough to fall in love and marry and spend a few good years under the same roof with a woman like Mattie Anderson.

Prophet sighed and shook his head as he blew another lungful of smoke into the darkness.

Maybe she had come along, indeed . . .

On the other hand, what if he was wrong? What if he liked Mattie more than he loved her? What if he'd just found her body uncommonly pleasing, and it was their unrestrained frolic that had clouded his brain? What if, after he'd settled down with her, he realized it was all a mistake?

Then where would he be?

He shook his head again, cursed.

But where was he now? He couldn't imagine being without her. When he thought of them separating, his heart felt as though an angry fist was ripping it from its moorings.

He stared at her lying curled in sleep, his pulse throbbing.

Was she the one?

If not her, who? If not her, was he destined to live the balance of his life alone, riding the long coulees for men with bounties on their heads? He had only so many years left. It wasn't a profession you could practice forever. Eventually, with age, your skills wavered, and you died bloody.

And alone.

But maybe that's what he'd resigned himself to.

Now, however, remembering the warm intoxication of making love to the girl slumbering on the other side of the fire from him, he didn't feel all that resigned . . .

He felt heady and charged with life and the urge to live and love and grow old with someone who loved him as he knew Mattie did. He could feel that love in his very fiber.

Would he be able to turn his back on it?

On her?

After another cigarette and another half a cup of coffee, the decision:

He just didn't know.

Despite the coffee and cigarettes, his eyelids grew heavy. He took a short walk around the camp; then, letting the fire burn down to two small, orange flames dancing along the edge of charred stick, he returned to his blankets. Mattie groaned and turned to him. She snuggled against him, resting her head on his shoulder.

She lifted her head, and opened her eyes, frowning at him.

"Are you all right, Lou?"

Prophet pondered. He felt his mouth curve in a smile. He also felt his brows beetle with a vague befuddlement. He stared at the stars. "Yeah. I don't think I've ever been finer, Miss Mattie." He kissed her temple.

She smiled, lowered her head to his shoulder, and curled one leg over one of his. "Yeah," she said, wistfully, dreamily, with vague befuddlement. "Me, too."

They slept.

Chapter Nineteen

Two days later, Prophet, Mathilda, and Frank Beauregard, who had been growing increasingly smelly since they'd dropped down out of the high, cool country, trotted into the yard of a saloon and whorehouse just south of Denver.

The low-slung cabin, barn, and several log and adobe outbuildings had once been a stage relay station for Wells Fargo out of Denver, but since the First Transcontinental Railroad had spread its tentacles from Cheyenne clear into New Mexico, this leg of the stage line had been rendered defunct.

The place looked abandoned. Weeds had grown up around the bases of all the dilapidated buildings. The cabin was sun-blistered to the dull gray of a cloudy sky and was missing half its shake shingles. The porch sat askew on crumbling stone pylons, and the steps were rotting. But someone still lived and even worked here.

The former Wells Fargo stage relay station was owned by the man who'd been the agent here for Wells Fargo. Grover Billings was an ex-buffalo hunter whose face had been badly scarred when another hunter, jealous of Billings's dalliances with the other hunter's buxom daughter, resulting in the proverbial bun in the girl's oven, threw molten shot in Billings's face when they'd both been swilling potent sour mash one late winter's night on the Texas Panhandle.

Always cautious, one hand on his holstered revolver, Prophet surveyed the yard.

A few horses stomped around the hitch-and-rail corral. One was down and rolling on its back, probably scratching where a saddle had recently been strapped. Two more switched their tails at the hitchrack fronting the cabin. Those were the only movements around the place now at ten thirty in the morning, only a few puffy clouds sliding slowly across the otherwise faultless blue sky.

"Miss Mattie, darlin', I know the place don't look much better than a wart on a crone's neck, but you're about to be treated to the best antelope stew this side of the Mississippi River and north of the Brazos. Only one man ever made stew better than Grover Billings, and that was a Mex down in San Marcos, Texas. But after the mouse population grew to ghastly proportions in and around the town due to a noticeable lack of kitty-cats, Rawhide Sanchez's prizeworthy stew fell out of favor. In fact, a passel of chafed citizens from the Coalition of Civic Pride and Enhancement, intent on putting San Marcos on the map, saw that ole Rawhide was tarred, feathered, and run out of town on a greased rail!"

"Oh!" Mattie exclaimed, looking as though she'd swallowed something rotten.

Prophet chuckled, removed his hat, and sleeved sweat from his brow. "Ole Rawhide took his wife and six kids to Dallas where, I'm told, the feline population has dwindled and the mice are as thick as ants on honey bread!"

Prophet set his hat on his head, and howled.

"That is not a true story, Lou Prophet!" Mattie insisted, glowering at him. "Why, it's no truer than that one you told the other night about the bear you supposedly wrestled in such an improbable place as—what did you say it was called? The Slap 'N' Tickle Saloon?"

"Oh, that one's as true as me sittin' here now!"

Mattie arched a schoolmarm's brow. "And the one about

Rawhide Sanchez's stew?"

Prophet flushed, sheepish, but before he could speak he looked away, frowning. "What was that?"

"What was what?"

The sound grew louder—a muffled chugging. A train whistle blew—a long wail followed a short one.

"Ah, the Santa Fe flier out of Denver. Here she comes."

The train swung into sight from behind the barn and corral, tracing a broad curve out away from the old stage relay station, swinging west and south. Black smoke gushed from the locomotive's diamond-shaped stack to form a long, sooty, buffeting flag over the tender car behind the engine. Again, the engineer blared the horn, setting one of the corralled horses to buck-kicking angrily, flinging its rear hooves in the train's direction.

"Goddamnit to hell!" came a man's bellicose shout from the direction of the cabin to Prophet's and Mathilda's right.

"Oh, boy—hold onto your hat," Prophet said.

"What . . . ?"

The cabin door slammed, and a beefy gent in a soiled apron ran down the porch steps, Billings's face appearing as though it were covered with one half of a Halloween mask. The man was bald on top, with curly gray hair covering his ears and trailing out behind him as he dashed off the steps. The two horses tied to the hitchrack reared and whinnied at the man's bluster.

He ran awkwardly into the yard, pausing once to pick up a fist-sized stone.

"Bloody fuckin' iron hoss!" The saloon owner ran past Prophet and Mathilda and into the brush at the yard's western perimeter. The man stopped and cocked his arm back and hurled the stone toward the train curving away from him. The stone landed only a good quarter mile short of its mark, invoking only the indignant chittering of a prairie dog. *"Bloody fuckin' piece of useless scrap-iron son of a bitch!"*

The horn blasted again—two quick shorts and one long. The engineer was jeering. From this distance, Prophet couldn't tell for sure, but he thought he saw the blue-clad engineer poke his head out of the engine's side window and raise his forearm and middle finger.

There was one more rollicking toot, and then the locomotive pulled its eight-car combination around a bluff studded with cedars, and was gone.

Red-faced, Billings swung around and kicked a cedar root twisting up out of the edge of the yard. He started back toward the cabin, scowling, muttering angrily. Apparently, he hadn't noticed Prophet and his comely trail partner sitting only thirty feet behind him, the girl stitching her brows.

Mathilda turned to Prophet, parting her lips to speak, but the bounty hunter held up one hand and gave her an easy smile. When Billings had stomped back into the cabin, Prophet said, "It's best to let ole Grover blow off steam in private . . . no pun intended."

"I don't get it," Mattie said as they rode their horses toward the hitchrack. "Why did that man throw that rock at that train?"

"Grover had him a nice business here before the iron horse came through. A stagecoach rolled through here three, sometimes four times a week. Grover fed the passengers and put 'em up overnight. A good business for an ex-hide hunter with only half a face worth lookin' at. Then the stage company pulled out and ripped up his contract. Now he's just got a backcountry saloon with a leaky roof. Serves stew and cheap whiskey to the occasional passin' horse-backer, and sells pokes off three fat whores sportin' fewer teeth than your average toddler."

Prophet swung down from his saddle, shaking his head.

He tossed his reins over the hitchrack and then helped Mattie off the back of her mare. Mattie turned toward where the train had disappeared, tucking strands of her long hair behind her ears.

Her features had acquired an expression of grave consternation. Prophet tied her horse and loosened its saddle cinch.

He saw that Mattie was still staring toward the train.

He placed his hand on her arm. "You all right, girl?"

She turned her despondent gaze to him. "The train just reminded me we'll be parting soon."

"Yeah," Prophet said. "It did me, too." He slung the saddlebags containing the Wells Fargo loot over his left shoulder. "Come on inside. Let's get some stew in our bellies. We'll feel better."

Mattie nodded.

As Prophet started up the splintering porch steps, he glanced over his shoulder at the girl and slid his shotgun around in front of him. "Stay behind me till I know it's all clear."

"You think . . . ?" Mattie said, tentatively, not completing the question.

"I think I got history," Prophet said. "Meaning that no bounty hunter hunts bounties long without making an enemy here and there. Never mind I got a sizable cache of loot on my shoulder"—he cast a smile at Mattie—"and a pretty girl on my arm."

He winked.

Mattie flushed and snorted.

Prophet stepped inside and looked around. There were only three customers in the shabby, shadowy place. One sat in a back corner, half-concealed by an arrow-shaped, deep-purple shadow and golden streams of glaring sunlight angling through a sashed window.

From what the bounty hunter could see of the gent, he was a smallish *hombre* attired in the range gear of a cow waddie. He was busy petting a gray cat in his lap, both boots crossed on the chair across from him. His head was dipped down toward the cat, the wide brim of his hat concealing his face. A wooden bowl and coffee cup sat on the table before him.

The two other customers were older men in shabby suits and Stetson hats. They sat to Prophet's left, near the front of the shack, leaning forward, holding each other's counsel. They both looked at Prophet, turned their mouth corners down as though with disdain, then resumed their low-toned, businesslike conversation.

To the right was the long plank bar, behind which Billings stood, his back to the door. He was shoving wood into the range's firebox. A large iron kettle bubbled away on one of the range's lids while a large coffee pot sat on a warming rack, pushing steam from its spout.

Prophet gave Mattie the all clear with his eyes, then walked over to the bar.

"Mornin', Grover."

Crouched before the range, Billings glanced at Prophet, his blind eye rolling whitely in its wrinkled socket. He winced as though he'd just spied a sand rattler slithering through his door. "Ah shit—it's you. Wasn't you just through here, Lou?"

"No, I wasn't just through here, Grover," Prophet said, indignant. "I haven't been *through here* in months."

"Oh . . . uh . . . well, sorry, Proph." Billings closed and latched the firebox door, straightening. "It's just that whenever I see you, it seems like you're courtin' trouble." The man's lone good eye landed on Mattie. It widened as well as brightened. "Well, well . . . if this is trouble you're courtin' today, Lou, I'd say trouble got a whole lot better lookin'!" He laughed. "Is this here the infamous Vengeance Queen, Lou? I heard a lot about her but never had the pleasure."

"No, this ain't Louisa," Prophet said. "I don't know where the sassy Vengeance Queen is keepin' herself these days. I half-expected to run into her by now. She's probably out wrasslin' porcupines or some such, just to keep her dander up. I reckon our trails will cross again soon, though."

Prophet wrapped an arm around Mattie's shoulders. "Grover Billings, I offer you the pleasure of meeting Miss Mathilda Anderson of St. Paul, Minnesota. Mattie, meet Grover Billings of . . . of . . . well, of this place here." Prophet glanced around, brows arched wryly. "Grover's been tryin' to wipe the Atchison, Topeka and Santa Fe Railroad off the map one stone at a time!"

Billings grumbled and snarled as he shook Mattie's hand, then grinned as he sized the girl up brashly. "Nice to make your acquaintance, Miss Mattie. How is it that you found yourself in the unfortunate position of ridin' alongside this big ugly Georgia catamount? You ain't wanted by the law, are ya?" He chuckled.

"Long story," Prophet told the man. "Suffice it to say, we're both emptier'n a dead man's boot. Hope that's your famous stew on the stove there, Grover. I been braggin' it up to Mattie."

"That it is."

"We'll each have a bowl and a cup of your equally infamous mud."

"Comin' right up, Lou."

Prophet led Mattie to a table near the bar, and pulled a chair out for her. When she'd taken the seat, Prophet sat with his back to the bar, so he could keep an eye on the other customers as well as on the front door and windows. He wasn't expecting trouble this close to Denver, but he knew from experience that not expecting trouble often hailed it.

He draped the saddlebags over the back of the chair to his left. He laid his Richards on the table to his right, within a quick reach if he should need it.

Billings brought the stew along with a quarter loaf of crusty brown bread that Prophet was surprised to find not moldy or speckled with dead boll weevils. The stew was the only thing that Billings made that was worth eating. Prophet and Mattie ate hungrily. When the famished duo finished their meals, Billings brought the pot over to freshen their cups, then took away their dishes.

When he'd retreated into his back room, Prophet glanced around the cabin. The three customers who'd been here when he and Mattie had first arrived were still here, the businessmen conversing seriously, the lone cowpuncher still sitting at the back of the room.

The cat was no longer in the lone rider's lap. He was slumped low in his chair, head back, hat pulled down low over his eyes, arms crossed on his chest. His boots were crossed on the chair across the table from him.

A snooze.

Prophet turned to Mattie, who was staring into her cup as though deep in thought. Prophet leaned forward. He reached across the table and took her right hand in his. He was about to speak when he thought he saw the lone rider at the back of the room shift in his chair and turn his head toward Prophet and Mattie.

Eavesdropping?

When Prophet looked directly at the gent, however, the puncher was as still as he'd been a moment before—appearing sound asleep behind his hat.

Prophet looked at Mattie again.

He was having trouble finding the words he wanted to say. Suddenly, his ears were hot and his heart was racing. His palms were sweaty.

"Lou?" Mattie said, regarding him dubiously from under her brows. "What's wrong?"

"Mattie?"

She dipped her chin and turned her head slightly to one side, her eyes locked on his. "Yes, Lou? Is there something you wanted to say?"

Prophet cleared his throat. He was holding her hand in both of his now, brushing his thumbs across her knuckles. "Yeah . . . there is."

Why was his heart racing? It felt like an over-stoked locomotive about to blast its way out of his chest.

"All right, then. Spit it out. I don't recollect seeing you this tongue-tied . . ."

"Mattie Anderson, I . . . I would like very much if you. . . ."

A man's shout from the front yard cut him off. *"Prophet?"*

The bounty hunter jerked his startled gaze to a near window. A cold fist tightened around his gut.

He'd been so busy trying to find the words to ask Mattie to marry him that he'd neither heard nor seen the seven horseback riders ride into the yard and spread out in a line about thirty yards before the saloon.

To a man, they wore Pinkerton's shields on their chests.

The lead rider, who Prophet recognized as the hired gun Leonard Kilroy, cocked his bearded head angrily and yelled, "Get your ass out here, Prophet. And bring the loot!"

CHAPTER TWENTY

Grover Billings bulled out of the curtained doorway behind the bar and strode along the counter to the front window, staring anxiously out. "Ah, shit—*now* what kind of trouble have you brought, Lou?"

Prophet released Mattie's hand and sat back in his chair, staring out the dirty window at the seven men lined up in front of Billings's saloon. "Ah, hell," he said, chuckling despite not finding any humor in the situation, "that ain't trouble. That's just Leonard Kilroy and his pards wantin' to talk about old times." He smiled reassuringly at Mattie. "That's all it is."

Mattie didn't look reassured. She was staring out the window, eyes bright with anxiety.

"Goddamnit, we're tryin' to have a business conversation over here, bounty hunter!" This from one of the two men who'd been having a serious discussion. He was pushing sixty—gray-headed and gray-bearded, his blue eyes bright with anger. "We didn't come here to discuss army remounts just to get in the middle of some gall-blasted gunfight between Pinkertons and a lowly *bounty hunter*!"

Obviously, Prophet's reputation had preceded him, as it often did.

"Ah, hell, I ain't as lowly as some say, you old horse trader," Prophet growled, glancing sheepishly at Mattie. She was still staring anxiously out the window.

"Prophet!" shouted Leonard Kilroy. "You hear me in there?"

"I'm comin', I'm comin'," Prophet said with a sigh, rising and grabbing his shotgun.

He looped the Richards over his right shoulder and slung the saddlebags containing the loot over his left shoulder.

"You stay here, girl," Prophet said. "If there's any shootin', crawl under a table and stay there—all right?"

Mattie looked at him, swallowed, and nodded. "Be careful, Lou."

Prophet strode to the front of the cabin. Billings was staring out the window to his left, cursing under his breath. "By god, Lou," he urged, "don't you shoot up my place!"

"Don't tell me," the bounty hunter said. "Tell it to them boys out there."

He opened the door and stepped out onto the porch. That fist tightened around his gut when he saw all seven men—Pinkerton hired guns—sitting their horses facing him, all holding rifles across the pommels of their saddles. They were spaced about seven feet apart. He could tell from their expressions that if he didn't hand over the money and likely Beauregard himself, this was going to get nasty.

He wanted to do everything he could to keep Mattie from getting hurt, but he just didn't know if he could bring himself to turn the loot over to bounty-poaching thieves. Thieves were what these men were, despite the badges on their shirts. Hired guns. Shootists. No better than Dodd. Prophet recognized several others besides Kilroy, who sat at the center of the pack on a fine black stallion.

Kilroy was long-haired and mustached, and he wore a long cream duster over a three-piece suit and string tie. His wool trouser legs were stuffed down into high-topped black boots. Maybe in his middle thirties, Kilroy had once been a deputy under Pat Garrett down in New Mexico. He and Garrett had had a falling out, though the circumstances of their disagreement were murky. Some said Kilroy had been straddling both sides of the law in Lincoln County, leaping back and forth to the one most lucrative.

Now he was a Pinkerton . . .

"Hi, Leonard," Prophet said, grinning and waving. "How you doin'? It's been a while."

"Shut up and turn over the loot. We'll be takin' Frank, too."

"Now, that's not fair, Leonard," Prophet objected. "I took ole Frank down fair and square. And I've confiscated the loot to turn over to Wells Fargo my ownself." He patted the bulging pouch hanging from his right shoulder. "First come, first served. I don't think Mister Pinkerton would approve of his men poaching bounties. Might get around. Make his esteemed company look not quite so esteemed, after all."

"Prophet," Kilroy snarled, "you're so full of Rebel bullshit, you're gonna float into the nearest privy pit. Pinkerton don't care how we get the job done just as long as it gets done. Now, Wells Fargo hired him to retrieve the loot. Paid a hcfty price up front. And that's what we been ordered to do. If the trail took us all the way down to Old Mexico, well, then, we was supposed to go down and chomp chili peppers and brush up on our Mexicano, sure enough."

The man to Kilroy's left—Cliff Bohanon out of Arizona—leaned forward against his saddle horn and added, "And if it means kickin' the shit out of both ends of a big, stupid, plug-ugly, ex-Rebel bounty hunter, then we're supposed to go ahead and soil our boots."

Bohanon spat a stream of chaw to one side and ran his fist across his narrow mouth.

A couple of the others chuckled at that.

"Now, that ain't fair," Prophet objected again. "Shit, it's seven against one!"

"So what if it is?" Kilroy said.

"So, it just ain't fair," Prophet insisted. "How 'bout if we do it this way—if you're man enough, Leonard . . ."

"Do it what way?" Kilroy asked, curling his upper lip.

"You and me will go at it right here in the yard. No shootin'. Just fisticuffs. The winner gets to keep . . . or take, as the case may be . . . the loot and the whiffy Frank Beauregard hangin' across his saddle there."

"How 'bout if we just shoot you down like the dirty Rebel cur you are," Kilroy said, jutting his dimpled chin angrily, "and *take* the loot *and* ole Frank hangin' across his saddle there? Don't *tell* me it wouldn't be fair, because I'm tired of *hearin'* that, you fuckin' moron!"

"Well, damnit," Prophet said, indignant, "it just wouldn't, Leonard, and you know it!" He shrugged and cut a challenging grin. "But if you're scared and a little short on honor, then, hell, go ahead. I mean, you are a Yankee, after all." Prophet spread his arms. "Go ahead and shoot a man in cold blood, you chicken-livered son of a bitch!"

Kilroy's cheeks colored above his beard. He looked around. The other six men were looking at him, brows arched. The grinning man next to him, Bohanon, leaned out to one side to spit another stream of chaw in the dirt.

"Godamnit!" Kilroy said, furious. He swung down from his saddle, red-faced, three veins forking in his left temple. He tossed his reins up to Bohanon, who caught them against his chest, grinning.

Kilroy stomped toward Prophet and stopped about halfway between his black stallion and the cabin's rickety porch. "Well, don't just stand there and piss down your leg. Get down here, you big, stupid, Rebel son of a bitch!"

Prophet grinned. He slung his shotgun behind his back and walked down the porch steps. He strode out to where Kilroy was crouching and raising his fists, moving his head and his feet as though dodging phantom blows.

He stepped toward Prophet, cocking one arm and bunching his lips.

"Hold on, hold on," Prophet said, stepping back.

"What is it?" Kilroy snapped, lowering the arm he'd cocked.

"My hat." Prophet removed his hat. He went back and set it on one of the porch steps, then started toward Kilroy again. "I don't want to get blood on it."

"Good thinkin'!" Kilroy glanced at the others and laughed. He lurched toward Prophet, bringing a haymaker up from his heels.

Prophet easily ducked the blow, saying, "I meant your blood."

Kilroy's arm made a *whoofing* sound as it connected with only air where Prophet's head had been. Prophet raised his head and his fist and landed a crunching blow against the side of Kilroy's mouth.

Both lips burst, blood washing across the lower half of the Pinkerton's face. A broken tooth oozed out with the blood and stuck against the bloody corner of the man's mouth.

Kilroy grunted and stepped back, eyes snapping wide.

Prophet stayed with him, smashing his face with his left and then his right and then his left again, keeping his own boots with Kilroy's, so that if you were watching only the two fighters' feet, you'd have thought they were dancing.

Kilroy screamed, backstepping, stumbling, arms pinwheeling, eyes wide in horror.

Smack. Smack. Smack. Smack-smack-smack!

SMACK!

Kilroy screamed and dropped to his butt.

His face looked more red than brown. Both eyes were quickly turning to pink, egg-shaped lumps.

Prophet towered over the sitting man, boots spread wide. As he cocked his right arm for another crushing blow, Kilroy threw his arms up and said, spitting blood down his chin and chest, "Enough!" He threw his arms up in surrender. "Stop!" he wailed.

There was the metallic rake of a rifle being cocked.

Prophet swung his head to his right to see Cliff Bohanon aiming a Henry rifle at him, cheek snugged up against the rear stock, one eye narrowed over the cocked hammer as he stared down the long, octagonal barrel at Prophet's face.

A rifle barked.

Prophet flinched but kept his gaze on Bohanon.

Bohanon's head jerked violently sideways, blood and brains lapping from his head's right side, from a hole above that ear. The blood and brains splashed onto the shoulder of a rider sitting six feet off Bohanon's right stirrup. That rider looked from Bohanon to his blood- and brain-splattered shoulder, and yelled, *"Jesus Christ!"*

Bohanon triggered the Henry sagging in his arms. Behind Prophet there was the dull clink of breaking glass. From inside the cabin issued a girl's scream. That scream was like a cold steel rod shoved up Prophet's backside.

Before him, the six mounted Pinkertons were trying to keep their jittery horses under control. Bohanon sagged down the right side of his horse and landed in the dirt with a dull thud, eyes rolling back in his head. At the same time, another rider cursed and, holding his reins taut in one hand, guided his rifle toward Prophet with his other hand.

Prophet slid his shotgun around to his chest, grabbing the blaster around the neck of its stock, curling his finger through the trigger guard as he thumbed both hammers back to full cock.

Boom!

The rider aiming his rifle at Prophet flew back off his saddle with a clipped scream, the flaps of his duster lifting like the wings of a bird taking hasty flight.

Another rider turned his horse and rifle toward Prophet.

Boom!

That rider's mouth formed a broad O as he disappeared, triggering his rifle at the sky, his horse giving a shrill whinny and leaping high off its front hooves. When the horse dropped its front feet back to the ground and galloped away, Prophet saw its bloody rider still rolling in the dust a good twenty feet away.

Prophet tossed the gut-shredder back behind him and palmed his Colt, clicking the hammer back and looking for another target.

"Enough!" This from Kilroy, who was climbing to wobbly legs, spitting several more teeth out on a stream of liver-colored blood. *"Enough!"* He threw up his arms and shook his head. "No more!" His words were garbled around a mouthful of blood and broken teeth.

The other riders—three were still mounted—were checking down their dancing mounts and glaring at Prophet. Now they lowered their rifles. Kilroy staggered over to where his horse stood a ways behind the others, reins dangling. The horse shook its head anxiously, whickering.

"Enough," Kilroy said, dragging his boot toes toward the horse, glancing back at Prophet, both eyes swollen to slits now, his lips looking like two bloody rags.

His horse shook its head again, and, afraid of the bedraggled rider stumbling toward him, sidled away.

Kilroy stopped and shouted as though his mouth were full of marbles, spitting more blood, *"Someone grab my fuckin' horse!"* His voice was as shrill as a coyote's yap.

One of the others rode over and grabbed the black's reins and handed them to Kilroy, who climbed heavily into the saddle. He turned once more to Prophet. It was impossible to tell his expression due to his swollen eyes and torn lips. His face was a mask of humiliation and misery.

"Fuck!" he shouted, throwing his head back and spitting the epithet at the sky.

He turned his horse toward the northern trail and rammed his spurs savagely against the black's loins. The others followed him, glancing back owlishly at the bounty hunter. One turned his gaze toward the barn.

Prophet looked toward the barn, then, too, and saw a slender female figure in a checked shirt, brown vest, and tight denim trousers standing before the corral. Long, golden-blond hair curled onto the Vengeance Queen's shoulders. She stood with one hip cocked, her Winchester repeater resting on her shoulder. Her snuff-brown Stetson shaded her face.

A brace of fancy, silver-chased, pearl-gripped six-shooters bristled on her slender hips.

"I'll be damned," Prophet said, half to himself, realizing that he was looking at the half-concealed diminutive "cow puncher" who'd been sitting back in the cabin's shadows.

Prophet remembered the scream he'd heard a moment ago, and swung around and ran up the porch steps and into the cabin.

"Mattie!"

He looked around, his heart pounding.

"Mattie!" he yelled again, louder.

"Christalmighty!" Grover Billings growled, poking his ugly face above the bar, looking around warily. "Is it over?"

"Where's Mat—?"

"Here." It was Mattie's voice.

Prophet's heart hammered again, this time hopefully.

"Where are you, girl?"

"Here," she said, louder. He saw her crawling out from under the table she and Prophet had been eating at. "I'm here." Her eyes were wild, and her hair hung in mussed strands across her face.

Prophet dropped to both knees beside her, placed his hands on her shoulders, and raked his gaze up and down her body. "Are you all right? You aren't hit, are you?" He ran his hands down her back, feeling for blood, finding none.

Mattie stared at him from beneath her brows. "Lou?"

"Yes, darlin'?"

"I'll marry you on one condition."

Prophet slowly shaped a shocked but delighted smile. "Anything."

"That you give up this nasty business. I don't want you ending up like Frank Beauregard." Mattie's eyes filled with tears.

Prophet laughed and drew her to him, hugging her tightly, rocking her from side to side. "You got it, darlin'!" He laughed again. "I'm done with bounty huntin'!"

He kissed her lips, long and deep, then pushed her away from him, and winked. "Come on outside. There's someone I want you to meet."

Prophet drew the girl to her feet, and they walked out onto the porch. Hoof thuds rose. A rider on a brown-and-white pinto was just then galloping out of the yard, heading south, blond hair bounding across Louisa's slender back and shoulders.

Prophet frowned. "Well, I'll be damned."

"Who's that, Lou?"

"The person I wanted you to meet." Prophet stared after the dust cloud the Vengeance Queen was trailing as she dwindled into the distance. "Oh, well," he said, turning to Mattie. "Some other time, I reckon. She can be funny."

Mattie gazed up at him uncertainly. "Where are we going to go, Lou? What are we going to do? After we're married, I mean . . ."

"I don't know," Prophet said, casting one more puzzled

glance toward where Louisa's dust cloud grew smaller and smaller. He smiled down at Mattie once more. "Let's get old Beauregard and the loot to the Wells Fargo office in Denver, and find out."

★ ★ ★ ★ ★

The Devil's Fury

★ ★ ★ ★ ★

Chapter One

There is nothing quite like the ratcheting snarl of a coiled diamondback to send fear into a man like a hot Apache war lance being driven into a hot, beating heart.

Friends and relatives . . . if there are any relatives here . . . we have gathered here today at the invitation of Louis Hammond Maxwell Prophet and Mathilda Lenora Anderson to share in the joy of their wedding.

The sound is something akin to coarse sand poured slowly through a hollow gourd and the ratcheting click of a gun hammer drawn back to full cock. If you could marry those sounds and give them two beady copper eyes, flat with passionless savagery, two long curving white fangs, and a flicking button tail rising from the end of a serpentine body coiled like cold, scale-covered, sand-colored hemp, you'd have the very essence of what a man fears most in this world.

You'd have the essence of what jerked Lou Prophet out of a dead sleep in the Mexican desert with a yelp.

This outward celebration that we shall see and hear is an expression of the inner love and devotion that Louis and Mathilda have in their hearts for one another . . .

Prophet turned to see the copper eyes glowing at him from a dark nook in the nest of volcanic rock he'd holed up in. The viper was coiled tightly, looped upon itself, head sliding slowly toward where the bounty hunter slouched against the rock, blood running down from the deep gash in his forehead, into his right eye, and down his cheek. He couldn't see through that eye. Only the left one.

That wasn't good. Being right-handed, he was also right-eyed.

I, the Reverend Ezra Thaddeus Waggler, believe marriage is of God, and that Mathilda Anderson and Louis Prophet have come here today to stand before God, who is truly Holy, and me, desiring to be united in this sacred relationship of marriage . . .

Slowly, Prophet slid his Colt from the holster thonged on his right, denim-clad thigh. Oh so very slowly, pressing his tongue taut against the back of his cut and swollen bottom lip, he clicked the hammer back.

As he did, he kept his eye on the snake, which kept both eyes on him. The snake's forked, colorless tongue tested the hot desert air, following the tongue toward its target, which was likely the vague, sunburned shape of a man and the smell of several days of desert sweat and soiled buckskin and denim and the spine-splintering fear of certain death . . . or something worse than death.

Now, Lou, Mattie—will you please turn and face one another and join hands to express your vows of love and devotion each to the other?

The diamondback shook its button tail again.

I, Lou Prophet, take you, Mathilda Anderson, to be my wife . . .

The revolting sound turned Prophet's blood cold. He stretched his lips back from his teeth as he slid the cocked Colt across his belly toward his left side. The snake was coiled in a nook behind the bounty hunter, over his left shoulder. He could see the viper in the corner of his left eye. It moved its head and slithering tongue forward, forward . . . ever closer . . .

. . . to have and to hold from this day forward, for better or for worse, for richer or for poorer . . .

The bounty hunter knew the serpent would strike at any

second. He had to get the gun across his body and aimed behind him before he did. A snake bite on top of his other sundry injuries would without a doubt be the last nail in his already sanded and varnished proverbial coffin.

. . . in sickness and in health . . .

Boom! Boom! Boom-Boom! Boom!

Prophet had fired half-blind, afraid to make any sudden moves lest the viper should sink those razor-edged fangs into his left shoulder. Now, as the echoes of his gun reports still banged around inside his battered head, he turned to see the snake in several ragged, bloody pieces behind him. The head was still opening and closing its mouth, as though chewing something, and the button tail was still writhing.

But for all intents and purposes, the beast was dead.

. . . in sickness and in health, I promise to love and cherish you . . .

From somewhere around the rock nest, a man's distant shout made its way to Prophet's ringing ears. His shots had alerted his hunters to his position.

"Damn."

Wincing against the rotten-egg odor of powder smoke, he punched out the spent shell casings and replaced them with fresh from his shell belt. More shouts rose on the hot Mexican wind. The shouts were in Spanish.

Running footsteps grew louder. Spurs rang. A boot kicked a rock. The rock rolled past where Prophet was hunkered down in the stone outcropping rising from a spur of a remote Mexican mountain range.

I, Mathilda Anderson, take you, Lou Prophet, to be my husband . . .

Prophet flipped the Colt's loading gate closed and spun the cylinder as a stocky Mexican in deerskin *charro* slacks and calico shirt came running up on Prophet's right from around a bulge of sandstone. The man turned his head toward Prophet. His eyes widened beneath the broad brim of his steeple-crowned sombrero.

He brought the two pistols in his hands around as Prophet's Colt went to work once more, shredding the Mexican's heart, blowing the bloody bits out his back, and punching him off the edge of the escarpment.

Chapter Two

The Mexican screamed as he tumbled backward into thin air, waving his arms as though trying to swim. He turned two slow backward somersaults before hitting the cactus-spiked desert below and lying spread-eagle on his back between two ocotillo plants.

"Shit," Prophet spat, edging out of his hiding place and looking around. He sleeved blood out of his right eye until he could see with it, albeit blearily.

"Santiago?" a man shouted above and behind him.

Prophet whipped around as another Mexican showed himself, a sombrero flopping down his back. The Mexican's dark eyes found Prophet. He raised the sawed-off shotgun in his hands but did not get the hammers cocked before Prophet capped his Colt's last cartridge.

The Mexican screamed, bounced off a rock formation behind him, and sagged forward. He tumbled straight down the escarpment toward Prophet, rolling several times, loosing dirt and gravel in his wake. A six-shooter was ripped out of a holster on the man's shell belt. It bounced along beside him.

The Mexican hit the escarpment floor two feet to the right of Prophet's right boot with a loud thud and a heavy sigh.

Prophet looked down at the Mexican wincing up at him through crooked teeth, brown eyes glazed in death. Prophet's own ten-gauge lay across the man's belly, hanging there by the thick leather lanyard looped around the dead Mexican's pocked and pitted neck.

"That ain't no way to treat a good Richards coach gun, you cork-headed son of a bitch," the bounty hunter said, holstering his Colt to reach down and lift the Richards from the Mexican's bloody chest. He pulled the lanyard up from around the dead man's head, then used the man's own cotton slacks to clean the blood off the ten-gauge's stock and iron barrels and receiver.

He'd dropped the barn blaster on his run across the desert, as the cutthroats had been closing on him like wolves closing on an injured fawn.

. . . *to have and to hold from this day forward, for better or for worse, for richer or for poorer* . . .

Prophet broke open the shotgun to make sure both barrels were loaded, then snapped it closed. He looped the lanyard over his head and right shoulder, adjusted the angle of his sweaty, salt-rimmed, funnel-brimmed Stetson on his head, and then began hoofing it off across the spur, angling southeast, crouching, keeping his head below the edge of the rise on his left.

The Mexicans had come from that direction. They'd run him out of Santa Rosaria. He'd thought he'd lost the pack of ten or so in these badlands he was now traversing on foot, having left his mount, Mean and Ugly, as well as the Richards, in the village after being surprised by Wolcott's gang.

But Pinkerton Agent Dean Wolcott was a determined son of a bitch. The reward on Prophet's head was enough to keep him stalking his quarry even deeper into Mexico, risking wild-assed Apaches and the fury of the Mexican government.

Wolcott and his Mexican cohorts had kept scouring the rough terrain until it had kicked up Prophet's sign—maybe a boot print or blood from his deeply cut temple, which continued to ooze blood—once more.

. . . *in sickness and in health, I promise to love and cherish you.*

Movement just ahead.

Prophet stopped, dropping to one knee.

He sleeved sweat and blood from his brow—the notch in his temple needed cleaning—and peered through some wiry brush standing atop a low, crumbling sandstone shelf ahead and on his right. He could see two straw sombreros jostling behind the shrubs, maybe thirty feet away and moving in Prophet's direction.

The bounty hunter glanced behind him. The outcropping in which he'd blasted the diamondback rose like sun-bleached dominos, vaguely forming a rectangle atop this narrow ridge. The saffron desert yawned below to the south, relieved by the swimming tawny lines and wayward shadows of distant ranges hovering just above the cactus-bristling desert floor. The second man he'd killed lay where Prophet had left him, stretched out in the sun as though napping with his eyes half-open.

When Prophet was relatively sure he wasn't being flanked, he licked his lips, rocked the coach gun's heavy hammers back to full cock one at a time, and moved slowly forward.

How could a man ever be sure about anything south of the border? he mused half-consciously. He winced when gravel ground beneath his boots. He was a big man and not as light on his feet as he should be for a man who'd been hunting others with prices on their heads—not unlike the price on his own head now—for more years than he cared to think about.

He'd tried to get out of it, though. The profession. Damn, if he hadn't tried to leave it behind . . .

With this ring, I, Lou Prophet, seal my promise, to you, Mathilda Anderson, to be your faithful and loving husband, as God is my witness . . .

He parted branches of the wiry brush with the Richards's double barrels and moved steadily, slowly forward. The two Mexicans were moving toward him, looking warily around, holding Spencer carbines in their gloved hands. Brass cartridge casings decorating their bandoliers glittered in the harsh sunlight.

They were coming around opposite sides of a ten-foot-tall ocotillo. Both turned their heads at the same time to see Prophet stepping out around his own covering brush. The one on Prophet's right gave a yowl and snapped his rifle higher.

The ten-gauge blast of buckshot picked him up and punched him back out of sight.

The other had just begun to tighten his right index finger on his own carbine's trigger when Prophet pulled the Richards's second trigger.

Boom!

The second Mexican's rifle barked, the slug careening wide as the shooter was blasted out of sight to lie somewhere back with the other dead man.

With this ring, I, Mathilda Lenora Anderson, seal my promise, to you, Lou Prophet, to be your faithful and loving wife, as God is my witness.

The bounty hunter moved quickly now, knowing that the twin blasts would bring Wolcott and the others. He ran as hard as his wobbly legs would take him—up another low shelf and then along a trail that wound westward along the crest of the spur.

As he ran, glancing cautiously behind him, hearing men shouting in Spanish but seeing none of the others, yet, knowing they were coming, he breeched the Richards. He shook out the spent wads, plucked two fresh ones from the loops on the lanyard, and thumbed them into the barrels.

He'd just gotten both wads seated and was snapping the gut-shredder closed when a rifle barked behind him. The slug spanged shrilly off a rock just ahead and to his left. The ricochet broke a lobe off a pipe stem cactus.

Prophet stopped, wheeled, caught a glimpse of a deerskin vest trimmed in silver, and a velvet sombrero, and let another fist-sized clump of ten-gauge buck carom through the brush, evoking another scream even as Prophet turned forward again and continued to run.

Another figure appeared on his right, leaping up from between two rocks. Prophet extended the Richards in his right hand, squeezed the trigger, and saw the assailant throw his rifle high above his head as he flipped a backward somersault in midair before rolling off down the slope toward the canyon yawning below.

The sound of the blast, like the crack of doom, rocketed skyward, dwindling slowly, echoing . . .

Mathilda Lenora Anderson and Louis Hammond Maxwell Prophet, you have come here today to stand before us and before God and have expressed your desire to become husband and wife . . .

Three or four rifles opened up behind Prophet.

The bullets whistled and screeched through the air around his head, hammering rocks and clipping brush and cactus stems. Several plumed dust and gravel around his boots, one nipping his right heel, tripping him up and hurling him forward. He fell, rolling violently down a rocky hill, wincing and yowling as stones and cactus bit into him.

As he rolled to a stop, grunting and wheezing, his heart fluttering in his chest, a familiar voice rose from above: "Prophet, you crazy son of a bitch, you either tell us where the money and the girl are or I'm going to gut-shoot you and leave you here for the wolves!"

Prophet scrambled behind a rock. He pressed his back to the rock, wrapped his hands around the Richards, and caught his breath.

"Kiss my ass, Wolcott!"

He snaked the Richards around the side of the rock and hurled buckshot back up the slope toward where he could see the vague figures of several men peeking out through clumps of brush or from around rocks. One man screamed in agony.

"My eye!" He was an Anglo; he wailed in English. "My eye! My eye!"

A voice that Prophet recognized as Wolcott's shouted, *"Move on the son of a bitch! Vamos!"*

You have shown your love and affection by joining hands, and have made promises of faith and devotion, each to the other, and have sealed these promises by the giving and the receiving of the rings . . .

"Shit!" Prophet bit out, quickly breaking open the Richards and punching out the spent wads.

As he did, he glanced around the rock. A good half-dozen men—no, more like eight to ten men, Mexicans and a few Anglos, all part of Wolcott's hastily thrown-together posse—were running down the slope now, weaving around rocks, firing Winchesters or Spencers or Sharps carbines.

Before he had to pull his head back to keep from getting it blown off, Prophet glimpsed Wolcott himself—a seasoned former lawman of questionable repute who now worked for the Pinkertons.

Prophet had fought against him during the War of Northern Aggression. Wolcott had been a brash first lieutenant while Prophet had climbed no higher in rank than sergeant but had been bucked back to corporal for fighting and general insubordination, which was in keeping with the surly dispositions of most of the sprawling, raggedy-heeled Prophet clan hailing from the mountains of northern Georgia.

Having fought on opposite sides of the war and then having come west around roughly the same time and crossing paths occasionally, there was no love lost between Prophet and Wolcott.

And now Wolcott had him. The Pinkerton's mercenary, ragtag army, put together hastily both north and south of the border, would have the bounty hunter surrounded in seconds.

Likely dead in less than a minute. Prophet wouldn't give Wolcott the satisfaction of taking him alive.

Prophet eared the Richards's hammers back until they caught.

He unsnapped the keeper thong from over the hammer of his holstered Peacemaker.

Then he got his boots set beneath him.

"All right," he said. "All right . . ."

He was about to bound to his feet, shooting, when a loud cacophony rose from behind him. It was the deafening *rat-tat-tat* of a Gatling gun. Prophet put his head down and stretched his lips back from his teeth, waiting for the bullets to smash into him, rending flesh and obliterating bone. He could feel the reverberation of each angry report through the ground beneath his boots.

The firing continued, nearly drowning the bellowing cries and shrill screams of the men who'd been running down the hill. None of the bullets tore into Prophet.

Incredulous, he looked up, poking his hat brim back off his forehead and stared ahead and to his right, where the Gatling's smoking maw spat fire as it rotated, hurling lead off Prophet's right shoulder toward the slope behind him. The gun and the man turning the machine gun's crank were all but concealed inside the branches of a dusty mesquite.

Prophet turned his head to his left, to stare over his shoulder at the slope.

"Retreat!" Wolcott shouted. "Retreat. *Retirada!*"

The Gatling gun cut two men down as Prophet watched. They'd wheeled to hightail it back up the hill, but now they were punched to the ground, screaming, rolling on down the slope.

The bullets continued to chew into the rocks, kicking up dust and sand around the four men who'd already fallen to hang up against boulders and brush clumps. The last of the survivors leaped back over the crest of the rise and disappeared.

The Gatling gun fell silent.

The silence on the lee side of the storm was deafening.

Prophet's ears rang.

He turned back around to stare at the Gatling's maw. The barrel rose with a squawk of the swivel. Smoke wafted around it. Several men bounded out of the brush and rocks around the gun—Mexicans, all—and ran past Prophet, yelling like wolves on the blood hunt.

They ran up the slope, shooting Wolcott's fallen, making sure they were buzzard bait. Then they continued up the slope. There were a half-dozen, maybe closer to ten.

As he stared dubiously toward the slope, something moved in the corner of Prophet's left eye. He wheeled, lowering the Richards defensively. Someone was moving out of the brush swathing the Gatling gun. She shoved a branch out of her way, let it whip back into place behind her, and shook her long, thick, yellow-blond hair back from her shoulders.

The Vengeance Queen stood staring at Prophet, one of her slender hips cocked, her head canted uncertainly to one side. She wore a ratty wool poncho and faded denims. Her legs were long and lean. Her man's hat shaded her symmetrical face with its long, persnickety nose and misanthropic eyes.

The lumps of her proud breasts pushed out her calico blouse and her poncho. Louisa Bonaventure's twin, silver-chased, pearl-gripped Colts glittered on her shapely hips.

Prophet gazed at her, blinked, turned away, turned back to her, then blinked again.

"You ain't here. It's this notch in my noggin. I'm addlepated an' seein' things. You ain't way down here in Mexico."

Louisa strode toward him, her rich lips compressed in a straight, disgruntled line. She stopped before him, gazing up at him curiously and with her customary reproof.

"I thought you got married," she said. "What happened?"

Therefore, it is my privilege as a minister and by the authority given to me by the State of Colorado, I now pronounce you Mr. and Mrs. Lou Prophet. Lou, you may kiss your wife.

"Ah, shit," Prophet said.

Chapter Three

Three months earlier . . .

Prophet clinked his wine glass to Mattie Anderson's.

"To us," he said. And while the next words were a bit harder to get out, as though the bounty hunter's tongue had suddenly swollen, he managed to say them without mangling them too badly: "To our w-wedding tomorrow . . . and to the long, happily m-married life we have ahead of us, Miss Mattie."

Mattie clinked her glass to his and smiled, her eyes glittering in the wavering light cast by several hurricane lanterns arranged around the crude, earthen-floored room. "To us, Lou."

She lifted her glass to her lips, and sipped. The glass was probably one of the only two fine, bona fide wine glasses in the entire little jerkwater of Broken Knee, Colorado, south of Denver. The full-hipped young half-breed girl who waited tables here in the eatery with the curious name of Ma McDonald's Ornery Chicken Inn & Café had rummaged around for the glasses for a good twenty minutes before finally hauling them out of a back room steamer trunk, looking a little weary from the toil.

Prophet had bought a bottle of good French wine a couple of days ago in the bustling little mining city of Leadville, when he and Mattie had been riding out of the mountains from Dead Skunk Gulch. The bottle had cost him a pretty penny, and he and Mattie were not going to slurp the precious liquid out of dented tin coffee cups.

This was a celebration. Lou Prophet, ex-Confederate soldier and soon-to-be-ex-Confederate bounty hunter, and Miss Mathilda Anderson, formerly of St. Paul, Minnesota, but with a brief, ill-fated side trip through Dead Skunk Gulch, Colorado, were hitching their stars to each other's wagons.

They had some celebrating to do, by god.

Tomorrow, Lou Prophet was hanging up his Richards double-bore sawed-off shotgun for good, taking his bounty hunting shingle out of his proverbial window, and marrying Mathilda Anderson.

It was time.

It was high time.

The devil, as per his and Lou's arrangement in accepting the bounty hunter's soul in exchange for giving him several good years on this side of the sod, good years in which he'd hunted men mainly for bankrolling the good times—drinking, loving, gambling, and generally taking it easy for long stretches in New Orleans or San Francisco, a nubile pleasure girl on each arm—had given Prophet his due. Prophet had felt he'd earned those good times, having survived the horror of the war in which he'd seen so many young men of his own southern ilk and even from his own family killed in the most hideous ways imaginable.

While he yet owed the fork-tailed Mr. Beelzebub a long peck of time shoveling coal down below, he still had a few years left on this side of the sod. He'd make the best possible use of those years by settling down and marrying the good woman he'd found quite by chance in Mattie Anderson.

His good times would continue, as per his and Scratch's agreement. This was part of his and Old Nick's deal—he and Mattie and at least a few good years of scratching out a living together somewhere quiet, far from the violence of the stalking trail and the ever-present stench of death.

Hell, maybe he and Mattie would even sow a few sprouts

together, though neither one of them had broached that subject yet.

They had time.

Plenty of time. Mattie was young, only in her early twenties, and Prophet was far from over the hill. Though the hardships of his business often made him feel like an old, old man on his last legs, he was still several years shy of forty.

"Are you sure, Lou?"

Mattie's voice had nudged him from reverie.

Prophet reached across the table and took her hand in his. "I couldn't be surer, Miss Mattie."

A frown cut an upside down V between her brows. "What about . . . what about that young woman from Dead Skunk Gulch? The one you wanted me to meet."

Prophet had wanted to introduce Mattie to his bounty hunting partner, Louisa Bonaventure, who'd shown up unexpectedly in Dead Skunk Gulch just in time to help keep Prophet from cashing in his chips during a furious gun battle for the loot he'd confiscated from the robber and killer, Frank Beauregard.

But when Prophet had led Mattie out of the stage relay station to make the introductions, Louisa had been riding away. He'd thought . . . or hoped . . . that he and Mattie would run into the Vengeance Queen on their ride out of the mountains. But they had not.

Something told Prophet that Louisa had already known, or at least sensed, how it was between him and Mattie. And she'd wanted to make a clean break. So she'd just ridden away.

That was like Louisa.

Deciding to hitch his star to Mattie's wagon and leave the bounty hunting profession for good meant he was leaving his old bounty hunting partner and oft-time lover, as well. That part made Prophet feel bad.

But Mattie's hand in his felt good. He caressed it with his

thumb, and smiled. "She was my partner."

Mattie gave him a sidelong look. "Just your partner?"

Prophet sighed, shaking his head. "No, Mattie. She wasn't just my partner."

"I see."

"Does it matter? It's you I love."

"Does she still matter to you, Lou?"

"She'll always matter to me, Mattie. But it's you I love."

Her eyes probed his. Her mouth corners rose, and she curled her thumb up over his first knuckle. "I'm glad she still matters. It tells me what kind of man you are. And, no," she said, shaking her head and smiling, "it doesn't matter to me. Maybe just a little. But not enough to keep me from walking down the aisle with you, Lou Prophet, and becoming your wife."

Prophet leaned across the table and kissed her. He held the kiss, enjoying how she returned it, moving her lips against his, until someone cleared her throat. Prophet pulled his head back from Mattie's and looked up to see the round-faced half-breed girl standing by their table, holding two steaming platters in her small, brown hands.

Those hands were shaking slightly.

The waitress wasn't looking at Prophet and Mattie. Her head was turned to stare at two men sitting in the deep shadows on the other side of a smoky lamp bracketed to a square-hewn ceiling support post. Prophet couldn't see either of them clearly—he could see only that one had short, curly hair and a short, light-brown beard. The two were talking in low, conspiratorial tones over their plates.

Prophet glanced curiously at Mattie, who returned the look.

"You all right there, sweet pea?" he asked the waitress, whom he'd thought he'd heard the cook call Wilomena. "Wilomena, honey?"

She jerked her gaze to Prophet. Her dark eyes were cast with apprehension.

Quickly, she set the steaming plates down in front of Prophet and Mattie, turned away, and, nervously rubbing her hands on her apron, hustled into the kitchen through a swinging door behind the long wooden lunch counter. Just before she'd disappeared, she'd cast a wary glance at the two men seated in the shadows.

Prophet shuttled his own glance to the pair, one of whom was staring at him now. The man quickly turned away, looking sheepish. Prophet riffled through the faces he stored in the file drawer of his brain. It was important for a man-hunter to have a good memory for faces. Man-hunters just naturally made enemies, and it was always good to recognize those around you who might be out to drop the hammer on you.

Prophet gave Mattie a carefree shrug. He refilled his and his betrothed's wine glasses, then grabbed his napkin. He set the napkin back down on the table and made as though to dig into his supper, but then said, "Forgive me, sugar, but I'd best pay a visit to the privy so's I can do this fine plate with all the surroundin's the justice it deserves."

"Okay, Lou, but hurry so your food doesn't get cold." Mattie gave him a playful smile over the rim of her wine glass. "Or me, either."

Prophet gave her a wink. He took his hat down off a peg in a near support post, adjusted his Peacemaker thonged on his right thigh, and headed down the long, shadow-murky room. He had to duck a little to keep his hat crown from raking the low ceiling.

When he got outside through the back door, he closed the door and then hurried to a window in the side of the building. Keeping his hat in his hand, he peered back into the eatery, where one of the two men who'd been sitting in the shadows about eight feet from Prophet and Mattie rose from his own table and grabbed his hat. He was about six-feet, broad through the shoulders and waist, and he had close-cropped red hair and a red beard. He was also tricked out with two hoglegs—at least, Prophet could see only two poking out from beneath the hem of his wool coat. He thought he could see a knife sheath, as well.

As the beefy gent walked past Mattie, who sat sipping her wine, he stopped suddenly, turned back to her, smiled, and gave a flirtatious bow, spreading his arms wide.

For a second, Prophet's heartbeat quickened, and he began sliding his hand toward his holstered six-shooter. But then the beefy gent walked away from Mattie's table, heading toward the back door. Prophet pulled his head away from the window, donned his hat, and walked back around to the rear of the building.

It was good and dark, so he could see only the outlines of a woodpile, some scrub brush, and the privy standing about twenty feet out from the eatery's back door, at the end of a well-worn path.

He drew up behind firewood stacked near the back door. From inside came the thumps of the beefy gent's boots. The thumps grew louder until the door squawked open. Peering around the side of the stacked wood, Prophet saw the man's thick silhouette against the eatery's murky umber light just before the man stepped outside, donning his hat and closing the door behind him.

The man turned toward the privy, pausing a moment to slide both of his revolvers from their holsters. Prophet heard the ratcheting clicks as the beefy gent cocked both pistols. As the man started walking slowly toward the privy, aiming both guns straight out in front of him, Prophet stole up behind him and rammed the barrel of his Colt into the small of the man's back.

"No sudden moves, now, Wade Kuhn, or I'll blast a hole

through your backbone you could drive a train through. Believe me, you don't want that . . . not that you'd be alive to hear the whistle. Just the idea, though, is ugly to contemplate—ain't it?"

"Ah, hell, Prophet."

"Uncock them irons and toss 'em away."

Wade Kuhn cursed again. Prophet heard the clicks as the pistol hammers were depressed. Kuhn was about to flip one away when Prophet heard the faint ring of a spur behind him. He winced, and started to turn around.

"No, no, no, no, no, Lou," a menacing voice said into his right ear. "Don't turn around. I ain't any better lookin' than the last time you seen me."

"Eli Snow, I take it?"

"You got it."

Kuhn chuckled victoriously as he stepped away from Prophet, turning toward the bounty hunter and cocking his pistols again. Snow reached around in front of Prophet, jerked the Peacemaker out of his hand, and tossed it away. He slid the bowie knife from the sheath on Prophet's shell belt, and tossed it into the darkness.

Both men, small-time long-coulee riders—rustlers and claim jumpers, mostly—faced Prophet now.

"You're right," the bounty hunter said to Snow. "The last time I seen a face like yours, it had a hook in its mouth." The side of Eli Snow's face, mainly the left cheek and that side of his neck, had been badly mangled when, caught long-looping a rich rancher's prized bulls, he'd been wrapped in barbed wire and whipped with braided quirts.

Snow didn't take kindly to Prophet's insult, however. He stepped forward and rammed his fist deep into the bounty hunter's solar plexus.

"There you go, Lou," Snow said as the wind was slammed out of Prophet's lungs. "How do you like that?"

Prophet dropped to his knees, gasping and gagging.

He glanced up at Snow. "You can beat me all night, but it ain't gonna do nothin' for your looks, Eli."

Kuhn dropped to a knee beside Prophet. "Where is it?"

"Where's what?"

"We know you got the money Frank Beauregard stole off that train. We know you got Beauregard's body, too. Got a two-thousand-dollar reward on it! We also know that as soon as you got to town today, you sent a telegram to the big chief in Denver askin' for a marshal to ride down to Broken Knee tomorrow and take both off your hands."

"You stupid bastard—you must've fallen on your head one too many—"

Kuhn cut him off with a harsh kick to Prophet's left side.

Prophet lowered his head again, gasping. He looked up at Kuhn glaring down at him, and said, "You hogwallopin' scalawag. Why don't you get a job?"

"You seem kinda close to that purty li'l gal in there, Prophet." Snow tossed his head toward the café. "If you don't bring us to wherever you stashed the money—"

"All right, all right," Prophet raked out, holding an arm taut across his injured ribs. "Leave her out of it. I'll take you to the damn loot."

Kuhn grabbed Prophet's left arm, hauling the big bounty hunter to his feet.

Snow rammed his pistol into Prophet's side and said through gritted teeth, "Let's go. Make it fast. No tricks, either, Proph, or we'll shoot you and come back for the girl. Get it?"

"If you do anything to harm that girl, killin' me ain't gonna be enough to save your worthless asses, because I'll haunt you from the grave."

"Tough talk," Kuhn said. "Just show us where the money and

Beauregard is, and maybe you won't have to try to make good on it!"

Prophet grimaced at the pain in his ribs, then slogged off toward the hotel, the only one in town, where he and Mattie had secured rooms. The two tough-nuts walked several paces behind him, pistols aimed at his back.

As he walked through the alley along the side of the restaurant, Prophet silently chastised himself for not taking better care of Beauregard's loot. He'd thought he and it would be safe here in Broken Knee. That's why he'd stopped here rather than continue north to Denver, where more men like Kuhn and Snow might be waiting for him.

He'd figured that news of Prophet's having brought down Beauregard and securing the outlaw's loot had by now made its way down out of the mountains, likely well ahead of Prophet, Mattie, and the loot as well as Beauregard's smelly carcass.

Broken Knee might have been home to a hundred souls, tops. And until Prophet had spied Kuhn and Snow in the restaurant, he hadn't seen anyone who looked like they didn't belong here. And by then it was too late. He'd let his guard down.

He hated having to turn over the loot after he'd gone through so much to get it. But in the process of running the loot and Beauregard down, he'd met Mattie.

The loot and Beauregard could go to hell. Neither was important anymore. Only Mattie was important. He'd turn the loot and Beauregard's carcass over to Kuhn and Snow, and he and Mattie would get married tomorrow and go on about their new life together, far away from men like those now shadowing Prophet with their guns drawn.

Chapter Four

There wasn't much to Broken Knee, an old hide hunter's camp and a stopping-off place for prospectors venturing farther west or south. Most of the badly weathered log cabins were abandoned. The communal windmill stood in the center of town, the few remaining wooden blades creaking dully in a desultory night breeze.

The only hotel stood just down the main street and on the other side of it from the Ornery Chicken, most of the buildings around it long-abandoned and boarded up. There was no town marshal—hadn't been one here in years, since the Texas trail herds had stopped passing through on the way to Denver, so the lack of any local law enforcement probably emboldened Kuhn and Snow even further than their initial scheme for getting rich quick on stolen bank loot.

Pop Calloway was sitting out on the boardwalk fronting the hotel, his round, steel-framed spectacles glinting in the light cast from the front windows of the adobe brick saloon abutting the hotel on its right. Pop was smoking his briar pipe and enjoying the warm breeze from his well-worn bench near the hotel's front door.

"What in tarnation . . . ?" the old man said when he saw Prophet, Kuhn, and Snow marching toward him out of the darkness.

Kuhn shoved Prophet up onto the boardwalk and aimed his

gun at the old man on the bench. "Shut up, Pop! Got it? Just shut up!"

Pop shrank back on the bench, his spectacles glinting.

While Prophet fumbled with the doorknob, Snow leaned in toward Pop and said, "You keep your mouth shut, Pop. This old hotel of yours would go up like dry kindling in a wildfire if someone was to take a match to it—savvy?"

Pop shrank a little farther back on his bench and didn't say anything.

"It's okay, Pop," Prophet said, not wanting the old man hurt. Pop had been an old rawhider in his day, all horn and gristle, but that day had been over before the last of the buffalo had been slaughtered on the western plains. He wasn't up to doing anything by way of tipping the scale in Prophet's favor. Not without getting himself hurt, anyway.

Prophet strode past the front desk in the hotel's pantry-sized lobby, and up the stairs. There was no lamp to light the stairwell, which was nearly as dark as the inside of a glove. Prophet considered making a move on the narrow stairs, but when he glanced furtively over his right shoulder and saw that both Kuhn and Snow, anticipating such a move from the big bounty hunter, were staying just out of Prophet's reach, he nixed the idea.

Prophet continued to the top of the stairs. Pop had lit a lamp bracketed to the wall in the second-story hall. The lamp was turned low, but it gave enough light for Prophet to see the door to his and Mattie's room. Prophet plucked the key from his pocket, fought with the rusty lock for a time, his two assailants cussing and stomping around behind him, then shoved the door open.

Kuhn pushed him through the doorway. He and Snow followed him into the room. Kuhn walked to the dresser, turning up the wick on a lamp. The wan glow spread, hazing shadows this way and that.

"Where is it?" Kuhn asked, his voice pitched with anxiousness. "Come on—where is it, Prophet? Under the bed? Where?"

"The closet yonder."

Snow stepped back, wagging his pistol at the door to the left of the bed. "Well, don't just stand there with your thumb up your ass. Fetch it!"

"Yeah," Kuhn said, chuckling eagerly now. "Fetch, boy! Fetch!"

Snow snickered.

Prophet suppressed the burn of anger threatening to flame in his belly. He had to think about Mattie. He had to turn over the Beauregard loot to these scoundrels, despite how it pained him right down to his toes, and get back to her. By now she was probably wondering what had happened to him.

Prophet walked up along the bed's left side to the closet door, and opened it. The saddlebags hung from a peg inside the closet. Both bags bulged with stolen train loot.

Prophet turned to Snow, who had followed him to make sure he wasn't about to pull any tricks. Behind Snow and behind Kuhn, who was flanking Snow near the open door, a shadow moved. A shadow shaped liked a young woman.

There was a female grunt and then the dull thud of something heavy hitting something yielding.

"Ohh!" shrieked Kuhn as he staggered sideways, dropping his pistol with a clattering plunk.

Snow turned quickly with a start. Prophet dropped the saddlebags and lunged toward Snow, grabbing the man's gun with his left hand, angling the barrel away from him, and slamming his right fist against Snow's jaw. Snow triggered the pistol into the wall to Prophet's right, the blast filling the room.

Mattie screamed and dropped the heavy china pitcher she'd brained Kuhn with.

"Mattie, get out of the way!" Prophet bellowed as he hammered Snow's jaw once more.

Snow stumbled straight backward. Prophet ripped the man's Remington from his hand. Snow righted himself, shouting, "You son of a bitch!"

He shucked his second Remy from its holster angled for the cross-draw on his left hip.

"Don't do it, you damn fool!" Prophet yelled.

Snow didn't take his advice and bought a bullet to the belly for his noncompliance. As the echo of Prophet's Peacemaker rocketed around the tiny room, Snow stumbled farther backward, triggering his second pistol into the floor between his boots.

He fell back against the wall, dropping the second Remy, groaning and clutching his belly.

"Ohhh!" he bellowed miserably. *"Ohhhh!"*

Prophet hurried over to where Kuhn was kneeling on the floor at the end of the bed, near the outside wall, as though in prayer. He was sandwiching his battered head in his hands as though fearing it would break into pieces if he didn't.

Prophet quickly defanged the man, jerking a second pistol and a knife off his cartridge belt, and tossing them both under the bed. Then he went over and picked up the gun that Kuhn had dropped when Mattie had brained him. He clicked the hammer back and aimed the popper at Kuhn.

Mattie, who had retreated to the hall, ran into the room and wrapped her arms around Prophet's waist, pressing her cheek to his chest. "Are you all right, Lou?"

"I'm all right, darlin'," the bounty hunter said, pressing his hand to the back of the young woman's head. "Thanks to you. That was a foolish move but I reckon it turned out all right."

Mattie looked up at him. "We still have the money, don't we?"

"Oh, yeah—we still have the money. How did you know . . . ?"

"I figured something was up when those two left the café just after you did. When I got to the back door, they were already herding you up toward the main street." Mattie shrugged. "So I followed . . . hoping I could be of help."

Prophet chuckled. "Well, you sure were, honey. I'm glad you didn't get hurt in the process, though. You could have been, you know. That was right foolish!"

"Well, it's done, now. And we still have the money. To give to the marshal, of course."

"That's right," Prophet said, leaning down to press his lips to her forehead. "We still got the money to turn over to the marshal. It would rankle me for the rest of my days if these two had hornswoggled us out of it."

"Oh, fuck!" Snow was down on his knees and one hand now, clutching his other hand to his belly from which his innards were oozing. "I'm on my last legs here, you son of a toothless old whore!"

Prophet gave Mattie a gentle shove away from him and scowled down at the slow-dying Snow. "I was born of Ma Prophet, and she was married to Pa Prophet, so I'll thank you to not call me the son of a whore or a bastard or even a son of a bitch. Especially in front of the woman who is about to be my wife. You're dyin', Snow. If I was you, I'd work on purifyin' my thoughts, maybe askin' forgiveness for my sins, not the least of which is you died in the commission of—stealin' stolen money."

"Shit, this hurts. Ever been gutshot? It really hurts!"

"Oh, Lord," Mattie said.

"Honey, why don't you go on back to the café? Have Wilomena heat up our supper. I'll be along shortly."

"Are you sure, Lou?"

"Sure I'm sure." Prophet kissed her and nudged her toward the door.

Mattie went out, looking anxiously over her shoulder, then drifted off down the hall.

Another face appeared in the doorway. This was the craggy countenance of Pop Calloway. "You okay, Lou?" He and Prophet had known each other for years, as Prophet frequently stopped here on his man-hunting expeditions about the west.

"I'm all right."

"I'm not all right, goddamnit!" bellowed Snow.

"You don't look all right," Pop told the gutshot man, adjusting his glasses on his nose.

"I'm not all right, you dried up old bean. I'm dyin'!"

"You look like you're dyin'."

Kuhn was down on all fours, shaking his head as though to clear it. Prophet nudged him with his boot toe. "Hey, Kuhn."

Kuhn turned his head to him. "What?"

"Get up."

"She brained me good—that girl of yours."

"I'll brain you again if you don't get up."

"I think she might've cracked my skull."

"A hard wooden head like yours would be tough to crack. You drag Snow outside. I don't want him dyin' in here. This is our room—mine an' the girl's. We're gettin' married tomorrow."

"I heard. Congratulations, you peckerwood," Snow choked out. "You don't want me dyin' in your honeymoon suite—that it, Prophet?"

"That's pretty much the size of it. Sorry if it sounds harsh."

"Fuck you!" Snow said, glaring up at Prophet.

Then his arms and knees gave way beneath him, and he lay flat on his face, dead.

"Shit in a bucket," said Kuhn.

"Drag him out of here," Prophet said.

"What am I supposed to do with him?" Kuhn asked.

"Bury him."

"This time of night?"

"I don't care what you do with him, just get him the hell out of here!"

Kuhn cursed and then found his flattened hat, reshaped it, and donned it. He picked up Snow's ankles and dragged the dead man out of the room and down the hall.

"What a mess," Pop said, staring down at the trail of blood and guts on the floor.

"Sorry, Pop."

"I'll get a bucket." The older man looked at Prophet. "What the hell were they after, Lou?"

"I'd just as soon keep that under my hat, Pop. But I'll tell you if you'll keep it under yours." Prophet knew he could trust Pop Calloway.

"You know I will."

Prophet told Pop about the loot. He returned the bulging saddlebags to their peg in the closet, and closed the door.

Pop whistled and shook his head. "You sure lead an eventful life, Lou."

"Yeah, well, that's about to come to an end."

"Why—just because you're gettin' married?" Pop threw his head back and laughed. "Why, you damn fool—you're just gettin' started!"

He gave Prophet an affectionate punch on the arm, then left to find a bucket.

Chapter Five

Three months later . . .

"Never mind," Louisa said. "Tell me about your big life change later. We have to get out of here. There's a *rurale* contingent riding herd on these parts."

"Who's *we*?" Prophet said, glancing at the slope behind him where Louisa's Mexican cohorts had disappeared after Wolcott's bunch.

"Later, Lou. The shooting might have drawn the *rurales.*"

Louisa had been dabbing at the gash on Prophet's forehead with a polka-dotted red handkerchief. Now he grabbed her wrist and slitted his lids at her curiously. *"Rurales?"*

Louisa nodded. "A whole pack of the unsavory characters. That's why I threw in with some friends."

"With some friends . . ." Prophet shook his head, staring at his old partner incredulously. He hadn't seen her since he'd watched her ride out of Dead Skunk Gulch back in Colorado, when he'd wanted to introduce her to Mattie. "I don't understand—what in the hell are you doin' down here in the first place? Did you follow—?"

Louisa placed two fingers on his lips. "Like I said, Lou—later." Her friends were coming back, jogging down the slope. Some were jogging past her and Lou, heading into the brush and rocks from which they'd appeared. "We have to pull foot."

"I need a horse."

Louisa was heading back toward the Gatling gun. She glanced over her shoulder and shaped a coy smile. "Whistle."

Prophet scowled at her. Then he stuck two fingers in his mouth, and whistled. A guttural snort sounded somewhere ahead. Hoofbeats. Then Mean and Ugly ran around a spur of rock and cactus, the lineback dun's reins tied around the horn of Prophet's saddle. The horse stopped six feet from the bounty hunter and bobbed his head in greeting, arching his tail and snorting.

"Well, I'll be damned," Prophet said, running a hand down the horse's long snout as the dust rose around him. He'd left the horse at the livery barn in Santa Rosaria. When he'd seen Wolcott, he'd had no time to fetch his own horse from the stable, so he'd leaped onto the first one he'd seen, and had fled the village as though the devil were nipping at his heels—which, in a sense, he had been.

In the person of Pinkerton Agent Dean Wolcott.

Wolcott's men had shot the horse out from under Prophet a couple of miles back.

Prophet led his trusty though ugly and ill-tempered dun around a clump of brush to see Louisa climbing onto the seat of the wagon in which the Gatling gun was housed, bristling like a brass and iron insect in the box. A stocky Mexican wearing a red bandanna over his lower face sat to Louisa's left, holding the reins of the single cream barb in the traces.

Prophet's head was swirling with questions. "How . . . ?" he said. "How in the hell . . . ?"

"Later!" Louisa yelled.

The stocky Mexican shook the reins across the barb's back, and the barb leaped forward. The wagon and the Gatling gun bounded out of its nest and rattled off across the rough terrain, following a narrow, winding course between rocky spurs.

Prophet swung up into his familiar saddle, on the back of his familiar horse, but he felt as disoriented as ever. The braining he'd taken when he'd fallen off one of the scarps he'd run across, trying to avoid Wolcott's gang, gave him a topsy-turvy feeling. The sun wasn't helping. Throwing Louisa into the mix—Louisa and her Mexican "friends"—merely added to the dream-like unreality.

It was like one of those dreams in which you find yourself with familiar faces in unfamiliar places, running for your life without quite remembering why.

Prophet clucked to Mean and Ugly, and the horse responded eagerly, breaking into a gallop. Horse and rider followed a twisting course between rocky escarpments. The wagon appeared ahead, jouncing and rattling over the rocky terrain. The horseback Mexicans galloped ahead. Prophet wondered where they were going, feeling oddly apprehensive as well as grateful to have been saved from certain death at the hands of Wolcott's men.

At the same time, he was down here to find his young wife, and so far he'd heard only rumors of her whereabouts but had been unable to follow up on those clues because he himself had found himself the target of a manhunt.

He hipped around in his saddle to stare behind him.

He hoped Wolcott was off his trail for good. If that meant the lawman was dead, so be it . . .

The bounty hunter turned his attention forward as he followed the Mexicans and the wagon bearing Louisa and the stocky *hombre* up out of the badlands and onto a flat stretch of open desert nearly as rugged. They swung onto what appeared a broad, ancient watercourse paved with fine black sand and followed it between low banks shaggy with palo verdes, mesquites, barrel cactus, and Mormon tea.

A jagged, darkly ominous mountain range loomed ahead.

They followed the watercourse's curving route for nearly a

half hour, by turns galloping and then cantering their horses. Not long after the lead riders had started galloping after a ten-minute canter, they slowed. The gap between them and the wagon narrowed.

Prophet drew Mean and Ugly to a slow walk, canting his head to one side, frowning curiously ahead along the wash, wondering what had slowed the group again so soon after starting another run. He maintained a distance of about fifty yards between himself and the wagon that continued rattling away from him. As he slow-walked the dun ahead, following another long curve in the watercourse, he could better see the eight or nine Mexican friends of Louisa sitting their horses side by side, in the middle of the old streambed.

They'd come to a dead stop.

Thirty to forty yards ahead of them was another group of riders. These riders were clad in the dove-gray uniforms and straw sombreros of the Mexican *rurales*—the Mexican rural police force.

"Shit."

Quickly, Prophet reined Mean and Ugly sharply right. He trotted the horse to the southern bank of the old riverbed, hoping the *rurales* were too far away to have seen his move. He urged the horse up the bank and followed a narrow trail littered with javelina scat through desert shrubs and cacti for forty or fifty yards to the south, away from the wash. He rode toward the mountains for another hundred or so yards before swinging back toward the watercourse.

He rode what he thought was maybe halfway back to the old riverbed before stopping. He swung down from the saddle and dropped the reins.

Mean would stand where his reins lay until Prophet whistled for him. Most horse traders worth their salt would have led the dun off to the nearest glue factory long ago. He was hammer-headed, ewe-necked, and spiteful. His ears and neck bore scars from fights with other horses, most of which he'd started. He had the walking gait of a Brahma bull. Few riders unaccustomed to his uneven bone structure could ride him for more than a mile before feeling like their joints were being ground to putty. (Prophet had acquired him years ago after losing at poker while drunk, trading away a sleek mount with thoroughbred blood.)

But Mean and Ugly was surprisingly fast, dependable, and stalwart. He was also surprisingly smart.

Too smart, sometimes . . .

Mean whickered curiously as Prophet swung the Richards over his neck and right shoulder, and slid his Winchester '73 from his saddle scabbard.

"Easy, boy," the bounty hunter said, running a gloved hand down the mount's sweat-silvered neck. "I'm gonna hotfoot ahead and see what's what, though I gotta admit I'm just a mite tired of all the horseshoes that's been throwed into our trail since we left Broken Knee. I got bigger fish to fry, goddamnit."

He removed his spurs and dropped them into a saddlebag pouch. He patted the horse's neck once more, tugged affectionately on a battle-scarred ear, then walked away. Mean stared at his retreating figure, skeptically twitching his ears and switching his tail.

As Prophet strode slowly through the chaparral, desert birds piping around him, he automatically breeched his shotgun to make sure it was loaded. Then he slid the gut-shredder back over his right shoulder and wrapped both hands around the Winchester. He quietly racked a cartridge into the action, then lowered the hammer to half cock.

Ahead, voices rose.

Prophet climbed a sandstone knoll capped with black volcanic rock.

On the other side of the knoll, two men were conversing in

Spanish. Arguing, they were speaking too quickly for Prophet, whose understanding of Spanish was of the cow-pen quality, to decipher more than a few words. Mostly, it seemed, the two conversers were casting doubt on the purity of the other's bloodline.

Prophet got himself seated near a notch in the volcanic rock, doffed his hat, and peered cautiously into the wash below. Thirty yards away, the two groups sat their horses, facing each other over a ten-foot gap. Louisa's so-called "friends" were to Prophet's left. Nine *rurales* were on his right.

The *rurale* leader was short and thick, neckless, and with a large paunch pushing out his gray uniform tunic. Gold sergeant's chevrons adorned the sleeves. He was bearded, and he wore a black patch over one eye. Long, thick, curly brown hair tumbled down from his sweat-stained sombrero.

He was arguing with the tall Mexican whom Prophet assumed was the leader of Louisa's group.

The *rurales* flanking the sergeant were younger, but they all wore similarly seedy looks. They were holding either Spencer carbines or old-model Springfields, and to a man they appeared not only ready, but eager, to use them.

Though Prophet couldn't understand much of what either of the two arguers was saying, it was obvious there was no love lost between the two groups.

After a loud back-and-forth haranguing, the "conversation" abruptly died, as though the leader of Louisa's group and the *rurale* sergeant had run out of insults or wind or both. Then the sergeant said with hard, quiet menace, "Antonio, you son of a diseased whore—what makes you think you can steal our Gatling gun and get away with it?"

Antonio wore a drooping mustache and two silver-chased pistols on his hips, in black holsters trimmed with silver *conchos.* He wore a gaudy black sombrero with elaborate silver stitching along the edge of the brim. He grinned wolfishly and glanced at the wagon sitting thirty yards behind him and the other members of his group, and said something like, "What—*that*? We found it in the desert and were wondering who it belonged to, Sergeant! There is no reason to get your drawers in a twist!"

The sergeant lifted his chin to yell at the man driving the wagon. "Anselmo, bring it up here!" To the men sitting their horses before him, he warned, "Antonio, make sure your men keep their hands away from their weapons, or we'll blast you out of your saddles and leave you to the javelinas!"

The *rurales* flanking the sergeant snapped their rifles to their shoulders, pumping cartridges into the actions. Their horses started at the sudden movements, but the men checked them down with brusque tugs on the reins. The horses of Louisa's friends bounced around a little, as well. One whickered testily.

Antonio glanced back at Anselmo, and tossed his head carelessly toward the sergeant, indicating for him to comply with the *rurale's* wishes. Louisa sat easily on the seat beside Anselmo, who had lowered his neckerchief to reveal his hawkish face. Louisa's Winchester lay behind her on the hard wooden seat, only the breech and rear stock showing. The Vengeance Queen lounged forward, elbows on her widely spread knees, gloved hands loosely intertwined.

She kept her head down. The wide brim of her hat hid her face.

As the men ahead of the wagon parted to make room, Anselmo shook the reins over the cream's back. The horse clomped forward, its shod hooves clanging on rocks. The wagon lurched and rattled along behind it. The *rurales* also broke into two groups and came around to both sides of the horse and wagon, nearly surrounding them. The sergeant rode around to Louisa's side, facing the bounty hunter watching from the escarpment. The others held their rifles on Louisa's friends as though daring them to make a move on them.

Anselmo drew back on the cream's reins. Horse and wagon stopped.

The sergeant gestured with his arm, and two *rurales* rode over to the wagon box near the Gatling gun. One stepped out of his saddle into the box and gave the gun a cursory inspection. He turned to the sergeant, and nodded once.

The sergeant rode up closer to Louisa's side of the wagon, and drew rein near the cream's hip. He stared down at Louisa. *"Quien es esta?"* Who is this?

Louisa lifted her head slowly, the hat brim rising.

The sergeant sucked a long breath through his teeth. "Ah . . . *chica rubia*!"

From Prophet's vantage, the Vengeance Queen's eyes were cool, lips expressionless, maybe a little bored. She could have been waiting for a train.

The *rurales* near the sergeant canted their heads to get a better look at the pretty blonde on the wagon seat. A couple glanced at each other, grinning lustily.

"*Madre* Maria is smiling on you, eh, Anselmo?" asked the sergeant, keeping his glinting eyes on the Vengeance Queen. "The mother of Jesus has given you a pretty friend. Who is she? She is certainly not from around here. Maybe from across the border, eh?"

"Sí, sí," said Anselmo, grinning up at the sergeant. "*Madre* Maria is smiling on me, Sergeant." He wrapped an arm around Louisa's shoulders, drawing her to him affectionately. "Meet my new wife, Sergeant. Isn't she splendid?"

The *rurales* glanced around at each other, smiling in delight of the pretty young woman in their midst, but also with skepticism.

"Your new wife, eh, Anselmo?" said the sergeant.

"Sí, sí," said Anselmo. "My new wife. We are on our way to

celebrate our union!"

"On your way to celebrate your union," the sergeant said, chuckling, his eyes lustily raking the Vengeance Queen up and down. He continued to grin, but his voice was pitched with menace. "Where did you find this new this wife of yours, Anselmo?"

"Find her?" Anselmo frowned, shook his head. "Oh, no, Sergeant. I didn't find her. She found *me.* She is very intelligent. She knows a good man when she sees one. When she saw me, right away she begged me to become my wife!"

"Begged you to become your wife, huh?" The sergeant glanced around at the other *rurales.*

They all had a good laugh at that.

Prophet's heart thudded heavily. His right index finger caressed his Winchester's trigger. Hell was about to pop.

Chapter Six

The sergeant kept his gaze on the Vengeance Queen, whose mouth corners lifted a rare smile of their own as she leaned close against Anselmo, resting one hand on the pot-gutted Mexican's chest. Anselmo kept his left arm wrapped around her shoulders.

"Like I said, Sergeant," Anselmo said. "She is very intelligent. She knows a good man when she sees one!"

"If she knows a good man when she sees one, Anselmo, you old outlaw—what is she doing with you?"

The others chuckled.

Anselmo's brows beetled. *"Que?"*

"You are twice her age." The sergeant's eyes continue to rake Louisa's slender but supple body. Prophet thought he could see more sweat oozing out of the large pores in the man's pitted cheeks, could smell the goatish lust rising from the old reprobate.

Jealousy bit Prophet deep. Though much had come between them, he was not surprised to find himself still feeling both proprietary and protective of his pretty sidekick.

"And this *rubia* . . ." the sergeant continued, "her beauty is quite rare for these parts. She is from north of the border. That much is obvious."

"So she is, Sergeant," Anselmo said. "So she is. Anyway, we would love to stay and converse, reminisce about old times, but like I said, the *chiquita* and I have much to celebrate!"

Anselmo took up his reins and was about to shake them over the cream's back, when the sergeant aimed his cap-and-ball revolver at Anselmo's head, and clicked the hammer back.

"Hold on, you old outlaw. We aren't done here. Not only have I found you with my stolen Gatling gun, but with a pretty blonde from the other side of the border. We have much to discuss, Anselmo. Perhaps we'd better all ride down to the *rurale* outpost at San Miguel. I think Colonel Quintero would be interested in conducting an interview with you and the *chica rubia.*"

Prophet wasn't sure but he thought Anselmo's face dropped.

One of the *rurales* aimed his rifle at the head of one of Louisa's friends, and shouted what Prophet roughly translated as, "If you lift that rifle any higher, you miserable dog, I will drill you a third eye!"

The man who'd been inching up his rifle barrel let it drop back down to his saddle pommel.

The sergeant kept his cocked revolver aimed at Anselmo. "How would you like that, you pig-fucking asshole? How would you like to go down to San Miguel and speak with Colonel Quintero about the Gatling gun and the *chica rubia*? I hope she has her permission papers for crossing the international border."

Anselmo stared back at him, stone-faced.

"You don't like that idea, eh, Anselmo? No, I didn't think you'd like it very much. Not after the colonel lined up your three cousins in front of the cemetery wall and blasted them all to *el Diablo*! And he's vowed to do the same to you!"

The sergeant threw his head back, laughing.

He cut the laughter off abruptly and switched his gaze to Louisa. "Colonel Quintero would very much enjoy the pleasure of the *rubia.* As would I." He depressed the hammer of his old Colt, lowering the pistol to his thigh. "I tell you what," he said in a throaty voice almost too low for Prophet to hear. "How about if your lovely bride pleases me right here? If she pleases me well enough, right here in front of your men and mine, then I will think about merely confiscating the Gatling gun and letting the rest of you . . . and the *chica rubia* . . . continue on to your celebration? Huh? What do you say to that offer, Anselmo?"

Anselmo said nothing. He merely glowered at the sergeant.

The sergeant looked at his men, and said, "If any of Anselmo's dogs moves a muscle, shoot them!"

Then he gigged his horse up to the side of the wagon. He stepped smoothly off into the driver's box to stand towering over Louisa, his own heavy gut sagging, turning the square, gold buckle of his shell belt nearly upside down. Louisa leaned away from him, curling her nostrils at the ugly man.

Prophet lifted his rifle, clicking the hammer back to full cock. His heart thudded heavily, angrily.

The sergeant smiled lewdly down at Louisa as he unbuttoned his fly.

"Very pretty lips," he told her. "What a pity to waste them on that old coyote there beside you."

Louisa glared up at him as he reached in and pulled his pecker out of the open fly of his pants.

Prophet poked his Winchester's barrel through the notch, then began to line up the sites on the sergeant's face, just beneath the broad brim of his straw sombrero.

"There, now," he said, smiling proudly down at his jutting organ. "Pretty good for a man of my age, eh?" He pivoted his hips to show himself to the others. They chuckled, snickered, laughed. They cut fleeting gazes from Louisa's friends, whom they kept their rifles on, to the sergeant.

The sergeant grabbed Louisa's arm, drew her off the seat beside Anselmo, and forced her onto her knees before him, on the floor of the driver's box. He placed his right hand against the back of her head, drawing her face toward his jutting shaft.

"Make it good, now, *chiquita!*" He laughed through his teeth. "And I won't take you to San Miguel!"

"You pig," Prophet raked out as he aimed down his Winchester, careful so the sun didn't reflect off the barrel.

As he planted his sites on the bridge of the sergeant's nose, the sergeant tipped his head back slightly, slitting his eyes and spreading his lips back from his teeth in satisfaction. His lower jaw began to sag. Prophet began to take up the slack in his trigger finger.

Suddenly, the sergeant jerked his head up, eyes snapping wide, mouth opening in horror. The man's shrill, girlish cry reached Prophet's ears a quarter-second later.

Befuddled, Prophet lowered the Winchester slightly, staring curiously toward the wagon. The sergeant stood with his hands over his bloody privates. Meanwhile, something shiny flashed in Louisa's right hand. Then she lifted her left hand as if to show something to the sergeant. Prophet saw blood dripping off what appeared to be the sergeant's appendage.

Louisa tossed the appendage up to the sergeant. It bounced off his chest and dropped to the floor of the wagon.

The sergeant danced in place, screaming shrilly.

"Christ!" Prophet snapped his Winchester to his shoulder, quickly lined up the sites again on the sergeant's face, and fired.

The sergeant's head jerked back. The man lowered his hands from his bloody crotch, and fell backward over the side of the wagon. The sergeant's nerve-racking screams and Prophet's rifle shot had set the horses of both the *rurales* and Louisa's friends to dancing.

The noise had also jerked the gazes of all the horseback riders toward the wagon. Now, however, seeing the sergeant lying dead on the ground and somehow believing Louisa's friends were responsible, the *rurales* began bearing down on their opponents once more. Rifles thundered, smoke and flames lapping from the barrels.

Louisa's friends screamed as they flew out of their saddles.

Prophet picked out a *rurale,* and fired. He picked out another one, and fired. He dropped two more and was about to drop another but the Vengeance Queen, firing both her pretty Colts from one knee in the wagon's driver's box, beat Prophet to the punch. She sent more lead hurling toward the *rurales.* Prophet did, as well.

The horses screamed and danced and buck-kicked as the men flew out of their saddles. The cream in the wagon's traces rose onto its back legs, clawing at the sky with its front hooves, whinnying horrifically. The wagon brake kept it from bolting more than a few feet ahead, dragging the wagon.

Finally, Prophet's Winchester clicked, empty.

At nearly the same time, he heard Louisa's Colts' hammers ping benignly onto empty chambers, one after the other.

The bounty hunter lowered the rifle and peered through his own wafting powder smoke through the notch. A few saddleless horses were running, fear-crazed, around the wagon. One was dragging its rider, whose boot had gotten hung up in a stirrup. The horse galloped away, the rider bouncing along the ground beside it.

Most of the *rurales* and Louisa's friends lay motionless. One *rurale* was writhing around on his back, shouting Spanish epithets at the sky. Prophet walked down the butte and into the wash. He strode up to the *rurale,* whose guts were dribbling out the gaping hole in his side, and finished him by drilling a .45 round through his head.

The man sighed and lay still.

Prophet turned to Louisa, who had gotten down out of the wagon and was now trying to calm the cream, cooing to it, running her hand down its snout. "Easy. Shh. Easy there, boy."

Prophet looked at Anselmo. The Mexican sat on the wagon

seat as though he was ready to take up the reins and be on his way. But the only place he would ever be on his way to again was the place where dead men go. A dark, puckered hole above his left eye dribbled blood down along the side of his nose, around his mouth, and down his chin. From there it dripped to his chest.

The man's eyes were open. He seemed to be staring over the jittery cream's head and at something far away beyond Prophet and the Vengeance Queen.

"Sorry about your new husband," Prophet said to Louisa. "He's seen better days."

"That's all right," Louisa said, stepping back to begin reloading one of her pretty pistols, flicking the loading gate open and shaking out the spent shells. "I was wondering how I was going to get out of this one." She crooked a droll smile at Prophet. "Now I don't need to wonder anymore."

Prophet was looking around at the dead men. "Maybe you all weren't such good friends, after all?"

"Oh, I wouldn't say that." Louisa was punching cartridges through her Colt's loading gate, steadily turning the wheel. "But I think they probably thought we were better friends than I wanted us to be. I met them in Santa Rosaria. It was just after you'd been run out of town on that proverbial greased rail you're always talking about. I told them I needed some help. They wanted to know what I'd give them in return for that help."

Louisa flicked the Colt's loading gate home, raised the pistol to her ear, and spun the cylinder, enjoying the whine of a fully loaded wheel in the way that only someone who lives and dies by the gun can. "I didn't come right out and promise anything, mind you, but I might have said enough to give them the wrong impression about how friendly I might or might not be after the sun went down."

"You charlatan!"

Louisa dropped her loaded Colt into its holster, shucked the other one, and began giving it the same treatment as the first. She looked at Prophet, slowly shaking her head. "Do you have any idea the trouble you're in?"

Punching fresh brass into his Winchester, Prophet glanced around at the blood-soggy ground. "Even a fool would have some idea. So, yeah, I guess I got some idea."

He punched the last round into the receiver, racked it, off-cocked the hammer, and punched one more round through the gate. He strode up to Louisa, and looked down at her. She was in his shadow now, the dry breeze playing with her hair. "I got a ton of questions, including how in the hell you knew I was down here. But the only one I need answered right off is: Do you know where Mattie is?"

Louisa dropped the second pistol into its holster, and looked up at Prophet staring down at her gravely. "I think so." She swung around and climbed into the wagon. She gave Anselmo a hard shove. The dead Mexican folded over the side of the wagon and hit the ground with a crunching thud, dust rising around him.

She released the brake and took up the reins.

"Follow me."

She shook the reins over the cream's back, and the wagon rattled on up the wash.

Prophet stared after her, frustrated. Finally he whistled for Mean, who came galloping up with a dubious cast to his gaze, shaking his head at the smell of fresh blood.

"Yeah, I know," Prophet told the horse, swinging into the leather. "Gettin' right whiffy on the lee side. I got a feelin' it's gonna get a whole smellier before the wind clears!"

He and the colicky dun galloped after the wagon.

Chapter Seven

Three months earlier . . .

"Therefore, as it is my privilege as a minister and by the authority given to me by the State of Colorado, I now pronounce you Mr. and Mrs. Louis Prophet." The Reverend Thaddeus Waggler grinned, showing a badly rotted front tooth. "Mister Prophet, you may kiss your wife."

The minister closed the Good Book in his hands and plucked the half-empty beer schooner off the bar behind him.

The plump, bottle-blond whore who was standing up for Mattie slapped a hand to her mouth to squelch a heartfelt sob.

"Shut up, Mary," said the man standing up for Prophet—sitting down, rather, because he was too drunk to stand. His name was Ephraim Wannamaker, who was the sole proprietor and operator of the Western Livery & Feed Barn. "Don't be a distraction!" He berated the whore, then tossed back a half a shot of rye.

"Kiss my ass, Ephraim!" Mary bellowed, plump cheeks red with sudden fury. "Who died and made you the fuckin'—?"

"Miss Mary, please!" urged the reverend over the rim of his frothy glass. "If you must quarrel with Mister Wannamaker, could you at least wait until we're done tying the knot here?"

"Harump!" said the whore, slapping the bar's crumbling planks. Then she beamed again at the newlyweds, and stifled another sob as tears dribbled down her cheeks.

Prophet turned to Mattie, who held a bouquet of spring wildflowers in her hands. Prophet had picked the flowers earlier that day by the creek that skirted the southern edge of Broken Knee. He'd made sure she'd at least had flowers, because the other wedding accommodations were less than perfect.

There was no church in Broken Knee, so Sunday church services, weddings, and funerals were held in the Shady Lady Saloon, a humble affair even by Broken Knee standards, owned by Stenson Albright, who now sat behind the bullet-pocked piano with a beer of his own, ready to spring into action with the traditional wedding march. A proper minister lived nowhere between Broken Knee and Denver, so Ezra Waggler, a drunken ex-buffalo hunter, ex-prospector, and pretty much ex-everything else including, so he said, ex-Lutheran minister, stepped in when a sky pilot was needed.

Whether or not the new state of Colorado really did give Reverend Waggler authority to perform weddings was in some dispute, but not enough to deter Prophet and Mattie from going ahead and marrying here in Broken Knee rather than traveling up to Denver and risk being caught in a whipsaw of outlaws and possibly even bounty hunters clamoring for the Beauregard loot.

They wanted no more surprises—at least, not of the blood and thunder kind. They'd had plenty of that up around Dead Skunk Gulch.

Prophet wasn't exactly dressed for the occasion, either. But the reverend had lent him a suit coat, which was only a couple of sizes too tight through the shoulders and short in the sleeves. Some might have said it clashed a little too startlingly with his trail-worn, sweat-stained buckskin tunic and faded blue denims with threadbare knees, but there was no one here to make the criticism. At least he'd had a bath and had pomaded his hair with oil he'd cadged from the hotelier, Pop Calloway, who sat smiling by the batwings, puffing his pipe.

Pop's mottled brown mutt lay curled next to Pop on the floor, asleep with its snout on its paws.

Mattie was not decked out in traditional wedding attire, either, but the cream, blue-laced frock she wore with a cameo-studded choker around her neck made her more than presentable here in the Shady Lady. The eager bride's dark-brown hair was pinned into a stately roll atop her lovely head, and Mary had limned her lips and brushed her cheeks with red paint that sharpened her natural robustness and complemented the gleeful glimmer in her eyes.

Prophet kissed his bride.

"Lou Prophet's married," said Wannamaker drunkenly, blinking his eyes at the kissing couple. "Lou Prophet—married. Imagine that!"

"Oh, shut up, you old sot!" admonished Mary as Prophet and Mattie continued to kiss, engulfed in each other's arms. The whore was gazing at them yearningly, both knuckles pressed to her cheeks, sobbing. "Beautiful," she sobbed. "So beautiful!"

Wannamaker climbed heavily to his feet, blinking his eyes as though to clear them. "Lou Prophet—married. Never thought I'd hear them words uttered in the same sentence." He ambled across the room past Pop Calloway, and stumbled through the batwing doors. He staggered off the deteriorating covered boardwalk fronting the saloon and stumbled into the street, yelling, "Lou Prophet is married! Lou Prophet is married. Jumpin' Jehosaphat—*Lou Prophet is married!*"

He punctuated that last with a shot from the old Remington he carried in a badly worn union-issue cavalry holster slung low on his right thigh.

"Lou Prophet is married!"

Bang!

"Lou Prophet is married!"

Bang!

"Did you hear that, everybody—Lou Prophet is married!"

Bang! Bang!

"By god—I never thought I'd live to see the day when Lou Prophet got hisself hitched!"

Bang! Bang!

As the last two shots rang out, setting Calloway's dog to barking raucously inside the saloon, staring into the street from beneath the saloon's batwings, the bald, barrel-shaped Stenson Albright hammered away at his piano with a loud but flat-footed version of the "Dulciana Wedding March," nodding and grinning from one cauliflower ear to the other.

Pop Calloway howled and clapped, stomping his boots while his dog stood beside him, barking toward the street.

As Prophet turned toward the batwings, offering Mattie his arm, Mary began tossing the rice she'd poured into a battered bowler hat on the bar. The rice rained down around the newly married couple, bouncing off their shoulders and peppering their hair.

Above the dog's raucous barking, the piano's bellicose hammering, and Pop's howling, Prophet said to his wife, "Shall we, Mrs. Prophet?"

"We shall, Mr. Prophet."

Arm in arm, they walked proudly across the room, through the batwings, which the beaming Pop Calloway held open for them, and out into the street. Wannamaker stood in the middle of the street, surrounded by mostly abandoned, scruffy-looking, sun-bathed buildings, reloading his old conversion six-shooter from the loops on his shell belt.

As he did, Prophet and Mattie headed south along the street, which was deserted except for one gray-haired old woman in a blue shawl and poke bonnet standing under a badly faded sign reading MRS. TATE'S LADIES' WEAR, shaking her round, jowly head in remonstration of the raucous, midweek activity transpiring in and around the town's only remaining watering hole.

Calloway's dog followed the slow-strolling newlyweds, barking and wagging its tail. When Wannamaker got his pistol reloaded, he resumed triggering shots into the air and howling, but by this time Prophet and Mattie had retreated to the cool, relatively quiet confines of their hotel room, where Prophet wasted no time undressing both himself and his glowing bride.

They climbed into bed, engulfed each other in their arms and legs, and did not surface for the rest of the day and night except to sip whiskey and demolish the large platters of steak and beans that Calloway brought up to them from the Ornery Chicken. The playful, occasionally raucous, sounds of their lovemaking could intermittently be heard from one end of Broken Knee to the other.

More than a few times throughout the day and deep into the night, the couples' howling and laughing and the hammering of the bed's headboard against the wall woke Calloway's cur from a dead sleep. The mutt stood barking defensively up the murky stairwell until Pop threw a shoe or a newspaper at him.

Aside from the dog, no one complained. Not even Mrs. Tate, who secretly pined for the days when revelry was far more common in Broken Knee, which had mostly fallen into funeral ruination. Lou and Mattie were Pop's only customers, and, like Mrs. Tate, Pop enjoyed the cacophony, which reminded him of more lucrative days as well as his own more sensual past.

The intermittent bouts of lovemaking died for the night just after one a.m. when, worn out and more than a little inebriated, the newlyweds fell asleep in each other's arms. Then only the coyotes could be heard, yammering in the distant hills broadly capped by a vast, black velvet sky liberally dusted with glittering sequin stars, although no one was listening to the coyotes except maybe Calloway's old dog.

Lou Prophet certainly didn't hear the coyotes. He didn't hear anything at all until, finally aware of the warm sun branding the side of his face through a window, he also became aware of rapid sniffing sounds. Breath that smelled of rancid meat assaulted his nose.

Opening his eyes, the bounty hunter saw Pop Calloway's dog staring at him from over the edge of the bed—two worried copper eyes hovering just inches away from Prophet's. The dog's black, leathery nostrils were working, sniffing.

Seeing Prophet now staring back at him, the dog gave a low, frightened yip, and turned away. Claws scratched and clattered across the floor as the cur made a hasty retreat, mewling and groaning deep in its chest. The scratching dwindled to silence.

Prophet lifted his head, immediately hardening his jaws against the sledgehammer being bashed through the top of his head, shattering his brain plate. At least, that's how violent the hangover felt. He lowered his forehead to the bed and waited for the misery to abate somewhat, though it didn't by much at all, before he lifted it again and turned to peer behind him.

Mattie's side of the bed was empty, the covers thrown back. The room's door yawned wide. Prophet saw something else that he thought must have been a mere distortion of his vision caused by the hangover, which continued to hammer rusty railroad spikes through both ears and into the back of his head, not to mention both eyes.

He blinked, brushed sleep crumbs from his eye corners, then opened the lids once more.

"Shit," he said when he became relatively certain that he was, indeed, seeing a pair of men's pointed-toed, black stockmen's boots angled toe down on the other side of the open doorway. The bottoms of the boots faced Prophet. Whomever wore them lay belly down on the hall floor, just outside Prophet's and his new wife's room.

"M-Mattie?" Prophet said, still looking around, his lips stretched with the misery of the hangover. "Mattie—are . . . you here?"

He'd been lying diagonally across the bed, naked beneath the covers. Now he tossed the covers aside, dropped his feet to the floor, and pushed up with a groan. He stood on the side of the bed opposite the door. Flares flashed in front of his eyes. The floor pitched beneath his bare feet like a ship on choppy waters.

He leaned forward, steadying himself against the wall. His guts heaved. What felt like warm mud sloshed heavily around inside his belly. For a moment, he thought he was going to puke.

His mouth was dry. His tongue tasted like a dead rat that had lain too long in the hot sun. He didn't remember ever being this hungover. Maybe back during the war when he and his squad had stumbled across a southern Tennessee root cellar stashed with several crocks of sour mash, and they'd made a party of it . . .

Cymbals crashing between his ears, he stumbled around the bed, heading for the door. As he did, he glanced toward the closet where he'd stashed the Beauregard loot. The door was open about six inches. Disregarding the loot for now, he stepped into the hall.

"Pop!"

It was Calloway who lay in the hall, belly down against the base of the wall. The old man's dog cowered in the shadows near the stairs beyond him, whining. The old man's briar pipe protruded from the right rear pocket of his canvas trousers.

"Pop!" Prophet said, dropping to a knee beside the old hotelier.

Calloway groaned, and moved a little. Blood oozed from a

cut in the back of his head, visible through the blue-gray strands of his hair. The old man lifted his head, turned over, rolling a shoulder up against the wall behind him. He looked as bad as Prophet felt. He lifted a hand to the back of his head.

"Jesus, Pop—what the hell happened?"

"Christalmighty—how long I been lyin' there?"

Hearing Pop's voice, the dog gave an eager yip and came running, wriggling its entire body and wagging its tail.

"You tell me," Prophet said. "When did you come up here? I didn't hear a damn thing!"

"I believe that. You were really sawin' away," Pop said, leaning back as the dog licked his face and mewled happily. "Melvin, where in the hell were you when I needed you, you worthless cur? Out huntin' rabbits half the night, no doubt . . ."

"Pop, what happened?" Prophet squeezed the old man's upper arm. "Where's Mattie?"

The old man looked blearily up at him. "You didn't see or hear none of it?"

"No! Where's Mattie? Who knocked you out?"

"I don't know!" the old man cried. "It was dawn, but it was still dark. That lawman from Denver woke me up to find out what room you two was in, and then he came up to pound on your door. I was just gettin' back to sleep when I hear a terrible commotion. The girl screamed and then somethin' hard hit the floor up here. I come up to check it out, an' . . ." Pop looked around as though to get his bearings. "An' here I am." He winced as he rubbed the back of his head. "With one hell of a goose egg!"

"What lawman are you talkin' about, Pop?"

"The one from Denver."

"I got that much. A deputy U.S. marshal?"

"Yeah. St. Vincent, I think he said his name was. George St. Vincent. George Patrick St. Vincent. Used all three names like he was mighty proud of each and every one."

"Where is he now? Where's Mattie?"

"I don't know where in the hell either one of 'em is, Proph. It was dark when I got up here. When I opened the door and stepped into the room, someone laid into the back of my poor ole noggin' with something damn hard. That's the last I remember. Melvin must've come in from huntin' this morning to find me up here. Get away, now, Melvin—good Lord, your breath smells like you been chewin' on the devil's ass!"

Prophet rose with another groan as pain continued to make mush of his head, and stumbled into the room. He grabbed his balbriggans off a chair, and pulled them on. This was much too dire a situation to continue in his birthday suit. Next, he pulled his socks on, cursing. He looked at the closet door again. A heavy dread flowed through him while a witch's chill breath puffed against the back of his neck.

He walked to the closet, wrapping his hand around the knob. He took a moment to steel himself, then jerked the door wide.

"Christ!" he said, staring down in horror. "The Beauregard loot is gone. But I think I just found George Patrick St. Vincent."

Chapter Eight

If the man sitting on the floor with his back resting up against the closet's back wall was Deputy U.S. Marshal George Patrick St. Vincent, then St. Vincent was . . . or had been . . . a jowly man with a neatly trimmed salt-and-pepper beard, long gray hair, and pale blue eyes.

His hair was extremely thin around the crown of his skull. His hat lay on the floor to his left. He was clad in whipcord trousers and a wool coat over a pinstriped shirt and leather vest to which was pinned the obligatory moon-and-star badge.

He appeared to be in his late thirties or early forties, his broad, rugged face leathery and pitted. A star-shaped scar was stamped into the center of his forehead.

His head was tilted nearly to his right shoulder. His half-open eyes stared opaquely down at the floor to the right of his boot tucked up close to his butt. His arms dangled straight down his sides, hands resting palm up on the floor.

Prophet couldn't see a gun on the dead lawman. No shell belt, either. He'd apparently been hit with the same pitcher that Mattie had laid out Kuhn with. This time, however, the pitcher had broken.

The pieces, both large and small, lay on the floor between St. Vincent's worn, low-heeled, gold-buckled boots. Some of the shards were red with blood. Whoever had killed St. Vincent had likely kicked the shards into the closet after they'd heaved the body into it, trying to buy as much time as possible for themselves.

Time to get away.

Time to get away with the money and Mattie . . .

"Oh, my," Pop Holloway said, peering around from behind Prophet. "Oh, my."

Prophet swung around, grabbed the old man's spindly shoulders, and shook him gently. "Pop—think. Someone must have followed St. Vincent up the stairs. They followed him here . . . to this room. They were after the Beauregard loot. They got it, and they got Mattie, too. Did you see anyone else? Anyone besides St. Vincent?"

"Hell, no," Pop said. "Like I told ya, Lou, I was almost back to sleep when I heard the girl scream and then the . . ."

He let his voice trail off, turning his head to one side, frowning, listening to more than one pair of boots thudding on the stairs. Prophet released the old man's arms and walked to the door, poking his head into the hall to see two men walking toward him, silhouetted by the yellow morning light filtering up the stairwell behind them.

The men angled over to where Prophet stood in the open doorway.

The first man was Prophet's height but older—mid to late sixties, rawhide tough. Dressed stylishly in a doeskin vest and black foulard tie, high-crowned, cream Stetson. Good pants, polished boots. He had the look of a man accustomed to wielding authority.

He looked Prophet's tall, broad, longhandle-clad frame up and down, wrinkling his nose with disdain. He looked over Prophet's right shoulder to see Pop Holloway sitting on the bed behind the bounty hunter, dabbing at the back of his head with a handkerchief.

"What happened?" the man asked in a deep, resonant voice.

Prophet looked at the younger, slightly shorter man behind the older one, then returned his own critical gaze to the older one, and said, "Who the hell are you?"

The older man gave a soft, defeated chuff through his nose and smiled without humor. "We're too late, aren't we?"

"Depends on what you're talkin' about. Too late to open Christmas presents? Yep, by god, you are."

"She's gone."

"Who's she?"

"We both know who she is, Mister Prophet. What has she done?"

Prophet was so befuddled by all that had happened, as well as the nearly overpowering pain inside his skull, that when the newcomer placed his hand on his chest, he stepped back without resistance. The man took one step into the room and looked toward the closet where the missing Beauregard loot had been replaced by one dead deputy U.S. marshal.

"Oh, Christ." The man turned to Prophet. "St. Vincent?"

Prophet glowered at him. "Who're you? And how do you know who I am . . . who he is?" He gestured toward the closet.

The older newcomer turned to the younger one, also stylishly dressed, and said, "Donald, find us a couple of fresh horses. We're pulling out in a half hour. Hurry, now, son. *Pronto!*"

"You got it, Father!" Donald hurried toward the top of the stairs.

Pop Calloway rose from the bed, glanced at the dead man in the closet, then walked to the door. He was holding his handkerchief to the back of his head. "I reckon I'd best find someone to haul the dead federal out of here."

"You'd best get a sawbones to look at that cut, Pop," Prophet told the old man.

"Sawbones? Shit," said Pop, ambling off down the hall. "We haven't had a sawbones in Broken Knee for many, many moons.

Come to think of it, we ain't had a murder here for that long, neither . . ."

Prophet turned to the newcomer, who, appearing in deep thought, took a seat in a brocade-upholstered armchair near the door. He crossed one leg, sissy-like, over the other, and dug a meerschaum pipe and a leather tobacco sack out of a pocket of his fancy vest. Prophet's frustration, confusion, and worry about Mattie caused his anger to flare.

"I asked you a question, Mister," he barked. "Who are you? I ain't gonna ask you again. My head hurts and there's a side of a dead government beef in my closet. As if that ain't bad enough, my wife is gone."

"Yes, and she won't be back." The newcomer was thoughtfully filling his pipe. "You can bet the seed bull on that."

When Prophet opened his mouth to speak again, the older man said, "Pull your horns in, Mister Prophet. We're on the same side here."

"What side is that?"

"The side that's been hornswoggled by"—he waved his hand holding a silver match case—"by that *wife,* as you call her in all your naiveté."

"In all my *what*?"

He thought he might know what the man had said, but he'd never heard the word in question pronounced the way this fussy stranger just had.

"The name is McCourt. Harland McCourt." He snapped a match to life on the wooden chair arm, and touched the match to the chopped tobacco heaping up above the rim of the gaudy porcelain meerschaum. "I learned about you from the U.S. marshal in Denver. He told me he'd sent a man here to retrieve a pair of saddlebags filled with stolen train loot. I ranch in western Kansas, a couple days' ride from here."

He had the pipe going now to his satisfaction and was looking around for somewhere to discard the match.

"Okay, I'm with you so far," Prophet said, leaning against a bedpost, arms crossed on his chest. There were so many more important things to worry about that he did not feel self-conscious about standing there clad in only his threadbare balbriggans and socks. "What about Mattie?"

"Mattie, eh? So, that's what she's calling herself these days?" McCourt gave an ironic snort.

"What the hell are you trying to say? Her name is not really Mathilda Anderson?"

McCourt puffed his pipe, withdrew it, and chuckled. "No, I'll say it's not. It is Abigail Justice. She is from western Arizona. At least, as far as I know. Her trail is as murky as the North Platte River during the spring runoff!"

"What're you doing here, McCourt?"

"I've had men looking for that woman . . . Mattie, as you know her . . . for several months. A business associate of mine saw you and her riding in the mountains last week. He sent me a telegram alerting me to that fact. He recognized Abigail from my description. He also recognized you, as I guess you are a man of some significance out here."

Again, McCourt raked his gaze skeptically, reprovingly, across the bounty hunter's crude, coarsely attired frame, then took a few more puffs from his pipe. "My man had been privy to the story going around that you'd found stolen train loot and were taking that loot to the U.S. marshal in Denver. Apparently, many men had been seeking same. Anyway, I and my son, Donald, traveled to Denver hoping to meet you there. I am quite good friends with U.S. Marshal Henry Todd. I've been checking in with him every day, inquiring about you and Abigail, whom you of course know as—"

"Mattie," Prophet finished for him.

"Yes, Mattie. However, I guess I inquired too late yesterday to learn that Todd had heard from you, that you were holed up down here in Broken Knee, awaiting one of Henry's deputies to come and retrieve the loot. You see, I'd hoped to ride down here with Deputy St. Vincent and make sure that that . . . that . . . *demon woman*—god blast her vile soul!—was brought to justice. Apparently, Henry did not fully understand the significance of the woman I had told him about. Did not understand how duplicitous she is . . . shrewd . . . cunning . . . malevolent . . . downright deadly. It seemed to have slipped his mind that he was to inform me about your whereabouts and that he had sent a man down here to retrieve both!"

McCourt had riled himself into a full-on tizzy. He had both feet on the floor, and he was leaning forward, red-faced, gesticulating with the hand holding his pipe. "That woman killed my son!"

"What?" Prophet said, finding his battered brain unable to swallow what he'd been told. "Mattie? No!"

"She married him. For his money. For his *family* money. Charles ran the mercantile in Sand Bluff. I own it. A year and a half ago, he fell in love with the pretty young woman who'd come to town from Missouri . . . as she told everyone . . . to teach school."

"Missouri? She told me she was from Minnesota."

"She told many people many things, Mister Prophet. She's been doing so since she was in swaddling clothes, so I've come to understand, having thoroughly investigated her rancid, crooked past."

Prophet was getting tired of hearing all of these attacks on Mattie's character. He didn't even know this man. For all Prophet knew, this man, McCourt or whoever in hell he was, might have instigated the stealing of the Beauregard loot as well as the taking of Prophet's wife.

He walked over to the rancher, reached down, and grabbed a

fistful of the man's tailored shirt. He cocked his other fist with menace. "Listen here, you damn rooster. I'm gettin' tired of hearing all your crowin' about my wife."

"Your wife—ha!"

"How 'bout if I just switch your ears around for you?"

"Do so if that'll make you feel better, Mister Prophet. But I assure you it won't change anything about Abigail Justice. I will guarantee you that. She came to Sand Bluff pretending to be a schoolteacher. She caught my son's eye, and they ended up married. Charles broke his leg when the floor in the mercantile attic gave way beneath him . . . under very mysterious circumstances, I might add . . . and she used the occasion of his being bedridden and helpless to drug him, suffocate him while he was asleep, and run off with the fifteen thousand dollars he had placed in the mercantile safe to pay for a load of freight being shipped from Council Bluffs.

"She probably came out here sniffing around for another man who would help her disappear. Possibly posing as a mail-order bride, which she has done before. *Twice* before, to be exact. Or, rather, as far as I know. I have no idea the circumstances of your meeting her, but rest assured, you're lucky you're still alive, Mister Prophet, though you do look rather worse for the wear. Tell me, did you have some trouble waking up this morning? Where were you when all of this was transpiring?"

He flung a hand out to indicate the dead marshal still sitting in the closet with his knees drawn up to his chest. The lawman looked like an overgrown, well-attired schoolboy being punished for placing frogs in the girls' privy.

Prophet released the rancher's shirt. He lowered his clenched fist and stepped back. He raked a weary hand down his face. "I . . . I slept through it."

"Sniff the glass you last drank out of."

"What?"

"Go ahead—sniff the glass."

Prophet looked at the man skeptically. Grumbling, perplexed, and in pain, he walked over to the small round table between the bed and the wall, lifted the goblet he'd last drunk whiskey from, and sniffed. He made a face.

"Does it smell a little like licorice with a hint of juniper?"

Prophet turned to give the man a dubious look.

McCourt nodded. "Wormwood mixed with Moon of Bathsheba—in the same family as the poppy plant first cultivated by the Egyptians. Powerful aphrodisiac when taken in very small quantities. When you bump that amount up to, say, a teaspoonful, it knocks you into a sleep deep enough to kill."

Prophet set the glass back down on the table. He moved to the end of the bed, and sank down on it. He leaned forward, placed his elbows on his knees, and raked his hands through his sleep-mussed hair.

"I'm findin' all this just a little hard to take, McCourt."

"I don't blame you. Miss Justice is a very good actress. My son swallowed her story hook, line, and sinker. An innocent farm girl from Missouri who attended a small teacher's college in Little Rock before coming west to teach the children. I was suspicious of her even before my son married her, but Charles wouldn't listen to my concerns. I had no firm evidence to back them, just a *feeling* that she was something other than what she claimed. Maybe she was just too sweet . . . too innocent. Too pretty. Too good a teacher. *Too much* in love with my boy . . . whom she killed. She's quite insane."

Prophet looked at the man. He didn't want to believe McCourt but he felt himself beginning to. Maybe deep down in his bones he himself had suspected that Mattie was a little too good to be true.

"After my boy died, I hired the Pinkertons to trail her. They couldn't find her. She seemed to have vanished for two whole years. God knows where she was holed up. They did, however, backtrack her all the way to Arizona, where she was raised. When she was very young, she left home and lived by scheming wealthy men out of money—wealthy *hacendados* in Mexico."

"Where in Arizona?"

"A desert ranch south of Tombstone. It's still there. Her father is a drunk. A couple sons live on the place with him. Outlaws, not surprisingly." McCourt raked a finger through the reddish gray muttonchop running down the left side of his face. "Don't feel too foolish, Mister Prophet. You're not the first man she caused to fall in love with her. It's my assumption that she ran into especially deep trouble in Mexico—maybe she murdered one of those wealthy Mexican ranchers—and that's when she fled north to live by her vile wits in Kansas and Colorado."

Donald's voice sounded in the street below the window. "Father?"

McCourt knocked the meerschaum's spent ashes into his hand, rose, and stuffed the pipe into his vest pocket. "Time to run that catamount to ground."

The rancher turned toward the door.

"Hold on," Prophet said, rising. "You know where she's headed?"

"Like I said, she was born and raised in Arizona. I suspect that after all the trouble she's gotten into here, and having had to kill a deputy U.S. marshal, there's a chance she'll head back in that direction. Most mountain lions, when they've raised particular havoc and know they're being hunted, usually head back to the security of their best-known territory."

McCourt lifted his hat, running a hand through his thinning hair. "Not to worry. My son and I have tracked her this far. Wherever she's headed, we'll run her down."

"If you catch her, what do you intend to do with her?"

McCourt hardened his jaws. "Hang her from the nearest tree!"

Chapter Nine

When McCourt had gone, Prophet lay back on the bed, trying to take in all that he'd learned about the woman he'd married less than twenty-four hours ago.

While he lay there, three beefy townsmen came and dragged the dead lawman away, casting wary, skeptical glances toward Prophet, who remained on the bed, staring at the ceiling as though trying to make some sense out of particularly obscure hieroglyphics.

Thinking was not the big man's strong suit at the moment. He still felt confused and disoriented. But he realized now that only whiskey in astronomical amounts and on an empty stomach could make him sleep through what he'd slept through a few hours ago and make him feel the way he felt now. His head felt like a large tender heart sending out spasms of raw, unadulterated agony with each logy beat.

Mattie . . . or Abigail, or whoever in hell she was . . . had poisoned him. He'd gotten her down out of the mountains only to have her double-cross him and abscond with the money. She'd headed into the mountains in the first place to become Shep Hatfield's wife—and, likely, to hide away from the authorities—only to find a man every bit as wicked and shrewd as she herself impersonating the man she'd gone there to marry.

The man, Shep Hatfield, whom Frank Beauregard had killed.

Prophet sat up, chuckling. The laughter made his head ache worse, but he couldn't help it. He leaned forward, took his tender head in his hands, and cut loose with several deep guffaws.

Oh, the irony.

Prophet had thought he'd rescued an innocent rabbit from a snake pit. As it turned out, he'd fished out the vilest serpent in the entire damned hole. Hell, this one had even caused him to tumble for her. Not only tumble for her but to marry her!

Prophet laughed again, gritting his teeth at the cracked bells tolling misery between his ears.

Had she only married him to torture him?

What other reason could there have been? She could have slipped him that nasty potion into his whiskey at any time.

Instead, she'd married him. When she'd risen from bed this morning to abscond with Beauregard's loot, she'd been unfortunate enough to run into the deputy U.S. marshal who'd been sent down from Denver to retrieve it. So, probably having waited for the man to give his back to her, she'd broken that pitcher over his head.

"Oh, Christ," Prophet growled, rising tenderly and walking over to the window. He shoved the flowered curtain aside and stared down into the street, which was brightly sunlit now. Squinting, trying to dull the javelins of agony piercing his pupils, he stared into the country beyond Broken Knee.

Where had she gone?

As his eyes surveyed the countryside and anger and humiliation continued to flare inside him, he was vaguely aware of another emotion, as well.

Worry.

After what she'd done to him? After she'd double-crossed and poisoned him and killed St. Vincent?

Why worry about her?

It made no sense. But by god, he did.

Probably because he still knew her as young, innocent

Mathilda Anderson from St. Paul, Minnesota, and hadn't quite worked his mind around whom she really was. He hadn't had time.

When he'd tamped down his emotions and began to let some clear thinking sift its way through his battered brain plate, he realized he couldn't lounge around here all day, licking his wounds. She'd taken the money, and he had to get it back.

Also, despite what she'd done, and because she had meant so much to him, and because he for some reason didn't want to believe that just a little of Mattie Anderson didn't genuinely exist somewhere inside whoever she really was, he couldn't let the McCourts hang her. He had to run her down himself, secure the Beauregard loot once again, and bring her to justice—alive.

Maybe most of all, he had to hear her story from her own mouth. Until then, he might never be able to truly believe it.

He began stumbling around looking for his clothes, still about half drunk, he realized. He felt as though he'd not only been poisoned but brained by something large and hard. He also realized his feelings were hurt.

Had it really all been a sham?

He had to see her. He had to hear from her own lips, which had once tasted so sweet . . .

He dressed and buckled his shell belts around his waist—one for the Peacemaker, the other for the Winchester. He looped the Richards over his head and right shoulder, taking one more slow appraisal of the room that had seen so much happiness—at least on his part—only a few hours ago but that had suddenly turned into a hall of mirrors as well as a death and torture chamber.

He drew his hat down low on his forehead, went out, and descended the stairs to the little lobby where Pop Calloway sat in a deep leather chair, a water glass half-filled with what looked like whiskey in one hand, an old *Rocky Mountain News* in the other.

"Did you have that head looked at?" Prophet asked him.

"By who?" Calloway said with a scowl. He looked Prophet up and down, the bounty hunter loaded for bear. "You goin' after her?"

"Sure as hell."

Prophet opened the door.

"She was a pretty little thing, wasn't she?"

Prophet glanced back at Pop, who pursed his lips and shook his head in bewilderment. The old man's expression summed up the bounty hunter's own feelings on the subject so simply and poignantly that he had to swallow down a taut lump in his throat.

He went out and, squinting against the brassy western sunshine, crossed the street at an angle, heading for the livery barn. He saddled Mean and Ugly, slid his Winchester into its saddle scabbard, and hung the Richards from the horn. He bit out a curse when he remembered that in his addlepated state, he'd left his bedroll and saddlebags in his room. Sometimes he stowed that peripheral gear with his saddle and his horse, sometimes he took them to his hotel room. This time, because he hadn't been sure how long he'd be in Broken Knee, he'd taken them to his room.

He left Mean ground-tied a few yards inside the barn's open double doors, returned to the hotel, and retrieved the bags and bedroll. When he dropped back down to the hotel lobby, Pop's empty glass sat on the broad arm of the chair. The old man's head was drooping toward his chest and he was snoring.

Prophet gave a wry chuff and headed outside.

As he crossed the hotel's small front veranda, a man in a long, brown linen duster and tan Stetson and holding a Winchester up high across his chest walked out of the livery barn's interior shadows. He stopped between the open front doors and cocked the rifle loudly.

"Hold it right there, Prophet, you son of a bitch!"

Prophet thought he recognized the voice but he couldn't place the man's face. It didn't help that he was obscured by the thick shadows cast by the livery barn above and behind him. Prophet was in no mood for introductions.

He stuck two fingers into his mouth and gave a short, high whistle.

From inside the barn rose a horse's whinny. Hooves thudded. Mean and Ugly burst out of the shadows behind the man standing between the open doors. The man swung his head in surprise, but he didn't get his rifle turned before the horse bulled into him from behind.

The man screamed as the horse hammered him to the ground and then trampled him, sending him rolling in a cloud of dust, his hat and rifle flying. Mean galloped to the hotel, reins leaping along the ground behind him. Prophet jumped down the hotel's steps in a single bound, grabbed the horn, poked his left boot through the stirrup, and swung into the saddle.

"Let's go, boy—*hy-ahhh!*"

As the dun leaped off its rear hooves into an instant, ground-devouring gallop, lunging forward with each thrust of its shod hooves, Prophet leaned down and grabbed up the reins. He'd just gotten both ribbons in his left hand when he saw movement ahead and left—a man stepping around the side of an old false building façade, holding a rifle. As the man began lowering the rifle's barrel, aiming toward the street, Prophet snapped up his Peacemaker, aiming at an angle across his chest.

He cut loose three quick shots, unable to aim accurately from his jouncing, fast-moving perch. He heard at least one bullet hammer the façade with a dull thud. One of the other two must have hit its mark. The man screamed, *"Shit!"*

The rifle clattered to the roof. As Prophet galloped on past the façade, heading south along Broken Knee's main street, he glanced back to see the shooter turn a somersault off the building's roof to land on his back in the street, where he lay without moving.

Beyond him, the man Mean had nearly ground to dust and horse apples was up and running toward Prophet, raising his rifle and shouting, though Prophet couldn't hear what he was saying above the thunder of Mean's pounding hooves. Prophet triggered his Peacemaker's last three shots along his back trail, and the man with the rifle ducked and ran for cover.

Prophet holstered the Colt and crouched low over the dun's billowing mane as Mean chewed up the trail, the terrain dancing past on both sides.

"Now, who in the hell was *that*?"

Chapter Ten

Three months later . . .

Prophet leaned forward against the remote Mexican cantina's bullet-scarred table and probed his bandaged forehead with his fingers. He winced at the pain shooting back through his temple to his left ear.

His poor head had taken more abuse in the past few months than most pumpkins on any given Halloween . . .

Glancing up and peering into the smoky room's dense shadows, he said, "Don't look now, *chiquita,* but a couple of your admirers are about to present themselves. They look a little miffed they missed your coming-out party."

Two Mexicans had risen from a round table in a rear corner of the earthen-floored room. One stood hitching up his dirty canvas trousers while the other stood staring through the smoky gloom toward Louisa, mashing out his cornhusk quirley on the table near his wooden *pulque* cup. He blew two streams of smoke through his nostrils.

He stretched his lips back from his teeth, though there was no white there to speak of, which meant either that his teeth were far from white or he didn't have any. When he and his *amigo,* who was six inches shorter than he, walked up to his and Louisa's table, Prophet saw that he did indeed have teeth, but no front ones. The only teeth visible were a couple of poor chipped leaning stubs poking up from the bottom gums and two grim-encrusted eyeteeth poking down from the upper gums.

One of the eyeteeth had been broken in half.

Both men wore long, black mustaches. Their hair was long and peppered with lice. Sombreros dangled down both Mexicans' backs from thongs around their necks. Their dark-brown eyes were rheumy from too much *pulque* or tequila, which were the only drinks served at the cantina, though Prophet would have killed for a cold ale.

"Pardon us, *amiga, amigo*—we don't mean to interrupt," said the tall Mexican, whose face was long and horselike, his badly sunken cheeks so pitted, he looked as though he'd taken a load of double-ought buck from close range. He seemed handy with English, albeit with a heavy accent. A border *bandito,* most likely.

He opened his mouth to continue, but Louisa interrupted him with a very cool, "You are interrupting."

The tall Mexican's ingratiating smile faded without a trace. His round-faced friend made a gurgling sound in his chest, his thick hands sliding slowly around on his cartridge-laden shell belt. Both men wore two visible pistols in old but well-oiled holsters.

"We interrupt only to offer you good money, *señorita.* You see, it is seldom we get a pretty *gringa* down this way."

"Oh, boy," Prophet groaned, leaning forward and taking his head in his hands again. Softly, he said, "Backwater, friend. *Por favor,* just backwater." The last thing he needed at the moment was more trouble.

"What does he say?" asked the shorter Mexican. "Back . . . the . . . water . . . ?" He glanced at his taller friend. "No *comprendo.*"

"What he's saying, *amigos,*" Louisa said, "is it would take a whole lot more money than you two could ever make in your entire lowly, miserable lives—even if you lived to be a hundred, which I doubt will happen—for me to join you out in the stable yonder . . . which I gather is what you're asking, right?"

"Oh, boy," Prophet groaned again.

The two Mexicans stared down at Louisa in grave silence. There were several other customers in the cantina, and they'd been conversing in low tones.

Now, however, silence descended on the room. Smoke billowed from cigarettes and cigars. It hung like several giant spider webs, and it smelled like pepper. A couple of beams of bright, golden sunlight angled through the cantina's two dirty windows, making the shadows even murkier in contrast.

Flies buzzed.

Somewhere in the room, someone broke wind.

Outside, a mule brayed distantly.

"You are most impolite, *chiquita,*" said the taller Mexican.

"I am."

"Most impolite," said the shorter Mexican, who had an absurdly round face and no chin to speak of. "We might be able to overlook it, *chiquita,* if you were to join us in the stable. I believe you will enjoy it. In fact, we think you can do much better than how you are doing here . . . with this big, ugly *gringo* who looks stupid and smells bad."

He slid his fishy, brown eyes toward Prophet.

"Hey, now," Prophet said, indignant. He lifted an arm to sniff the pit.

"Oh, I know I can do better," Louisa said. "Believe me, I'm on the scout. But you two toothless privy rats are not the ones to trim my wick. So, as my friend here says, backwater unless you have a hankering to turn belly up."

The tall man sucked air between his grimy eyeteeth, narrowing his eyes. Both gestures were snakelike. The shorter Mexican compressed his lips. His eyes blazed. A nerve twitched in his left cheek.

Prophet sighed. "Now, fellas . . ."

He intended to say more but then the taller Mexican slapped

his right hand to the holster positioned for the cross-draw on his left hip. Prophet didn't know how she did it, but the Vengeance Queen managed to lift one of her own silver Peacemakers without appearing even to move. Even to twitch. It was as though time stopped for one second, and when it picked up again a second later, she had that pretty popper up and roaring, stabbing yellow flames into the dingy room.

Pow-Pow! Pow!

The room seemed to jerk with each deafening blast.

The tall Mex twisted around and dropped to one knee. He'd taken the first two shots in the gullet. The stocky Mexican flew straight back, rolling ass over teakettle over the table behind him, where two older Mexicans had been playing a bone game, before, realizing they were in the line of a lead storm, they'd scrambled to safety.

"Dog-fucking *puta* bitch!" the taller Mexican wailed, trying to bring his long-barreled Schofield around.

Still sitting, Louisa aimed straight out over the table, narrowing one eye and compressing her lips. Her Colt roared again. The bullet painted a puckered purple whole in the taller Mexican's forehead, punching him down hard on the floor where he lay on his back, quivering.

Prophet looked around the room, the Colt still smoking in Louisa's hand. She was waiting to see if any of the other customers were going to join the fray. None did. In fact, the place emptied itself out in about five seconds, six or seven men scrambling out both the front and rear doors. One fleeing customer knocked against a table in his haste, tipping over a cup.

Liquid dribbled onto the floor.

Suddenly, Prophet and Louisa were the only ones in the cantina. Except for the rotund *hombre* who ran the place. He rose heavily, breathing hard, from where he'd cowered behind one of the stout barrels holding up his makeshift bar. The big man surveyed the room with a sigh, then ambled out to begin dragging off the dead, taller Mexican who was adding the fetor of fresh blood and viscera to the cantina's potpourri of wretched stenches.

The bartender cast several skeptical gazes toward the Vengeance Queen, who flicked open her Colt's loading gate. She shook the spent cartridges onto the table, where they rolled around between Prophet's tin cup of tequila and Louisa's tin cup of water. (She did not imbibe in "spirituous liquids" and looked down her nose at those who did.)

"Now, where were we before we were so grievously interrupted?" she asked, knocking the last empty shell casing out of her Colt's wheel.

"You were going to tell me where Mattie was."

"No." Louisa set four fresh cartridges from her shell belt onto the table, bullet end up. "You were telling me about Wolcott."

Prophet sighed. Nothing got past his partner. "Well, it was him who ripped down on me in Broken Knee. I thought I recognized the voice but I couldn't see his face or no Pinkerton badge. The other fella—the one I drilled—was Wolcott's Pinkerton partner, Harrison Lamb. Wolcott took it right personal, Mean and Ugly stompin' him into the dirt and then me killin' Lamb, though if I hadn't killed him he for damn sure would have killed me.

"Stupid son of a bitches didn't leave me no choice. They could have just talked polite, and then Wolcott wouldn't have had to chase me across the country and into Mexico. But I reckon he thought I had . . . and still have . . . the Beauregard loot. That I killed St. Vincent to keep the loot for myself!"

Prophet threw back half his tequila shot and watched the big bartender drag the shorter Mexican out the back door, again casting wary looks toward the Vengeance Queen, who ignored him.

"Then you headed to Denver," Louisa said.

"I followed three sets of tracks to Denver. Mattie's and the tracks of the McCourts. Lost them there in that mess of humanity Denver is becoming. You know, if it weren't for the good liquor and even better parlor girls, I'd never step foot in that smelly perdition."

Prophet looked at Louisa. She stared at him as though he were a saddle gall she was trying to figure how to medicate.

"Anyway," he said, "as I was sayin' . . . I headed north to Cheyenne. A ticket agent told me a girl matching Mattie's description had headed up that way. Well, that turned out to be a wild goose chase. Finding neither hide nor hair of her up that way, I headed back to Denver and did some detective work. Turns out she and both McCourts had been spotted by a couple railroad employees boarding trains for parts south. Apparently the McCourts were hard on her heels. I figured the old rancher had been right, after all—she was headed home."

Prophet looked up and cleared his throat when the bartender came back in, huffing and puffing as though he'd run a long ways. "Pardon me, *amigo.*" He held up his empty cup and gave a beseeching grin. *"Por favor . . . ?"*

The sweating, breathless barman came over, muttering Spanish epithets under his breath and casting more dubious glances Louisa's way, and replenished Prophet's drink. The bounty hunter quickly threw half of it back. He knocked his cup against the barman's bottle, before the man could walk away. The man eyed the level of the tangle-leg in the bottle, gave his head a single wag, and splashed more tequila into the bounty hunter's cup.

He turned away and held out his hand for payment.

Prophet dug into his jeans pocket and placed a gold coin in

the man's thick palm.

"You're a good man," Prophet told the barman as he shuffled off. "Sorry about my partner here. She has the social skills of a snake-bit grizzly with its ass on fire."

"You're getting drunk," Louisa accused him.

"Medicine." He pointed at the bandage on his forehead.

Louisa rolled her eyes. "You headed south from Denver on the train. That was nearly three months ago."

"Well, I lost Mattie's and the McCourts' trail somewhere in New Mexico. I ended up getting some more bad information that sent me into northern Arizona. Before I could get back on the right trail again, Wolcott caught up to me. Or got close. As did a couple of deputy U.S. marshals. Apparently, there is now a three-thousand-dollar bounty on my head for the murder of George Patrick St. Vincent as well as the Pinkerton, Harry Lamb . . . not to mention the little matter of the Beauregard loot, which I ain't seen since Mattie poisoned me back in Broken Knee and lit out with it."

Louisa rolled her eyes, shook her head, nudged her hat off her head to let it dangle down her back, and caressed her temples.

Prophet said, "You think *you* got a headache. Now you know how *I* feel! It took me all of six weeks to shake that Pinkerton and the U.S. marshals, and just after I finally did and picked up Mattie's trail again—thank the good Lord you don't see too many pretty young ladies traveling alone in the southwest—Wolcott picked up my sign in southern Colorado. Only now he was runnin' with a small army of Mexican and *yanqui* cut-throats! Boy now, there's a feller that holds a grudge! He followed me all the way down here!"

Prophet reached over and closed his hand around Louisa's left forearm. "She's down here, isn't she? I heard from a couple of furloughed soldiers they seen a pretty gal dressed to the nines and fitting Mattie's description heading for the border some months back. She asked them where she might be able to hire a couple of troubleshooters to guide her into Mexico."

"She's down here," Louisa said.

"How do you know?"

"After I left you and your"—Louisa smiled ironically, caustically—"*gal* in Dead Skunk Gulch, I headed south myself. I got as far as Lordsburg and decided to head back north. I had a funny feeling about you and this gal of yours."

"A jealous feelin' you mean." Prophet smiled and sipped his tequila.

"No," Louisa said, wrinkling a nostril in disgust at him. "It wasn't jealousy. I always figured that if you decided to settle down and get hitched it would likely be to some pretty vixen who'd pull the wool over your eyes and leave you in a howling heap, just as it turned out this girl did."

"I might have howled for a while, but I pulled out of the heap."

"It doesn't look like it to me."

"God, I missed you!" he said with irony.

Louisa raised her water cup in mock salute. "Of course you did."

Prophet leaned forward. "Where is she?"

Louisa opened her mouth to speak, but just then a faint rumbling rose in the distance. It grew gradually until Prophet began to feel the vibration through the floor beneath his boots.

"What the hell is that?" he said, turning to a dirty front window.

Chapter Eleven

As the rumbling grew loud enough for Prophet to recognize the thunder of many horses, the barman gasped and shuffled through a curtained doorway behind the bar. He returned a moment later hefting a five-gallon wooden bucket in both hands. Milky *pulque* lapped over the top of the bucket, dribbling onto the floor. The barman lifted the bucket onto the bar as the horseback riders galloped into the yard fronting the cantina.

As Prophet and Louisa watched through the window, the fifty or so riders reined up in the yard, clay-colored dust billowing around them. Their horses—all short, willowy mustangs—were sweat-leathered and mud-streaked. They'd been ridden hard a long way.

"Well, I'll be damned," Prophet said, apprehension tickling the base of his spine.

The riders gathered in the yard were all dressed in similar dove-gray uniforms as those of the men Prophet and Louisa had left in bloody heaps along their back trail, maybe five miles away from this lonely cantina servicing a mountain crossroads. This larger group was led by a tall, lean drink of water with a colonel's gold eagle insignia on his shoulders and gold braid trimming the crown of his straw sombrero, also decked out with the insignia of the Mexican Rural Police.

"Rurales," Prophet said, raking a hand across his mouth. "Shit."

He was glad now that Louisa had had the foresight to leave

her wagon with its contraband Gatling gun in a draw behind the cantina, partly concealed by mesquite brush. Still, he reached down to the holster thonged on his right thigh, intending to unsnap the keeper thong from over his Peacemaker's hammer.

He stayed the movement when Louisa said softly over the rim of her water cup, "Relax, Lou. Enjoy your tequila."

Prophet frowned at her. *"Rurales."*

"I know."

"You know these fellas?"

"By reputation only—so far."

Prophet was about to ask her what she meant by that, but then something caught his attention out the window. The colonel gigged his grullo mustang over to where Prophet's mount was tied to a hitchrack in the shade of a sprawling cedar. The colonel examined Prophet's horse, noting the Richards hanging by its lanyard from the saddle horn. The bounty hunter wished he'd had the foresight to hang the gut-shredder around his neck where it could do him some good.

However, down here in Mexico displaying too many weapons could mean to some you were asking for trouble, and he'd meant to avoid as much more of that as possible. Instead, he'd tied Mean where he could keep an eye on both the horse and the Richards and his Winchester.

Prophet's gut tightened as the colonel leaned down for a closer look at the shotgun. The bounty hunter's gut tightened another couple of notches when the man plucked the shotgun off the horn, hung it over his right shoulder, then, with a grim set to his mouth beneath a dragoon-style, black mustache, galloped over to the front of the cantina. He swung lithely out of his saddle and tossed his reins up to a young *rurale* wearing a corporal's stripes on his sleeves.

He said something in Spanish too rapid-fire for Prophet to

make out. Two young *rurales* swung down from their saddles. So did one older man, a sergeant in his fifties. He was shaggy-headed and fat. He wore a bowie knife in a scabbard strapped to one of the cartridge bandoliers crossed on his lumpy chest.

The apprehension tingling along Prophet's spine grew more keen. He lifted his cup to his lips, sipping the tequila.

As he did, the colonel clomped up onto the stoop fronting the cantina and then pushed brashly through the swinging front doors. Spurs rang in belligerent tones. The four underlings marched in behind the colonel, the two youngest men moving to the bar where the barman was just then setting a gourd dipper onto the planks beside the bucket.

The two young *rurales* hefted the bucket off the bar, one also grabbing the dipper. They carried it between them as they headed outside to the cheers of the other *rurales* now eagerly dismounting their sweaty mustangs.

Meanwhile, the colonel and the fat sergeant stood near the bar, staring into the shadows obscuring Prophet and Louisa, where the two bounty hunters sat in the room's front corner, near the window, their backs to the wall. The colonel held Prophet's savage-looking shotgun in both hands across his chest, as though to show it off. The leather lanyard/shell belt hung down against the *rurale's* flat belly.

Louisa stared stonily back at the man from beneath the brim of her Stetson. Prophet did likewise. He could sense the Vengeance Queen's calm collection as she sat there to his left. He doubted it was an act. She had the nerves of a puma, Louisa did.

His own guts, however, were twisting around like baby snakes. He'd spent enough time in Mexico to know the reputation of the *rurales*. He'd crossed trails and locked horns with them more than a couple of times. If he was the type to notch his pistol grips, his .45 would be notched with more than a few for the *rurales* he'd left dancing with el diablo.

More than just those still giving up their ghosts along his recent back trail . . .

The colonel strode forward, squeezing Prophet's barn blaster in his long-fingered, gloved hands. The *rurale* officer was darkly handsome but with copper-tinged eagle eyes. A strange cipher—a double cross jutting from the base of a horizontal figure eight—was tattooed on his forehead. The sergeant walked along beside him but not with near as much grace as did the tall colonel, who stopped about six feet away from Prophet's and Louisa's table.

He appraised the two *gringos* for a time, the brunt of his attention lingering on the comely *gringa,* before saying in nearly unaccented English, "And you are . . . ?"

Prophet said quickly, "Bill Smith. This is Annabelle House. We're American." Bill Smith, long dead, had been a friend of his during the war. Annabelle House had been a pretty girl he'd sparked back in Georgia. The names had somehow leaped onto Prophet's tongue.

"Of course you are," the colonel said coldly, his eyes sliding quickly back to Louisa.

Prophet said, "And you are . . . ?"

"I am Colonel Rafael Treviño Quintero. I am in charge of this area. That means I am always on the lookout for people who should not be here. More specifically, *gringos* who have crossed the border without papers." He extended his right hand. "May I see your papers, *por favor* . . . Señor Smith and Señorita House?"

Oh shit, Prophet said to himself, glancing at the double-barreled gut-shredder now resting in the crook of the colonel's left arm.

Prophet gave a wooden smile and began sliding his right hand back down toward his Colt. "Now, look, Colonel. Surely we can work this—"

Louisa cut him off with: "I believe our mutual acquaintance, *Doña* Nazaria Salazar, will vouch for my and Mister Smith's authorization, Colonel Quintero." She offered a self-assured half-smile and raised her cup to her lips.

"Ah," said the colonel, a line cutting into the skin between his eyes, slightly ruffing the strange tattoo. "*Doña* Nazaria." He scrutinized Louisa more closely, and then Prophet, who was smiling mildly but holding his breath, his trigger finger itching as it rested on his thigh above his Colt. "Well, then. *Sí.*"

He leaned forward and placed the shotgun on the table. "I will leave you folks to your beverages and wish you a delightful stay in our fair country."

He lifted his hat by its crown, gave Louisa a lascivious wink, and reset the hat on his head. He turned and glanced commandingly at the sergeant, whose own dark eyes were riveted on the comely *gringa,* and started toward the door.

The sergeant smiled as he continued to stare at Louisa, as though he was wanting to say something but wasn't sure what. Something told Prophet the sergeant had about as much of a working knowledge of English as the bounty hunter had of Spanish.

Finally, the sergeant smiled, parroted the colonel's hat gesture, and hurried off to rejoin his superior outside, where their lesser lights were taking turns dippering up the *pulque* while their horses drew water from stock troughs.

Prophet turned to Louisa, frowning. "Not that I mind the name-dropping, mind you—hellfire, not at all—but who on God's green earth is this Sister Nazaria . . . ?"

"Salazar," Louisa said, calmly sipping her water and staring across the room with a bland expression. She kept her voice low, even. "Later, Lou. Later."

Prophet glanced out the window, where Quintero was just

now dippering up his own portion of *pulque* while the lower ranking men conversed in jovial tones around him, some tending their tack or their horses or both. After what seemed an hour but was probably only fifteen or twenty minutes, the *rurales* tightened their saddle cinches, dropped the gourd into the empty *pulque* bucket, mounted up, and rode away to the east in the same way they'd ridden in—as though the devil's hounds were nipping at their heels.

Prophet let out a long sigh of relief. "Now, what in the hell was that?"

"My, you're chatty these days," Louisa said, rising quickly from her chair and adjusting her Colts on her hips, beneath the striped serape. "Since you've gotten hitched, I can hardly get two words in edgewise. Come on!"

"*What?*" Prophet stared incredulously after her as she took long strides, her spurs chinging raucously, across the room and out the door. He stared after her, scowling his indignation. "Wait! What in tarnation . . . ?"

He stopped just outside the cantina as Louisa continued taking those long strides on those well-turned legs, the legs of a young woman accustomed to riding roughshod in the saddle, toward a crumbling thatch-roofed adobe stable. She pulled one of the stable doors open and disappeared inside.

Prophet swung the Richards over his head and shoulder and strode toward the stable. He stopped to peer through the open door just as Louisa appeared in the thick interior shadows, mounted atop her brown-and-white pinto, which she'd apparently left there, saddled.

Louisa kicked the other door open, and the pinto broke into a lunging gallop.

"Come on, Lou! Quit lollygagging!"

"Christ—where to *now*?"

"You want to find your wife, don't you?"

Prophet stared after her, a cloud of dust quickly obscuring her retreating, jostling figure. "Of course, I do!"

Louisa glanced over her shoulder at him, and beckoned. "Then come on, you lummox!" She and the pinto dropped down a slope and were gone.

"Shit!" Prophet ran over to where Mean and Ugly stood hitched, eyeing his rider skeptically. "Your guess is as good as mine, ole son."

He swiped the reins off the hitchrack, swung into the leather, and touched the dun with his spurs. Mean lunged into a rocking gallop, and soon Prophet was eating the Vengeance Queen's dust.

When he drew up to within twenty yards of her, it became apparent that she was, in turn, eating the *rurales'* dust. In fact, as he gained the top of a low, rocky rise, he could see the gray-clad *rurales* a quarter mile ahead, pulling a thick, tan dust cloud along behind them.

They were galloping full out, leaning forward across the jostling manes of their mounts. They were crossing a rocky desert valley colored red by the sandstone formations cropping up around them. Far beyond loomed a high, dark ridge running north to south along the horizon. Around Prophet, charcoal-gray shadows stretched a little longer every minute as the sun quartered westward.

Here and there in isolated pockets were the saffrons and the salmon greens of desert flora. Prophet heard the fleeting ratcheting of an indignant rattlesnake somewhere to his right, and then it was gone as the desert wheeled past him.

The bounty hunter wasn't sure how far he and his partner had traveled—a couple of miles, at least—before they neared the top of a low rise, and Louisa checked her pinto down ahead of him. Prophet blew a sigh of relief as he pulled back on his reins. Mean and Ugly gave his own grateful whicker. The horse had more bottom than any other mount Prophet had known, but he wasn't accustomed to the desert, and Prophet had felt the horse tiring beneath him.

The heat beat down relentlessly out of a sky the color of a newly minted penny.

Louisa led the pinto off to the right of the old freight road they'd been following. She tied the pinto in the shade of a high jumble of desert boulders about forty yards from the trail. Prophet did likewise with Mean, and looked at Louisa. She doffed her hat, sleeving sweat from her forehead.

"What's goin' on?" Prophet wanted to know.

But she only said, "Come on," a little breathlessly and then swung around and began climbing the rise. "Bring your glass."

Prophet cursed again, wearily. His head aching dully, he fished his spyglass out of his saddlebags and followed her.

At the crest of the rise, he stopped and dropped to a knee to Louisa's left. They both crouched behind a buttress of solid sandstone, but there was a three-foot gap in the rock between them. When she doffed her hat to lie belly down and stare through the gap, Prophet did likewise.

He gazed down the other side of the rise from which he now heard the crackling of gunfire. Louisa reached over and plucked his hide-wrapped spyglass out of his hand, shucked it from the case, and telescoped it. She aimed the glass to the north.

The yips and yowls of crazed men now joined the frenzied pops of gunfire. A woman screamed shrilly.

"Good Christ," Prophet said, gritting his teeth as he slitted his eyes against the sun's watery haze. "What in hell is happening down there?"

Louisa shoved the glass at him. "Take a look."

Prophet glanced at her dubiously, then pressed the glass up to his right eye. As he adjusted the focus, several wagons swung into view. They were lined out on a dull yellow trail cleaving the valley and obscured by chaparral. The *rurales* were spread out widely now, descending on the freight train. Smoke puffed from the barrels of their pistols and rifles as they fired on the freighters.

The freighters, some wearing steeple-crowned sombreros, were firing back, the wagons stopped, several men running out from the wagons and returning fire. The *rurales* continued to whoop and holler like marauding Apaches.

As Prophet watched, two freighters went down in a hail of gunfire. Another man, standing in the driver's boot of the second of the three covered wagons, jerked back clutching his belly. He dropped his rifle, then stumbled forward to pitch face first onto the ground.

A young, dark-skinned woman in a low-cut Mexican blouse stood where the dead man had been standing a second ago. She was screaming and gesturing beseechingly with her arms. One of Quintero's men rode up to the wagon, grabbed her skirt, and pulled her out of the boot. He rode away with the girl kicking and screaming as she lay belly down across the pommel of his saddle.

The shooting and yelling and screaming continued for another five minutes. Then the shooting dwindled to random, intermittent pops. Through the sphere of magnified vision, Prophet watched three *rurales* leap into the driver's boot of each wagon. Soon, all three wagons were barreling in Prophet's direction, the horseback *rurales* leading the way.

Behind them, the elongated lumps of eight or nine men lay unmoving in the desert.

Prophet lowered the spyglass, reducing it. The sun was liable to reflect off the lens and give away his and Louisa's position.

"What in the hell?" he asked Louisa. "So, the *rurales* are up to no good. Attacking freight trains headed for the border, most like. What's this got to do with Mattie?"

Louisa rose and walked over to a large boulder leaning out from the crest of the rise. The thunder of the *rurales* grew louder. Louisa placed her hand on the side of the boulder and leaned out away from it to stare toward where the trail cut through the escarpment.

The hoofbeats continued to grow louder. Beneath them came the frenetic clattering of the wagons.

The *rurales* appeared about fifty yards beyond where Prophet and Louisa waited behind the boulder. Quintero was at the head of the pack galloping back in the direction from which they'd come. Two of the riders held squirming young women across their saddles.

A few seconds after the last of the horseback riders galloped back toward the west, the first of the wagons appeared, the *rurale* driver cracking a blacksnake over the backs of the four mules in the traces.

Then the second wagon appeared. Then the third. The mules ran full out, ears laid back against their heads.

The wagons barreled off after the horseback *rurales.*

Soon Prophet could only see the white canvas covers of the wagons, only barely hear the receding thunder of hooves and ironshod wheels. Louisa pushed away from the boulder. She'd started to head back to her pinto, but Prophet grabbed her arm and pulled her toward him.

"Enough of this, goddamnit! Where is she?"

Louisa regarded him gravely, shaking her head once. "I lied. I don't know. But we're about to find out. The *rurales* will take us to her."

"How do you know?"

"Trust me."

Louisa jerked her arm free of Prophet's grip and continued toward where their horses were tied in the shade of the upward thrust of boulders.

Louisa had taken half a dozen sure steps when she stopped with a surprised gasp.

A man had just stepped out from a boulder ahead of her. A lean, mustached man in canvas trousers and suspenders over a dark wool shirt to which was pinned the copper shield of a Pinkerton agent.

Agent Dean Wolcott loudly cocked the Winchester in his hands and said, "Hold it right there, Vengeance Queen. The goose chase is over."

CHAPTER TWELVE

Prophet began to slide his hand toward his .45.

"Nuh-uh—don't do that, Prophet." The voice had come from Prophet's right, where two more men stepped out of the shade of another boulder. "I'd have to kill you, and it ain't nice to poison buzzards." He squinted skyward. "Even if they is just Mescin buzzards."

This was Deputy U.S. Marshal Merle Krueger—a big, ugly man with small, seedy eyes and a girlish mouth. The man standing next to him, broader, shorter, and darker, was Krueger's half-breed tracker, Stew Pot. His real name was Isaiah Smoking Kettle but his love for food, as proven by his sagging belly, had inspired someone somewhere in Smoking Kettle's past to hang the Stew Pot handle on him.

He didn't seem to mind. He was always smiling. He wore a flat-brimmed, flat-crowned black hat with a thong of braided crow feathers dangling against his buckskin-clad chest. The hat was trimmed with small bone amulets and dyed porcupine quills. He smiled amiably now, propping one moccasin-clad foot on a rock, while opening and closing his hands around his Sharps carbine, the rear stock resting on his raised thigh.

"You two ain't supposed to be down here," Prophet said. "I'm tellin' the Mexican authorities on you. You're both gonna get taken to the Mexican woodshed, and they don't mollycoddle, these Mexicans."

"You ain't supposed to be down here, either, Proph." Dean

Wolcott's fair face, usually clean-shaven but now owning a good two weeks of sandy whiskers, was badly blistered by the Sonoran sun. "And you're the one headed for the proverbial woodshed . . . for the murder of my friend and partner, Harry Lamb. And for running off with the Beauregard loot."

Prophet said, "Most dogs wouldn't be low enough to call Harry Lamb a friend, Dean. You know that."

"Ain't nice to slight the dead, Proph," Wolcott said, smiling.

"Before you settle up for Lamb, it's my priority to bring the killer of George Patrick St. Vincent to justice," said Krueger in his raspy growl, smiling frigidly at Prophet. "The world's better off with Lamb where he is, though I know that don't make me popular with you, Wolcott, to say so, but this bounty hunter killed a federal marshal."

"I didn't kill St. Patrick," Prophet said. "And I didn't run off with the Beauregard loot."

"Oh, no?" said Krueger. "Then who did?"

Prophet winced, raking a thumbnail down his unshaven cheek. "My . . . wife."

"Oh, sure—blame the women." Stew Pot spoke with the odd rhythms of the Northern Plains Indian, cheeks deeply dimpled as he grinned. "That's the way to do it, Prophet." He winked at the bounty hunter.

Wolcott said, "All right, all right—enough palaver for the moment. You two unbuckle your cartridge belts and toss them over to Krueger. Any fast moves by either one of you, and I'll drill you." He stared pointedly at Louisa. "Don't think I won't, Miss Bonaventure. You and I have never met." He grinned lewdly as his eyes dropped to Louisa's chest. "If we had, I'd remember. But I've heard your reputation, so I'm on my toes with you as I am with your big, ugly friend back there."

"You ain't so purty yourself, Dean." Unbuckling his shell belt, Prophet gazed at the bloody bandage wrapped around

Wolcott's neck, above his tightly wound and knotted red neckerchief.

The man also had a nasty gash slanting diagonally across his left cheek. Both wounds courtesy of Louisa's friends, the bounty hunter assumed.

"And that bullet burn on your face could use some stitches, looks like, or you're gonna be even less purty than you are now."

He tossed his gun belt over to where Krueger and Stew Pot were standing about fifteen feet to his right.

"Don't worry about me, Prophet," Wolcott said, keeping his rifle aimed at the two bounty hunters. "You just better hope the hangman's in a generous mood the day he hangs you. I hear that executioner they got up in Denver doesn't like to snap a fella's neck right away. Likes to watch him dance. Sick son of a bitch!"

"I killed Lamb in self-defense," Prophet said. "He gave me no choice. And he sure as shit didn't identify himself, just like you didn't." He turned to Krueger. "And I did *not* kill St. Vincent."

"I know, I know—your wife did." Krueger laughed. He tossed a set of handcuffs onto the ground at Prophet's feet, then another set at Louisa's feet. "Put those on."

"Why her?" Prophet looked at Wolcott. "What's she being charged with? All she did was save me from you."

"Then that's what she's charged with," said the Pinkerton. "Saving you from me." His eyes glittered as his gaze danced across Louisa once more. "Besides, she's far too pretty to be on the run alone in Mexico."

"You're a goat," Louisa said.

Prophet looked at the cuffs. His innards recoiled at having his hands bound. He'd be relatively defenseless. Defenseless in Mexico. Christ!

He put the cuffs on. So did Louisa, casting him bitter glances as though this were his fault.

Stew Pot led up Prophet's and Louisa's horses, tossing them each their reins. Then he and Krueger retrieved theirs and Wolcott's mounts. When they were all together again, standing around with their five horses, Krueger said, "Now, all you have to do is lead us to the Beauregard loot, and we'll get the hell out of this godforsaken desert once and for all."

He looked around, shaking his head. "Shit in a bucket—I hate Mexico. I've a mind to write off the loot and head north with Prophet."

Wolcott shook his head and gritted his teeth. "Forget it. It's as much your duty to retrieve the Beauregard loot as it is mine, Krueger."

He wagged his Winchester at Prophet's and Louisa's horses. "Get mounted. No foolin' around, now. The sooner you take us to the loot, the sooner we'll be the hell out of this canker on the devil's ass. Can't say as I like Mexico any better than Krueger does. Them *rurales* was led by Colonel Quintero. He don't like *gringos.* In fact, that gold train they just robbed was haulin' gold north from an American-owned mine."

"We're right friendly with Quintero," Prophet said.

"We know." Krueger grinned. "We was on a hill above the cantina. We had you glassed the whole way." He frowned. "Why was you in such an all-fired hurry to get after him? Has the heat turned your brains to *menudo*? Most folks ride the *other* way when they see Quintero!"

"My partner here," Prophet said. "I think Louisa's taken a shine to him. Somethin' about a man in uniform, I reckon."

Louisa said to Wolcott, "Look, if we follow Quintero, he'll lead us to the loot."

"What're you talkin' about, pretty girl?" This from Krueger, suspiciously. He was sucking on a pebble, rolling it around from one side of his girlish mouth to the other. "Are you tellin' us that Quintero has the Beauregard loot?"

Prophet arched a curious brow at his partner. "Yeah, is that what you're sayin'?"

"In a manner of speaking."

"Why don't you speak it in a manner we can understand?" Wolcott narrowed his eyes at the pretty bounty hunter, keeping his carbine aimed at her breasts pushing out her serape in twin delectable cones. "Unless you're just tryin' to lead us into a hell we ain't likely to get shed of . . . so that you two can get the loot for yourselves and have you a fine old time down here in Mexico."

Louisa said, "I don't like the idea of riding into that hell any better than you do, Wolcott. I don't know if Quintero has the loot, but if we follow him, I'm convinced we'll at least be close to it."

"Wait," Krueger said. *"What?"*

"That don't make no sense to me at all," said Wolcott.

"We don't have time to debate it," Louisa said, urgently. "The sooner we get on Quintero's trail, the sooner we'll have the loot." She glanced at Krueger, quirking a wry grin. "And you can take this big, ugly lummox back to Denver and throw him that necktie party you're so fired up about."

Prophet glowered at her.

Krueger looked at Wolcott. Wolcott looked at Krueger.

Wolcott, being the sharper of the pair, and Stew Pot, being a subordinate tracker, seemed to be unofficially in charge. Where Krueger and Stew Pot had met up with Wolcott was anyone's guess and not something Prophet was overly concerned with at the moment. They'd all been after him, believing he'd lead them to the loot, so he supposed their trails had been likely to cross sooner or later.

Krueger hiked a shoulder.

Wolcott wagged his rifle at the horses once more. "All right—get mounted. Don't try anything. I'll have this carbine aimed at your backs the whole way, and I can shoot the eye out of a turkey buzzard in full flight from two hundred yards away!"

"This is goddamn, crazy," Prophet said, riding with his reins in his teeth, his cuffed hands hooked over the saddle horn.

They'd run their horses a quarter of a mile and were now cantering, saving them, following the tracks of the *rurales* as they headed back toward the cantina.

"Pure *loco,*" the bounty hunter said around the reins, glancing at his partner riding just off his right stirrup. "You realize that, don't you?"

"Hey, no talking up there!" Krueger yelled behind Prophet.

Wolcott rode behind Louisa. The half-breed tracker, Stew Pot, took up the rear. As usual, he was grinning as though he had a seedy secret and was wanting to tell but couldn't because then the joy would be gone.

Ignoring Krueger's order, Prophet said to Louisa, "What do them *rurales* have to do with Mattie?"

"Did you hear the good marshal, or didn't you?" Wolcott asked.

"Or are you just trying to buy time?" Prophet said, lowering his voice one octave, keeping his eyes on Louisa. "Is that it?"

The Vengeance Queen was staring over her pinto's head at the ground, frowning. The frown bit deeper into the skin above the bridge of her nose. She drew back on the reins she held in her cuffed hands. "Whoa!" she said, slowing the mount, curveting, blinking against the dust wafting around her.

While the others slowed their own mounts, Louisa neck-reined the pinto into a sharp circle, continuing to cast her puzzled gaze upon the ground. She looked back behind Stew Pot. "They left the trail. We lost their tracks."

She batted her heels against the pinto's ribs and galloped back in the direction from which they'd come, brushing past hers and Prophet's captors.

"Hey, where do you think you're goin'?" Krueger bellowed, raising his Winchester to his shoulder, cocking it.

Prophet ground spurs into Mean's flanks. The dun whinnied and bounded into the side of Krueger's piebald.

The lawman's rifle cracked, flames lapping skyward, as both man and beast screamed. Mean drove them both to the ground. Krueger gave another scream as the piebald landed on his left leg.

"You son of a bitch!" the lawman bellowed as the horse scrambled back to its feet, whickering and shaking itself. The saddle slid down its side. On the ground, Krueger reached for the Colt on his left hip.

Wolcott plunked lead into the ground near Krueger's right hand. Dirt spat across Krueger's broad, ugly face. Shaking his head and blinking grit from his eyes, the lawman left his pistol in its holster and jerked an enraged look at the Pinkerton.

"What the fuck you think you're doin', Wolcott?"

"We're down here for the fuckin' Beauregard loot, you moron! We ain't gonna get it back without Prophet and the split-tail!" Wolcott canted his head toward Louisa sitting her pinto a dozen yards back along the trail, looking bored.

Krueger slid a glare at Prophet. His eyes were as bright as isinglass in direct sunlight.

Wincing against the pain in his right leg, he heaved himself to his feet and turned toward Wolcott. "I think I just figured out why gettin' your slimy Pinkerton hands on the Beauregard loot is so all-fired important to you." He managed a chill grin. "They're offering you a bonus for bringin' it back—ain't they?"

Wolcott regarded him incredulously. Then he smiled, and snorted. "Okay. All right. Sure, they're offering a bonus. The agency has a reputation to uphold. They want the money back at all costs. So they sent me—the best agent in the southwestern district. And, you bet, they're offering a reward to make sure I see the job through to the end. They often do that."

"How much?"

"What?"

"How much cream they gonna plop onto your pie?"

Wolcott flared a nostril. "That's none of your business."

"Listen, you slimy devil," Krueger said. "You want me to help you get the loot back? Well, the loot ain't as important to me as gettin' this killer of a deputy U.S. marshal back to Denver to shake hands with the federal hangman."

"It's in your interest to retrieve the Beauregard loot, too, Krueger." Wolcott leaned forward, jutting his chin with anger. "It's your job!"

Krueger spread his badly chapped lips in a devilish smile. "How much?"

"I told you—none of your business."

Krueger kept smiling. "How much?"

Wolcott stared at him. He glanced at Stew Pot, who sat his horse a ways off the trail, leaning forward against his saddle horn, grinning.

"Four thousand," Wolcott said, barely loud enough to be heard against a sudden breeze gust pelting desert grit against them all.

"I want half," Krueger said.

Wolcott compressed his lips. He looked at Prophet sitting behind Krueger. Krueger's horse had wandered off the trail a ways and stood pulling at a patch of dry brush, its saddle hanging.

"I'll give you a thousand," Wolcott said. "Not a dime more. Now get back on your horse, you simple fool, and—"

"Half. Fifteen-hundred for me. Five hundred fer the breed."

Krueger jerked a thumb at Stew Pot, who didn't seem to mind being relegated to the smallest cut of the pie.

"A thousand. You can two split it however you want."

"Two thousand or I'm gonna take my prisoner back to Denver right now. Me an' Stew Pot. You don't seem near grateful enough to me an' Stew Pot for ridin' up just in time to save you from them Mescins."

"Oh, I think I'm grateful enough. Considering . . ." Wolcott glanced at the rifle he had aimed at the lawman's belly.

"So, what?" Krueger said. "You gonna keep that aimed at both me an' the breed the whole trip? Gonna sleep with one eye open?" He chuckled. "Shit, first chance that savage gets, he's gonna cut your tongue out, dry it on a rock, poke a string through it, and wear it around his neck."

Wolcott narrowed his eyes and flared his nostrils at Krueger. "All right. Half. But you don't deserve a penny of it. You're a disgrace to that moon-and-star you're wearin'. Now, get back on your horse, you ugly bastard."

Limping, casting indignant looks at Prophet, Krueger gathered his rifle and his hat, reset his saddle, and climbed onto his pie's back. He spat and turned to Prophet again. "You and me are gonna have to come to an understandin'."

"Anytime you wanna take these cuffs off, Krueger, we'll do that." Prophet smiled.

Krueger spat again. "Now then," he said, filling his lungs with air. "Where we goin'?"

"The tracks are here," Louisa said, glancing off across the desert. Apparently, the *rurales* had left the trail and were heading south.

Prophet rode up to her. She looked at him fixedly, her blank gaze acknowledging what he'd done for her back there. He shook his head, dismissing it. She'd done the same for him.

They touched spurs to their mounts' flanks and started south.

"Simple fools," she said, glancing over her right shoulder and shaking her head. "Utter, simple fools."

"I heard that!" Krueger yelled behind her.

Chapter Thirteen

"We'd best be careful," Prophet said as long shadows leaned out from towering cliff walls to either side of him, Louisa, and their three unwanted trail mates. "It'll be dark soon. If they haven't gotten to where they're goin', they'll be campin' out. We don't want to ride up on 'em. I'd rather ride up on a pack of Mexican mountain lions dancing over fresh kill than that Quintero. He had a look about him."

He was remembering the strange tattoo, the flat raptorial eyes.

Louisa didn't say anything. She was thinking about something. Prophet wasn't sure what, but he had a feeling that what distracted her was not only the *rurales* or Mattie or the loot they were after.

Wolcott, Krueger, and Stew Pot rode behind him and the Vengeance Queen, looking owly. They were thinking they were being led in circles. If the chase didn't end soon, Prophet knew the pot was going to bubble over, like it almost had when he'd bulled Mean into Krueger, injuring the lawman's leg.

They rode a little farther.

They stopped to water themselves and their horses, taking quick, water-preserving sips from their canteens, then continued riding. When the large fireball of the sun blazed especially brightly from the tip of a towering black western peak, then abruptly disappeared, shadows slid across the copper ground as though some god had knocked over his black ink-bottle.

The shadows spilled clear to the eastern horizon just above which a single star flickered to life.

As Prophet's group topped a rise, the bounty hunter hissed through clenched teeth, "Back, back, back!"

They reined around and galloped several yards back down the rise.

"What is it?" Wolcott said.

"A couple campfires yonder. They must've holed up for the night."

"All right," Louisa said, swinging down from her pinto's back. "That means we camp, too."

"Who's givin' the orders here?" Krueger objected.

"I am." Wolcott tossed his saddle on the ground and looked from Prophet to Louisa. "You two gather firewood. We'll have us a small cook fire. The breeze is out of the south so the *rurales* shouldn't smell the smoke. Stew Pot will tend the horses."

"Stew Pot's my man," Krueger said. "He listens to my orders only."

Tossing his bedroll down by his saddle, Wolcott laughed without mirth.

Krueger nodded at Stew Pot. The grinning half-breed gathered up the reins of all five stripped horses, and led them down the rise.

Prophet turned to Wolcott. He held out his cuffed hands. "If you want us to root around for wood, take these off."

The Pinkerton hiked a hip on a large rock and cocked the Winchester in his hands. "Forget it. Get to it. I don't want you out there in the dark. You might get ideas, though where you'd run to, cuffed in the darkness without your horses, without *water,* would be straight to hell. So keep that in mind."

Prophet cursed under his breath and began stumbling around in the semidarkness, looking for wood. The man had a point. Even if his and Louisa's hands weren't cuffed, running would be counterproductive.

They gathered wood from around a stand of mesquites and palo verdes stippling a shoulder of the rise and lining the meandering wash in which they set up camp. It was a well-protected bivouac, covered on one side by the desert scrub, on the other side by boulders that had likely washed down the ancient streambed when the arroyo was not just sand and gravel flecked with dinosaur bones but a free-flowing watercourse draining the distant mountains.

When they'd gathered enough wood, Wolcott said with customary conceit, "Now, I think I'd like to be served this evening by a woman. Miss Bonaventure, would you do the honors of building a fire? Keep it low now. We don't want any more of your friends running up on us out here. Then I think I could stand some coffee and beans, maybe a little cornbread. You'll find the makings in my saddlebags. I like to come prepared."

He smiled jeeringly and leaned back against a boulder.

Prophet gritted his teeth for the imminent retort but was surprised when Louisa merely smiled and said, "I'd be happy to. But if you want me to be your kitchen slave, I'll need my hands free." She held her cuffed wrists out to Wolcott.

"Forget it."

"Cook your own supper then."

Louisa plopped down by the mounded wood and crossed her legs Indian style. She nudged her hat off her head and shook out her hair.

Krueger laughed. "You want me to make her? I bet I can make her. Shit, I bet I can have her followin' me around like an orphan puppy dog, you give me fifteen minutes back in the brush with her."

"Oh, it wouldn't take you that long," Prophet said.

Krueger puffed out his chest at him. "Remember, you an' me

is gonna understand one another."

Prophet held up his cuffed wrists again. "Any time."

Wolcott scowled down at Louisa. Her blond hair shone in the fading velvet light.

"You are a prime bitch." He looked at Krueger. "Tie Prophet good and tight to that mesquite over there. His ankles, too."

While Stew Pot held his rifle on Prophet, Krueger tied him with his own saddle rope to a mesquite at the edge of the arroyo, wrapping the rope around the tree and Prophet's belly. Then he tied the bounty hunter's ankles together.

When Krueger stepped back, grinning jeeringly at Prophet, Wolcott turned to Louisa.

"Get up."

Louisa rose.

To Krueger, Wolcott said, "Take her cuffs off."

"I'd like to take more than her cuffs off," Krueger said.

While Wolcott stepped back, aiming his carbine at Louisa's belly, Krueger stepped forward a little warily and unlocked the Vengeance Queen's cuffs. As the bracelets fell away from her wrists, she said, "Boo!"

Krueger jerked backwards with a startled grunt.

Louisa smiled.

Wolcott chuckled.

Stew Pot sucked an amused breath through his scraggly teeth.

Krueger glared at Louisa. "How 'bout if I take you off in the brush and teach you some respect?"

"How 'bout if you do that?"

"That's enough," Wolcott said. "Don't tangle with her, Krueger. I got a feelin' you've met your match."

"Oh, you think so, do ya?"

To Louisa, Wolcott said, "Just get a fire going. I'm hungry, an' I need some coffee. I got two extra canteens there—since the men your Mexicans killed had no more use for them."

"You're the boss," Louisa said.

Prophet's lower jaw sagged at her composure. It wasn't like her to take orders from any man without trying to cut his privates off.

As the Vengeance Queen, dutiful as any squaw, set to work building a fire and making supper, Wolcott, Krueger, and Stew Pot sat around with their rifles resting across their knees, watching her. She removed the cumbersome *poncho,* tossed it over a rock, and rolled up the sleeves of her man's cotton shirt. The first several buttons of the shirt were undone, offering a good look at her cleavage and the first swell of her breasts.

She moved like a cat, flexing and stretching as she worked and allowing the shirt to draw taut against her bosoms.

She appeared to be totally immersed in her chores. But Prophet knew that she was very much aware of the lusty, glowering stares of the men seated at three points around her and the short, crackling flames of her supper fire.

When she bent forward, they canted their heads to get a better look at her firm, round ass, which her faded denims caressed lovingly.

Krueger pulled a bottle out of a saddlebag pouch, uncorked it, and took a drink. He smacked his lips and held the bottle up so Prophet could see it in the flickering firelight.

"Want a drink of my firewater, Lou?"

"Sure, I'll have a drink."

Krueger laughed and pulled the bottle back against his chest, cradling it protectively. "Prisoners don't get none. Ha!"

"Krueger, stop pullin' my leg!"

"Pass it over here, Krueger," Wolcott said, reaching for the bottle while keeping his eyes on Louisa.

"Hold on," the lawman said, and took another long pull.

He handed the bottle to Wolcott, who cleaned the bottle's lip thoroughly with his gloved hand before drinking. He passed the whiskey over to Stew Pot.

The men drank and watched Louisa cook. Prophet had to smile, watching her work. He'd never known her to take such interest and care in cooking, but she boiled and then fried a pan of beans like she did it every night, though Prophet knew that when out on the trail she mostly lived on hardtack, wild vegetables, and jerky. She didn't often risk a campfire. She could go a long time without anything to drink except water.

When the beans were done, she bowled them up and passed them around, making sure each man got a good look down her shirt. She brought a smoking bowl and a spoon and a steaming cup of coffee over to Prophet.

"You be careful," he warned her, keeping his voice low. "You hear?"

She offered a coy half-smile, then returned to the fire where she refilled the men's coffee cups from the pot she'd boiled on a tripod.

She took a bowl of food, sat on a rock, crossing her long legs, and ate.

The men ate, grunting and snorting and belching, casting frequent looks at the pretty blonde, the fire's orange flames dancing across her cameo-pin face and glistening in her hair.

"Damn good," Wolcott said, dropping his spoon into his empty bowl and tossing both down at Louisa's feet. "Now you can clean up."

Krueger tossed his own bowl and spoon over to Louisa. "I could get used to havin' a split-tail around the camp. She's right handy."

Louisa pretended to ignore them.

While she cleaned the cooking gear with sand and piled it near the fire, the men passed the bottle around again, and watched her, their eyes hungry and growing hungrier for female companionship.

Louisa stood and stretched, leaning back at the hips, thrusting her breasts out.

"Anything else?" she asked.

Stew Pot got up, handed the whiskey bottle back to Krueger, and walked around the fire to move up on Louisa from behind. He wrapped his arms around her waist and nuzzled her neck.

"Knock it off," Louisa said, briskly, pushing the half-breed away.

"Time for us to take a little walk, see the stars," Stew Pot said.

"You heard her," Wolcott said thickly, watching them. "Knock it off, Stew Pot."

Krueger picked up his rifle, cocked it, and, resting it across his lap, aimed the barrel at Wolcott. "Let him be."

Wolcott frowned at him. "Put that down."

Krueger smiled.

Stew Pot continued to rough up Louisa, who made a good show of being unable to handle him. She groaned and made a show of shoving him away, but he kept clinging to her, pulling her arms down, drawing her back against him while he nuzzled her neck and nibbled her ears.

Go easy, girl, Prophet silently urged his partner. *Be careful, now . . .*

"Take her yonder," Krueger told Stew Pot. "You loosen her up for me, take a little of that hump out of her neck. Make her purr like a kitten for me. That's how I like 'em."

Still standing behind Louisa, Stew Pot suddenly wrapped his arms around her tightly, and lifted her off her feet.

"No!" Louisa said, twisting around and jerking up her right knee, aiming for the half-breed's privates. Stew Pot had been ready for the move. He sidestepped her and renewed his hold on her.

Prophet's gut tightened anxiously. His partner was no longer *pretending* to be manhandled. Stew Pot outweighed her by a good hundred pounds, and her fighting skills were no match for his.

Wolcott, whose rifle leaned against the rock he was sitting on, glared at Krueger. "Call him off, you fool. She's the only one who can lead us to the Beauregard loot!"

"You worry too much, Wolcott. We're just gonna take some sass out of her, that's all. She'll still lead us to the Beauregard loot. You bet she will!"

Again, Louisa tried to knee Stew Pot, but he kept his legs pressed too tightly against hers. She jerked her head back, managing to draw her arm back out of his grip. She swung her right fist forward.

It cracked sharply across his left cheek.

Stew Pot laughed. Then the laughter was gone and he shaped a savage expression before backhanding Louisa so hard that the smack sounded like a small-caliber pistol shot.

"Oh!" Louisa said.

Her head whipped back, hair obscuring her face.

"You bastard!" Prophet turned to Krueger. "You get him off of her, Krueger. You'll get no Beauregard loot unless you call that dog off her right now!"

Krueger ignored the bounty hunter.

Stew Pot backhanded Louisa once more. She sagged in his arms.

Stew Pot gave another laugh, crouched, pulled the Vengeance Queen over his right shoulder, and carried her past Prophet and into the mesquites behind him. She was draped across the man's broad shoulder, limp as wet wash.

"Let her go, you son of a bitch!" Prophet yelled. "Let her go, or so help me, I'll kill you slow, you fuckin' savage!"

Stew Pot's heavy footsteps dwindled gradually to silence.

Chapter Fourteen

The fire crackled in the otherwise silent night.

Krueger kept his rifle on Wolcott. Both men were staring off toward where Stew Pot had carried Louisa.

Krueger shaped a drunken, slit-eyed smile. "Well, now—hear that? I think they're gettin' along just fine."

Wolcott stared in silence. Then he chuckled. "Well . . . maybe you're right. Let's flip to see who goes second."

"Forget it," Krueger snapped at the Pinkerton. He aimed his rifle at Wolcott's head. "This Winchester says I get her next!"

Prophet's heart thudded. He had his head turned to stare into the darkness over his left shoulder. No sounds. Damn her. He'd warned her, but just like she always did, she'd thought she was smarter than he was. Now she had herself in a pickle.

Prophet turned to where Krueger sat on a rock by the fire, six feet from Wolcott. "I'm gonna kill you, Krueger. You hear that?" He could feel several veins bulging in his neck and forehead, and his blood roared in his ears. "I'm going to gut you and feed you to—"

A shrill scream cut him off.

Prophet turned his head to stare into the brushy darkness behind him.

"Louisa?" he said in a voice hushed with agitation.

The scream came again. The first part of it sounded female; the second part became the slightly lower-pitched, chortling wail of a male in agony.

"Bitch!" Stew Pot screamed. He sobbed. "Ohhh—you *bitch*!"

Krueger lurched to his feet. So did Wolcott. Both men ran toward the mesquites. Krueger tripped over a rock and fell with a wail. Prophet raised his tied ankles as Wolcott was about to run past him into the brush.

Prophet's boots caught Wolcott's. The Pinkerton tripped, fell, and rolled, dropping his rifle.

"Fuck!" he cried.

A shadow moved out of the darkness over Prophet's left shoulder. Louisa raised her arm.

A pistol flashed, popped.

Wolcott grunted. There was a thud as his head hit the ground.

Krueger had gained his feet and was stumbling around, trying to pick up his rifle.

Louisa's pistol barked again, the flash coloring the brush around her orange for the briefest of quarter-seconds. Krueger twisted around and fell on the fire, smashing the tripod standing over it. He lay in the fire on his back, jerking wildly as he died, gasping, clawing at the air, and burning.

Louisa walked over and looked down at him.

"Pull him out," Prophet said. "I'm gonna need the key to these cuffs."

Louisa turned her mouth corners down in disdain. Then she grabbed the still-jerking man's ankles, and pulled him out of the fire. His clothes were burning. She tamped them out with Krueger's saddle blanket, then dug the key out of his pocket.

She walked back over to Prophet, dropping to a knee.

"I just knew you were gonna put the hurt on ole Stew Pot," he said, chuckling and shaking his head. "Didn't doubt it a bit!"

Louisa unlocked the cuffs. Prophet tossed them away.

"What did you do to him, anyway?"

"Gelded him with a rock. Then hit him over the head with it."

Prophet grinned. "Ain't you a caution." He dug his folding bowie knife out of his pocket and used it to cut away the rest of the ropes. "Only problem is," he said, walking over to their gear piled on the ground near the fire, "them *rurales* might have heard the commotion."

He found his guns among Krueger's tack and strapped his Colt around his waist. He strapped the shell belt housing cartridges for his Winchester around his waist, as well, then looped the Richards's lanyard over his head and shoulder. Louisa was rummaging around the dead men's gear for her own weapons.

When Prophet had slid his bowie knife back into its sheath and he saw Louisa checking the loads in one of her silver-chased Colts, her rifle leaning against a rock beside her, he kicked out the fire.

"We'd best do a little reconnaissance," he said quietly, looking around at the dark night.

The only sounds now were the breeze in the treetops and the soft crackling of the dying coals.

Prophet made sure his Peacemaker and rifle were loaded, then stole up the rise. He could hear Louisa fall into near-silent step behind him. She could move like an Apache, that girl. Sometimes she could move so quietly it was downright unsettling.

He found himself glad to be back on the warpath with her, despite all that had happened. Despite Mattie . . . or whoever the so-called Mathilda Anderson really was.

Who in hell was she, anyway?

Gaining the crest of the rise, he dropped to one knee and peered down the other side of the rise and out onto the night-cloaked flat stretching away like black velvet below. The *rurales* had three fires going. They were mere pinpricks of flickering orange light from this distance of a quarter-mile away.

They could have heard Louisa's shots from that distance. The question was, would they bother inquiring about them? Doing so in the dark might be too risky. If they decided to check, they might wait until dawn.

There was a good chance they'd ignore them, Prophet thought. This country was teeming with *banditos.* Quintero might shrug off the shots he may or may not have heard as a disagreement between border bandits, and leave them at that.

Prophet turned to where Louisa knelt in a cavity surrounded by slab-sized boulders, a sky glittering with sequin stars arching overhead.

"What do you think?"

"About what?"

"About Quintero?"

"I think Quintero has one thing on his mind—or maybe two things. He's not going to worry about a few gun pops up here. Besides, he and his men are probably good and drunk. He has the arrogance of power."

Prophet considered that, and nodded. He turned to Louisa again, a blond shadow beside him. "What are those two things on his mind?"

"Gold and women." Louisa frowned. "Maybe three things."

"What's the third?"

"Did you see that tattoo on his forehead?"

"Uh-huh."

"It's a symbol of your friend, el diablo."

"Thought it looked familiar. I seen it on a cabin door or two back in Appalachia. What's this Quintero fella up to, anyways?"

"Quintero robs American-owned gold trains as they head out of Mexico for Arizona. He kidnaps women on both sides of the border, and uses those women to satisfy his men or to sell to others or . . ."

"Or what?"

"He sacrifices them to your pal, Scratch."

"No shit?"

"Quintero's a satanist. He belongs to an ancient satanic cult, one that originally started in the Catholic Church. He's a true believer. Pure crazy. With the devil's help, he's trying to build up enough wealth and power to fuel his own revolution down here."

Prophet rubbed his chin. "Sold his soul to the devil. Depraved bastard."

"Imagine that." Louisa turned to Prophet in the darkness. Starlight shimmered in her eyes. "I think he's got your wife, Lou."

Prophet's voice was low, flat. "What makes you think so?"

"After I left you in Colorado, I came down here to investigate Quintero. I'd heard about his female sex slave operation. The kidnapping and the sacrifices. There's a nice-sized bounty on his head . . . back in Arizona. He crosses the border now and then for *gringas,* who are worth more than Mexican girls in the Mexican sex slave trade.

"I saw a young woman who looked like Mattie when I was riding through Arizona. I followed her down here. I didn't know what she was up to or if she was really who I thought she was. I'd only seen her from a distance in Colorado. But then the hotel she was staying at was raided by *rurales.* Several young women were taken away. They were taken south."

"South *where*?"

"I don't know. I would have followed but I ran into trouble of my own. A group of ungentlemanly sorts came after me, having recognized me as one of the two bounty hunters . . . the second one being *you* . . . who killed a goodly number of their gang up in Montana. So I had to skin out and hole up for a while. That's when I saw you in Santa Rosaria . . . on the run from Wolcott."

"But you think Quintero will lead us to Mattie."

"That's what I'm thinking. It's a possibility, anyway."

"What about the Beauregard loot?"

"I don't know. But if we find Mattie, or whoever she is, we'll likely find the loot, too."

"Shit." Prophet sagged onto his butt, and leaned back against a boulder. "So . . . we wait and follow Quintero at sunup. Hope he leads us to Mattie."

"Right."

Prophet looked at his partner. "I'll be ding-dong-damned."

"What?"

"Here I thought you were just out to help me find Mattie. Out of the sheer kindness of your heart." Prophet smiled knowingly, shaking his head slowly. "I should have known."

Louisa beetled her brows. "What?"

"You're on the blood trail. Quintero's trail. You're out to kill that demon-lovin' *rurale.*"

Louisa gave one of her supreme, shrewd smiles.

Prophet sighed and tossed a pebble into the darkness. "Oh, well—best not to look a gift Vengeance Queen in the mouth, I reckon."

They didn't speak for a time. They sat staring toward the *rurales'* fires.

Louisa's voice was soft and intimate in the quiet night. "Do you love her, Lou?"

Prophet looked at her, then looked down. "I did. Leastways, I thought I did. Now I don't know what to think."

"You want her back?"

"I don't know what in hell I want. I know I want the loot back." Prophet sighed. "As far as Mattie goes . . . I reckon I just want to know who she really is. I want to know why she did what she did. I never would have figured her for . . . for a killer."

"You also want to know if she really loved you."

Prophet looked at his partner again, then doffed his hat and set it in his lap. "I reckon." He raked a hand through his hair in need of a trim. "Ah, shit, Louisa—I been seven kinds of a fool. I don't know how it happened. I really don't know how it happened. I don't think I was even drunk through most of it!"

"I know how it happened."

Prophet looked at her, one brow arched.

Louisa hiked a shoulder. "Deep down, you're a good man. It might be hard to see it in you at times . . . when you've got your pockets full of reward money and you're in some town somewhere, 'stompin' with your tail up,' as you call it. Taking full advantage of your own arrangement with Scratch. You're a bit wayward in your ways, uncertain in your convictions, free with your money as well as with your love, which isn't usually very long-lasting, and you've way too much taste for—"

"Wait," Prophet said irritably, cutting her off. "Is there gonna be a compliment here somewhere or this just another trip to the woodshed?"

"Deep down—well, not all that far down, actually—you're a good man. You don't like killing. You don't even like stomping with your tail up overmuch. At least, you've gotten tired of it. So without even realizing it, you were looking for someone to settle down with."

Louisa sighed and looked down at the pretty Colt she was absently twirling with one finger. "And I wasn't that woman."

"Is that why you rode away from Dead Skunk Gulch so fast?"

"Yes." Louisa slipped her pistol back into its holster. She nodded and looked up at Prophet staring down at her.

She sucked in her lips. A couple of tears glistened in the starlight, rolling down her cheeks. "I felt bad that I hadn't been the one you were riding away with. That I never could be." She sucked back a ragged sob. "When deep down I've wanted it so much."

Prophet brushed a tear from her cheek with his thumb. "We

done tried that before."

"I know."

"Shit."

"Yeah, well." Louisa drew a deep breath, placed a hand on his cheek, and gazed into his eyes. "But I'm here now. Yes, I'm going to kill Quintero. And I'm going to help you get the stolen money and your reputation back, you big lummox. And your woman back, too, so we can get that part of it settled, as well."

Prophet smiled. "Thanks."

"You'd do the same for me."

"I don't know." Prophet chuckled. "That's a mighty tall order." He chuckled deeper down in his chest, wagging his head.

"What's funny?"

"It's kind of hard to take seriously a gal who promises to help me get my reputation back . . . after she's killed a deputy U.S. marshal, a federal tracker, and a Pinkerton agent who was cock of the walk back in Chicago."

"They had it coming," Louisa said casually. "Besides, nothing counts in Mexico."

Prophet found himself staring into her eyes. It was a cool desert night, but he could feel the heat coming off of her. He could smell the warm musk of her. He thought that as they sat there, gazing at each other in the darkness, as her chest rose and fell more heavily. He knew his own breath was growing more labored.

At the same time she started to reach out to him, he reached out to her. As she placed her hand on his thigh, he wrapped his big paw around the back of her head and drew her toward him.

They kissed gently at first.

Then hungrily, entangling their tongues.

Prophet could feel his denims tighten. He released her, drawing his head back from hers.

"This ain't no time," he said, turning away, clearing his throat, trying to suppress the lust that had ignited inside him.

"No, it's not." Louisa removed his hand from her thigh and turned her head to stare toward Quintero's encampment.

They reached for each other again at the same time, kissing almost violently, grinding their mouths together, poking their tongues deep into each other's mouths. Louisa unbuckled one of his cartridge belts. She had no trouble. She'd done it before.

She unbuckled the other belt and then unbuttoned his pants, pausing to press her hand against the growing hardness behind his fly.

They both wrestled his jeans and summer underwear down to his ankles. Then Louisa rose, kicked out of her boots, and pulled down her own denim trousers and cotton drawers. She kicked them away and, wearing only her blouse and serape, sat down on top of Prophet, her bare legs straddling his.

She reached for him. He was standing at full mast.

Prophet groaned as she wrapped her hand around him and rubbed him against her furred portal, grunting as she did so. Groaning. Sighing. Sucking sharp breaths through her teeth.

Finally, she lowered herself over him. Slid down, down, farther down, until she was sitting on top of him. He was deep inside her. She held there, sandwiched his big face in her hands, and kissed him tenderly.

"I missed you, Lou," she whispered.

"I know you did, Louisa."

She chuckled as she rose on her knees, sliding back up to the end of his manhood. "You're a bastard."

"You're gettin' right blue-tongued, Miss Louisa." He reached up under her serape and blouse, sliding his hands up her flat belly and beneath her chemise to massage her firm breasts, the nipples jutting.

"Nothing counts in Mexico," she said.

"Not true."

"What does?"

Prophet rolled his thumbs across her distended nipples. "This does."

She moved up and down on him.

Their blood rose, passions climbing, until they had to clamp their hands over each other's mouths to keep from howling like rapturous coyotes and waking half of Mexico.

Prophet woke when the sky was periwinkle blue. He lifted his head to see a wash of pink stretching low across the eastern horizon. He and Louisa were lying together in their niche in the boulders atop the rise. She had her head on his chest, her body curled against him.

She was sound asleep. He could feel the warmth of her breath through his shirt.

It was chilly, but they were safe and warm here in the rocks. The fatigue of his long, trying journey pulled him back down into cozy slumber with Louisa. His eyes snapped open when he heard an odd sound. He blinked against the slanting morning light. A shadow moved over him. His heart hiccupped when he saw a broad-shouldered figure silhouetted against the sky, staring down at him.

The man wobbled on his feet and hips as though drunk.

Prophet blinked, at first slow to comprehend that the man was not part of some crazy desert dream spawned by his battered head and the haunted Mexican desert. Then, when Stew Pot began lifting his arm slowly, as though the pistol gripped in his right fist weighed thirty pounds or more, Prophet rose with a dizzying leap.

Louisa lifted her head with a gasp.

Stew Pot puffed out his cheeks. He grunted and groaned. His eyes rolled around in their sockets. Blood shone on his caved-in left temple. It spoked out around the savage wound, dripping into that eye.

Prophet jerked the gun out of the half-breed's grip.

Stew Pot groaned, ground his teeth, then stumbled backward, and fell in the rocks. He lay still.

"Well, I'll be," Louisa said. "I was sure I'd killed him."

"Well, maybe you'd better make sure next time," Prophet grouched.

Louisa gritted her teeth and slanted her eyes at him. "Let's not start counting each other's mistakes, partner. I have a feeling the tally at the bottom of my column would pale compared to the one at the bottom of yours."

Bile bubbled in Prophet's guts. So much for their enchanted evening together. A new day, a new fight. "That's a low one even for . . ."

He let his voice trail off as he stared off to the south.

"What is it?"

Prophet lifted a hand to shade the hazy morning sunlight from his eyes. "Quintero's bunch. They're gone."

Chapter Fifteen

Prophet and Louisa picked up the *rurales'* tracks where they found the still-smoking coals of the group's campfires.

Quintero's bunch—a dozen men, at least—had continued south.

The bounty hunters followed the tracks through the morning and into the afternoon, when a mass of low, angry-looking clouds paraded like warships into the long valley between ragged, sun-blasted mountain ranges. Rain slashed furiously out of a sky bellowing thunder and hurling pitchforks of lightning as though it was determined to make a name for itself.

During the worst of the monsoon storm, Prophet and Louisa had to take cover with their horses under a mantle-like ledge bulging out of a sandstone cliff wall. They'd been following an arroyo that had been dry just an hour ago. Now that arroyo frothed like milky tea in the deep cut that curled only a dozen or so yards from the base of the cliff.

Rain pocked the surging floodwaters like large-caliber bullets. The current roiled with driftwood and entire cactus plants and large chunks of sandstone ripped from the ravine's wall.

It all jounced downstream toward where Quintero was probably holed up, as well.

Prophet stood with Louisa between their frightened horses. He held Mean's reins with one hand while he rolled a quirley and licked it closed. He scratched a lucifer to light on his thumbnail and stared down from their perch at the swollen arroyo below.

Beyond the arroyo, desert brush, willows, palo verdes, and mesquites rolled away to the far ridge that shone beyond the shimmering cream screen of the rain.

He could feel the storm's fury through the soles of his boots. The smell of brimstone tanged his nose.

Everything seemed bigger and more violent in Mexico. The mountains and the rivers seemed older. The sky vaster. The men more savage. He'd be glad to have the Beauregard loot back and get the hell back across the border, though he knew it was all an illusion. The land that the U.S. occupied was no less old or savage than the land down here.

Still, north of the border was home. Mexico was a brooding, foreign land. A haunted land, as well. He always sensed it as soon as he stepped across the boundary line. It was as though he was stepping into some taboo land. A land of black magic and nightmares.

Why had Mattie come here? Come here *alone*? The money would have stretched farther down here, but there was a good chance she, a pretty young woman alone, wouldn't live to spend it. Wouldn't live to hold on to it and keep her life in the process.

Maybe she just hadn't known how dangerous it was.

Likely, she was already dead. If so, Prophet would never hear from her why she'd done what she'd done. Why she'd married him only to skip out on him with the Beauregard loot. If she'd been going to take the loot, she could have taken it before going to the trouble of the so-called ceremony in Broken Knee. Hell, she could have brained him while he'd slept on one of those nights they'd been traveling and camping in the mountains.

Maybe killing the marshal and taking the money had been a moment of insanity that she'd lived to regret . . . Foolish to hold onto such a thought. Or such a hope. Everything was changed now. He'd loved her, but she'd obviously not loved him enough to stay with him even for a little while. She'd obviously had her eye on the loot with a mind to take it.

Now she was a thief and a killer.

"What are you thinking, Lou?"

Prophet blew smoke out into the hammering rain, and hiked a shoulder. He stared off toward the distant mountains. "About how the stakes always seem higher down here."

"You could turn around," Louisa said. "Go back. Leave the money. It's not your job to get it back."

"Yes, it is."

Louisa turned her mouth corners down, and gave a nod.

Then she frowned, looking around warily. "Why do I have the feeling we're not alone?"

Automatically, Prophet removed the keeper thong from over his Colt's hammer, and slid the piece from its holster. He cast his gaze about, frowning. But there were only the horses and he and Louisa here, and the rain that appeared to be letting up some.

Louisa turned and walked along the base of the cliff. As she left the shelter of the mantle-like shelf, rain ticked onto her hat. She disappeared around a bulge in the sandstone wall. Prophet looked around; then, relatively sure no one was on the lurk in his immediate vicinity, he followed Louisa around the bulge.

She was crouching now, one hand on her knee, the other hand filled with a silver-chased revolver. She was peering into what appeared a notch cave. The oval-shaped opening was maybe five feet high. Prophet crouched, as well, and peered into the cave.

"Holy shit," he said.

"I was right. We weren't alone."

Inside the cave, a human skeleton sat on a bed of bone-white gravel, leaning back against a stone wall. The remains were of a partly mummified Apache still dressed in a calico blouse, dark-blue sash, and deerskin leggings. High-topped moccasins were folded down at the white knobs of the knees.

The stitching along the top of the left moccasin had unraveled, revealing what remained of a toe—the white bone showing through a thin covering of brick-red skin. A maggot was crawling along the edge of the tear.

The Apache still had some hair hanging in thin patches here and there about the skull capped with a thin layer of leathery hide. The hair sprouting from those patches had grown long. It was grizzled and gray and didn't really look like hair at all. A frayed red flannel bandanna held the hair back from the skeleton's forehead.

The eye sockets were dark and empty. The Indian's nose was almost entirely weathered away.

There was a ragged-edged, quarter-sized hole in the calico blouse about four inches down from the partly exposed breastbone.

"He died slow," Prophet mused. "And alone."

A depression settled heavily onto his shoulders, made even heavier by a welling loneliness. It was then that he realized why he'd married Mattie. He didn't want to die like this Apache.

"Christ," he said.

Louisa placed her hand on his forearm, and gently squeezed. "Come on, Lou. Let's find the Beauregard loot and get the hell out of here."

"Yeah," Prophet said, staring at the long-dead brave, repressing a shudder. "Let's do tha—."

He stopped, then turned back to peer into the cave, frowning.

"Wait."

"What?"

"Look."

He pointed at the symbol carved into the cave wall, just over the dead Apache's left shoulder. It was the same double cross jutting from a lazy figure eight.

"Quintero's tattoo," Louisa said.

Prophet dropped to a knee and picked up a handful of the gravel paving the cave floor. He sifted the white dust through his fingers.

"This ain't gravel," he said.

"No," Louisa said. "It's . . . bone."

Prophet turned his hand upside down, letting the ancient human bone dust drop back down to the cave floor. He gave a shudder and looked at Louisa, who said, almost breathless, "They performed sacrifices here. Long ago. Long before this Apache, wounded in some battle, crawled in here to die."

"Yeah."

"Let's get out of here, Lou."

"Yeah."

Prophet turned away from the makeshift grave and walked back to where their horses waited, ground-reined. The rain had quit entirely now, so he and Louisa filled their canteens from a *tinaja* swollen from cliff runoff, then swung up into their saddles.

They pushed hard for the rest of the day, following the *rurales'* tracks clearly delineated in the mud hugging the swollen wash. More rain came an hour after Prophet and Louisa had lit out from the Apache's ghastly grave, but not as heavy as before.

Night closed down over the desert.

Still, they rode. By the time they booted their mounts down off a low rise toward the lights of a small village, the rain had turned to a fine mist. The closer they rode to the village, the stronger came the smell of supper fires rife with the tang of seasoned meats and perfumed with burning piñon.

Like most villages in Mexico, this one had the look of age. The stout adobe dwellings, cracked and teetering, some fronted by brush *ramadas,* sprawled across the brushy hills with no apparent strategy.

Prophet rode stiff-backed in his saddle as he and Louisa negotiated the muddy street meandering through folds between the hills. Light spilled from cantinas and whorehouses, as did the muffled sounds of revelry and the strumming of a mandolin. Somewhere in the populated hills comprising the town, a baby cried and a man was shouting in a voice teeming with anguish for a woman or a girl named Maribel.

"Mary-bellll!" he cried, then louder, shriller, "Mary-*beeellllllll!*"

"Mattie," Prophet whispered, looking around, wondering where he'd ever find her, if find her he would. "Mattie . . ."

"Hold on," Louisa said.

Prophet turned to her. She'd stopped her horse a ways behind him.

She looked around to see if anyone was listening, then said, keeping her voice low, "We can't just go riding up to the nearest *rurale* post. Remember, Quintero has seen us."

"What do you suggest?"

"We stable our horses and get the lay of the land."

"What does that mean?"

"We tread softly, you fool. We don't just ride up to Quintero and ask for your woman and then shoot him."

"All right." Prophet looked around for a livery barn. He turned back to Louisa. "But she ain't my woman. I 'spect she never was."

"She was. But something happened."

"How do you know?"

Louisa shrugged a shoulder, looked him up and down, and quirked a shrewd half-smile. "I know."

They rode a little farther up the street. What appeared a livery barn sat off to the left, abutted on the near side by a stable constructed of tightly woven ocotillo branches. The barn was a stout adobe structure, badly pitted and pocked, with one gaping crack running down the front wall near the corner. The crack had been stuffed with mud and straw.

A withered old man sat in a cane chair outside the double doors. He was singing softly, almost under his breath, to someone strumming a guitar in the shadows off the barn's far side.

All that Prophet could see of the guitar player was the glowing orange coal of the man's quirley when he inhaled on it, then the pale smoke blowing out into the shadows. A small cat was hunkered on the old man's left shoulder. As Prophet and Louisa turned their horses toward the barn, the cat rose to its feet, humped its back, and arched its tail at the strangers.

From up in the barn's loft came the low groans and sighs of what could only have been a couple making tender love.

"Hola," Prophet said to the old man, who reached a gnarled hand up to sooth the cat on his shoulder. "Can we stable our horses here?"

"Of course, *señor. Señora.*" The old man gave Louisa a gentlemanly dip of his raisin-like gray head. He smiled and poked a crooked finger at the open loft doors above. "Please, do not be offended. My daughter is, uh, entertaining her *novio.*" Boyfriend. "Her mother will not allow them to even hold hands in our *casa.* He is from the wrong side of town, *entiendes*?" Understand?

He lifted his hands in supplication. "I allow them time here in the barn. It is safe and quiet and"—he smiled whimsically—"I am old enough to enjoy the sounds of young love."

He glanced around, smiling beatifically. "A lovely rain, eh? Did you ride far in it?"

"Far enough," Prophet said.

The strumming of the guitar continued, maybe slightly louder than before but not enough for Prophet to notice the change except in a vague, fleeting way. The guitar player was also humming. The strains were bittersweet, appropriate music for such a brooding, quiet night in Old Mexico.

Prophet swung down from his saddle and handed Mean's reins to the oldster. Louisa did the same. "A big group must have ridden into town ahead of us," she said, spreading her boots a little farther than shoulder-width apart, planting her gloved hands on her slender but nicely rounded hips, and staring out at the night-cloaked village.

"Sí," said the old man, leading the horses through the open doors. "A big group." As he began to unsaddle Louisa's pinto, he glanced toward the two bounty hunters. "You have ridden down from the border, uh . . . for a reason?" He smiled, one bleached-out eye glinting bashfully, trying to take any possible edge off the impoliteness of the question.

"As a matter of fact," Prophet said, taking out his makings sack. He glanced at Louisa. "What was the name again, pard? *Dona . . . ?*"

"*Doña* Nazaria Salazar," Louisa said.

"*Doña* Nazaria, that's it," Prophet said. "That's the name. My partner here has a good memory. And she's right purty to look at—wouldn't you say, *Señor* . . . ?"

The guitar player played several quick, raucous chords. Then the guitar fell silent.

The old man looked worriedly at Prophet and Louisa and led both horses off, muttering, "I wouldn't know anything about that. I wouldn't know anything, *Señor* . . ." His voice dwindled to silence as he led the horses off into the barn's dark bowels.

Prophet glanced at Louisa. She arched a brow.

The rain ticked down from the barn's eaves. The sound of gentle, passionate lovemaking continued in the loft. Those were the only sounds until the guitar player resumed playing. This time it was the Confederate song, "Dixie to Arms."

The guitarist sang along with the jovial strumming of the old, familiar strains:

"Southrons, hear ye Country call ye! Up!
Lest worse than death befall you!
To arms! To arms! To arms! In Dixie! Lo!
All the beacon fires are lighted,
Let all hearts be now united!
To arms! To arms! To arms! In Dixie!"

Prophet glanced at Louisa once more, skeptically. Then he strode slowly along the front of the barn toward the shadow-cloaked side from which the guitar strains were rising, improbably jovial and, under the tragic circumstances of the war itself, solemn. At once grave and jeering to Prophet's ex-Rebel ears.

As the singer sang the chorus, Prophet unsnapped the keeper thong from over his Colt's hammer and slid the big revolver from its holster.

Chapter Sixteen

"Advance the flag of Dixie!
Hurrah! Hurrah!
For Dixie's land we take our stand,
To live or die for Dixie!
To arms! To arms!
And conquer peace for Dixie!"

Prophet stopped at the corner of the barn and pressed his Colt's barrel to the back of the neck of the man sitting in a chair there, leaning forward and holding the guitar across his knees.

The bounty hunter clicked the Peacemaker's hammer back. "Who the hell are you?"

The man stopped singing. As Prophet stepped around in front of him, the man lifted his head topped with a dusty, salt-grimed Stetson that had seen far better days. His smile displayed a full set of relatively healthy teeth in a young, handsome face with friendly eyes. "Who—me?"

"Is there anyone else skulkin' around in these shadows over here but you?"

The young man looked around. "Uh . . . no . . . no, I don't reckon."

Louisa moved up to stand beside Prophet. Her pistols remained in their holsters, but she'd tucked her serape behind them and placed her gloved hands on the grips. She turned her head to cast a cautious glance into the street, then shuttled her gaze back to the guitar player.

Still, the rain ticked down softly. The mist hung like smoke in the air.

In the barn loft, the lovers were cooing and chuckling in postcoital bliss.

The young man with the guitar shrugged his shoulders and said, "I'm called different things here an' there. Mostly, I reckon they call me the Rio Concho Kid."

"The Rio Concho Kid, eh?" Prophet said.

"Sure enough, Mister Prophet."

Prophet frowned, glancing again at Louisa. "How do you know me?"

"Oh, I reckon I study up on folks." The Rio Concho Kid pinched his hat brim to Louisa. "Hello there, Miss Bonaventure. How are you this rainy Mexican evenin'?"

He spoke with the soft, velvety drawl and self-deprecating vowels of a Texan, his slitted eyes sending lines of easy affability slanting up under his sandy eyebrows.

Louisa canted her head to one side, scowling down at him uncertainly, one spurred boot cocked forward.

"Studied up on her, too, did ya?" Prophet said.

The Rio Concho Kid grinned again, and shrugged. He was not as bashful as he wanted others to believe. "You two ain't hard to study. I've crossed your paths here and there. You two are on them paths a lot, as I am, though I reckon you'd have no reason to notice me the way I noticed you—you bein' famous an' all."

"What are you doing down here?" Louisa asked him.

"Same as you . . . maybe."

"Let's see," Prophet said keeping his Colt aimed at the Kid's head. He seemed harmless enough, despite the pistol he wore in a holster strapped to his thigh, but Prophet wasn't taking any chances. Especially not in Mexico.

"I overheard you mention *Doña* Salazar."

"What's it to you?"

The Kid hiked a shoulder. "That's the person to know down here . . . if you're down here for what I'm down here for . . . and for what I'm guessin' you're down here for." He grinned. "Unless I miss my guess."

Prophet scowled his frustration. "I'll tell you what *we're* down here for but only if you tell us what *you're* down here for first!"

"Oh, for Pete's sake," Louisa said, glancing around to make sure they were still alone. The lovers were chatting in the barn loft, their attention on only each other. "We're looking for a young woman. *His* young woman." She gave Prophet a quick sneering, accusing look. "We think Quintero took her."

"If a young woman's been taken," said the Rio Concho Kid, "then it was likely Quintero who took her."

"Who is *Doña* Salazar?" Louisa asked him.

Prophet turned his befuddled scowl on his partner. "Don't you know?"

"I just heard she was working with Quintero. I never learned how. I assume she's part of the slave trade."

"Oh, yeah, she's part of the slave trade, all right," the Kid said.

Prophet wagged his pistol at him. "You know why *we're* down here. Now, why are *you* down here?"

The Kid glanced around cautiously and then began strumming his guitar again, very softly, to cover his words. "I'm lookin' for a gal named Peggy. Prettiest girl you ever seen. Blond hair, blue eyes, a spray of freckles across her cheeks. She was taken off the Gladstone Ranch in southern Arizona. *Rurales* got her. I trailed them . . . and young Peggy . . . here."

"Why?"

"I was workin' for Mister Gladstone. I, uh . . . sorta took a shine to Miss Peggy. I'm here to get her back and to settle up with Colonel Quintero."

"Ain't that a coincidence?" Prophet said, jerking a thumb at his partner. "She wants to snuff the bastard's wick, too."

"No disrespect, Miss Vengeance Queen," the Kid said in his humble way, "but only if you can beat me to it."

"I can handle that," Louisa said, narrowing her eyes.

"If you're after Quintero," Prophet said, "what're you sittin' around out here for, strummin' your guitar?"

The Kid shrugged. "I reckon I been waitin' for you two. Didn't know you were comin', but I knew I needed help. Here I thought I was just building up the courage to make my play. Now I know that I was waitin' for you two all along. Ain't that somethin'?"

Prophet stared incredulously down at the seemingly good-natured young man. "Kid, I don't know what to make of you."

The Kid raised his hands and smiled his calculated, self-effacing grin. "That's all right, Mister Prophet. I don't know what to make of myself most of the time." He looked at Louisa. "You wanna get the lay of the land, do ya?"

"You got good ears," Louisa told him.

The Kid rose from his chair. He dropped his quirley in the dirt and mashed it out with his boot. He scooped a bottle up off the ground, held it up to Prophet, and grinned.

The bottle in the crook of his left arm, the guitar resting on his shoulder, the Kid walked into the barn. Outside, Prophet could hear him talking in Spanish to the liveryman. The Kid reappeared a moment later, then canted his head to one side, indicating that Prophet and Louisa should follow him. He walked into the dense shadows along the side of the barn, heading for the rear.

Again, Prophet and Louisa shared a conferring glance. Louisa shrugged.

Prophet adjusted the Richards slung behind his right

shoulder, brushed his hand across his Peacemaker's grips, and tramped off after the Kid. Louisa fell into step behind him. Their boots made squelching sounds on the damp earth. Wet grass soaked their pants cuffs. The storm seemed to have passed, leaving the ground soggy in its wake. Here and there, rivulets gurgled.

The Kid remained about ten yards ahead of the pair as he led them around the village's perimeter. It was hard to see out here, random flares and outdoor fires offering the only light, but the Kid paused now and then to point out rain-soaked rubble in their path.

As he walked, working up a sweat despite the cool, damp night, Prophet could occasionally hear isolated outbursts of Mexican revelry in the village sprawled off to his right and below the trail he and Louisa were traversing, behind the Kid.

Fifteen or twenty minutes after they'd left the barn, the Kid stopped on a steep, rocky rise overlooking a deep canyon.

He dropped to a knee.

Prophet and Louisa followed suit. Prophet was breathing hard. He wasn't accustomed to walking much farther than across your average street, exchanging one saloon for another. If he had to travel any farther than that, he usually forked leather and rode. The heavy, humid air made exertion even more of a chore.

Louisa wasn't breathing hard at all as she knelt to his right, looking coolly around. Prophet silently cursed her. The Kid uncorked the bottle he'd been carrying, and offered it to Lou, who took it.

"This'll put the wind back in your sails, Mister Prophet."

Prophet took a couple of sips, letting the tequila burn down his throat and spread a refreshing, relaxing glow through his belly. He took one more drink, caught Louisa looking at him reprovingly, then, his ears warming slightly with chagrin, gave the bottle back to the Kid.

"Thanks," he said. "I needed that."

The Kid offered the bottle to Louisa who merely glowered at him.

"An abstainer, eh?" the Kid said, and took a couple of his own pulls from the bottle.

"What're we doing here?" Louisa asked, grumpily.

The Kid rammed the cork back into the bottle and looked down into the canyon on the far side of the rise. There was a building down there—a barrack-like adobe structure lit by torches. Several outbuildings and corrals flanked it.

"See that down there?" the Kid said. "That's the local *rurale* outpost. That's where Quintero and his men hole up when they ain't off raidin' gold trains or crossing the border looking for *gringas* for their slave trade."

Prophet's heart quickened. "So that's where he brings 'em. That's where he's got Mattie, most like."

"No." The Kid lifted his head to stare up the rise behind the *rurale* outpost. "That there is where he stows his captives."

Prophet stared. He'd thought he'd seen only a couple of feeble stars up that way, but now with closer inspection, he saw a large building silhouetted against the sky. The flickering orange lights fronting it were probably torches lighting an entrance.

"The Convent of St. Theresa," the Kid said. "Only, it ain't a convent no more." He looked at Prophet and Louisa, each in turn. "More like the house of the devil these days. In fact, it's been the devil's hell house for near on a hundred years."

Prophet poked the skin above the bridge of his nose. "When we seen Quintero, he had a tattoo on his forehead. We saw the emblem inside a cave."

"Double cross rising from a lazy eight," Louisa added.

The Kid nodded. "You'll find the same hoodoo emblem carved into the convent's front doors. You'll see it branded into the . . ." The Kid paused, gritting his teeth as though not much caring for what he was trying to find the words to express. ". . . into the hindquarters of the girl captives."

"Christ," Prophet said, raking his hand along his jaw.

"You'll find it in caves once used for ceremonial sacrifices. I've seen it on canyon walls nearly as far north as the border. Never knew what it meant till I came down here looking for Peggy and ran into an old man, a former priest at the church up there at the convent. The old *padre,* nearly deaf and blind and wracked with guilt by all he'd seen and done, filled me in like he was givin' confession. He's dead now, and I hope the poor, guilt-ridden devil's been shown some mercy."

"Tell us about *Doña* Nazaria Salazar," Louisa prodded.

"She's the head *honcho* up there." The Kid jerked his chin toward the convent, which was little more than a bulkily foreboding silhouette on the ridge behind the *rurale* outpost. "It's the devil's convent now. *Doña* Salazar has been the lead practitioner of a demon cult that was brought over here from Spain a long time ago. You don't hear much about it. The Catholic Church is ashamed that the cult grew up like a cancer inside it, its flame kept alive over the generations by a small but persistent number of priests and nuns seduced by Lucifer.

"This place used to be a bona fide Catholic convent and mission. But when Sister Salazar came here nigh on fifty years ago now, she spawned an insurrection amongst a few nuns and a few priests, as well as many poor, downtrodden peasants easily swayed by the liquor and prostitution she avowed—all the carnality that the Catholics *dis*avowed so long ago—and turned the place inside out. Like I say, it's the devil's house now."

"How did she come to throw in with Quintero?" Louisa asked.

"Easy," the Kid said, then smiled coldly. "Quintero is the bastard spawn of that place. Of some poor girl, kidnapped long ago, probably near as long ago sacrificed to the devil after giving birth. Quintero was raised by *Doña* Salazar. Together, they kidnap women, bring 'em here, drug 'em, and prostitute 'em to Quintero and his men and to rich, depraved bastards from ranchos around here or to wealthy government scoundrels who travel here from Mexico City. There's a long list o' them sickly perverts. When the girls outlive their usefulness or they get some disease or become in the family way, they're sacrificed."

Louisa looked at him in shock. "You mean the sacrifices are still happening?"

"Oh, sure. According to this old priest, they drug the so-called sacrificial lambs, lay 'em down on the altar, pray over 'em for a time, then slide a jewel-encrusted stiletto through their heart. They pass a chalice filled with the victim's blood, believin' it's the blood of Satan himself. They got 'em a whole cemetery behind the place, filled with them poor girls they sacrificed. I've been there. I've seen 'em. None of the graves are marked. Just the same, you can see the depressions—some very old, you can tell."

His sorrow showing through his devil-may-care veneer, the Kid shook his head and gritted his teeth. Prophet thought he saw a glistening tear dribble down his cheek. "So help me, I hope that ain't where Miss Peggy is. She's a sweet gal. Innocent-like and good. She don't belong there. But then . . ." He returned his flinty gaze to the black convent on the ridge top. "She don't belong in there, neither . . . branded like common stock and used for"—he shook his head in frustration—"wickedness."

Prophet thought of Mattie treated similarly. Bile burned in him. Even after all she'd done—the conniving and killing and riding off with the loot and leaving him holding the bag, so to speak—even after all that, he couldn't bear the thought of her being treated so savagely.

He had to get her out of there.

Now, having learned what he'd learned about the Convent of St. Theresa, Prophet had a notion he was going to give Louisa and their new friend, the Rio Concho Kid, a run for their money in seeing who would kill Colonel Quintero first.

Chapter Seventeen

Two nights later, a woman screamed, *"Bastardos!"* at the top of her lungs.

She sobbed and then cut loose with a maelstrom of Spanish, which Prophet roughly translated as, "You are filthy pigs—both of you! Never come back—do you hear?"

Men's laughter rose from the small cantina on the far side of the street from where Prophet and the Rio Concho Kid crouched behind rain barrels. Prophet shared a glance with the Kid.

After two days of planning their move to get Mattie and Peggy and the Beauregard loot back, they were about to put that plan into action. Around an hour ago, they'd seen the two *rurales* ride up to the little whorehouse/cantina here on the edge of San Miguel. Now Prophet watched as the *rurales* stumbled out through the crude wooden door, their gray uniforms making them look like oversized pigeons in the dark night.

The cantina was a two-story adobe. From a lamplit open window in the second story drifted the sobs of a young woman—probably one of the *putas* who'd entertained one or maybe even both of the *rurales*. Apparently, the *rurale(s)* had treated her shabbily, which didn't surprise Prophet.

He'd learned over his past two days here in San Miguel that Quintero's *rurales* were more *banditos* than lawmen, and they'd all taken sacred vows to adhere to the black rights of the satanic cult practiced up at the old convent, which was overseen by

Doña Salazar and Colonel Quintero. Prophet had seen the devil's tattoo on several *rurales* he'd observed strolling around town. Like Quintero, they all wore them on their foreheads.

Now the young whore was sobbing and the madame was mad as hell, and Prophet couldn't help shaping a devilish half-smile as he silently promised both women that the *rurales* would soon get the justice they deserved.

All of them.

Every last demon-worshiping son of a bitch, including Quintero himself.

The *rurales,* gray silhouettes from Prophet's distance of forty feet, stopped outside the cantina lit by dull lamplight radiating from behind dirty windows. One yelled back at the madame, laughing and cursing the woman as well as the *puta,* while the other one finished rolling a quirley. Both staggered as though drunk. When the one had finished building his cigarette, the other one scraped a match to life on a post holding up the boardwalk roof, and touched it to the other man's smoke. Both men cupped the flame, shielding it against a dry breeze shepherding paper trash along the street.

Staggering around, chuckling and conversing in low tones, spurs trilling on the boardwalk, the *rurales* raked their reins off the hitchrack and swung up onto their horses. One had trouble. As his mount backed away from the hitchrack, the *rurale* hopped on one foot, the other foot caught in the stirrup.

The other man laughed. The *rurale* with the caught foot cursed the other one. Just as he was about to swing his right boot over his horse's rump, he gave a shrill cry as Prophet reached up, grabbed the collar of the *rurale's* tunic with one hand and his cartridge belt with the other hand, and jerked him out of his saddle.

The *rurale* hit the ground with an indignant cry. He rolled, got his knees under him, and was about to lunge at Prophet when the bounty hunter swung the rear stock of the Richards forward from behind his right shoulder. The stock smashed into the *rurale's* left temple with a crunching thud.

The *rurale* dropped without a sound.

Prophet glanced to his left in time to see the Rio Concho Kid struggle for a second with the other *rurale,* whom he'd also pulled out of his saddle. While the *rurale's* horse danced and shook its head, the Kid got his arms around the *rurale's* neck and gave a savage backward jerk.

There was the grinding crack of the *rurale's* neck snapping like dry kindling. The *rurale* collapsed into the Kid's arms, the Mexican's arms sagging straight out from his shoulders, like broken wings.

Prophet and the Kid each dragged their respective dead man back into the alley they'd been waiting in. Prophet could see the tattoo in the forehead of the man he'd killed, just above the dead man's rolled-back eyes—the double cross jutting from the lazy eight.

He and the Kid dragged thc still-convulsing cadavers just beyond the alley mouth, into the liquid shadows there, then ran back into the dark street and grabbed the reins of the *rurales'* horses. When they'd tied the reins to a hitchrack, they looked around to make sure no one had seen the attack—or at least that no one intended to intervene.

The street appeared deserted. Save for the ratcheting of the breeze, some accordion music rising from the far end of the village, and a couple of dogs barking in the hills, the night was quiet. The *puta* was no longer sobbing in the whorehouse's second story.

Prophet and the Kid returned to the alley and quickly got the two dead *rurales* out of their gray tunics. Prophet pulled on the tunic of the man he'd killed while the Kid slouched into the tunic of the one he'd snapped the neck of. Prophet tried to button his tunic. No doing. He couldn't get the two sides of the undersized garment to meet.

"Shit." Prophet looked at the Kid.

The Kid was just finishing buttoning his own appropriated tunic, which fit him nearly perfectly. The younger man lowered his hands, looked at Prophet, and chuckled softly. "You'd best lose some weight, Lou."

Prophet cursed again under his breath.

"Never mind. It's dark." The kid set his *rurale's* sombrero on his own head. "No one's gonna notice the fit of your clothes if we move fast. We just gotta get into the compound of Quintero's headquarters. Through the front gate and up into the guard towers. Just wearin' this much gray and these sombreros should do the trick. It's a pretty dark night."

Prophet shook his head. "Damn risky, though. High odds."

"This ain't your first trip to Mexico, is it, Mister Prophet?"

Lou lashed the thong of his own sombrero beneath his chin, then grabbed his Winchester from where he'd leaned it against an alley wall. "What do you think?"

As the Kid strode toward where the *rurales'* horses waited, he glanced over his shoulder. "Then you know the odds are always higher down here."

"Yeah," Prophet said, stuffing his own hat into a saddlebag pouch. "I was just tellin' my partner that very thing." He took the reins of his borrowed horse and swung into the saddle. He looked over at the Kid mounting beside him. "Hey, Kid—would you mind callin' me Lou or Proph or even son of a bitch? I don't much cotton to bein' called Mister. It makes me feel old, and I ain't *all that much* older than you."

He slid the *rurale's* rifle from its scabbard and tossed it into the alley, then shoved his own Winchester into the boot.

"I don't know," the Kid said, frowning as though to consider the request. "That don't sound respectful, addressin' a man of your years by his first name." Then he grinned.

Prophet cursed and chuckled as he swung his horse into the street. He knew nothing about the Kid. Not even his real name. He knew only that the Rio Concho Kid must be a romantic devil to have come all this way, risking life and limb, to rescue the daughter of the rancher he worked for.

He must have been as romantic as Lou Prophet himself.

As they turned their horses toward the west, Prophet and the Kid pulled back their reins at the same time. Two human-shaped shadows stood on the whorehouse/cantina's front boardwalk. Prophet's hand went to his Peacemaker's grips. He dropped the hand back down to his thigh when he saw a rotund, middle-aged woman in a skimpy red dress standing there with a shawl about her shoulders, gazing toward him. A small Mexican girl, wrapped in a blanket, stood beside and a little behind the madame.

She, too, stared at the two strangers who'd just killed the *rurales.*

The women said nothing. Just stared, their eyes vaguely questioning, uncertain.

Prophet pinched the brim of his stolen sombrero to the pair, then touched spurs to his stolen horse's flanks, and galloped off to the east, his mount's shod hooves clacking on ancient paving stones and cobbles. He and the Kid slowed their horses when the village's stock pens and crumbling adobes slid back away along both sides of the trail.

Off to the left, the whitewashed adobe wall encircling the *rurale* outpost shone pale in the darkness. The headquarters building itself rose above and behind it, in the center of the yard sparsely stippled with ragged desert trees and a few cacti. When Prophet and the Kid came to a fork in the trail, they took the fork's left tine and headed toward the wooden gate in the adobe wall.

The gate was guarded by two *rurales* with rifles. They were both smoking. Prophet could see the orange glows of their quirleys when they drew on them. Gray smoke billowed in the darkness around the guards' sombreros.

One guard was tossing stones in a desultory way, side-armed. The other sat on his butt, his back against the adobe wall. The two were conversing in Spanish—arguing, rather. It wasn't a heated argument, but only the mild disagreement of two bored *rurales* on guard duty when they and their superiors knew damned good and well that no one around San Miguel was bold and/or stupid enough to attack the outpost. Everyone knew Quintero's reputation. The *peons* in this neck of Mexico fairly quaked in their sandals at the mere mention of the colonel's name. And that of *Donã* Salazar, most likely. These two could have been up at the convent or in the village, cutting their wolves loose. Instead, they were here at the gate, bored out of their gourds.

Prophet and the Kid lowered their heads, letting their sombrero brims hide their faces. They rode slowly toward the gate. Prophet crouched forward slightly, sitting loose-jointed in the saddle. He wanted to appear half pie-eyed. The Kid was doing the same.

"What do we have here?" asked one of the guards in Spanish. "You two back so soon? The tequila must have been running freely at Mother Ricardo's, eh, *amigos*?"

"Antonio, you never could hold your panther piss!" jeered the other *rurale*.

He and the other man laughed. The one who'd been throwing stones pulled the gate open and continued his friendly argument with the other *rurale,* who remained sitting with his back against the wall. Prophet and the Kid rode on through the open gate. The bounty hunter glanced back as the *rurale* closed the gate behind them.

Prophet slowed his mount and poked his hat brim up off his forehead. He and the Kid and Louisa had studied the layout of the *rurale* outpost several times over the past two days, by daylight from the ridge to the west. The barrack-like building stood straight ahead, its windows lit, in the center of the compound. A few desert shrubs stood around it. Men were talking as they lounged on a front veranda. The flag of Sonora snapped in the night breeze.

The stables and a munitions house flanked the main building.

Two low guard towers stood about six feet back from the wall and about forty yards apart. They were now directly to Prophet's right. Each thatch-roofed tower platform housed one Gatling gun and a guard.

Prophet figured the guns and towers were a necessary precaution against an unlikely set of *banditos* storming the outpost for the gold that Quintero was widely known to have stored up at the convent.

The Kid had investigated Quintero thoroughly. He'd learned that no one in the past five years had ever made a play for the colonel's gold. One reason for that was Quintero's formidable reputation throughout northern Mexico. No one wanted to butt heads with him—not even his superiors in Mexico City. Not even the *federales.*

Another reason the outpost was given a wide berth—the convent was said to be cursed. Most good Catholics wouldn't go near *Casa del Diablo,* as the convent was widely now known throughout Sonora. Only the bad Catholics—mostly wealthy, corrupt, and arrogant businessmen and politicians—paid furtive, proscribed visits here, lured by the dark fruit of the young, branded women promised by *Doña* Salazar.

Prophet steered his horse toward the far guard tower. The Kid steered his own horse toward the near one. Prophet gritted his teeth. He was waiting for someone either behind or ahead of him to see that he and the Kid had steered their horses off the trail that curved around the front of the outpost's main building toward the stables flanking it. He looked up at the far tower's platform to see if the guard up there was watching him. He couldn't tell. He could see only shadows beneath the thatched roof.

When Prophet had his horse within fifteen feet of the base of the far platform, a voice behind him raked cold fingers against his spine: "Hey, *amigos,*" one of the gate guards called. "Are you so drunk you've lost your way?" His voice was high and shrill with mocking laughter.

"No, no, no," the Rio Concho Kid called as he swung down from his saddle. "I have brought Pedro the bottle he requested from the village!"

At least, that's what Prophet thought he'd said. His nerves were jerking around beneath his skin, making it hard to translate. As the bounty hunter dismounted his own horse, the gate guard said in the same shrill, mocking voice as before something akin to: "That is not Pedro in the tower, *pendejo!* You are a drunken fool!"

He glanced back at the other guard, and they both had a good laugh at the Kid's expense.

Calmly, Prophet slid his rifle from its scabbard and pumped a round into the chamber. He looked up the tower ladder as the *rurale* manning it crouched to peer down at him, scowling, showing the white line of his teeth as he said incredulously, "What the fuck . . . ?" Or something like that.

To which Prophet, aiming his Winchester straight up the ladder and planting the beads on the *rurale's* face silhouetted beneath the broad brim of his sombrero, replied with two quick rifle blasts.

The *rurale* jerked back away from the hole and then, switching directions, stumbled toward it, his boots thudding on the platform. Prophet stepped back as the *rurale* fell out of the tower to pile up three feet in front of the bounty hunter's boots with a solid thud and a wheezing sigh.

Chapter Eighteen

Prophet glanced toward the Kid, who just then raised his own rifle and fired up into the guard tower looming over him. The guard in the tower screamed. Boots thudded loudly. The guard dropped down over the tower's backside to land the same way his cohort had.

Yelling incredulously, the two gate guards ran through the gate they'd shoved open, raising their own rifles. Prophet and the Rio Concho Kid cut down on them at the same time, sending them both flying back toward the open gate, rolling, dying . . .

More shouts and yells rose from the blocklike post house.

So far, so good.

Prophet sent the Kid a quick salute. Taking his rifle in one hand, he began climbing the tower ladder. As he climbed, he peered between the wooden rungs toward the post house. *Rurales* were storming out of two doors, one on each end of the building, shouting and raising rifles or drawing pistols from holsters. Shadows dashed past lighted windows.

Guns began flashing and popping from the scrum of *rurales* now running toward the guard towers, some in their confusion running toward the open gate, believing that's where the threat lay. A bullet clipped a ladder rung two inches from Prophet's boot just as the bounty hunter gained the platform.

"Cuttin' it a little close, maybe," Prophet muttered, leaning his rifle against the rail to his right.

A dove-colored cloud of jostling shadows ran outward from the post house, flames lapping from pistols and rifles. A couple of bullets chewed into the rail around Prophet's tower. A couple more plunked into the underside of the brush roof above the bounty hunter's head. One spanged off the housing of the Gatling gun just as Prophet reached for the handle.

He jerked his hand back as though from a hot stove, then grabbed the gun, raised its brass snout, slanted it down toward the oncoming crowd of yelling *rurales,* and turned the crank.

As the machine gun commenced roaring and lighting up the area around the tower, spitting red flames, a similar roaring kicked up from the tower to Prophet's left. The bounty hunter turned the crank and swiveled the canister from left to right and back again, grinning in satisfaction as the *rurales* were blown off their feet and sent rolling in the dark dust, bellowing and cursing.

Prophet glanced toward the Kid's tower, grinning again as he saw jets of fire licking out into the night from beneath that tower's thatched roof, pale smoke wafting thickly. Prophet hadn't fired a Gatling gun in years, and the thrill of it caused him to cut loose with ripping Rebel yells as he gritted his teeth and turned the crank over and over again . . . until the gun clicked and fell silent.

The clip poking up from the canister housing was empty.

A few seconds later, the Kid's gun stopped hiccupping, as well.

Prophet's blood was up. "Take that, you demon-worshippin' dogs!" he shouted, reaching for his rifle.

He cocked the long gun, snapping the rear stock to his shoulder. He stared out over the rail of the tower, blinking against the peppery odor of burned powder. He could see a good dozen *rurales* lying sprawled on the ground, some with their bodies twisted together. A couple were crawling and howling. Several others ran back toward the safety of the outpost building.

Prophet and the Kid opened fire with their rifles.

When Prophet had emptied his Winchester, all of the *rurales* were on the ground. Only one was moving, crawling on hands and knees toward the towers, sobbing and cursing, obviously disoriented.

Prophet rested his rifle on his shoulder and drew his Peacemaker. He started to point the weapon at the wounded *rurale* but stayed the movement when the rattling of a fast-approaching wagon rose in the darkness. The rattling grew louder. The wagon appeared, racing toward Prophet from behind the outpost building. Louisa sat in the wagon seat, yelling at the two horses hitched to the doubletree, shaking the reins over their backs.

The crawling *rurale* stopped crawling to look off toward the oncoming wagon. He opened his mouth to scream but didn't get the sound out before the horses hammered into him, trampling him savagely beneath their galloping hooves. The wagon's left front wheel finished the *rurale* off, leaving him in a rumpled, dusty heap.

Just beyond him, Louisa stopped the wagon and looked up at the towers.

"If you two want a ride, you'd better get down here pronto!"

Prophet gave an ironic snort and grabbed his rifle. He and the Kid leaped off the ladders at the same time, ran over to the wagon, and jumped into the box. Louisa whipped the horses into gallops once more.

On his knees in the box, on the wagon's right side, Prophet grabbed the side panel to keep from getting thrown out. The wagon bounced over several dead *rurales* as it turned sharply onto the trail leading behind the outpost building toward the northern ridge.

Staring toward the building, Prophet saw two *rurales* run out the near front door, raising rifles. He and the Kid dispatched them with crackling rifle fire. And then the wagon caromed around the side of the outpost building and was heading for the ridge beyond, covering the fifty yards of open ground in fifteen seconds.

They tore past the stables and corrals and then started up the incline toward the convent. The trail curved sharply as it climbed the ridge. When the wagon reached the crest, the two horses were blowing. Louisa turned the wagon and stopped, setting the break.

She grabbed her rifle off the seat beside her.

Prophet and the Kid, kneeling side by side in the wagon box, stared at the convent. It was a large, towering, stone structure blocking out the stars. The church was on the left side of the building. Two Spanish gothic towers jutted skyward, above the trinity of deeply recessed wooden doors. The doors had three stout chains threaded through their heavy iron handles.

That would be where the gold was stored.

The convent part of the structure was a rectangular extension to the right. There were two doors at the tops of two sets of high stone steps fronted with statues of *Madre* Maria. One door was near the church part of the building; the other was at the end of the convent part.

The place was eerily silent. It was the silence of catacombs.

The breeze blew up dust in the large yard fronting the building. Down in the village, several dogs were barking wildly, likely having been stirred up by the shooting.

Prophet stared at the vast, sepulcher-like place down the barrel of his cocked Winchester, pulse beating in his ears. The Kid had informed him and Louisa that they would meet most of the resistance at the outpost. But surely there were a few *rurales* up here, as well. If not enjoying the pleasures of *Doña* Salazar's sex slaves, then certainly guarding the gold.

Where was Quintero? The Kid, having reconnoitered the outpost and the *Casa del Diablo* for several days, had determined that Quintero spent most of his time up here when he wasn't out raiding. The Kid thought Quintero must live up here . . .

Suddenly, the door at the top of the near steps opened with a squawk of heavy, rusty hinges. Prophet rose to a standing position, and aimed his Winchester at the dark figure that stepped out of the doorway, silhouetted against the dimly lit entrance behind it. The figure appeared a nun in a habit, but Prophet couldn't see clearly in the darkness.

The figure just stood there for a short time. Whoever the figure was turned and walked back into the building. He or she left the door open. The open door seemed an invitation. An invisible arm, beckoning.

Apprehension drew Prophet's shoulders taut. He glanced at the Kid, then at Louisa, then leaped out of the back of the wagon.

A chill breeze rose, sweeping dust and pine needles and grit. It moaned around the tops of the giant spires towering above the old Spanish church.

Louisa and the Kid climbed out of the wagon. They moved up to stand on either side of Prophet, who was absently shoving fresh cartridges into his Winchester while he studied *Casa del Diablo.* A strange smell emanated from the place. He couldn't place it, but it was nothing derived from the natural environment. The cloying odor was drifting out of the heavy door that remained open, showing the arched doorway framing dim, wavering, orange-yellow light within.

"I don't like it." Louisa looked up at Prophet. "I don't like it at all."

Prophet glanced at the Kid, one brow arched in question.

The Kid stared stone-faced at the building that fairly radi-

ated a palpable evil. "All I know," he said with a sigh, "is that Peggy is most likely in there somewhere. And I ain't goin' nowhere without her. I ain't goin' nowhere until I know Quintero is dead."

"Yeah, well," Prophet said, sliding his gaze across the dark exterior of the place, "I ain't goin' nowhere until I have Mattie. And some answers. And the Beauregard loot. Them's what I came here for, and I reckon an open door ain't gonna deter me. The door's open, so I'm walkin' through it." He pumped a cartridge into his Winchester's action and started forward. "Might not walk back out it," he said, staring straight ahead. "But I'm goin' through it, by god."

Prophet walked up to the steps. Louisa and the Kid fell into line behind him, all walking slowly, tensely, rifles ready. Prophet licked his lips, tightened his grip on his rifle, adjusted the position of the shotgun slung over his right shoulder, and walked up the steps, taking them two at a time—fluid movements that kept the Winchester steady in his hands.

Inside opened to a foyer with a high, arched ceiling. Crude religious paintings adorned the walls—badly faded, frames cracked and rotting, one canvas torn, the picture hanging by one spike in the pocked and pitted adobe wall. Torches flared in brackets to Prophet's right and left as he entered the vestibule.

Here, the foul odor grew more intense. Prophet began to identify the mélange. It was the stench of cook fires, stale liquor, tobacco, sweat, excrement, sex, and death . . .

A broad stone stairway climbed the foyer's right wall. Prophet stopped near the bottom of the steps, wondering if he was meant to go up the stairs or take the hall that appeared to lead out of the foyer. But the hall was as dark as a cave. A torch wavered from a bracket at the top of the stairs. Like the door, it seemed to beckon him.

He glanced back at Louisa and the Kid flanking him, then

climbed the stairs, moving more slowly now, quietly, vaguely noting the crumbling state of the stones beneath his boots. Part of the stone rail had cracked and tumbled onto the risers. At the top of the stairs, he found himself in the mouth of a high-ceilinged hallway. There were doors to his right and left—tall, stout doors made of oak and bearing strong hinge bands.

As Prophet began walking down the hall, boots crunching debris littering the hall's floor, he could hear strange, echoing sounds emanating from the doors around him. Moaning sounds. Wailing sounds. Shrill cries as well as hysterical laughter. The sounds were muffled by the heavy doors, but Prophet thought he detected both men's and women's voices.

Men and women in the throes of rabid lovemaking.

Behind one door, a man coughed. Glasses clinked together, as though liquid was being poured. A woman spoke in a slow, hushed, intimate voice. The man laughed and then the woman laughed, as well. Her laughter betrayed her youth—just a girl, most likely.

Prophet continued walking, glancing over his shoulder at the two behind him. As the Kid walked along beside Louisa, he tipped his head to each door that he passed, shaping a befuddled, frustrated frown. He was listening for Peggy's voice.

The torches on the walls to Prophet's left and right were widely spaced so that when he left the light of one torch, there were several steps of near-total darkness before he reached the light of the next torch. He walked through such a darkness now, squinting to see ahead of him, the hair along the back of his neck pricking with cold fear.

When he stepped into the light of the next torch, he stopped abruptly, his heart quickening.

The nun stood before him, at the base of another set of steps running up the wall to her right. Prophet couldn't see her face clearly, only her habit-swaddled outline, until he took another few steps.

He stopped again. His breath caught in his throat when he saw the eggshell-white eyes set in deep sockets. The nose was long and beaklike. The skin was drawn taut across sharp cheekbones. It had the color of mahogany and the texture of ancient leather. The thin lips were stretched back from small, yellow, leaning and rotten teeth.

Prophet couldn't tell if the old nun, whom a bodiless voice told him was *Doña* Salazar, was smiling or grimacing. The tissues in her face were so taut that any other expression except a smile or a grimace was likely impossible. She had her arms, clad in the baggy sleeves of the black habit, folded across her middle. Now she used one to gesture up the stairs.

Prophet stepped wide of the old woman, instinctively repelled by her. If the air in this House of the Devil was foul, then the stench emanating from *Doña* Salazar was even fouler. It threatened to burn Prophet's eyes until he was ten steps above her and continuing up the stairs.

He turned into a giant, cathedral-like room, and stopped abruptly again.

Two statues, each maybe fifteen feet tall, stood to either side of him, at the entrance to the vast room. One statue depicted a badly defaced Jesus in flowing robes, arms upraised as though to give blessing. A rope had been thrown around one of these upraised arms and tied off below. Dangling from the end of the rope twisted into a noose was the rancher who'd visited Prophet in Broken Knee—Harland McCourt.

McCourt had been hanged several days ago, judging by the man's stench, which only heightened the sour reek of rot in this obvious perdition. His face was badly swollen and purple, curled tongue protruding as though in a stony wail, eyes nearly bulging out of their sockets.

The other statue was a badly defaced Mother Mary. Hanging from the rope draped around her neck was McCourt's son, Donald. The younger man's body had twisted around on the rope so that his back faced Prophet, as though he were ashamed to show his face. The bounty hunter knew who he was just the same.

He'd kicked out of one of his black, high-topped boots, which lay on the floor near one of Mary's stony, sandaled feet.

"Christ," Prophet muttered, turning his gaze back to Harland McCourt.

"Friends of yours?" Louisa asked. She kept her voice low, but it still echoed in the vast, cavern-like room.

Before Prophet could respond, a man shouted from the room's far end, "Come, *amigos*! Come and get it while it's hot! There is much food here and since I have suddenly many fewer men than I did only an hour ago, there is much to go around!"

The shouts echoed crazily.

Prophet stared down the long, high-ceilinged room toward where two men in *rurale* uniforms sat at a long wooden dining table, dining. They were a long ways away, but Prophet knew that one was Colonel Quintero.

Chapter Nineteen

"Come, *amigos*! *Amiga!* Come, come—the food is getting cold!"

Quintero had risen from his chair, and he was holding a white napkin in one hand while beckoning with the other.

"Ven aqui!" He sat back down in his chair.

He went to work on the heaping plate of food before him.

Prophet shared a skeptical glance with Louisa and the Rio Concho Kid, then began striding slowly down the center of the room, which was obviously a dining hall. Most of the tables, however, didn't look like they'd been used in a long time. A fine layer of soot and dirt lay on all that Prophet could see in the shadowy gloom inadequately lit by flares mounted here and there on the high walls. There must have been around twenty of the tables, and each was no less than thirty feet long.

As Prophet approached the back of the room, he saw now that the lone man seated next to Colonel Quintero was the short, fat sergeant who'd joined him in the cantina, when Prophet and Louisa had first encountered the colonel. There was a large, steaming crock on the table between the two men, who were eating hungrily from wooden bowls. A round loaf of bread, half-devoured, sat on a cutting board beside the crock. There were two straw wine demijohns, and a wooden wine goblet stood near each man's plate.

As far as Prophet could tell, there was only one other person in the room. A short, heavy, moon-faced Mexican woman of early middle age in a loose gray smock and an elaborately embroidered skirt stood behind and between the colonel and the sergeant. She wore her hair in a neat roll atop her head, which was ensconced in a black lace *mantilla.*

She had her hands crossed before her; she hung her head with apparent deference to her superiors, but ready to serve. Behind her was a large, ornate credenza carved out of what appeared to Prophet's untrained eye a fine, exotic wood. Besides the tables and the crude wooden benches, the cabinet was the only piece of furniture in the hall. It was badly scuffed and scratched. Liquor bottles and candle sconces littered the top of it.

From somewhere came the soft chortling of pigeons. They must have been perched somewhere in the dark ceiling across which the torchlight flickered dimly.

A stone stairway slanted up the wall above and behind the credenza. Prophet could see a stone-railed balcony up there in the dense shadows. Cool feathers of dread brushed his spine. He had the feeling he was being watched from all angles.

There was a soft, scraping tread behind him. He and Louisa and the Kid all turned their heads to see the hideous old nun walking up behind them, nearly silently, with that same death's head grin as before on her wretched face. She stopped about ten feet away, lowered her chin, hiding her face in the habit's hood, and stood there like a silent, black ghoul.

Quintero stared at the newcomers, chewing, frowning.

"We have met before," he said, pointing his spoon, then spooning up more beans and meat. Juice from the food dribbled off his plump lower lip as he chewed. He narrowed his eyes and a shrewd smile lifted his mouth corners, raising the ends of his carefully trimmed mustache. "You placated me with the name of *Doña* Salazar."

His eyes flicked toward the old woman who stood behind the newcomers in ghoulish silence.

"I thought you must have come with more girls. *Gringas.* But, no. You come spitting fire." Quintero dropped his spoon into his empty bowl and sat back in his high-backed chair. "So, tell me . . . what is it you want? The gold? If so, you are wasting your time. It's not here. I have sent if off to my business partners in Guadalajara. Invested it. Gold does little good just sitting around. It must be used to grow more. My last run against those American imperialists was my last, I am afraid—at least, for a while." He sort of grimaced at that, then added, "At any rate, none is here. You have wasted a trip . . . and ammunition."

"We didn't come for here for the gold," Prophet told him. "We came here for the women . . . and a pair of saddlebags filled with money stolen off an American train."

And to kill you, you son of a bitch. He thought he'd save that piece of information for last.

"Ah. I see." Quintero nodded. He shared a glance with the sergeant who was still busy spooning beans and meat into his mouth with onc hand and dipping bread into the bowl with his other hand.

"We need to have a conversation, then," the colonel said. "But in order for that to happen, you will need to set your weapons here on the table."

"I bet you told that to them two hangin' around back there," said the Rio Concho Kid, jerking his head toward where the two McCourts hung from the statues.

"Out of the question," Prophet said. He aimed his rifle out from his right hip at Quintero's chest.

The *rat-a-tatting* thunder of a Gatling gun opened up in the balcony high above Quintero's table. The servant woman poked her fingers into her ears. A line of bullets chewed into the stone floor halfway between Prophet and Quintero and the sergeant's table. The bullets ripped apart the already cracked and chipped stone flags eight feet in front of Prophet, and sent rock shards flying.

Prophet squeezed his eyes closed and gritted his teeth against the deafening assault on his ears. Louisa and the Kid did likewise.

When ten or twelve shots had been fired, the Gatling gun fell silent.

The echoes caromed around the room. Prophet could smell the rotten odor of the smoke.

Pigeons flapped wildly against the ceiling as though searching frantically for a way out. Apparently they found one. Their warbling dwindled to silence.

The bounty hunter thought he heard the old nun cackling behind him.

"The next rounds," Quintero said from his chair, "will render a discussion impossible unless you think, *señores* and *señorita,* you can speak from the grave."

Prophet gave a deep sigh. The feeling of dread had now drifted to the small of his back, where it wrapped its cold fingers around his spine. He, Louisa, and the Kid had walked into a trap. He'd known it had been a risk, walking in here. Now he was sure it had been. He could try to take a shot at the shooter in the balcony, and then at Quintero and the sergeant, but he didn't know how many men the colonel had lurking in the room's thick peripheral shadows. He sensed there were several.

He looked at the Vengeance Queen standing to his right. She compressed her lips at him. Her chest rose and fell slowly. On Prophet's left, the Rio Concho Kid gave the slightest shrug, his expression stony, grave eyes wide and round beneath his Stetson's brim.

Prophet walked up and set his rifle on Quintero's table. He unbuckled his cartridge belts and placed them and the Peacemaker on the table, as well. He followed it up with the

Richards and his bowie knife.

He turned to Louisa and the Kid. Their faces were a little pale. Louisa muttered something to herself, and then she and the Kid stepped forward and set all of their own weapons on the table.

"There, now," Quintero said, lifting his goblet in mock salute. Prophet noticed that his hand was shaking slightly. "That is more like it."

"Let's get to it," Louisa said.

Quintero studied her. He quirked a mouth corner, sipped his wine, ran his napkin across his mustached mouth, and said, "You are beautiful." He shook his head in amazement, his eyes rolling brassily across Louisa standing before him.

Behind Prophet, the hideous old nun made a gravelly sound of restrained delight in her throat.

Louisa said nothing.

Quintero rose from his chair. He stumbled on a chair leg as he stepped out away from the table. He moved around it to stand in front of Louisa, looking down at her—a big, raptorial bird admiring its prey. The tattoo on his forehead seemed to have grown since Prophet had seen him in the cantina. Or maybe his head had shrunk.

He ran two fingers through her long hair hanging down her shoulder. Again, the hand shook. He had a palsy. Something wrong with him—more than just too much to drink.

"What are you doing here? You're certainly not looking for women." The colonel glanced at the sergeant. "Maybe men, eh?"

The sergeant snickered, feasting his glassy eyes on Louisa.

Louisa jerked her head back from the colonel. "I doubt I'll find any real—"

Prophet quickly interrupted her with, "She's here for what we're here for. The women and the money. Now, you said we needed to have a discussion. Let's palaver."

Quintero stepped over to stand in front of Prophet. "What two women are you here for?"

"One named Mattie and . . ."

"One named Peggy," said the Kid.

Quintero glanced at each man in turn, interest showing in his eyes. "I see. I see. Mattie and Peggy. Hmmm." He steepled two fingers against his lips, pondering.

"Mattie might be Abigail or some such," Prophet added, a little sheepishly. "I'll know her when I see her."

"And what is this . . . this *Mattie* . . . to you?" asked Quintero.

A woman's voice said, "His wife."

Heels clacked on the stairs slanting up the wall above the credenza.

Prophet's heart quickened as he watched the shadow descend the steps. Only when she was halfway down did the torchlight begin to reveal her in soft, glinting, all-too-brief flashes—the pleat of a dark skirt rippling about slender legs, a pale slender hand running lightly down the stone rail, a flash of cream neck above a white collar, the glint of a choker pin. Certain highlights in her brown hair pinned atop her head glistened like streaks of gold dust in a cave wall.

At the bottom of the steps, to the right of the table, she pivoted with her hand on the stone newel, and stood frozen. Her eyes were wide and dark there in the shadows, the torchlight flickering in them, dancing in her hair. She parted her lips. The light kissed them like a tender lover.

"Mattie?" Prophet heard himself say, thickly. His lungs were painful knots in his chest.

"No." She stepped forward, came into the edge of the sphere of wavering light, and stopped, her hands entwined before her belly. She stared toward Prophet, her eyes drawing up a little, catlike, at the corners. "No, not Mattie."

"Abigail Justice?"

"Mi amor!" Quintero strode to her, took her hand in his, and led her over to present her to his three guests. "Meet my new *amigos* . . . and *amiga.*" He smiled brightly at Louisa and then slid his smarmy, liquid gaze to Prophet. "This one is—"

"Lou Prophet," said Abigail Justice, her cold eyes on Prophet's. "Like I said, I married the fool."

The word was a harsh slap across Prophet's face delivered in a low, raking tone rife with both mockery and disdain. It was so cruel that even Louisa turned her head quickly to Prophet, as though to see how he'd received it.

Prophet choked back the ache, wrinkled a nostril, and put some steel in his voice. "I see you've been two-timing me, dear heart. After only one night of marriage. That's right cold even for a practiced confidence artist."

"I don't understand," said Quintero, shunting his puzzled frown between them. "You married this man, *mi amor.*"

"Sí," said the woman Prophet had known and couldn't help still knowing as Mattie. "It was a ruse. He had money. I wanted the money. So I married him, drugged him, and absconded."

"But only after killing a deputy U.S. marshal."

Mattie smiled coldly. "Forgive me. How could I leave that part out? The fool had no fear of a woman, I guess. Turned his back on me, and I brained him. Had a devil of a time getting him into that closet, but when I did, I was as free as the breeze."

"Where's the money?" Prophet asked her.

"*Sí,* where is the money, Abigail?" Quintero asked her.

"Gone." Mattie kept her eyes, which were not Mattie's eyes but the eyes of this woman Prophet didn't know—Abigail Justice's eyes—on Prophet, as though wanting to assault him with every word she had to confess, rubbing his nose in her ruse. "It was stolen from me in Arizona. Out of a roadhouse. I should have buried the loot in the desert, but I'd been doing that, and I had gotten tired of digging it back up. So I took a chance. A foolish chance."

She turned to Quintero. "It wasn't much. You're worth so much more, *mi amor.*" She hugged the colonel's arm and turned her winning, mocking smile on Prophet. "It was really nothing. To him, maybe . . . but not to us."

Quintero studied her skeptically. Slowly, the skepticism faded from his eyes, and his mouth broke into a delighted smile. He drew Abigail Justice to his chest and laughed loudly, "You've been a very busy girl, Abby! A very busy girl, indeed! But that's how I've always known you to be. Ever since we were but children! And that is why I am so very happy you chose to return to me."

A frown played across Quintero's hawkish features once more, and he turned to Abigail. "Even though you have, apparently, taken up for a time with this *gringo* . . . this *gringo* who killed so many of my men to get to you."

"I guess I left quite an impression," Abigail said. She turned to Quintero. "I assure you, however, *mi amor,* he meant nothing to me. Nothing at all."

Even though he'd tried to harden himself against her, the words were like javelins to Prophet's heart. He couldn't help remembering how they'd once been together . . . back in the Colorado mountains . . . back in Broken Knee.

"And now?" Quintero asked her, arching one black brow.

"And now even less," she said, the torchlight glittering in her slitted eyes.

Quintero slid his Remington revolver from the holster on his right thigh. He held it up in front of Abigail, butt-first. "Show me."

She glanced sidelong at him. Her lips parted to show the white edges of her teeth.

Quintero stretched his smile wider, and gave a slow blink.

"Show me how little he means to you, *mi amor.* And we will be off to Guadalajara together at first light."

Abigail returned the colonel's challenging gaze.

She glanced at Prophet.

Then she licked her lips, accepted the gun from Quintero, cocked it, and aimed it at the bounty hunter's broad chest.

Chapter Twenty

Abigail Justice squinted one eye as she stared down the Colt's barrel.

Prophet's heart shrank in his chest.

"No!" Louisa yelled, lunging forward.

At the same time, Abigail turned the pistol on Quintero standing beside her, and fired.

The blast was a sharp, resounding report in the cavelike hall.

Quintero yelped and stumbled backward. The gun had been so close to the colonel's chest that the flames from the blast set his tunic on fire.

Quintero screamed again as Abigail swung the pistol toward the sergeant, aimed again hastily, and fired. The sergeant flew back in his chair with a scream, he and the chair hitting the floor.

Prophet blinked, shocked. Then he remembered the Gatling gun.

"Mattie!" he shouted, and grabbed her around her waist.

He flung himself and the young woman across Quintero's table. He rolled off his shoulder, half-consciously positioning himself so that he'd hit the floor on the other side, which he did, Mattie landing on top of him. He grabbed the pistol out of her hand, rose onto an outstretched arm, and aimed at the balcony nearly straight above.

Torchlight glinted off the Gatling's brass canister as the gun was aimed toward him. He could see the man-shaped silhouette behind it. He fired at it three times.

There was an echoing scream, and then the *rurale* tumbled out of the balcony to hit the floor with a cracking slap of flesh and bone on stone.

In the corner of his right eye, Prophet saw shadows jounce out from the cavelike walls. Torchlight revealed gray-clad men with rifles. Yelling and shouting curses, they ran forward, snapping their rifles to their shoulders.

Prophet grabbed his own Colt. He, Louisa, and the Kid fired from over the table.

The thunder caused dust to sift from the ceiling.

The *rurales* screamed as the bullets punched them back into the shadows from which they'd emerged. Only a couple got off wild shots before their rifles clattered to the floor.

Silence.

Smoke webbed.

Beneath the silence rose the sounds of a distant commotion. There was apparently a great scurrying in the brothel part of the convent. Hearing the gunfire, the clients of the House of the Devil were likely scrambling to flee, dressing hastily and heading for their horses and buggies in the stables that, according to the Kid, flanked the old convent.

Prophet rose from behind the table, looking around. Louisa and the Kid did likewise.

"I have to find Peggy!" the Kid said, and leaped up onto the table and down the other side. He ran down the middle of the room toward the entrance marked by the statues and hanging dead men.

Prophet turned to where Mattie crouched beside him. He gave her his hand, and he led her out from behind the table. Louisa followed.

Prophet turned to his . . . who was she to him now? Surely, not his wife . . .

"Mattie," he said.

"Oh, Lou!" She sobbed and threw her arms around his neck. "I'm so sorry," she cried into his chest.

A hissing sounded behind her. A shadow lunged toward them. Before Prophet could move, the old nun had flung her right hand against the small of Mattie's back then pulled it away. Mattie jerked in his arms.

"Oh!" she cried.

The old nun stepped back, cackling. Torchlight glinted off the bloody blade she held up in her hands, showing it off.

Louisa palmed one of her Colts, clicked the hammer back, and fired.

The old woman was punched back off her feet to pile up on the floor in a crowlike, writhing mess. Louisa stepped up to her and emptied her Colt into the loathsome old devil.

"Mattie!" Prophet said, reaching around the young woman, feeling blood oozing out of her back. She was sliding down his chest, her wide, terrified eyes riveted to his.

"Lou," she gasped.

Gently, he crouched, and laid her down on the floor.

"Oh, Mattie," he said, reaching up to rip the neckerchief from around his neck. He wadded it up in his right hand and pressed it to the small of Mattie's back, over the wound that continued to issue hot blood.

Mattie lay on the floor, gazing up at him. Gradually, the terror left her eyes. She reached up and sandwiched his big face in her hands. "Just know this one thing . . . and it's true if nothing else in my life ever was . . . I loved you, Lou Prophet. That's why I did what I did."

"Oh, Mattie . . . I don't understand any of it!"

She blinked, shaking her head. "You had the lousy luck to fall in love with a devil, Lou. Isn't that funny?" She sobbed, and smiled as she gazed up at him through tear-glazed eyes. "And that devil fell for you."

Her head sagged back, and she lay still against the floor.

She didn't die that night. Nor the next one. But the third night after the dustup in *Casa del Diablo,* Mattie—whose real name was Abigail Justice—breathed her last in Prophet's arms.

He buried her in the sprawling, ancient cemetery behind the convent. He took his time, digging the grave good and deep, then covering it with heavy stones. He fashioned a wooden cross, mounted it at the head of the grave, said a short, silent prayer, told his wife goodbye, and walked over to where Louisa sat in the shade by her pinto and the tail-switching Mean and Ugly.

Louisa said nothing.

The bounty hunters mounted their horses and rode away from San Miguel and the empty shell that was all that was left of the blood-splashed *rurale* outpost as well as *Casa el Diablo.* The mysterious Rio Concho Kid had found Peggy and had taken her back to her ranch in southern Arizona. The other girls imprisoned in the devil's house had been given shelter by the villagers, who would continue to shelter them until their families came for them.

Prophet didn't start talking about Mattie until his and Louisa's second day on the trail north toward the border. Then he told her what Mattie had confessed to him as she lay dying in a room at the old convent.

"She grew up on a ranch in southern Arizona. Bad family. No mother. Drunken outlaw father. Barely survived several Apache attacks. Her mother was killed in one. Mattie was raped by the Indians and left for dead. When she was only fourteen, she fell in love with a brash young *rurale* lieutenant who patrolled the border near her ranch and she ran away with him.

"Came here to where he was stationed and was secretly growing his own army. The devil's army. Abigail Justice got indoctrinated by *Doña* Salazar just as Quintero himself had been. Worked for the old woman in the brothel. Became addicted to the potpourri of herbs and drugs the old woman used on her slave girls. Got addicted to living in that Sodom back there. Finally, though, she couldn't stand watching the sacrificial lambs get led off to the literal slaughter anymore, so she ran away. Headed north. Survived by her wits. Married men for their money, left some alive . . . killed one—Charles McCourt. That was his father and brother hanging from the statues."

Prophet reined Mean and Ugly to a halt on a rise overlooking a sandy gorge. He stared down at an ancient, falling-down shack nearly covered in sand and flanked by dusty willows and mesquites. Part of an old Mexican *rancho*, long abandoned. The wind was blowing, kicking up sand. There was nothing else down there. Just the ruined shack and the sand and the pervasive wind that haunted this part of the Sonoran desert, less than a mile south of the border.

Prophet swung down from his saddle. He squinted up at Louisa. "She said that when she became other people, like Mattie Anderson, it wasn't just an act. She *became* that girl, that Mattie, totally, so that she almost forgot who she really was. She made up everything about Mattie Anderson—her past, her family, how she thought and felt about things, her reactions to what happened to her. It was a way, I reckon, of escaping, at least for a while, who she really was."

Prophet turned to stare into the gorge at the ruined shack. "She claimed she married me because she honestly loved me. But she knew how she was, how she had the devil in her, and it wouldn't last. So she killed St. Vincent and took the money to finance her trip back to Mexico. She figured she belonged with folks like her—Quintero and *Doña* Salazar. Sodom had never really released its hold on her, though she didn't expect to find

Doña Salazar even crazier than before, and Quintero dying from Cupid's itch . . ."

"Syphilis," Louisa said.

"On the way down here, guilt got ahold of her . . . for how she'd betrayed me. So she buried the loot in the desert—here in that arroyo, according to the map she drew—believing there was half a chance I'd hunt her down and she could tell me where she'd buried it, so I could dig it up and clear my name."

Prophet glanced back at Louisa. "I don't reckon I should believe anything she said, knowin' now who she was." He hiked a shoulder. "But what the hell? Once a fool, always a fool."

Louisa quirked a one-quarter smile and shrugged.

"So," Prophet said with a sigh. "I reckon I'll go down and find out how big a fool I really am. Wait here with the horses, will ya, partner?"

He strode down into the gorge and returned twenty minutes later with the saddlebags draped over his shoulder. Then he and Louisa rode across the border and continued north to Denver.

ABOUT THE AUTHOR

Born in North Dakota, bestselling western novelist **Peter Brandvold** has penned over seventy fast-action westerns under his own name and his pen name, **Frank Leslie.** He is the author of the ever-popular .45-Caliber books featuring Cuno Massey as well as the Lou Prophet and Yakima Henry novels. Recently, with his first young-adult western, *Lonnie Gentry* and its successor, *The Curse of Skull Canyon,* he began publishing with Five Star. Head honcho at "Mean Pete Publishing," publisher of lightning-fast western ebooks, he lives in western Minnesota with his dog. Visit his website at www.peterbrand-vold.com. Follow his blog at: www.peterbrandvold.blogspot-.com. Send him an email at: peterbrandvold@gmail.com.

The employees of Five Star Publishing hope you have enjoyed this book.

Our Five Star novels explore little-known chapters from America's history, stories told from unique perspectives that will entertain a broad range of readers.

Other Five Star books are available at your local library, bookstore, all major book distributors, and directly from Five Star/Gale.

Connect with Five Star Publishing

Visit us on Facebook:
https://www.facebook.com/FiveStarCengage

Email:
FiveStar@cengage.com

For information about titles and placing orders:
(800) 223-1244
gale.orders@cengage.com

To share your comments, write to us:
Five Star Publishing
Attn: Publisher
10 Water St., Suite 310
Waterville, ME 04901